Praise for *A Rebel Heart*

"*A Rebel Heart* features characters with depth, a gripping plot with thoughtfully researched authenticity, and unexpected twists."

Booklist

"White bridges Union and Confederate in this charming post–Civil War inspirational romance."

Publishers Weekly

"The start to the Daughtry House series is a worthy read."

Romantic Times

"*A Rebel Heart* checks all the boxes on my wishlist for a satisfying novel. It brings a lesser-known slice of history to life and deals honestly with our national past. The characters are colorful and compelling, the setting richly painted, and the high-stakes plot carries the reader to the end without ever slowing down. Full of intrigue, grit, and grace, *A Rebel Heart* is Beth White at her finest. I can't wait to read the rest of the series."

Jocelyn Green, award-winning
author of *A Refuge Assured*

"With great skill, Beth White combines intriguing history with inspiring romance, and then adds a good measure of mystery and suspense to her newest novel, *A Rebel Heart*. From the first page to the last, readers will be wrapped up in Selah's quest to restore her family's stately Mississippi home and charmed by the touching romance. Levi's investigation to solve a series of robberies and find out who is behind the mysterious incidents that threaten Selah and her family will keep readers guessing and turning pages until the very end. Well done!"

Carrie Turansky, award-winning author of
Shine Like the Dawn and *Across the Blue*

"Pinkerton agent Levi Riggins stole my heart, beginning with his valiant rescue of Selah Daughtry after a train wreck in the opening scenes of *A Rebel Heart*. Selah couldn't help but lose her heart too, although she has more than one reason to be wary of the former Yankee officer. Beth White's careful historical research shines throughout this novel, as do her wonderful characters. Highly recommended."

Robin Lee Hatcher, Lifetime Achievement Award–
winning author of *You're Gonna Love Me*

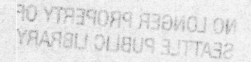

A
RELUCTANT
BELLE

Novels by Beth White

A RELUCTANT BELLE

BETH WHITE

Revell

a division of Baker Publishing Group
Grand Rapids, Michigan

© 2019 by Beth White

Published by Revell
a division of Baker Publishing Group
PO Box 6287, Grand Rapids, MI 49516-6287
www.revellbooks.com

Printed in the United States of America

Library of Congress Cataloging-in-Publication Data
Names: White, Beth, 1957– author.
Title: A reluctant belle / Beth White.
Description: Grand Rapids, MI : Revell, a division of Baker Publishing Group,
    [2019] | Series: Daughtry house ; #2
Identifiers: LCCN 2019012069| ISBN 9780800726904 (paper)
Subjects: | GSAFD: Christian fiction. | Love stories.
Classification: LCC PS3623.H5723 R45 2019 | DDC 813/.6—dc23
LC record available at https://lccn.loc.gov/2019012069

ISBN 978-0-8007-3621-7(casebound)

Scripture used in this book, whether quoted or paraphrased by the characters, is taken from the King James Version of the Bible.

The author is represented by MacGregor Literary, Inc.

19 20 21 22 23 24 25   7 6 5 4 3 2 1

This book is for L.G. and Cindy Catlett,
fine examples of my ideal reader.

PROLOGUE

June 1860

Tree limbs slapped Joelle's face as she ran through the woods behind the bathhouse. She could feel the underbrush snatching at her bathing costume, snagging the short, full skirt and balloon-like pants legs under it. Her tender bare feet slid on rotten leaves, tangled on some briars, and she fell hard. Rolling up onto her knees, she sat on her heels and stared at the scratches on her palms.

There was no reason to have run this way, into the woods, instead of along the path toward the road. No reason—except humiliation and horror. She could still feel the weight of that creature in her hair, a blob of sliminess on top of her head, flailing about in its own terror. Literally one of her worst nightmares come to life. It wouldn't have touched her hair, except she'd removed her bathing cap. "It's July," she'd retorted when Selah protested the immodesty, "hotter than blue blazes." She took off her shoes too and jumped into the pool.

Now she knelt on the forest floor, winded, panting, regretting that decision. The creepy feeling along her scalp, the bruises and scratches on her feet, were a terrible price to pay.

Somehow, some way, at some time when he least expected it, Schuyler Beaumont was going to pay. This was all his fault—him and his giant bullfrog. His idea of a joke.

Boys.

She and Selah and Camilla had been laughing over some silliness, when the frog crashed the party.

She put her stinging palms to her cheeks and shoved the angry tears away. Thirteen wasn't a baby, for heaven's sake. Control regained, she sucked in a deep breath. Frog successfully outrun. Now what? All desire to swim with the other girls was gone.

The sound of running footsteps through the woods made her leap to her feet.

"Joelle! Where are you?"

That was Schuyler, she could tell by the abrupt octave shift in the middle of the last word. She'd enjoyed teasing him about his changing voice for the last couple of days while his family visited from Mobile.

What if he had another frog? The hair on her arms lifted, and she took off running again.

He was upon her within a few seconds. "Joelle! Stop! I just wanted to say I'm—"

"Leave me alone!" As she whirled around, her hand hit him in the stomach.

He doubled over with an *oof*, and she stood there shaking like a jelly. Served him right.

Under the blond hair falling over his eyes, his face was red, the wide mouth clenched. "I said I'm sorry," he said through gritted teeth.

"That was a foul thing to do."

"Amphibian." He gingerly stood up, clutching his skinny middle.

"*Foul*, not *fowl*," she spat. "Horrid. Disgusting. Mean."

He flinched. "Yes, it was mean," he said quietly. "I apologized."

"And then made a joke."

"You're bleeding." He walked up to her and took her hands to turn them palm up. "Better wash this, or they'll rot and fall off."

She snatched her hands away. "Don't touch me."

His eyes were a dark, stormy blue-gray. It was the first time she'd been close enough to notice their color. She also noticed that she had to look up to meet them. He'd gotten taller over the summer.

Something shifted between them. His gaze dropped to her nose, then her lips. Then lower. She suddenly realized her dress was still damp, and inappropriate for mixed company. He was a boy. A *boy*, becoming a man.

She crossed her arms over her chest. "What's wrong with you?"

He shook his head. "I don't know." Now his voice was deep and rumbly, which rattled her even more.

"Well. Go home. I mean, back to the house. Just leave me alone."

"I can't leave you here by yourself. It's—it's not safe."

He had that right. She did not feel safe at all. Not that he would actually hurt her. He might scare her half to death, but he would never lay a hand on her in anger. When she thought of Schuyler, laughter came to mind. "I'm sorry I hit you," she blurted.

"I deserved it." He sighed. "Sometimes I do things without thinking about the other person's feelings. I know how much you hate frogs."

She blinked. "How did you know that?"

"Selah told Camilla a long time ago. They were laughing about it. I thought it was funny too."

Selah was Joelle's older sister, Camilla was Schuyler's, and they were best friends. "It's not funny," she said. "I have nightmares."

"Listen." He tilted his head for a moment, holding her eyes. The noises of the woods took over, birds twittering, a breeze rustling the leaves, and underneath it a harsh, monotonous cheeping sound.

She started to speak, but Schuyler held up a hand and walked over to a tree. He scooped something off a limb onto his palm, cupped the other hand over it, and came back to Joelle.

"Look," he said, showing her what looked at first like a large green bug. Then it moved and spread out, tiny fingers clinging to Schuyler's big, bony hand, throat pulsing. It was a tree frog. "See? Not scary at all."

Joelle stared, fascinated. "That's not what you put on my head."

"No, but it was his big, clumsy cousin." He grinned at her. "Kinda like me."

He had pretty teeth, too big for his face, but white and even in his sun-browned, ruddy face. Something about his smile moved her, scared her. "I've got to go. Selah will be looking for me."

"Let me walk you back." He deposited the tree frog on its limb and returned, wiping his hand on the seat of his pants.

They walked through the woods together in awkward silence, occasionally bumping elbows. They hadn't gone very far before Joelle was limping.

Schuyler halted to look down at her with a frown. "Where are your shoes?"

"In the bathhouse."

"Of all the—" He gave a grunt as if taxed beyond endurance and suddenly bent to put his shoulder against her middle, then stood with her flopped over his shoulder like a sack of meal.

"Schuyler! Put me down!" She elbowed his shoulder blade.

He kept walking. "I'm not going to take you home with bleeding feet *and* hands." Within a few yards, he was huffing and puffing. "You're heavier than you look," he observed with clear irritation. "Over a hundred pounds, I'd say."

"I told you to put me down. We can go slowly." The blood was rushing to her head. That was why she felt so flustered, with his arm hooked over the back of her legs and her chin bobbing against his back. She didn't know what to do with her hands.

He slowed and stopped. Letting her slide downward, he kept his arms around her, halting her when her toes just touched the ground. Which was a good thing, because she didn't think her knees would have supported her. She'd never stood this close to any male except her father, who wasn't much of a hugger.

Schuyler was tall and whiplash thin, smelling of something alien that she could only describe as fresh *boy*. His chin and upper lip, right in front of her eyes, bore a fine blond layer of hair that might have been called a beard, and his cheeks had begun to hollow, defining his jawline. His face was losing its babyish roundness.

She noted those details because she considered herself a writer, and writers noticed things about people. Even people she didn't like.

She reminded herself that she did not like Schuyler Beaumont. One did not kiss a person who had less than thirty minutes ago released a giant bullfrog upon one's head.

Kiss? Who said anything about kissing? Perhaps she'd said it aloud, for to her abject horror, he bent his head and pressed his lips to hers. And she let him. In a clinical, detached way, as if she floated above herself, she admitted that she might have encouraged him by putting her arms about his neck. His lips were as nice as his teeth, cool and dry and yet somehow warm as honey.

When he stopped—which didn't take long, she supposed only a few seconds—she lowered her hands and pushed at his chest. "Let me go."

He did, dropping her like a hot brick onto her bruised feet. "Joelle?" He looked as surprised as she felt.

She took a step backward. "If you tell anybody that happened—*anybody!*—I'll swear you're a liar. And then I'll come kill you in your sleep."

One

April 30, 1870

The writing was not on the wall. It came, rather, inscribed in Grandmama's spidery hand on a sheet of embossed stationery that likely cost more than the sumptuous dinner on the table. Still, it seemed Joelle had clearly been weighed in the balance and found wanting.

She laid the opera tickets, enclosed with the letter, beside her empty plate and reread her grandmother's missive. No, she hadn't misinterpreted the message. "'My dear grand-progeny—'" She looked up at the company assembled in honor of the opening of her school on the following Monday. "*Grand-progeny?* Is that even a word?"

"If it's not, it should be." Schuyler Beaumont—invited to the party because he had donated funds to enlarge the kitchen storage room and furnish it as a schoolroom—popped a whole lemon truffle into his mouth and mumbled around it, "Sounds like a Chinese emperor."

Gil Reese, young pastor of the Tupelo Methodist Church

and Joelle's longtime suitor, eyed Schuyler dismissively. "Obviously you've never been to China. My parents were missionaries there for a time, before I was born."

"Why would I want to go to China?" Schuyler licked sugar off one finger. "They eat dogs." He winked at Joelle's younger sister, Aurora.

Aurora giggled, but Cousin ThomasAnne McGowan, at the advanced age of thirty-three, well past the delights of juvenile humor, showed signs of succumbing to the vapors. Dr. Benjamin Kidd, seated in a neutral position at the foot of the table between Aurora and ThomasAnne, rolled his eyes at the comment and partook of truffles.

"Really, Schuyler." Joelle gave him an annoyed look. Seating him across the table from Gil—who clearly resented both Schuyler's hedonistic enjoyment of dessert and the splendid cut of his suit—had been a social gaffe her elder sister Selah would never have committed. Joelle had hoped to turn the minister's influential opinion in favor of the school, but escalating masculine competition threatened to turn her pleasant dinner into a gladiatorial spectacle. Hoping to deflect hostilities, she returned her attention to the letter. "Anyway, Grandmama continues, 'I have decided that you girls need a short vacation away from that rural mausoleum in which you have buried yourselves. I have arranged for you to take the early train to Memphis on Monday and have dinner with your grandfather and me. You will attend the opera *Cosí fan tutte* as my guests, then spend the night at McGowan House. Joelle in particular will enjoy the treat, as Fiordiligi will be played by the Italian soprano Delfina Fabio, who I understand is quite the modern darling.'"

Aurora shook her head so hard her coppery curls bobbed.

"It's a trap. If I get anywhere near Memphis again, Grandmama will guilt me into staying. I'm not taking that chance."

Joelle lowered the paper and looked at the tickets. "It's at the Greenlaw Opera House," she said slowly. "I really would like to go." Grandmama knew their weak spots. As much as she loathed crowds, Joelle was a pianist and singer herself and would adore to meet an opera star. "It's too bad Selah and Levi aren't here. They could go with me." Selah's new husband was a concert pianist (when he wasn't solving cases for the Pinkerton Agency), but the two of them were still in New Orleans on their honeymoon. Joelle looked at her cousin. "ThomasAnne—"

"Oh, no no no." ThomasAnne picked up her fan and plied it with desperate vigor. "Aunt Winnie gives me palpitations."

Nearly everything gave ThomasAnne palpitations.

"Well, I can't go by myself." Joelle tried to hide her disappointment.

"I have a suggestion," Doc said, giving ThomasAnne a heartening look. "Your aunt seems quite fond of Schuyler and me. Perhaps you'd allow us to go along with you and Joelle as escorts and, er, social buffers."

Schuyler put two more truffles on his plate. "I'd rather be shot at dawn than watch a lot of fat ninnies caper about in tights, caterwauling in some foreign language."

"I'm sure I can find someone to oblige you," Joelle said tartly, stung by his flat refusal.

His lips quirked. "You are too kind. But I was about to say, I can overcome my nausea, if you don't mind me meeting you at the opera house. I have to be in Memphis on Sunday for a fund-raising event for my father's gubernatorial campaign, and I'll be tied up through dinner on Monday."

He was so cocksure of himself, and everything had to be on his terms. Joelle was tired of tying herself in knots to accommodate him. "Don't put yourself out. I'm sure Reverend Reese would be happy to take the fourth ticket." She turned to smile at Gil.

Everyone looked at her in surprise. Reluctant to encourage Gil's awkward, persistent suit, Joelle rarely addressed him directly. But lately, in the face of Selah's delirious happiness— and more so in her absence—she had begun to feel an increasingly uncomfortable loneliness. This seemed a perfect opportunity to give Gil a chance. To see if she had missed a relationship that had been in front of her all the time.

Gil's mouth opened and shut a time or two. An attractive smile lightened his long, bony face. "Why, Miss Daughtry, I'm honored."

Joelle sought Schuyler's gaze. His beautiful, cleanly marked brows had drawn together over his nose. That was an encouraging sign. Maybe he could be redeemed after all. In a tiny corner of her heart, she couldn't help wondering if she might regret having so firmly shut him down.

May 2, 1870

Joelle adjusted the focus of the opera glasses Grandmama had loaned her for the evening. The mahogany paneling, gilt gaslight chandeliers, and velvet draperies of the Greenlaw Opera House blurred into the background of Schuyler's laughing countenance. He was golden himself, like Dionysus come down to carouse with mortal fraternity brothers. Clad with careless elegance in a well-tailored black suit and snowy linen, longish hair tumbling over his brow in burnished waves, he fairly glowed with joie de vivre.

He'd said he wasn't coming. What was he doing here?

"Joelle, are you not feeling well? Perhaps I could fetch you a lemonade."

Startled, she dropped the glasses and turned to find Gil already halfway out of his seat. All day, during the long train ride to Memphis and then dinner at her grandparents' house, he'd been even more attentive than usual.

"No, no, I'm fine." She forced Schuyler out of her mind.

"But you were growling. Or clearing your throat. I thought you might be about to—you know . . ." Gil's color rose.

ThomasAnne, seated to her left, looked at Dr. Ben, seated to her left. "Oh dear, I knew that fish at dinner looked suspect. Ben, maybe you should take a look at her."

Joelle had to laugh at her cousin's excessive concern. "There was nothing wrong with the fish. I'm just surprised to find Schuyler in the audience, after he carried on so the other night."

"Where is he?" Gil grabbed the glasses and began to search the audience.

"Down front with that pack of young men. The tall one in the middle with his cravat half untied."

"I don't know how you can tell that from the back." Gil handed the glasses back to her. "But I wouldn't be surprised. Beaumont is an undisciplined"—he stopped himself and glanced at ThomasAnne—"idiot."

Joelle saw no need to encourage Gil's incessant criticism of Schuyler. "Shh. The lights are dimming." The curtain opened, and she was soon lost in musical euphoria. Delfina Fabio lived up to her billing. Joelle might have her differences with her autocratic grandparent but could only be grateful for this unexpected treat. She would never have been able to afford the tickets, let alone the train fare, on her hotel manager's salary.

The lights came on for intermission, and she looked around to regain her bearings. Realizing Gil had been staring at her and not the stage, she jumped to her feet. "I need some air."

Gil rose. "I'll go with you."

"No, I have to—I need to—" She circled a hand vaguely.

Blushing, Gil dropped back into his seat. "Oh."

She'd almost made it out to the lobby when someone grabbed her by the arm. She whirled, jerking free of the drunk who had accosted her, and faced the untied cravat and stubborn chin of Dionysus himself.

"What are you doing out here by yourself?" he demanded before she could say a word.

Gently bred single women didn't wander around alone. She knew that. But the look of disapproval narrowing his blue-gray eyes was annoying.

"It's intermission. I'm doing what one does during intermission."

He eyed her suspiciously. "Women travel in packs. Where's ThomasAnne?"

"She's in her seat." She looked him up and down. And up and up. He was one of the few men of her acquaintance who towered over her nearly six-foot height. "But if we are being interfering and inquisitive, perhaps you'll tell me what has overcome your professed violent disdain for opera."

He stared at her, as if he couldn't decide whether she really wanted to know or had simply thrown out a verbal barb.

She wasn't sure of that herself.

20

Finally he said, "Hixon and Jefcoat and I came with General Forrest and his wife. I met them at the fund-raiser yesterday, and apparently Mrs. Forrest is on the opera board."

Nathan Bedford Forrest, one of the most celebrated Confederate officers to survive the Recent Unpleasantness, had retired to direct the post-war recovery of the South from his Memphis plantation. Rumors swirled regarding his involvement in vigilante groups like the Red Shirts and the Ku Klux Klan.

Joelle stifled hurt that Schuyler had accepted the Forrests' invitation after turning hers down. "I see. That's . . . interesting. In that case, please excuse me while I conclude my business." She dipped a pert curtsey and turned.

"Wait—Joelle, don't go like that." He caught her hand. She turned with a sigh. "What, Schuyler?"

"I told the Forrests about you and your sisters and the hotel, and his wife wanted to meet you."

"Really?" She bit her lip, the reporter in her coming alive. She could interview General Forrest and write a truthful article about him. Mr. McCanless, editor of the *Tupelo Journal*, would certainly buy such a hot-topic piece.

"Yes, but here's the kicker. We've all been invited to a party after the opera, hosted by this Fabio woman—the star of the show. I told the general how you love music. Wouldn't you like to come?"

She stared at Schuyler. There was something soft in his expression, almost as if he were trying to please her. Which was such an odd idea, she brushed it away as a quirk of her imagination. Schuyler rarely tried to please anyone but himself.

But getting to know an opera singer would almost be

worth the effort of staying up late and making small talk. "I suppose that would be nice," she said slowly, "if the rest of my party doesn't mind. Thank you for thinking of me. I'll meet you in the lobby when the opera's over. Now, if you'll excuse me, I'm in a hurry." Squeezing his hand, she whirled in the direction of the ladies' room.

Schuyler watched the back of Joelle's red-gold head disappear into the crowd milling about the lobby. Feeling rather strangled, he reached up to loosen his tie and found it, to his deep chagrin, already dangling against his shirtfront. He'd been so busy herding his friend Kenard Hixon out of the hotel bar and finding a hack for the opera that he'd had no thought for a mirror. No wonder Joelle had looked at him like something she'd just shaken off her shoe. She probably thought he'd taken a turn through the ale house himself.

Which, come to think of it, would have been a deal more fun than this highbrow snorefest. If he hadn't told Joelle he'd introduce her to the Forrests after the opera, he'd ditch the whole thing and go back to the billiards room at the Peabody. He glanced in the direction of the women's retiring room. He didn't like the thought of Joelle wandering about unescorted. He knew how well that dazzling exterior disguised her introverted soul. He could wait for her, walk her back to her seat.

But she'd probably challenge his "interference" again. How was a man to maintain a code of chivalry in the face of such manic independence?

So he made his way through the darkened theater, stumbling over indignant patrons who hadn't been cursed by acquaintance with Joelle Daughtry. He longed for simpler days when his major trial had been sailing a blockade runner across Mobile Bay under Union gunboat fire. Flumping into his seat between Hixon and the third member of their triumvirate, Jefcoat, who had just arrived, he scowled at the portly tenor carrying on in the limelight. Fabio the Fabulous, as the American press dubbed her, was nowhere in sight. He couldn't imagine why Joelle was so excited about meeting her.

"Where you been?" Hixon whispered, nearly singeing Schuyler's eyebrows with the alcohol on his breath. "Might've known you'd ditch ush in favor of shome sh-shkirt."

"That was no skirt, at least in the sense you mean." Schuyler elbowed his erstwhile fraternity brother. "Stow it before you get us thrown out."

"That wouldn' be shuch a great losh." Bitterness laced Hixon's tone. "You owe me a drink after thish."

"I think you've already reached your—"

"Shhhhh!" someone behind them hissed.

Schuyler slumped deeper into his seat.

Sometime later he awoke to thunderous applause and shouts of "Encore! Encore!" Circling his head to relieve the crick in his neck, he sat up. The entire cast had paraded onto the stage for an extravagant mass bow. Flowers flew over the heads of the orchestra, and the audience—with the exception of himself—came to its collective feet. The lovely dark-haired Fabio in her red velvet gown glided to stage center, where she kissed her hands with extravagant drama.

Thank the Lord it was over. He could find Joelle, take her to the Peabody, introduce her to the Forrests, and call it a day.

His father owed him one for this dangerous foray into enemy territory.

He stood up, looking for his two companions. Jefcoat was snoring like a freight train, head back against the seat, so perhaps he'd just leave him to sleep it off. Hixon was hunched over, elbows on knees.

Schuyler shoved him. "Hixon! Get up! It's time to go."

Hixon looked up, his face a strange greenish white above his thick beard. "I think I'm gonna be—"

Two

"JOELLE, YOU ARE ENTIRELY TOO DREAMY and impulsive," Papa had said to her the morning he sent her and Selah off to boarding school, as if it were a character flaw of which she should be mortally ashamed. "This is for your own good. Let go of your mama and get on that train with your sister, right now."

She felt something of that sense of dread as she threaded through the crowd leaving the theater, behind ThomasAnne, Gil, and Doc. Had she really agreed to attend an opera star's cast party at the Peabody Hotel? What if she wasn't dressed right? What if she tripped over her own big feet? What if she unintentionally said something insulting to the wrong person? Schuyler would be embarrassed, his father's campaign would be negatively affected, and the hotel would lose business.

Intelligent, levelheaded Selah or bubbly Aurora should have been chosen for this task.

As they reached the lobby, she tugged the back of Thomas-Anne's simple bolero jacket. "ThomasAnne, I need to tell you something. I ran into Schuyler during intermission. That's why I was late coming back into the theater."

ThomasAnne turned with a smile. "That's nice. Did you invite him to come to Aunt Winnie's house after the opera? You know how she dotes on him."

"No, I didn't invite him. I actually didn't think of it, though I'm sure he'll come by sometime tomorrow. I was just going to say, he invited me to a party at the Peabody. I'm to meet Miss Fabio and some of the other singers. Isn't that wonderful?"

ThomasAnne's naturally arched eyebrows rose nearly to her hairline. "Tonight? But it's nearly eleven o'clock! We can't go to a party. It's bedtime!"

"Well . . . Actually, he only invited me. You don't have to come."

"Oh." ThomasAnne blinked. "Certainly I don't mind, but what about your escort?"

"My escort?" She watched Doc and Gil strolling along in conversation a few steps ahead of them. "You mean Gil?" She hadn't considered how he might feel to be excluded. *Oh no*.

Apparently realizing the women had gotten left behind, Doc elbowed Gil and turned to see what was going on. "Is something the matter?"

"Joelle wants to go to a party," ThomasAnne said, looking troubled. "At the Peabody, with Schuyler." She made it sound like an orgy.

Doc looked concerned. "I'm not sure that's a good idea. Your grandmother will expect you to come home with us."

Joelle had somewhat expected these objections, had even considered letting her elders override her plans. But suddenly she remembered she was a modern twenty-two-year-old woman. A professional writer, a journalist. Why couldn't she go to a party if she wanted to? "I'm afraid I've already agreed to go. There comes Schuyler right now."

She saw his golden-wheat head weaving through the crowd. As he got closer, she realized he had his friend Hixon's arm draped over his shoulders, lugging him along like a sack of wheat. Hixon did not look well.

Schuyler gave Joelle a rather desperate look. "Wait there. I'll be right back." He hauled Hixon toward the men's room.

Joelle watched them go, mouth open.

"Joelle, you're not going anywhere with that reprobate," Gil said. "Look at the company he keeps."

ThomasAnne brought out her fan. "I need to sit down. I think I'm going to faint."

"I think we all need to sit down," Doc said grimly. "Reverend Reese, if you'll be so good as to secure a hack to take us all to McGowan House, I'll go to the cloakroom and find the ladies' wraps."

Joelle lifted her chin. "I would appreciate it if you'd collect my wrap, and of course you all are perfectly free to return to Grandmama's house. I'm going to the Peabody. But first somebody needs to go check on Schuyler and his friend." She looked at Doc.

Doc wavered. "Perhaps I should—"

"He got himself in this mess. He can take care of himself." Gil folded his arms.

Schuyler chose that moment to return, looking exceedingly harrassed. "Joelle, I'm going to have to take Hixon to our room before I can take you to the party."

She had made up her mind not to be coerced. "That's all right. I'll just go with you."

"Hixon will be fine in the morning, but he's not fit for female company right now." Schuyler shoved his hands into his already wild hair. "I'm not sure how long this is going to take."

Whose side was he on? "The others can drop me off at the Peabody," Joelle said. "I'll wait for you in the lobby."

ThomasAnne started bleating incoherent protests.

"You can't do that, Jo," Doc said, not unkindly. "As you can see, your cousin is worried about you. We need to get her home to your grandparents."

"I'll stay with her," Gil said suddenly.

A minute ago he hadn't wanted her to go. Now he stared at Schuyler like a bull ready to lock horns. Joelle did not fancy herself in the role of a cow. "Now wait just a—"

"That's not a bad idea," Schuyler said. "Y'all wait in the Peabody lobby, and I'll find you after I get Hixon settled." He wheeled off into the crowd again.

Gil cleared his throat and addressed Doc with assumed authority. "Joelle seems to have her heart set on absorbing as much of what her grandmother considers 'culture' as possible in one evening. Such an opportunity does not often come. Besides, I confess I should like to make the acquaintance of the talented Miss Fabio myself." He took Joelle's hand and tucked it into the bend of his elbow. "I'll chaperone her at the party and make sure she returns to McGowan House well before the stroke of midnight. After all, we cannot let our heroine's carriage turn into a pumpkin, can we?"

Joelle didn't relish being obligated to Gil, and she didn't much like fairy tales. But having committed herself, there was no backing down. Where was one's fairy godmother when one needed her?

As they entered the Peabody's luxurious lobby, whose golden chandeliers cast glittering light from the grand curving staircase to the massive front door to the gleaming walnut service desk, Joelle looked up at Gil. He might not be as extravagantly good-looking as Schuyler, but there was character in his bony face and kindness in his eyes as he glanced down to make sure she didn't slip on the polished marble entryway.

"Thank you for coming with me, Gil. I really appreciate it."

His expression brightened. "I'm happy if you're happy." He indicated a tufted brown velvet sofa just inside the door. "Why don't we wait here until Beaumont arrives?"

Joelle sat down, pulling her wrap about her shoulders. Though she wasn't cold, she definitely felt out of her element. She would be glad when Schuyler arrived. As much as he irritated her sometimes, his force of character had always served as a welcome buffer for her shyness.

"Are you comfortable?" Gil sat beside her, his shoulder brushing hers.

"Yes, thank you." She hesitated. "Gil, why did you really offer to come with me? I know you don't like parties."

He reddened. "Neither do you!"

"That's true, in the normal way of things. But I did want to meet Miss Fabio. If she comes to the hotel, she'll bring others with her. The word will get out. Besides, she seems like an interesting person. I enjoy talking to interesting people."

He looked as if he didn't believe her. "Interesting people are usually immoral."

Did he realize what he'd just said? She laughed. "That's

a bit of an overstatement. *I'm* not immoral! Don't you find me interesting?"

"Of course I do, I only meant—" His big hands gripped his knees. "You're not *that* kind of interesting. You're the perfect sort of quiet lady I enjoy spending time with."

"I was just teasing. But, Gil, I'm not the perfect anything." She sighed. "I have lots of faults that I'm trying to correct. Helping others, for example. I don't want to be selfish."

His gentle gray eyes were puzzled. "Joelle, I don't think of you as selfish at all. I've seen you trying to educate your slaves."

"They're not slaves!"

"I just meant, they work for you—and yet you take your lunchtime to help them learn to read and write. That's more than most people do."

"It's the *least* I can do. How can people take care of themselves if they can't read a contract or do basic arithmetic or even read the Bible? God's Word tells us to treat others the way we want to be treated."

"You're right, of course. I should put that in my next sermon."

"Yes, you should," she said quickly. "If Christians don't show love in these simple ways, who is going to? Why should Southern Christians stand back and let missionaries from up north come down here to do what we can do ourselves?"

"Joelle, what are you talking about?" He looked alarmed. And confused.

"The American Missionary Association has been sending teachers into Southern states to start schools since the war ended. I've been looking into getting connected with them." She'd been thinking about this for some time, and she was glad he'd brought the subject up. "But why can't we move my little school to our church? The building isn't used for anything during the week. It would be closer to the Shake Rag community, and even more people could come, adults and children! You could be the headmaster—"

"I'm not a schoolteacher! I'm a minister!" He took her hand. "Your intentions are good, but you haven't thought this through. Those people would be very uncomfortable in our church. I'll help you in any way I can, but it's best to move very slowly and carefully. Besides, haven't you already begun to add a schoolroom onto the Ithaca kitchen?"

"Yes, but we're not calling it Ithaca anymore. It's Daughtry House." Why couldn't he remember that? The name Ithaca reminded her of her father. She drew her hand away and folded her arms. "We've already started the renovations, thanks to Schuyler."

Gil frowned. "He's just trying to impress you."

Joelle snorted. "I doubt that. Whatever his reason, giving us the money was a very generous thing to do."

Gil was quiet for a moment, then said, "What about this? Suppose we get the church to take a collection on Sunday and donate it to your school?"

That was his solution? Taking a collection? "I suppose that would be nice," she said as enthusiastically as she could. She'd been trying to convey her feeling that she hadn't done enough to help those wronged by her family, but apparently she'd only succeeded in offending Gil. He wasn't a schoolteacher, and undoubtedly he had more important things to do, running a church—visiting the sick, praying for the dying, preparing to preach God's Word on Sundays.

Come to think of it, he had been a rock of comfort to her

family in the last two months as they'd dealt with burying their father, getting Selah and Levi married, and convincing Grandmama to return to Memphis. Gil had taken care of a myriad of details, notifying the newspaper, providing transportation, lending a word of counsel just when most needed. And she had taken him for granted.

Tonight he had gone out of his way to bring her into a social situation that clearly made him uncomfortable. Perhaps she should give him the benefit of the doubt.

"Listen, Gil," she said slowly. "I understand if you don't have the same passion for education as I do. Missions has lots of facets, after all. Just please don't look so scandalized when I take action on something I feel God wants me to do." She peeped at him from beneath her eyelashes. "All right?"

He chuckled. "I think you're a minx. Which is why I'm here tonight."

She brightened. "Minx" was a word usually reserved for the effervescent Aurora. Perhaps she herself was becoming a more normal girl.

Before she could respond—either appropriately or inappropriately—the exterior door swung open to admit a flustered doorman and three well-dressed young gentlemen in varying degrees of sobriety. Schuyler, the one in the middle, never looked up as he shepherded his companions in a lurching path across the lobby toward the stairs. How they managed to make it up to the second floor with limbs and crania intact Joelle would forever after wonder.

Her stomach sank.

"Oh my word," Gil said. "Are you sure you don't want to go back to your grandmother's?"

Schuyler was vaguely aware of the grandeur of his sur-roundings as he hauled Hixon through the Peabody's three-story lobby, trailed by Jefcoat. He couldn't help but be grate-ful for the plush Oriental carpet muffling their staggering ascent of the curving staircase and hoped they wouldn't all be thrown out for public intoxication. After zigzagging down the hall and struggling to unlock their guest room, he cast Hixon, fully clothed and already snoring, upon the four-poster bed.

Jefcoat wandered in and propped himself against the wall. "Hix won't like it that he's missing the party."

"Then he shouldn't have imbibed nearly a quart of Old Dominick's on top of a meal fit for Belshazzar's feast." Sometimes he felt like a nursemaid to two rich, overgrown children. "I suggest you lie down and sleep it off too," he told Jefcoat as he walked to the mirror to repair the damage to his neckcloth and hair. "Where have you been all weekend? I thought you were going to meet us for dinner before the opera. Even I know it's not good manners to come in after the intermission."

"Had a family matter to take care of." Jefcoat hiccuped. "Family first, you always say that."

"I suppose I do." Schuyler looked at him over his shoulder. "Have you had anything to eat today? Besides liquor, I mean?"

"Not since midday. But there'll be food at the party. Come on, let's go. I wanna see an opera star in person."

"You're going without me. I promised to meet Joelle in the lobby."

"Joelle? The red-haired bookworm?"

"The very same." He didn't know why Jefcoat's derisive tone was so irritating. He'd called Joelle a bookworm himself on multiple occasions.

"Pretty girl, if you like 'em tall and silent." Jefcoat pushed away from the wall, jerking his jacket into place. "Reckon she's got a speech impediment."

"You're a moron, Jefcoat," Schuyler said wearily. "Lock the door behind you. I'll see you when I see you." He quit the room, thrusting his hands into his pockets to keep from slugging Jefcoat on the way past.

Halfway down the stairs he started looking for Joelle and found her standing near the door talking to the preacher.

No, arguing with the preacher.

Her fists were clenched at her sides, her wrap had slid off one shoulder to hang like a bronze satin table runner down the front of her dress, and cobalt sparks kindled her eyes. She was fairly magnificent, and he couldn't help wondering what had set her off.

Unfortunately, he discovered himself to be the culprit. As he approached, Joelle caught sight of him, stepped around the preacher, and stalked toward him. "There you are!" she exclaimed.

He couldn't tell if she was angry or excited. Most likely both, he decided. "Yes, here I am. What's the matter?"

Joelle walked right up to him and stared into his face. She took a big sniff, turned around, and said to Reese, "I told you he wasn't drunk."

"What? Of course I'm not drunk!" Schuyler glanced at the preacher, who was scowling in deep suspicion. "Why would you think—Oh. Were you sitting here when I came in with Hixon and Jefcoat?" He laughed. "*You* try hauling a two-hundred-fifty-pound deadweight up two flights of stairs sometime and see if you can do it without leaning a little off-kilter."

"You'll have to forgive my reluctance to subject Joelle to your disgusting displays of bacchanalia," Reese said in a self-righteous tone.

"What was I supposed to do, leave him in the entryway?" Schuyler shrugged. "Maybe you treat your friends that way, but I don't. Thank you for keeping Joelle company. I suppose I owe you a favor. Good night, Reverend Reese." He took Joelle's sliding wrap off her shoulder and offered her his elbow.

"Oh no you don't!" The preacher stepped between them. "I'm not leaving her alone with you."

"Fine." Schuyler sighed. "Then you come too." Looping the length of satin about his neck in a jaunty fashion, he headed for the stairs.

Joelle caught up to him in a skip. "Wait, Schuyler! Is your friend—Hixon, is that his name?—is he all right?"

Pausing with a hand on the newel post, he looked down at her. The things she paid attention to sometimes surprised him. "That's his name, and yes, he'll be fine after he sleeps it off. Too much to drink at dinner. But I swear I didn't—" He caught himself caring too much about her good opinion. "I needed to keep my head squared away tonight. Mrs. Forrest is an upright Christian lady." He started up the stairs.

"Is she?" Joelle sounded curious. "I've heard the general is a hard-nosed businessman."

"He is, very clever, and he has influence in all sorts of places. I'd like to know your thoughts after you've talked to him. I'd thought he might support my father, but now I'm not so sure."

She gave him a funny look. "All right. Is that why you wanted me to come?"

"Partially. Mainly I just thought you'd enjoy the outing."

By now they had reached the first mezzanine landing. She had been silent so long that he looked down and found her smiling up at him. "I am enjoying it. I've never been to the opera before. Grandmama seemed pleased to have us visit and was in a charitable frame of mind at dinner. She was disappointed that you didn't come though."

"I'll go see her in the morning." Glancing over his shoulder to find the preacher several steps behind them, he leaned in and said softly, "I'm sorry you got stuck with him tonight. I didn't mean to goad you into—"

"Schuyler, you didn't goad me into anything! I invited Gil because I wanted to, and he was very kind to accompany me so that you could take care of Mr. Hixon." She looked exasperated.

"The only reason he did was to make me look bad. And to make sure you don't have too much fun."

"That's ridiculous." She laughed. "I didn't know you'd gotten so cynical."

"You don't know the half of it," he said, hunching his shoulders. "If you could hear these politicians I've spent the last three days with, it would curl your hair." He reached over and tweaked one of the strawberry ringlets bouncing against her neck. "Which would be a sight to behold."

"If they're so bad, why are you wasting your time with them?"

"My pa has asked me to keep my ear to the ground. I don't know what he's so worried about. People talk a lot of loud nonsense, but that's all it is."

"Do you think so?"

He glanced at her, noting the dainty way she lifted her skirts clear of the stairs, yet the directness and intelligence in her expression. Joelle had always been something of a mystery to him, a challenge he enjoyed unlocking. He sensed there was something doubtful behind her question, but they'd reached the top of the stairs and the suite where the reception for Miss Fabio was to be held. "It had better be," he said and knocked on the door.

Three

DAUGHTRY HOUSE WAS BEAUTIFUL in its own way, but the amenities of the Peabody quite took Joelle's breath away.

Finding herself in a high-ceilinged sitting room furnished with expensive tables, sofas and chairs, gilt-framed artwork and mirrors—not to mention the elegantly dressed ladies and gentlemen standing about—she gaped at a graceful wrought-iron staircase that curved up into a balcony railing fronting a row of second-floor bedrooms. The effect was somehow exotic and yet entirely American in its frank opulence.

As a liveried butler took her wrap and the men's hats, she made mental notes of what she would describe in her society article to come. Vaguely she was aware of Schuyler speaking to the butler, who pointed out a distinguished middle-aged couple standing under the central chandelier and then bowed himself away.

"Let me introduce you to Mrs. Forrest and the general," Schuyler said. Leaving Gil to follow, he offered an arm to Joelle.

General Forrest, tall and striking in his severe evening

dress, his silver-streaked dark hair brushed away from a handsome, hawkish countenance, greeted them as they approached. "Beaumont! Happy to see you made it down, after your friend's little . . . incident."

"Yes, sir, I'm sorry about that," Schuyler said with a grimace. "Hixon is upstairs sleeping it off."

Mrs. Forrest, an attractive woman dressed in sober brown bombazine, smiled at Joelle as Schuyler presented her and Gil. "We're happy you could come, Miss Daughtry. I've met your grandmother a time or two. Reverend Reese, welcome to Memphis." She looked up at her husband. "Bedford, what do you reckon has happened to Miss Fabio? Our guests are waiting to meet her."

The general glanced up at the interior staircase. "Here she comes right now."

And a grand entrance it was. What Delfina Fabio lacked in height she made up for in color and sparkle. Hips swaying, she descended on the arm of a portly mustachioed gentleman, her voluptuous form emphasized by the low-cut red velvet evening gown she'd worn for the curtain call. Diamond-studded combs ornamented her dark hair, and garnet sprays dangled from her ears and draped about her delicate neck.

The company burst into spontaneous applause. Joining in, Joelle glanced at Schuyler, expecting to find him gawking at the beautiful opera star.

He was, rather, smiling down at her. "Would you like to meet her?"

"Oh yes! But—"

He was already approaching the singer with his confident swagger and friendly grin. He bowed low. "Miss Fabio!

Mrs. Forrest was kind enough to invite me to be the first to welcome you to the American South. If I had not been an aficionado of the opera before, I certainly am now. Schuyler Beaumont at your service."

Delfina gave her escort a twinkling upward glance from her big black eyes. "Why, Poldi, *cara*, what delicious treats the Memphis Opera has to provide for us!" She dropped the man's arm to slink toward Schuyler, eyeing him like a tray of candy in a confectioner's window. "Is a pleasure, Mr. Beaumont. You must meet my manager, Mr. Volker." The implication was clear: Volker was not her husband.

Schuyler exhibited no discomfiture at such blatant flirtation. He laughed and shook hands with Volker. "How do you do, sir? I was just about to offer refreshment to my friends, at least one of whom is much more musically literate than I. Miss Fabio, perhaps you'd like to join us? Miss Daughtry is quite agog to meet you." He turned to wink at Joelle.

Delfina simpered. "I am happy to meet so educated admirer. Refreshment sounds lovely." Tucking her small beringed hand into his elbow, she allowed Schuyler to lead her toward the little group under the chandelier.

How does he do that? Joelle wondered. People simply melted under his charm.

Well, people except for Gil Reese.

"I told you she was immoral," Gil muttered under his breath. "Falling for that load of nonsense."

"Shhh!" She bobbed a curtsey as Delfina approached. "Miss Fabio, what a thrill to have seen you perform! I am Joelle Daughtry, and this is Reverend Reese."

"Happy to be acquainted, Reverend Reese." The singer gave him a dimpled smile, then extended both hands to Joelle.

"But you and I must be Delfina and Joelle, yes? I feel we shall be good friends, with the music to bind our hearts!"

Chuckling at this extravagant offer, Joelle returned the clasp of Delfina's hands. "I'm not sure what Schuyler led you to believe, but I assure you I'm the veriest amateur. Now, my sister's husband you should meet—our Levi is quite the concert pianist."

Delfina released Joelle and pressed her hands together at her bosom. "I wish to acquaint such an artist!"

"I'm sure we could arrange that," Schuyler said before Joelle could demur in confusion. "Perhaps when your engagement here is at an end, you would enjoy a short trip south. Miss Daughtry's family owns a lovely resort near Tupelo, Mississippi, and I feel certain you would find a most comfortable and restful sojourn there."

Delfina beamed at Joelle. "I would adore that of the most certain! But you must promise that your Mr. Beaumont would be there as well." She gave Schuyler a teasing sideways look. "Unless, my dear Joelle, he is perhaps your—your *spasimante*?"

"Oh no!" Joelle felt her face flood with color. "We are not betrothed! Schuyler is our family's business partner."

After a thoughtful stare, Delfina smiled. "I see," she said slowly. "Then I shall not worry to take him for a glass of something cold to drink. I am parched!" She bore Schuyler away to the refreshment table.

There was something dissatisfying about that exchange that Joelle could not quite put her finger on, but Mrs. Forrest claimed her attention, while Gil entered into a discussion of local politics with the general.

"My dear, are you feeling quite well?" Mrs. Forrest asked

sometime later, her fine eyebrows drawing together in motherly concern. "Perhaps you'd like to sit down while your young man fetches you a plate and a glass of lemonade." She touched Gil's sleeve.

Gil immediately looked around, contrition in his expression. "Of course. I'll be right—"

"What?" Joelle blinked, her attention returning to her hostess. "There's nothing wrong with me, I'm just . . ." How could she admit that she could not have named one item of any significance the good lady had rattled on about in the last fifteen minutes, but in her head she had created a nice outline of rebuttals to everything Forrest had said. "Well, perhaps I am a bit hungry."

As Gil disappeared into the crowd, she edged toward the closest chair and dropped into it. What was wrong with her that she couldn't even keep up her side of a simple conversation without drifting off into her own head? Resting her elbow on the arm of her chair, she laid her aching forehead in her palm. Maybe she should just ask Gil to take her home and forget this. Schuyler had gone off with the opera singer she came to talk to, and General Forrest clearly assumed she hadn't enough intellect to participate in a masculine exchange.

Then a random thought occurred, something that often happened when she was most discouraged. What would her mother have done in this circumstance? The consummate example of social grace, Mama had been adept at navigating difficulties without succumbing to self-pity or panic.

Find someone who is less comfortable than you and let them feel your love.

Mama had said it often enough, as the three girls grew

up, that Joelle could actually hear the soft, lilting musicality of the words. Joelle sometimes thought Mama directed them specifically at her because she was so inward, so self-contained. Able to play with dolls or paper dolls, or even sticks and leaves in the yard, for hours on end without talking to another soul, Joelle knew her mother worried about her middle child's social development.

Nothing wrong with the brain. Nothing wrong with the voice or body. *The child is just odd*, Papa used to say. And he would laugh.

And Joelle would flinch every time, though she never told anybody how much it hurt. Nobody but God, anyway.

And God always reminded her of her mother's gentle words. *Let them feel your love.*

All right then. She sat up and looked around for someone more uncomfortable than herself.

Downing his punch in one long slug, Schuyler tuned an ear to Delfina Fabio's Italian-accented and highly creative English syntax. He didn't know when he'd met a more irritating woman in his life. His effort to ensure that the singer came to visit Daughtry House seemed to have resulted mainly in her determination to make him her next American conquest. Every time he moved away from her, she shimmied closer, all but drowning him in some expensive Parisian scent. His head was beginning to pound from the effort to hold his breath and keep his eyes focused on something besides her nearly naked bosom.

And Joelle clearly couldn't care less. Leaving her in conversation with Mrs. Forrest and the preacher, he'd assumed she'd be able to hold her own until he returned. But a little while ago he'd caught a glimpse of her creeping around the edges of the room as if she were trying to escape. Then she disappeared.

Now he couldn't find her anywhere. Alarmed, he climbed two steps of the staircase behind him in order to gain a broader view.

Delfina followed, her head tipped in a coquettish fashion. "Mr. Beaumont, I am think you either try to take me upstairs to the bedrooms, or there is something interesting of the other side in the room."

"I assure you, I am not—" He looked at her and found her smile rather more amused than lascivious. "Oh. You're teasing."

She giggled. "Happy I am to discover you have the sense of humor. Most American young men would rather bed me than listen to me."

Though he appreciated her frankness, Schuyler couldn't think of two things that interested him less. As he tried to formulate a diplomatic reply, a crowd of men across the room shifted with a roar of approval, and he saw what had created such a stir. Joelle—looking, he was chagrined to note, competent, happy, and absurdly beautiful—leaned over an elaborately carved billiards table, aiming a cue at a white ball. Her apparent opponent, the execrable Andrew Jefcoat, stood behind her, keeping himself upright by leaning on his cue stick.

Schuyler scowled. This was . . . this was—not acceptable! He had sacrificed a significant amount of time and mental strain this evening for Joelle's benefit, and she had taken the opportunity to shark one of his best friends. Jefcoat would have no way of knowing Joelle had grown up playing the game under the tutelage of one of the master billiards players in the South. Her father the Colonel had had her own cue made when she was still small enough to need to stand on a box to reach over the table. She had memorized Michael Phelan's *Billiards without a Master* by the time she was ten. Nobody within a hundred miles of Lee County would take her on.

"Excuse me," he muttered to Delfina. "There is a situation I must attend to." Stepping past her, he shoved his way through the crowd. On the way, he passed the preacher, in earnest conversation with Delfina's mustachioed German manager. Schuyler halted. "What were you thinking? You let her go off by herself!"

"Who?" Reese looked irritable at the interruption.

"Joelle! Did you know she's in the corner, playing billiards with a half-drunk farmer?"

"Billiards? She was sitting right—" Reese looked around. "Where did she go?"

"Never mind." Schuyler continued his charge across the room, leaving Reese to follow if he chose. "Joelle! What do you think you're doing?"

Joelle looked up, startled, and as she did so the cue slipped and scratched the green baize surface of the table. She stared at the marred fabric in horror, then jerked upright. Her blue eyes spat fury. "Look what you made me do!"

"I'll pay for it." He snatched the cue out of her hand. "Jefcoat, how much have you lost?"

Jefcoat blinked owlishly. "Forty-five or so. She's pretty good, you know. I think she's got sixty-nine points already."

"I'm surprised it's not more than that. Here." Schuyler

pulled out his wallet, peeled off a couple of notes, and stuffed them into Jefcoat's breast pocket. "That should cover it. Go find something else to do. You're too drunk to play anybody with skill." Ignoring Jefcoat's protest, he took Joelle by the arm. "Come with me," he said grimly and towed her toward the door.

"I'm not going anywhere with you!" She dug in her heels. "Have you lost your mind?"

"Me? Ladies don't play billiards in public! Didn't your mother—or at the very least your grandmother or Thomas-Anne, or somebody with some common sense at that boarding school—teach you that?" Realizing he was shouting, and that people were looking at them, he let go of her arm. Leaning in, he moderated his tone with an effort. "Joelle, if you want to make a favorable impression for the hotel, you've got to *think*. Here in Memphis you can't behave like we do in the country, where everybody knows everybody else. Besides that, it's not fair for you to take advantage of poor Jefcoat. He's three sheets to the wind and would never be a match for you. His family doesn't have much money, and he can't afford—" The expression on her face stopped him. "I mean, you wouldn't know that, and . . . Joelle, please don't cry."

She blotted under her nose with the back of her hand. "You have just humiliated me in front of a hundred strangers. I'll cry if I want to." She heaved a shuddering breath. "Let me tell you something, you unmitigated arrogant beast. Andrew was standing against a wall without a soul to talk to. I recognized him as your friend and asked him if he'd like to join me in a glass of lemonade. *Lemonade*, do you hear me? Which we drank. Then he noticed the billiards table and asked me if I knew how to play. He seemed so shy, I could neither tell him 'ladies don't play billiards,' nor that I'd beat him like a drum in a military band within the space of five minutes. So we got up a game. I tried to lose, Schuyler! I tried! But when everybody started watching, something took over and I just couldn't do that to my father's memory. In spite of everything, Papa taught me that game, and it's the one good memory of him I have." She was openly sobbing now. "So excuse me if I go to the ladies' room and cry in private." She wheeled and stumbled away.

He let her go and met the wide-eyed gaze of Gil Reese. What had he just done?

Four

THE RE WAS NO PLACE TO GO.

Blinded by tears, Joelle was about to duck into a closet off the vestibule and indulge in a bout of weeping, wailing, and gnashing of teeth, when Delfina rescued her.

The singer's perfume preceded the comforting arm she slipped about Joelle's waist. "Ah, *cara*, the man they are stupid, is it not? But you must never let him see you crumple this way. Come to my room. We shall put the tincture of roses on your eyes and show who is the strong one after all!"

Joelle found herself whisked upstairs to a gold-and-turquoise brocade-appointed bedroom that could have graced a European palace. Delfina pushed her into a little dressing chair stationed at a mirrored table, handed her a soft, lacy handkerchief, and knelt to kindly pat her knee.

"I'm sorry," Joelle muttered. "I was only trying to be kind, and he took me so off-guard."

"Yes, yes, but it is because he loves you that he acts so, so . . . *pazzo*."

Joelle hiccupped on a laugh. "*Pazzo*—crazy indeed. But

you completely misunderstand. Schuyler does not love me. He thinks *I'm* the crazy one!"

"If you say so." Delfina shrugged. "In whatever case, you must be very careful with the tears. Useful they can be, of a certain, but not when one is truly exercised! *Mama mia!* Do not ever let a man think he give you real reason to cry."

"But I'm *angry!* I cry when I'm angry."

Delfina got to her feet and turned to rummage in the table's lap drawer. "Now that is a practical emotion. But if I may give a bit of advice from the acting school? Anger is best to present itself in cold, dignified—how do you say?—*altezzo.*"

"Hauteur?" Joelle sighed, twisting the handkerchief. "Delfina, I'm afraid I'm a terrible actress. I don't know that I have a haughty bone in my body."

"Then you must think of something that make you feel that way." Producing a small stoppered bottle, Delfina poured a little of the contents on the handkerchief and handed it back to Joelle. "Close your eyes and rest here for a few minutes. I leave you alone. When you feel better, you come down and show the hauteur to everyone—especially the beautiful crazy boy who make you so angry."

Delfina disappeared as if she were the incarnation of the fairy godmother Joelle had wished for earlier, leaving only the scent of roses and strong Parisian perfume in her wake.

Joelle sat stewing. She did not want to think. Thinking brought on poor decisions such as the one she had just committed. How could she not know ladies didn't play billiards at a party? Probably someone had said so at some point, when she was reading a book or thinking of something more interesting. Which brought her circling back to the original point.

Thinking was dangerous, and taking action was dangerous.

Except for the opera, which she had truly enjoyed, the whole evening had been one disaster after another. She hadn't even thought to invite Delfina to come to visit the hotel. Perhaps—

No. What she had better do was find Gil and make him take her home. Well, to Grandmama's house. She could write a thank-you note to Delfina later, when she'd had time to recover from her embarrassment.

Dabbing her eyes with the rosewater-soaked handkerchief, she rose and straightened her dress. She couldn't even face herself in the mirror.

Exiting the bedroom, she emerged on the landing and stood for a moment looking down on the party in the sitting room below. The general blur of color and motion reminded her of the kaleidoscope Papa had brought back from a trip to New York one summer. The billiards game in the corner had continued without her, Andrew Jefcoat having found a new opponent. There were, she noted with a shudder, no women in the group of onlookers circling the table.

Then she heard someone playing a piano and located a modified grand in a focal point near a curtained window. Delfina stood in its crook, the epitome of an artist prepared to engage an audience. She opened her mouth, and the rich voice rolled out a long, joyous opening "Ah!" then continued, "Je veux vivre, dans ce rêve qui m'enivre . . ."

I want to live in this dream that intoxicates me again this day! Sweet flame, I keep you in my soul like a treasure . . .

Transfixed, Joelle moved to the balcony railing and gripped it with both hands. She'd never seen a production of Gounod's *Romeo et Juliette*, but she'd once heard a senior student at boarding school butcher this aria in a recital. She'd asked her music teacher to lend her the music and privately played through it, imagining how it might be sung by a real soprano. Now she was hearing it.

Halfway through the song, she realized she was the only person looking at Delfina. Everyone else in the room directed a smiling gaze at a tall, lanky black-haired gentleman bearing a bouquet of roses up the curving staircase toward her. Gil. What was he doing? Oh, dear Gussie, now everyone was looking at *her*.

Gil kept advancing, up one step, then another, until he stood beside her, proffering the roses. "For you, Joelle," he said softly as Delfina kept singing. "I only wish they were as beautiful and innocent as you." His expression told her he knew she hadn't meant to make a spectacle of herself at the billiards table and that he would never argue with her in front of others. "This is the last time I'm going to ask you if you'll marry me. If you say no, I'll never bother you again. But if you say yes, and make me the happiest of men, I'll promise to treasure you as you deserve. You don't have to answer now. But I couldn't resist this opportunity to show you how much I love you."

Joelle looked at Gil, an explosion of unidentifiable emotions cascading from her aching head to her bruised heart and back again. She had thought about saying yes to him, more than once over the last month or so. Watching Selah and Levi together—and realizing she was no longer going to have her best friend's constant companionship—inevitably brought on a certain melancholy as she lay awake at night. If she married Gil, at least she'd have someone to talk to, on the rare occasions when she needed a confidant, and she could have tremendous influence for good as a minister's wife. Now, at this moment, she realized she loved Gil's humility, his tenderness, and the sweet, sweet words he spoke.

Against her will, her gaze searched the room for the one person she desired to witness this extraordinary display of devotion. He wasn't anywhere in sight.

Well, good riddance.

Resigned, she forced a smile for Gil. "Yes, I'll marry you."

Jouncing along in the carriage beside Gil on the way home, as emotion gave way to intellect, Joelle began to have some second thoughts. "Gil, were you offended by my behavior tonight? With the billiards game? You never mentioned it."

He sighed, taking her hand. "I was just worried. You know I love you and want to take care of you, and you have this tendency to wander about, saying and doing things without considering the consequences."

Well, that much was true. Maybe she did need him, to keep her from wandering into explosive devices like Schuyler Beaumont.

Gil, on the other hand, would be getting the bad side of the bargain. "Why do you want to marry me?" she blurted. "If I'm so much trouble, I mean."

"Why? Because you're—you're—" She could hear him gulp in the darkness of the carriage. "You obviously don't look in a mirror very often. Which—now that I think about it, that's a very good trait!" He sounded cheerful to have thought of something that wouldn't sound shallow. "You're modest and thrifty, as well as pretty! I know how much you love God's Word. You're devoted to your family, and I've seen you defend your poor cousin ThomasAnne. And as I said,

I admire your service to your slaves—I mean employees—teaching them to read, although I think you'll likely have to give that up when we get married, because you'll be much too busy with church work—"

"Gil." He talked a lot, when he got going. "Thank you, but I didn't want a laundry list of my attributes. I simply wanted to know how you feel."

"How I feel? I believe I said I love you. Twice."

She bit her lip. "Never mind."

They completed the remainder of the trip in awkward silence.

She looked up at him as he handed her down onto the drive path of her grandparents' house on Adams Avenue. "Gil, before you talk to my grandfather, I want to ask you something else."

"Before I—what do you mean 'talk to your grandfather'?"

"Well, you'll have to ask him for my hand, of course."

"Why? You're a grown woman."

In other words, an old maid. On the shelf. Most girls married before turning twenty, and Joelle had long passed that. She sighed. "He'll expect it." Grandpapa was *very* old-fashioned.

Gil audibly gulped. "All right. What did you want to ask me?"

"Never mind. It's not important." She was too tired and overwrought for any more intellectual conversation. "Well, there is a lot to talk about, but let's get this part of it over with." Grandmama was the one who was going to give her trouble.

"Are you sure?" Now *he* sounded uncertain.

"Just pay the cab and let's go inside."

They found her grandparents in the first-floor salon with Doc Kidd and ThomasAnne. The two women shared a settee near the open window, where lacy curtains fluttered in a desultory breeze. Gaslight from the wall sconces cast harsh shadows on Grandmama's craggy, aristocratic features but somehow turned ThomasAnne into an even more muted watercolor painting than usual. Doc was engaged with Grandpapa on the other side of the room, the two physicians nursing brandy snifters and carrying on a lively conversation, probably about catheters or cadavers or some such.

ThomasAnne jumped to her feet, clearly relieved at the arrival of another target for Grandmama's critical tongue. "Joelle! You're back! See, Aunt Winnie, I told you—"

"Yes, yes, I have eyes in my head, girl." Grandmama waved ThomasAnne back to her seat but continued to glare at Joelle. "Your grandfather was about to go out searching for you, and wouldn't that be a fine disaster if he should come to grief in some lowbrow neighborhood?"

Oddly heartened by this familiar harangue, Joelle laughed. "Grandmama, the Peabody is barely two blocks away, and nobody remotely lowbrow could afford to live in its vicinity. As you can see, Gil and I are perfectly fine."

With a loud "Hmph," Grandmama transferred her cobra-esque stare on poor Gil, promptly reducing him to a stammering mass of red-faced apologies.

"I told her we shouldn't—that is, it seemed perfectly innocent. I've always wanted to meet General Forrest and his wife. And Joelle would have been fine if Schuyler Beaumont hadn't—"

"Schuyler?" Grandmama pounced at mention of her favorite. "Then he was at the Peabody? Why didn't he come to see me?"

"I'm sure I don't—"

"Grandmama!" Interrupting Gil's spiral into incoherence, Joelle sank into the closest chair. The headache was turning into a migraine, and bedtime seemed nowhere in sight. "Schuyler begged me to give you his regards and to tell you that he will come to call. Gil, why don't you ask Grandpapa for a short audience?"

Grandmama, who was nobody's fool, pounced. "Audience? Do you mean *audience* audience?"

ThomasAnne looked confused. "What is an audience audience?"

"Gil." Joelle gave him a nudge. "Grandpapa is right over there."

He gulped. "Oh. Yes." He turned and stumbled away, muttering, "She already said yes. It's not as if he can—but what if he doesn't . . ."

"Did you already say yes?" Grandmama looked amused.

"Say yes to what?" ThomasAnne looked from Joelle to Grandmama and back.

"Yes. I did." Joelle shrugged.

"Joelle." Grandmama's eyes softened. "You can do better."

Joelle straightened. "He is a good man. He cares for me, and I—I care for him."

ThomasAnne gasped. "Do you mean—"

"Of course that's what she means, you twit." Grandmama sniffed. "I tried to tell you girls what would happen if you sequestered yourselves at that ramshackle plantation in the middle of nowhere. Why you wouldn't stay here after the war ended, I will never understand. But it's not too late. Your grandfather will refuse, and you can come have a season in Memphis this summer."

"I told you I care—"

"Hogwash." Grandmama rarely uttered vulgarities, and when she did, one had better listen. "You have simply given up. I wouldn't have suspected you of such spinelessness, Joelle."

She couldn't admit she'd agreed to Gil's proposal as a result of an argument with Schuyler Beaumont. "On the contrary," she said, "I find myself having to exert quite a lot of spine to overcome this unreasonable prejudice against a man of godly character and humble means. You, Grandmama, are a snob."

"I never claimed otherwise," Grandmama retorted. "But that has nothing to do with my concern that you are selling yourself at a woefully cheap price. You are not cut out to be a preacher's wife."

"What does that mean?"

"Can you actually see yourself hostessing ladies' missionary parties? Visiting sickbeds with tisanes? Decorating the sanctuary for Easter?"

Less than three months ago, Joelle had voiced almost those exact words to Selah. Still . . . "I imagine no one ever feels qualified to serve God when they are called. Even Isaiah said as much."

"'Woe is me, for I am undone,'" ThomasAnne said suddenly.

"Exactly," Joelle said. "And Moses stammered."

"You will be miserable," Grandmama said with the persistence of a dog with a fine bone. "You hate crowds, you despise public speaking, and preachers live in a fishbowl."

"But preachers' wives are expected to care for the poor, which will make my Negro school less of a scandal."

"Your—*what*?" Grandmama all but came up out of her chair.

"My Negro school. I've been planning and saving for it for quite some time. Schuyler is helping sponsor it." She didn't know why she blurted that last.

But it stopped Grandmama in her tracks. The Beaumonts were imbued with a cunning blend of educated culture, opportunism, and political savvy. Besides that, they were distant relatives via Schuyler's maternal grandmother. Still, the old lady looked skeptical. "Why on earth would he do that?"

Joelle remembered a rather facetious conversation she and Schuyler had had regarding the education of slaves, the summer after she and Selah were dismissed from boarding school. Their expulsion had resulted from Selah's championing of a certain liberal teacher who insisted there was no biological difference between black brains and white brains—and who had subsequently been fired for subversion. Sky had remarked that he'd once dissected an albino frog and a regular frog and couldn't tell their brains apart, and that one could infer the same would hold true for humans.

"Headmistress would say slaves are not human in the same way that you and I are," Joelle told him bitterly. "They can't be educated."

"Headmistress is full of beans," Schuyler had said, laughing.

Thinking of that conversation, Joelle smiled. "Who knows what mysterious elements lurk in Schuyler's brain? The important thing is that Negroes are free, and they can vote.

I believe they should be educated so that they can make informed decisions."

"Joelle, that is not your problem. *You* can't vote."

"Which is another unfortunate circumstance I hope to change."

Grandmama eyed her grimly, and Joelle was aware of ThomasAnne twisting her hands in an agony of discomfort. How did she and her opinionated grandparent always manage to find themselves at loggerheads after more than ten minutes in the same room?

She looked for a distraction and realized Gil was standing before her grandfather, turning his hat about in his hands, Adam's apple bobbing above his starched collar. Grandpapa reached up to shake hands, Gil dropped the hat on his own foot, and Doc picked it up, laughing.

"Congratulations," Doc said, rising to clap Gil on the back. "I never thought she'd say yes."

Well then, it was settled. Joelle could consider herself engaged.

Five

SCHUYLER AWOKE THE NEXT MORNING without a hangover—a state which might normally have been a relief, but which at present only indicated the sorry state of his social life. When a man let a woman influence him to the extent that getting roaring drunk lost its appeal, it was time to flee the area.

Thus his sanity was certainly in question when he found himself, at the unholy hour of nine a.m., fully dressed and bearing a posy of daffodils, at the front door of McGowan House on Adams Street.

"Good morning, Alistair," he said to the butler who answered the door. "Is Miss Winnie up and about yet?"

"Now, Master Sky, you know Mistress get up with the chickens. She in her parlor writing letters." Alistair smiled, eyeing the flowers. "You take those right on up, you know how she like a present. How about I bring up a tray of coffee and snickerdoodles?"

"You speak my language, sir." Schuyler headed up the stairs to the old lady's lair. He'd meant the flowers for Joelle, but a peace offering for the dragon wouldn't go amiss. He stopped halfway up and called over his shoulder, "Is anybody else with her?"

Alistair paused in the dining room doorway, dark eyes gleaming. "I think I saw Miss Joelle in the breakfast room. Did you hear what happened last night?"

He'd seen the whole thing. Watched it coming on like a freight train off the rails. He knew he'd upset Joelle by dragging her away from the billiards game. Generally he had more tact, but something about the idea of her flirting with Jefcoat had sent him into a spiral of insanity. Which had played right into the hands of the preacher. Apparently Reese had arranged that whole romantic opera scene with the manager, Volker.

He hoped that Joelle hadn't committed herself past redemption. And he hoped that she would forgive him.

"I heard there was an opera in town," he said, playing dumb.

"An opera and—but ain't my place to talk out of turn. Best let her tell you." The butler disappeared.

Schuyler continued lightly up the stairs. At the open doorway of Miss Winnie's sitting room, he halted to straighten his vest.

"Come in here, boy, don't stand there blocking the light." The old lady's crackly soprano made him laugh as he entered the room.

"Please forgive, ma'am. I just wanted to make sure I'm presentable." Bowing beside the desk at which Winifred Mc-Gowan sat like a black-clad myna, one gnarled claw grasping an old-fashioned quill, he proffered the flowers. "These are for you."

"Well, aren't you the smooth young commodore?" Miss Winnie laid aside her pen and took the flowers. "What are you doing up and about so early?"

"If I hope to be as wealthy as Mr. Vanderbilt one day, I must be early to work." Schuyler took a casual scan of the room. "I see the opera crowd have yet to rise."

"We were all up late last night." Miss Winnie gestured toward a chair. "Sit down and tell me why you failed to keep my granddaughter from betrothing herself to that young Ichabod Crane."

"I'm afraid I might have accidentally precipitated it." Schuyler wandered over to a bookcase stuffed with an assortment of souvenirs from the McGowans' Asian and European travels and picked up a Chinese wood block puzzle. When the old lady was quiet for a long moment, he looked over his shoulder.

"I had thought . . ." After a moment, she waved a hand. "Never mind. I see I was mistaken. Tell me about the Negro school."

Senility, he had heard, sometimes approached without warning, taking even the sharpest of elderly minds. "Perhaps you're thinking of someone else. Railroads and hotels are my milieu."

"Yes, of course, but Joelle said you've helped her fund a school for freedmen. I must say I'm surprised, for I'd thought your background not particularly suited to educational pursuits." She scowled. "And I wish you'd discouraged this nonsense. She's had her head in the clouds for far too long."

"Oh that. She asked if I had any ideas for her project, and the only thing I could think of was giving her some cash. I'd forgotten all about it." He set down the wooden puzzle and picked up the Japanese kokeshi doll beside it.

"How altruistic of you," the old lady said. "And convenient."

He turned, ready to argue, but Alistair stood in the doorway, a very odd expression on his generally bland dark face.

The butler held a silver tray bearing a small, plain white envelope. "Miss Winnie, there's a telegram . . ."

"Don't just stand there, bring it to me," Winnie said impatiently. "Where are the cookies?"

"It's for Master Sky." Alistair swung his gaze to Schuyler. "I'm sorry, sir. The morning paper just came too, so I didn't know until—" He swallowed. "I'm so sorry."

Something leaden dropped in Schuyler's stomach. "A telegram for me? Here?" Very few people knew of this trip to Memphis, and those who did would assume he'd be receiving mail at the hotel.

"Yes, sir." Alistair proffered the tray in the manner of one extending a deadly snake. "A messenger from the Peabody brought it."

Schuyler took the envelope with a nod of thanks for Alistair. "With your permission, ma'am?" he said to his hostess.

"Of course."

There was nothing to be afraid of, not until he'd read it. Still, his fingers trembled as he tried to open the envelope.

Joelle burst into the room. "Schuyler, wait, don't open that!" She reached him and snatched the telegram from his hands.

"What are you doing?" He grabbed and missed.

Stuffing the paper into the front of her dress, she backed

toward the door. "Come with me. I have to talk to you right now."

"Have you lost your mind?"

She looked a little crazy, curly red hair escaping from her sleeping braid, a day dress buttoned rather haphazardly over what looked suspiciously like her night rail. Her face was flushed, blue eyes swollen and watery. "Please. Let's go down to the parlor. Grandmama will excuse us, I'm sure."

To his astonishment, the old lady nodded. "I'll make sure you're not disturbed. Alistair, I'll want my cookies and coffee, if you please."

"Yes, ma'am." Alistair bowed and exited, a bizarre mixture of relief and sorrow etched in the lines of his face.

Schuyler followed Joelle down the stairs to the ground-floor parlor. Had she ended the engagement? Her grandmother hadn't indicated such. But why would she be so upset with him reading his own telegram? How would she know what was in it?

She pointed to her grandfather's chair. "Sit down."

He did so, noting that the whole room smelled of Dr. McGowan's tobacco, which also smelled like his own father's cigars. Schuyler had never seen Pa without a cigar either in his mouth or in his hand. "Joelle, what is going—"

"I'll tell you." She dropped onto the hassock at his knees and looked up at him with eyes like rain-washed lapis lazuli. "You shouldn't read this in the paper or in a telegram. I know Camilla meant well, but—" She took his numb, icy hands, which had been clutching the arms of the chair. Hers were warm, comforting. "Schuyler, something terrible has happened. You know your father was in Tuscaloosa this week, campaigning?"

He nodded, jerkily. "I was supposed to meet him there, but I had the chance to connect with General Forrest, so we decided—Pa agreed it would be a good idea. Is he hurt?" Ezekiel Beaumont was an indestructible force, like one of the trains he loved so much.

Joelle's fingers tightened painfully around his. "Schuyler, this is so hard, but your father is d-dead. Someone shot him while he was making a speech from his hotel balcony."

Trying to make sense of the words, he looked at her lips, noted their trembling tenderness. She had been his friend for his whole life, and yet how he loathed her in that moment. "That's a lie. I know I've hurt you and teased you, Jo, but that is beyond the bounds of cruelty."

"I wish I could make it not so." Her eyes, naked in sorrow, held his.

"Give me the telegram."

Slowly she reached into her dress and handed it over, crumpled and still warm from her skin. His hands shook so hard he couldn't get it open, so Joelle took it again, opened the envelope, and handed him the thin sheet of paper containing two sentences from his sister Camilla.

SCHUYLER SO SORRY TO TELL YOU PAPA HAS BEEN ASSASSINATED. COME HOME.

"How did you know? How did Alistair know?" Schuyler looked as if he'd run into a wall, and Joelle couldn't blame him.

"It was in the morning paper." Schuyler's father was a figure of statewide importance in Alabama, a leading candidate for governor.

"Wait. Alistair reads?"

He was grasping at nonsensical details.

She took the telegram from his unresisting hold, laid it on the side table, and took his hands again. "Grandpapa taught him," she said gently, "which is why it's so absurd for Grandmama to block my school. Never mind that. What do you want to do?"

He stared at her blankly. She'd never seen Schuyler cry, didn't expect him to do so now. But there should have been some emotion. Some anger. Something. Schuyler loved his father, admired him above any other man on earth.

She remembered how she'd felt after her own father fell from the cupola at Daughtry House. She hadn't seen it happen. In fact, she hadn't even known for sure that her father was still alive. But Selah had been the one to hold her as she discovered the truth about their father's insanity and villainy. And there had been a sort of cathartic grief that had gripped her during the days before and after the funeral, when the three sisters drew together for mutual solace.

There was no one here from Schuyler's family to stand with him in the face of this horrific blow. His mother had died when he was born. His older brother, Jamie, was holding down the shipping business in Mobile. Camilla was in New Orleans with her family.

Joelle didn't know what to do. If Gil were here, he'd pray or quote Scripture. Preachers were used to comforting the grieved. And when she married Gil, she'd be expected to do so as well. What a terrifying thought, comforting strangers.

But Schuyler wasn't a stranger. She'd known him practically her whole life, and their grandmothers were cousins. Which made her all he had at the moment.

"Schuyler, I think we should pray."

His lips tightened. "I have no desire—"

"I know you don't, but the very time you feel least like it is when you need it the most." That was what Selah said when they found out their mother had been brutalized and killed by Yankee marauders. And she had been right. The only way they got through that year had been laying their bruised souls at the feet of Jesus.

To her astonishment, Schuyler suddenly bent double over their joined hands, uttering a groan that sounded like rending cloth. "I can't, Jo," he choked. "You do it." She felt a splash of warmth against her hands.

She laid her cheek against the top of his head, wishing with all her heart she could take the sorrow from him. "Oh, God," she breathed. "Oh, God, I don't know what to say. Please help us." She lay there feeling him shudder, absorbing his tears.

Some time later he relaxed and turned his head. "I don't mean to be such a baby." His voice was low, gravelly. "You won't tell anyone, will you?"

"How could you think—"

"I don't really. I'm just so . . ." He sat up, dragging a sleeve across his face. "You asked me what I want to do. I don't know. I'm empty." He looked at her. "But I can't just sit here. Do I go for his body? Will somebody send him home?"

"I don't know." She felt helpless. "I wish Levi was here. He'd know what to do."

"So would Jamie. I've always been the youngest in the family. Somebody else makes the big decisions." He picked up the telegram and read it again. "Assassinated. Camilla wants me to come home. Where's the newspaper? I need all the details."

Joelle could almost feel her heart pumping pain through her body, and Schuyler's must be beyond comprehension. But at least he seemed rational. She got up to retrieve the newspaper from the breakfast room, where she'd been eating eggs and toast when Alistair handed it to her. She gave it to Schuyler, folded back with the pertinent article on the front page center. The headline was in one-inch type: "Candidate for Alabama Governor Shot By Unknown Assailant."

Schuyler's hands were steady now as he read. His thumb brushed across the photograph of his father accompanying the article. At last he looked up at Joelle. "Why? It doesn't make any sense. Pa is about as moderate as they come. Everybody likes him."

"Someone didn't." Joelle spoke the obvious. "Who hates him this much, Sky? Is there something your father espoused politically that made him a target of a person so mad?"

He shook his head, stubborn as usual. "Only a crazy person would do this, that's certain, and who can predict what they'll do?"

She had to be very careful here. Females weren't supposed to pay attention to politics, at least publicly. Everyone knew women influenced the voting practices of their men, but few were so bold or so unladylike as to express opinions on national- or even state-level topics. "What about railroad subsidies? It makes sense that Mr. Zeke would be in favor of them, considering your family's business interests. But there are a lot of folks radically opposed to government intervention in the transportation industry."

Schuyler would normally have given her one of his patented raised-eyebrow smirks, but understandably his sense of humor had abandoned him. "My father is not an opportunist. He is rather an advocate of Lockean free trade economics."

"Then perhaps some of those opportunists, as you call them, might have decided to eliminate an impediment to the government trough. Money is a powerful motive for treachery."

"That is a fairly astute observation." Schuyler rubbed his forehead. "I wish Levi were here too. He'd know how to pursue such a lead."

"Why don't you hire him—if, that is, you don't feel you can trust the investigation to local law enforcement?"

He stared at her so hard and for so long, eyes opaque as blue steel, that she inwardly shrank. She'd only been trying to help.

Finally he rose. "I don't know why I didn't think of it. I'll telegram Levi, and maybe he can come over to Mobile with Camilla for the—for the funeral." Extending a hand to pull Joelle to her feet, he drew her awkwardly into his arms. "Thank you for being here. Thank you for listening. Thank you for—" He stopped, abruptly. "Whoops."

"What's the matter?" She looked over her shoulder.

Gil stood in the doorway. He looked both disapproving and embarrassed.

Oh dear. Trying not to appear as if she had been caught in some illicit lover's embrace, she extricated herself with as much dignity as possible and curtseyed to her betrothed. "Good morning, Gil. We were just talking about you." He had at least crossed her mind. That had to count for something.

Gil's frown deepened. "Why?"

She prayed her burning cheeks would calm down. Drat

this red hair and fair skin. "Schuyler has just had some very bad news, and I was thinking you'd be a good person to talk to him."

"I'm sorry to hear that." Gil's face relaxed. "What happened?"

"Schuyler's father—"

"There's no need to bother the preacher," Schuyler interrupted, putting a hand on Joelle's shoulder. "I'm fine now, and I've got things to attend to, related to your suggestion."

The look in his eyes kept her from arguing. For all his gregariousness, Schuyler could be very private about some things. "All right. Please let me know if there's anything I or my sisters can do."

"I will." Schuyler squeezed her shoulder and quit the room.

She felt the loss of his warmth, but focused on Gil with an effort. "Schuyler's father was killed yesterday during a campaign speech in Tuscaloosa. It was in this morning's paper. The gunman slipped away in the crowd and hasn't been apprehended."

"That's terrible. I'm so sorry."

"Yes, it is terrible. He loved his father very much, and his family is close. I just tried—" She pressed her hands together in delayed distress. "I wanted to make it less painful than reading it in the newspaper. We've been friends for a long time."

"I thought you didn't like him."

"Why would you think that?"

"Because you argue constantly. About everything."

"Of course we argue. He's like a brother to me." She could still feel Schuyler's hair pressing into her cheek as he wept over her hands. She'd never had a brother, but that alternating aggravation and protectiveness she felt for him could be described no other way. Gil would just have to live with it. "Have you had breakfast?"

"I don't eat breakfast. I thought you might want to take a walk and discuss our marriage plans."

What kind of person didn't eat breakfast? No wonder he was so skinny.

"What is there to discuss? Well, other than who will perform the ceremony. Can a preacher marry himself?"

Schuyler would have laughed at the facetious question, but Gil seemed to take it seriously. "That's exactly the kind of thing I mean. Do you want to marry in the church or at Ithaca—I mean Daughtry House?"

She really didn't want to talk about it at all. "Let me think about it. Selah and Levi married at home, but I'm not sure I want that much hoopla."

"I thought all women wanted hoopla." He looked confused. "In that case, let's go ahead and get married here in Memphis. I don't think long engagements are a good idea anyway. Your grandparents' minister can do the service. Or we can go to the courthouse, whichever you prefer."

She felt unreasonably panicked. "No! Gil, I'll have to go to Mobile for the funeral, and—don't you see that we can't rush into things?"

"Rush?" He scratched his head. "We've known each other for ten years. But I guess if I've waited this long, another few months won't kill me."

"Exactly. Let's go back to Tupelo so I can make sure the hotel is in good order before I make the trip to Mobile. When I get there, I'll talk to Selah about wedding"—she circled her hand vaguely—"things."

"All right. Whatever you want, Joelle. I just want to make you happy." He bent as if to kiss her, but she dodged him so that his lips landed on her eyebrow.

"Thank you, Gil. That's very sweet." If he wanted to make her happy, he would go away and leave her alone. Since that wasn't likely to happen, she took him by the arm and tugged him toward the stairs. "Come on, Grandmama has cookies. You really need to eat something, or you're going to blow away in the next high wind."

Schuyler stood aimlessly outside the Memphis train station with his hands in his pockets.

The one thing he wanted at this moment—and the one thing he couldn't do—was to tell Pa he was in love with Joelle Daughtry, and wasn't that a staggering development after some twenty years of acquaintance, during which they'd rarely if ever participated in a civil conversation?

If he were already at home, he would dive off a pier into the bay and swim until he was exhausted, or row a canoe for hours, or go stomping around in the woods with Jamie. Instead, he must wait here for two hours for the next train headed south. This enforced introspection, after such a shock, was dangerous.

How could those two things—finding out his father was dead and that he was in love—have happened all but simultaneously? On second thought, perhaps the one had triggered the other. Lying under Joelle's silken cheek, unmanly tears wetting her dress, the realization that he'd never see his father again had caused something like Pauline scales to fall from his eyes. She cared about him, no matter what crazy backward arguments she slung at him on a regular basis.

And he'd lost her, to a man who deserved her infinitely more than an undisciplined, hubristic younger son like Schuyler Beaumont. He'd never own the right to hold her for more than a few seconds in a brotherly hug or pat on the shoulder. No more sharing private jokes or making up words or playing billiards after midnight.

No more praying together.

Probably it was that last thought that grieved him most. There was not another human being in his life who had the temerity or the insight to insist that he needed to bring his sorrow to God. And she was right. Those few minutes had broken him and seared him and set him on a path to healing.

He felt raw. What in the world was he going to do without Pa and without Joelle?

He could go home, draw on the strength of the rest of his family. Or he could take the next train to Tuscaloosa, claim his father's body, and find out who had committed the murder.

Of those two choices, the first seemed cowardly. He was tired of taking easy roads.

He straightened his vest and headed for the telegraph office. As Joelle suggested, he was going to need Levi's help.

Six

"NOW THAT I AM FREE, I will make the most of every opportunity to help my fellow man."

Joelle stared at the sentence Shug Pogue had just written
on the blackboard fixed to the back wall of the cookhouse
pantry. It made her heart pound with both pride and anxiety.
She had taught him to write, but she had not designed his
thoughts.

Selah had always told Joelle she would be a good teacher,
but she hadn't believed it. Or perhaps it was just that she
hadn't wanted to be a teacher. She slid her hand into her
pocket and fingered the red ribbon binding five letters she'd
composed first thing this morning, in answer to questions
regarding summer bookings at Daughtry House Hotel and
Resort. She had no particular passion for the hotel business
either. If anything, she resented the intrusion it made on the
things she really wanted to do.

What she dreamed of doing was writing a book like Mrs.
Stowe, or perhaps Mrs. Alcott, whose work she had devoured
under the influence of Miss Lindquist at the Holly Springs

Academy. But she'd resigned herself to the fact that her life was to be mainly composed of the boring and trivial. At least she was safe. She was engaged to marry a good man. The hotel was set to take in its first guests in June, just a few weeks away. Besides, look what had happened to Miss Lindquist: dismissed without a reference, for teaching her students to embrace rebellious female libertarianism.

Still . . . something about Shug's words on the blackboard challenged her complacency.

She clasped her hands at her waist in her best imitation of Miss Lindquist—calm, encouraging, attentive. "That is beautiful work, Shug."

Shug, six feet tall and skinny as one of the slats of the table at which he sat with the other students, gave Joelle his big grin. "Thank you, Miss Joelle. I know how much you like good writing. Is everything spelled right?"

"It's perfect." Shug's work was always perfect. He'd supervised the crew who put the new roof on the big house, as well as the main outbuildings, like this kitchen and the manager's cottage where the family lived. Part of his pay included lessons in reading and writing, which he took full advantage of, and which Joelle considered a fair trade for services rendered.

"My turn, Miss Jo!" Ten-year-old Tee-Toc Weber jumped to his feet and swaggered to the board. "I got a sentence better than that."

Amused, Joelle sat down at her little desk by the window to watch the boy carefully scrape words onto the board, tongue firmly between his teeth. She'd be astonished if he didn't one day become president of the United States. He was dark of skin and ragged of clothing, his wiry hair sawn off with a butcher knife in uneven clumps, but his mother saw that he was always clean and well fed when he appeared at the hotel every morning for work.

With a grand flourish of the last letter, he turned to read his words aloud. "A man who can read and write caint never be cheated."

Joelle bit her lip. He was so proud and so confident, she hated to correct him. But shoring up weakness would help none of the students looking to her for instruction. "The thought is beautiful and true. Can I help you a bit with the spelling and grammar?"

"Yes, ma'am, 'course you can. I want you to." Tee-Toc plopped back down on his bench, looking only slightly crestfallen.

"All right." She stood and went to the board. Pointing at the word "caint," she said, "This word is actually two words smushed together—*can* and *not*. So you've actually made up a word here, Tee-Toc." She grinned at him. "That's creative, but in formal writing you need to stick to the dictionary." When the boy laughed, she picked up a piece of chalk to write *can*, *not*, and *never* on the board. She circled *not* and *never*. "All right, now that we've separated your word into its proper pieces, you see that you have two negatives next to each other. You're good at math. What do you know about two negatives?"

Tee-Toc snapped his fingers. "They cancels each other out!"

"They *cancel*," Joelle corrected him. "But yes. So you need to leave out one of those negatives to make your sentence make sense. Write either 'cannot ever' or 'can never.'"

Tee-Toc nodded slowly. "I see. I think. There sure is a lot of rules for writing, ain't there?"

Joelle sighed. "There sure are. It's enough to give one a headache." On the bright side, however, Tee-Toc had just given her the lead line for an article she had been working on for the *Journal*. She had made notes all the way home from Memphis yesterday, ignoring Gil's persistent attempts to engage her in conversation. He'd finally given up and gone to sleep with his hat over his face to muffle his snores.

She shouldn't be so critical, she thought as she erased the chalkboard. A man with a nose that size was bound to snore. And wasn't that going to be lovely after they got married? He'd be snoring in her ear for the rest of her life.

"So, Miss Jo, you think I write good enough now to help Pastor Boykin run for state senate?"

Joelle turned to find Shug regarding her seriously, as were the three other men at the table. She put down the eraser and dusted her hands on her skirt. "Of course you do. But why don't you run yourself? You'd make a fine senator. You're honest and organized and good with details. The whole community respects you and your family."

Shug lifted his shoulders. "That's mighty kind of you, and I thank you for the good word. I might start with something a little smaller, here on the local level. Maybe tax collector. But the Reverend is head and shoulders above me, and we need men with his reputation and education to represent freedmen in Congress."

"Not just freedmen," she reminded him. "He'd be representing all of us."

"Yes, ma'am. That's why I think he's a good choice. His father was white, had him educated in that fancy military academy up north." Shug glanced at his brother-in-law, Clancy Crumpton, seated next to him. Clancy and his wife,

Shug's sister Neesy, had taken on management of the hotel dairy. "Ain't that right, Clancy?"

"Yup. He got family all up and down the river here in Lee and Union Counties. Ain't nobody got a sour word to say about him nor his wife and chirren." Clancy hesitated. "Me and Shug had a idea—you always saying you wants to help."

"Of course I do," Joelle said. "But you know women can't vote. I'm not sure how—"

"We heard you gon' marry the Methodist preacher," Shug said.

"That's true," Joelle said cautiously.

"Well then." Shug grinned. "He gon' do whatever you tell him—least, if things works for white folks like they does in my house."

Joelle laughed. "I'm going on that assumption myself. So what am I to convince Reverend Reese it's in his best interests to do?"

Clancy slapped one of his big fists into the other palm. "That pulpit of his, it be a powerful source of influence. If he use it the right way, we can bring the voting community together and elect good men who can help us right some of the wrongs been done, without making enemies in the process."

Shug nodded. "We seen you and your sisters work with the Lawrences and the Vincents to break down walls on both sides. I know it ain't easy, and I know it gon' take time to bleed out in the community and the county and the state. They's a whole lot of fear and resentment out there. But we got to start somewhere. We figure if anybody know how to make it happen, you would."

I'm just a woman, she wanted to say. Hadn't she already

done enough, writing anonymous articles in the paper and volunteering to teach? Besides, she was about to be occupied in planning her wedding—not to mention running a hotel in her sister's absence—and she despised confrontations.

But . . . what if she'd been placed in such a time as this, as had Queen Esther of the Bible? All she had to do was blink at Gil, and he would melt like butter in a Mississippi heat wave. Couldn't she at least ask him to see what he could do for Reverend Boykin and Shug?

She slowly nodded. "I can't promise anything, of course, but I suppose I could speak to him. Gentlemen, I promised my sister I'd accompany her to town for some kitchen supplies, so I'm afraid we must conclude our lesson for the day. I would like for all of you to develop these sentences into a full paragraph supporting your thesis, and have it ready for me tomorrow. And don't forget the mathematics assignment as well. You've done good work today."

Benches scraped under the rumble of male voices. Within a few moments the pantry was empty except for Joelle, left to tidy her desk. She hesitated, then sat down. Aurora could wait another half hour while she finished her article. She could turn it in while she was in town.

She worked on it for half an hour, then once it was done, scanned through to make sure there were no words left out or inadvertent grammar mistakes. Fortunately she'd been blessed with good penmanship and spelling skills. Satisfied that she could turn in her composition without embarrassment, she folded the pages and slid them in beside the letters in her pocket, then exited through the interior kitchen door.

Horatia Lawrence, the hotel's head cook and housekeeper, turned from the stove, where she'd been busy canning a giant kettle of blackberry preserves. "Lessons all done?" Horatia used a neat handkerchief to dab a trickle of sweat from her caramel-colored brow. "Maybe you'd like to taste a spoonful of this on a leftover biscuit."

Joelle's mouth watered. "Yes, ma'am, I surely would." She poked under the cloth covering a basket of bread on the big butcher-block table in the middle of the room. Opening the flaky biscuit with her thumbs, she cupped it in her palms near the kettle.

Smiling, Horatia spooned a sweet-smelling black blob onto the biscuit. "I could always count on you to be my taster since you was a little thing."

"It's a miracle I'm not round as a barrel of flour since you came back to cook for us." Joelle licked a drop off her thumb. "Mmm. That's heavenly. Can I take one to Aurora? She and I are about to drive to town to take care of the list you gave me this morning. Do you need anything else?"

"No, but check with Mose before you leave. He was in the chicken yard a little bit ago."

"I will. Let's fix a biscuit for him too."

Juggling the three biscuits in a napkin, Joelle left the kitchen and crossed the lawn toward the farm side of the property. She found Mose repairing the wire near the chicken yard gate.

He looked up, smiling around the pipe in his teeth. "Hope you got something edible in that napkin, little lady. My stomach's setting up a howl, and I got a ways to go before this fence is coyote-proof again."

"Horatia's cat-head biscuits and warm blackberry preserves. I'll share, if you'll promise to play your harmonica for me after supper tonight."

"Small price to pay," Mose said, tucking his pipe into his pocket.

Joelle handed over the treat. "Did we lose a chicken last night?"

"Two." Mose made a disgusted face. "Wyatt gon' have to go huntin' again."

"He won't mind. He should be home from school before too long. I'm going to town with Aurora. You need anything?"

He thought as he chewed on a bite of biscuit. "Some tomato seed, if Whitmore's got any. It's a little late for planting, but I lost some vines in that late freeze in April."

"All right. We'll be back before dinnertime."

"Y'all be careful. I told Nathan to look at the off rear wagon wheel, but I'm not sure he got to it this morning."

"I'll check with him before we go." She wandered on toward the big house, thinking if she could have picked a papa, Mose would have been her choice. And wouldn't that be odd? The image of her own father never came to mind without a burst of rage and sorrow. It wasn't just that he'd clearly adored the practical, math-minded Selah and gregarious, outdoorsy Aurora, while barely noticing his quiet middle daughter.

He'd forced Joelle to leave home for boarding school at the age of seven. Having no one but Selah close by to represent home had further cemented Joelle's tendency to retreat inward. In Holly Springs she'd made few friends. Other girls assumed she was stuck-up, proud of her so-called beauty, when in reality she was terrified of saying the wrong thing. Often she'd contribute a perfectly reasonable English sentence, causing her conversational partner to look at her as if a horse or dog had just spoken. Later she might find that one or more of her vocabulary choices had been a tad esoteric.

And so she would pretend to be stupid or bored and say nothing at all. Or she'd simply stay in her room with a book and her journal, or steal into the music room to play the piano.

At least Papa had seemed to enjoy her musical talent, she thought as she entered the big house through the back breezeway door. She'd even caught him wiping away surreptitious tears during the family's Wednesday musical evenings.

"Pete!" she called up the stairs as she reached the foyer. Aurora had gone by Papa's nickname for her since she was a baby, and Joelle seriously doubted she would ever answer to anything else. "Are you ready to go?"

Aurora came clattering down the stairs, pulling on her gloves. She always seemed to be dressed to the nines when they went anywhere. And she had a wide variety to choose from, for Grandmama had paid for her clothes while she lived in Memphis.

Halting at the bottom of the stairs, Aurora planted her hands on her hips. "*What* are you wearing?"

Joelle bristled. "I'm wearing what I always wear on a Wednesday afternoon."

Aurora walked over and twitched at Joelle's homely dark blue skirt. "I know you have something better than that. It doesn't even fit you. Look at it hanging off your hips. Go change."

Joelle looked down at her own faded day dress, suddenly aware of her extreme dowdiness. They'd all had new gowns made for the ball back in April—and she'd worn hers to the opera—but the expense of a complete new wardrobe would have to wait for the arrival of hotel income.

"I don't have anything to change into. And quit ordering me around. I'm in charge here."

Aurora's cinnamon-colored eyes lit with amusement. "Is that right? Well, my things are too short for you, but what about that travel dress that Selah—Oh. Selah wore it to New Orleans."

"Yes." Joelle sighed. "Her trousseau seemed to trump my need for a dress to wear to town. Nobody expects me to be a fashion plate, Pete."

"Have you thought about Gil? Now that you're engaged, people will be looking at you as the future pastor's wife." Aurora waved off Joelle's incipient objection. "Never mind, we'll take care of it today. And don't argue, I'll pay for it. Grandmama left me some funds for just this purpose."

Swallowing aggravation, Joelle followed her little sister out the front door. Once she sold the article in her pocket, she'd have funds of her own for a new dress. She'd been planning to spend it on new books for the school, but she'd be hog-tied if she'd let Grandmama pay for her clothes. Maybe Gil would loan them a few of his books until she could afford more. She made up her mind to speak to him about it this very afternoon. And while she was at it, she'd convince him to promote Reverend Boykin's candidacy for Congress.

Feeling paradoxically righteous and anxious, she let Aurora handle the reins and listened with half an ear to her sister prattling about fashion during the half-hour drive to Tupelo. She couldn't care less what clothes went on her body at this point. Gil certainly paid no attention to such worldly attributes. Schuyler sometimes tweaked her about her cuffs being buttoned wrong or her collar turned inside out, but he was in Mobile.

"I'm going to the funeral," she said suddenly.

Aurora turned to look at Joelle in high dudgeon. "If you're going to interrupt, you could at least say something cheerful."

"Funerals are not inherently a cheerful subject."

"Inherently? What kind of word is that?"

The look on her sister's face reminded Joelle very much of her boarding school classmates. "Never mind. I'm sorry I interrupted. What color feather did you say you were going to buy for your hat?"

Guiding the wagon around a giant rut in the road, Aurora sighed. "No, *I'm* sorry. Grandmama tells me I monopolize conversations. What funeral? Who died?"

"I told you about Schuyler's father. His whole family will be in Mobile. The hotel won't open for a month, so I don't see why I can't take a few days to be with them. Camilla will think it odd if no one from our family goes."

"Do you think I should go too?"

"I honestly would feel better about it if you'd stay to deal with hotel management, in case anything comes up. Selah and Levi will be on their honeymoon for another week or so."

"All right." After a pause, Aurora said, "Do you think Selah will abandon us and move to New Orleans with Levi?"

Joelle laughed. "Well, the wife generally goes wherever her husband goes."

"You know what I mean. They talked about Levi giving up the Pinkerton job and staying here in Tupelo, so Selah wouldn't have to leave the hotel. She worked so hard to get it going."

"We all did." Joelle sighed. "And I'm really worried you and I can't handle the practicalities without the two of them."

"Well, Mose and Horatia and Nathan and Charmion are

all still here. And surely Schuyler will come back, once the funeral business is over."

Joelle supposed he would. And she was engaged. To Gil. *The wife goes wherever her husband goes.*

Ugh.

The minute Schuyler laid eyes on Levi Riggins at the Tuscaloosa train station, he realized what he'd done. With the fresh eyes of one so recently cured of the blight of self-absorption, he saw a newly married man—less than two weeks, if his calculations were correct—torn from the side of his bride during his honeymoon. What sort of cad would do such a thing to a man he called friend?

The sort of cad, apparently, who was used to paying for whatever he wanted. But in response to Schuyler's wire, Levi had telegraphed back that he would meet Schuyler in Tuscaloosa, and there would be no money involved.

Now it was too late to withdraw the request for help.

Levi got off the train and strode toward Schuyler with his swinging horseman's gait, a hand held out in greeting. Schuyler took it without a word as Levi gripped his other shoulder.

"I'm sorry, my friend," Levi said gruffly, a painful acknowledgment of sorrow in the hazel eyes. "I can't imagine . . ." The hand on Schuyler's shoulder tightened.

Schuyler's throat closed. He'd not given in to tears since he'd wept in Joelle's lap, and he wouldn't do so now, no matter how comforting he found the sympathy of a friend. He dropped Levi's hand and stepped away. "Thank you. I'm sorry I rushed into asking you to come all this way. I've talked to the coroner, and he says the sheriff is a good man who's looking into the shooting."

"Don't be stupid. I bought a ticket as soon as I heard. Matter of fact . . ." Levi hesitated. "Keep this between us, all right? There's been a rash of this kind of atrocity, and Pinkerton has already been called in. So I'm on the payroll."

Schuyler glanced down the street. "That's where it happened. The balcony of the Old Tavern Hotel. He was giving a speech—" To his horror, his voice broke.

Levi overlooked Schuyler's struggle for control. "Yes, I'll want to talk to the coroner and the sheriff. But let's find somewhere more private, so I can ask you some pertinent questions about your father."

Schuyler cleared his throat. "I'm staying at the Tavern. As you might guess, the steak and ale's pretty good there."

"Then I'm your man. It's been a long trip up from the coast."

The two of them left the station and headed down Broad Street's tree-lined boardwalk to the famous hotel. From 1827 to 1846, when Tuscaloosa was the state capital, the Tavern had hosted quite a list of celebrated guests and now boasted such comforts as gas lighting, indoor toilet facilities, and a bath upon request. Schuyler had checked in last night and retired exhausted, but he'd lain in bed listening to the noise of the bar below, unable to shut down a flood of memories of his father's larger-than-life presence. He'd woken to sunlight flooding his room and kept himself upright all morning, as he'd told Levi, in the pursuit of what information he could obtain about Pa's murder.

By now, however, he was so weary it was all he could do to set one foot in front of the other. Still, he tried to think beyond himself. "I'm so sorry to have interrupted your honeymoon. Did Selah go home—to Tupelo, I mean—when you came here?"

"Yes, I didn't know how long this would take, and she's been concerned about Joelle getting overwhelmed with the hotel opening."

"Joelle is—I guess you could say she's coming into her own." Schuyler pictured her face as she'd given him the worst news of his life. "She's handling things just fine. She finally said yes to the preacher."

"The preacher? You mean Gil Reese?" Levi gaped at him. "Yes to *marriage*?"

Schuyler shrugged.

Levi whistled, giving Schuyler a look that he couldn't interpret. "Selah was right to worry. That's bad."

He had to agree, but what could he say that wouldn't sound like sour grapes? They walked on in silence.

As they sat down at a table in a back corner of the Tavern's dining room, Levi regarded him with concern. "You look like you've been on a five-day bender. Are you all right?"

Schuyler straightened his shoulders, swiped a hand across his bristly chin. He'd forgotten to shave. "Can't lie, this has rocked me. But my pa wouldn't stand for wallowing in grief. He'd want me locating the swine who did this and making sure he pays. So what do you need to know?"

Levi took a leather-bound notebook and pencil out of the inside pocket of his coat. "I made some notes on the train, trying to establish motive. I don't know much about your father, beyond what you told me when we first met in Oxford. I know you have an older brother, Jamie, and Selah introduced me to Camilla and her husband in New Orleans.

Your father, you said, tried to run the M&O through Ithaca but had to reroute when Daughtry wouldn't sell. So there were some business conflicts between the two?"

Schuyler nodded. "My family and the Daughtrys are shirttail kin, I guess you'd say. My grandmother and the girls' grandmother—their mother's mother, you know—were first cousins. So our mothers grew up as schoolmates and friends until they married and moved to opposite ends of Mississippi and Alabama. They continued to correspond and visit whenever they could, either at Ithaca or our home in Mobile—until my mother died when I was born. Then my grandmother kept up the connection, mainly for Selah and Camilla's sake. But Colonel Daughtry wasn't what one would call a friendly sort, even before the war. He was competitive, jealous, and guarded his property like a dog with a bone." He met Levi's eyes, wincing. "He would never have allowed you to marry Selah. It's a good thing he's gone."

Levi chewed on the end of the pencil. "He was a pitiful old man. But I'm glad I met him so that I understand a little of Selah's grief. In spite of everything, I could tell he loved his wife and daughters."

"Yes. But it's funny, when you look back on events that happened when you were a kid, things that didn't make sense come into focus. Like Daughtry's obsession with an heir to carry on his name. He treated Selah like a substitute boy, even had her educated that way. He more or less ignored Joelle, petted baby Aurora, and fell apart when the little boy died. Kind of explains his lapse in sanity when he thought the place was going to be taken over by the government." Uncomfortable with the melancholy turn of the conversation, Schuyler produced a sour grin. "In any case, despite the ties between our families, there was no chance Daughtry would let go of one square foot of that plantation, especially to an Alabama mercenary like my father—nothing personal, you understand," he added with a curl of his lip.

"Fair enough." Levi scribbled a note. "What about the M&O's buyout attempt of the Mississippi Central? Perhaps you could update me on that process."

"You think someone from the Mississippi Central might have killed him?"

"Sky, we have to consider everything at this point."

Schuyler rubbed his aching forehead. "My brother knows more about it than I do. The idea was to keep the competition from gaining strength. The transportation industry is already saturated here in the South, and consolidation is one way to curb that. Jamie's been in negotiations with the MC for some time now, but I don't know how it's going. I've been so occupied with the launch of the hotel . . ." And other things, things which he was embarrassed to talk about with Levi.

Eyebrows quirked, Levi waited for him to finish the thought, then glanced at his notes again. "All right. I'll talk to your brother when we get to Mobile."

"You're going to come to Mobile?"

"I wouldn't normally horn in on a family tragedy," Levi said, "but there are people there I'll need to question."

"You wouldn't be 'horning in.' I consider you family. I'm just surprised you're willing to leave Selah for that long. Newlyweds and all that." Schuyler grinned at Levi's flush. "Why don't you get her to come down with Joelle? We can put off opening the hotel for another month if we need to."

Levi considered him for a moment before answering. "You aren't the same man I met after the train wreck in February."

"Well, sooner or later a man has to grow up and adjust his priorities."

"True, but . . ." There was another long pause. "All right, I'll wire Selah before I visit the sheriff. Right now I need more information about your father's political dealings. That's the third strand of this snarl, personal and business being the first two. I understand he was running for governor."

"Yes, he was concerned about rail subsidies and gradually came to the conclusion that if he was going to stop it, he'd have to step in and do something from the inside. Though they're similar in many ways, Alabama politics have always been more complex than Mississippi's. My father was a Whig who converted to conservative right before the war. People in the upper parts of the state, the cotton kingdom, called people like us in Mobile—who'd made our money in other ways—elitists."

Madly taking notes, Levi looked up at that. "Different flavors of Southern aristocrats, huh?"

Schuyler made a face. "I suppose you'd say that. But during the 1860 presidential election, everything boiled over. Moderate ex-Whigs, like my pa, and folks in the border states created the Constitutional Union Party in an effort to skirt the issue of slavery. They were adamantly opposed to sectional extremism and, I suppose, considered cooperationist at the time."

Levi lowered his pencil. "Wait—did your family not own slaves?"

Schuyler laughed. "That's where my own crazy grandma comes in. I'm sorry she passed on, because you two would have gotten along famously. Pa's money came from transportation, not cotton. We had a few house slaves, owned by my grandmother—at least I thought so. Turns out she had set them free the minute my grandfather died, and they stayed with her to help run a leg of the Underground Railroad."

"But your father—"

"The old man was cagey over the issue. Had no personal love for the institution but was reluctant to dictate his convictions to his neighbors. He opposed secession, but gave in to the inevitable when Lincoln won the 1860 election. Pa was publicly called a traitor and a 'scalawag.' If he hadn't jumped in to offer rail transport for Confederate troops and supplies and funded Jamie's free trading, the whole family would have faced exile." Schuyler wiped his face again as buried memories surfaced. "My sister being caught spying nearly undid us all. If Jamie and I hadn't—" He stopped, reminded that, though he liked Levi, he was talking to a former Union officer.

"I'm listening."

"Well, let's just say Jamie and I were involved in projects that ensured our survival."

Levi gave him a wry, sympathetic smile. "So your father's politics were, as you say, fairly complex, which could make him the target of violent conservatives."

"I don't know." Schuyler shook his head. "The Constitutional Union Party fell apart when the war started, and Pa was running as a moderate conservative. He'd managed to cobble together a lot of support at the bottom of the state."

"Still. As I've been told over and over, people are good at holding grudges in the South."

Schuyler mentally sifted through the top layer of his father's multitudinous acquaintances. "I suppose you're right. I'll think about it and let you know if someone has a particular ax to grind."

"Please do. Meanwhile, since we're here, I want to go up to the balcony and look around." Levi closed his notebook and stuffed it back into his jacket. "You don't have to come—"

"I'm not that fragile." Schuyler shoved his chair away from the table and rose. His father's last hour had been spent on that balcony. Running away would not change the fact that he was gone. "Let's go."

Seven

"YOU'RE GOING TO MEET ME HERE in an hour, aren't you?" Aurora glared at Joelle for all the world as if she were the elder, by at least a couple of decades. In fact, at that moment she bore an uncanny resemblance to Winifred Pierce McGowan at her most autocratic.

They stood outside the Whitmore Emporium, just down from the hitching lot where they had left the wagon.

"I said I would. I'm going to the post office." Joelle scooted across the street before Aurora could argue. She *would* go to the post office—after she stopped by the newspaper office.

No one except Levi knew of her hidden penchant for journalism. A couple of months ago, he'd caught her coming out of the building that housed the *Journal*, when she was supposed to be shopping for ball dress materials. The trouble with Levi was that he noticed everything. Also, he had a perfectly charming, insidious way of eliciting information that one had sworn never to reveal.

It was a skill that Joelle was determined to learn, as it seemed eminently useful to the job of reporting.

Fetching up outside the newspaper office, Joelle straightened her hat and looked down with new diffidence at her attire. Perhaps Aurora was right, and she should at least look like she hadn't come down to her last penny when visiting her one real source of personal income. Would her editor be more or less likely to pay her what she was worth if she appeared not to need payment?

That being a question she felt unprepared to tackle—and rather beyond her control at any event—she pasted on her best bright smile and pushed open the door. "Good afternoon, Mr. McCanless! How are you today?"

"Well, if it isn't the Concerned Citizen!" McCanless took off his spectacles and propped them atop his balding head. "Have you another opinion article for me today? That last was quite a doozy. Advertisements are up this week."

Joelle looked over her shoulder to make sure she had not been followed in. "I have two articles, but neither is an opinion piece. One is a society report of the opera I attended on Monday, and the reception for Miss Fabio. The other is heavily researched, with quotes from several scholarly sources. I have been corresponding with professors at Harvard and Yale, as well as the Medical College of Louisiana."

"Have you now? Let me see." McCanless extended an ink-stained hand.

Joelle pulled her articles from her pocket and handed them over. As the editor lowered his glasses and began to read, she wandered about the office, picking things up and examining them. There were piles of books everywhere—*Journey to the Center of the Earth* and *Twenty Thousand Leagues Under the Sea*, *Goblin Market* by Christina Rossetti, *Lorna*

Doone, and tucked behind a cigar case, *Incidents in the Life of a Slave Girl*—

"Mr. McCanless, have you read this?" Joelle turned with the Harriet Jacobs memoir in her hand.

"What's that? No, my wife handed it to me and said I should read it. Extremist claptrap."

"Could I borrow it?"

He shrugged. "You can have it." He stabbed her article, lying on his desk, with a penknife. "You seem to have a soft spot for black folk."

She lifted her chin. "Matter of fact, I do. The ones I know, anyway. Which is why I believe they deserve an education."

"Sure they do. Just not on my dime. They got to work for it, just like I did."

Joelle thought about ten-year-old Tee-Toc Weber, clambering on the roofs of Daughtry House Hotel from four a.m. until high noon, then spending his lunch hour in the kitchen pantry learning to read and write and do sums. "I never suggested they didn't need to work to earn an education. The point of my article is that Negroes can learn as easily as we can, and they should not be prevented from doing so, if we want that section of the electorate to cast informed votes."

McCanless removed his spectacles and rubbed his forehead, leaving a purple smear between his eyebrows. He looked mildly satanic. "This is a well-written piece, Miss Daughtry. And it's going to stir enough controversy—which sells papers—that I'm willing to print it. But you won't be taken seriously if you continue to publish anonymously. I think we should create a pseudonym for you."

"A pseudonym?"

"Yes, a *male* pseudonym, to be precise. We'll say you're

from . . . over in Hernando. Far enough away, but close enough to a Yankee stronghold that you're not likely to be weaseled out."

Joelle tried to find holes in the suggestion. "That would be lying. I'm fixing to marry a preacher."

The editor laughed. "Soon as you get married and start having babies of your own, you're going to be too busy to educate black children or write much more than your weekly grocery list. Why not enjoy your freedom while you've got it? Women have been taking pen names for decades. I know how much you admire Mrs. Alcott. Even she did it."

"Mr. McCanless, I'm tired of hiding what I write. It's exhausting."

He blew out an exasperated breath. "It's as much for my sake as yours. The stuff about the railroad is common dialogue and needs to be debated publicly. But this—" He thumped the papers in his hand. "If anyone suspects I'm paying a female to nudge public opinion in this liberal direction, we could both be socially ostracized, if not in actual physical danger."

Joelle laughed, but when the editor failed to respond with so much as a smile, she realized he was serious. "Mr. McCanless! People already think Selah and I are half crazy, hiring our former slaves as employees. I hardly think one article—"

"That there, young lady, is the problem. You're hardly thinking. I'm afraid I'm going to have to insist. If you want me to buy this piece, it's going to be under the name of . . . T. M. Hanson. Contributor from DeSoto County. There you go."

Joelle thought about the books and paper and ink and chalk she needed for her class. She thought about how much she wanted that article in print. She thought about Aurora waiting for her at the Emporium.

"I don't have time to argue with you," she finally said. "Just give me the money, and you can assign the article whatever byline you wish." Perhaps she'd caved in too quickly, but she was not argumentative by nature—except with certain obnoxious dandies—and she didn't want to cause Aurora to ask nosy questions.

A few minutes later, she left the office, wadding a roll of banknotes into her reticule. Having learned her lesson from that fateful encounter with Levi, she looked both ways to make sure the sidewalk was clear before making her way to the post office.

This was most likely a pointless errand, since Wyatt always brought the mail home with him after school, but she'd used it for her excuse to shake Aurora long enough to deliver her article. She'd have to at least show her face to Mr. Carpenter, the postal agent and Tupelo's only trained telegraph operator. Otherwise, Aurora would somehow dig her subterfuge out of her and ask a hundred questions, and Lord knows Joelle was a terrible liar. Gil would probably consider that a virtue, but it was downright inconvenient at times.

"Good afternoon, Mr. Carpenter!" The hissing and chugging of steam, the screech of brakes, and the sound of cargo slamming into cars and onto wagons followed her into the little office next to the train station. She shut the door behind her, glad to escape the smoke and congestion of the terminal. "How are you today?"

A slight, sandy-gray-haired man turned from his occupation at the telegraph key. "I'm happy as a pig in slop to see you," he said, leaning on the counter, a smile on his genial, clever face.

Joelle had always liked the postmaster, who had been a friend of their family since she was big enough to sit in her mama's lap and come to town. He'd never failed to produce a stash of horehound drops from under the counter for her and her sisters, and Joelle had a well-known fondness for the strong flavor.

"Has Wyatt come by for the mail yet?" She stopped short of the counter, already turning to head back to the Emporium.

"Yes. But wait—Miss Joelle, there's a telegram for you!"

"What?" She reversed direction once more. "For me?"

"Yes, it's from your sister. She says she's—but here, read it for yourself." Carpenter handed her a sealed telegram and watched her handle it gingerly. "It won't explode," he added with a smile. "I'm glad you came in, since Wyatt has already come and gone. Now I won't have to send someone all the way out to Ithaca—I mean, Daughtry House."

"Indeed," she said dubiously, breaking the seal. "I hope nothing's wrong." She read the telegram and looked up at the postmaster, feeling a smile break out on her face. "Selah's coming home! Oh, I missed her so much!" She'd grown to love and appreciate Aurora's bossy little self, but there was nobody like calm, wise, practical Selah.

"It's odd she's returning to Tupelo without her husband. Especially considering this wire he just sent to her." He handed Joelle a second envelope, addressed to Selah Riggins. "You'll make sure she gets it, won't you?"

"Yes, sir, of course I will." Joelle poked both telegrams into her reticule. Levi had cautioned her about Mr. Carpenter's tendency to share contents of private correspondence. That was illegal, of course, and he could get into trouble if it were proved. She didn't want to believe her old friend would betray the sworn confidentiality of his post. "I'm not sure what their plans are at the moment. I'll just have to ask her when

I see her, won't I? Her train will arrive tonight, so I'm sure we'll see you when we come back for her. Thank you for the good news, Mr. Carpenter! Good afternoon!" She bobbed a quick curtsey and flitted out the door onto the boardwalk.

One thing was clear: Levi had gone to help Schuyler, and Selah was coming home to occupy herself in his absence.

Joelle broke into a little jig of happiness. Selah was coming home!

Tuscaloosa County Sheriff Conrad Stevens wiped his dripping face with a large handkerchief he'd pulled from his coat pocket. There wasn't much humidity on this mild May morning, even standing in the sun that flooded the balcony, but Schuyler supposed the middle-aged law officer's portly bulk under a wool suit could create the sweat beading his high forehead and dampening the heavy beard and mustache.

Or perhaps it was the pressure of dealing with an assassination and riot upsetting the peace of his jurisdiction.

"Professional rioters," Stevens growled, stuffing the handkerchief back into its pocket. "You never saw such a mess in your life."

Levi, leaning against the back wall of the balcony with his notebook and pencil in hand, straightened. "What do you mean, professional rioters?"

"Listen at that accent." Stevens glanced at Schuyler. "Why you want to bring a Yankee into this?"

Schuyler shrugged. "Smartest Yankee I know. He's . . . my lawyer." He knew not to volunteer Levi's connection to the Pinkerton Agency.

"Fair enough." Stevens picked through his words. "Hard

to say where this thing started. Well, obviously it happened at that cursed rally on Monday—the one your pa spoke at—but I got a feeling it goes back even further than that. Comin' and goin' between here and Montgomery, folks trying to get the mayor replaced." The sheriff took out his handkerchief to mop the top of his head. "Like I said, it's a big mess."

Schuyler rolled his shoulders, trying to relax. He had to keep a clear head. "What's all this got to do with my father's murder?"

"I'm getting there, hold your horses." Stevens hitched up his pants. "Your pa had been invited to make a speech at this rally sponsored by the mayor—that's Mr. Thad Samuel," he said to Levi, who was taking notes. "The idea was to promote Alabama 'coming out of isolation, trying to heal up the wounds left by the war.'" He was clearly quoting someone else's rhetoric, and his broad face reddened in some unidentified emotion. "Now, I'm not saying he's wrong. But I'd warned the mayor it was a mistake to bring in a white politician from the southern part of the state, not to mention those two colored Lincolnites. Turns out I was right. The longer your pa talked, the more restless the crowd got. I was standing on the porch below with my deputy, trying to keep people from busting into the hotel."

"Wait," Levi said. "Names. Who were the other speakers, the two freedmen?"

Stevens seemed to consider how many more details he should share. "One was a state legislator from Randolph County, a Reverend Josiah Thomas, the other a militia officer named Sion Perkins. Both were well dressed and well spoken, I have to admit—I met them when they arrived that morning. But your father was first on the program, the idea being to warm up the crowd with a couple of jokes and what-not. Then Perkins starts in with how 'Ku-Kluxing has got to stop.'" The handkerchief reappeared. "Hoo-boy. That was not well received from a colored man in a uniform. There was armed white men in the crowd, and they didn't look friendly. But the Negroes started hollering agreement. Before I could stop it, pushing and shoving commenced, gun butts started swinging, and then there was a shot fired. All, uh, perdition broke loose. Women was screaming, more gunshots, and the riot rolled. My deputy and me gave the signal to a few men I'd temporarily deputized ahead of time. We all waded in and tried to break it up. Seemed like it took forever, but the whole thing probably only lasted ten minutes."

"What about the men up here?" Imagining that wild scene below as his father must have seen it, Schuyler leaned on the balcony rail, trying to catch his breath. "One of those gunshots was aimed this way."

"Beaumont," Levi said quietly, "I'll ask the questions."

"I'm all right." Schuyler straightened.

"I got up here as fast as I could," Stevens said. "But by then your father was dead. Mayor Samuel tried to stop the bleeding, but the shot had gone to the heart. Another bullet grazed the Reverend's arm. Perkins wasn't hit at all."

"Injuries in the crowd?" Levi asked.

"Bumps and bruises on a handful of white folk. Three Negroes injured by gunfire. Two more dead."

Levi nodded. "Tell me about the men in custody. You said they're in bad shape. I assume they were identified as start-ing the violence?"

"Not yet. I'm getting there. So, yeah, I interviewed wit-nesses until nightfall. And then things got worse. Somebody comes running to the jail, hollering that the mayor's livery stable is on fire. I go running down there, and it's a madhouse, horses screaming, flames threatening to jump to adjacent buildings." The sheriff's face blanched at the memory. "I swear I didn't know but what the whole town was gonna burn down. Fortunately, the firemen got the livery under control before anything else caught."

Meanwhile, his father lay in the mortuary—while Schuyler attended an opera and flirted with an entertainer at a Memphis luxury hotel. Wasn't he just the most outstanding son God ever created?

Stevens didn't seem to notice his agitation. "It was near two o'clock in the morning before everything calmed down again. Next morning somebody reported having seen Thomas, Perkins, and a white schoolteacher named Lemuel Frye skulking around the livery before dark. Mr. Frye had been involved in some sort of racial to-do earlier in the spring. So I brought 'em all three in for questioning. The federal circuit judge will be in town Monday morning for a hearing."

Schuyler looked at Levi. "I'll have to take my father's body back to Mobile."

"Like I said, I'll go with you to talk to your brother, then come back here for the hearing if I need to." Levi tucked his notebook back inside his jacket. "Are you ready to go to the mortuary?"

Schuyler looked down at his hands, clenched on the balcony rail. "I'll never be ready for that, but let's get it over with."

Eight

JOELLE PAUSED OUTSIDE THE EMPORIUM. She couldn't wait to tell Aurora that Selah was coming. But patronizing the Whitmores' establishment had become awkward for the Daughtrys, ever since Levi had mortally insulted Mrs. Whitmore at the ball they'd held at Ithaca to introduce the hotel to the community. Of course Elberta Whitmore more than earned the insult with her sniggering remarks about Selah and ThomasAnne. And Levi could be excused by his love-drunk condition.

Still, the prospect of purchasing salt and woolen goods from a woman who glared at one with the gimlet eye of Medusa was bound to put a damper on a body's eagerness to shop.

Taking a deep breath, she went inside and stopped in her tracks. "Gil! What are you doing here?"

"I'm buying socks. Fortunately, once I have a wife, I won't have to purchase them myself." Gil smiled at Joelle, as if she should take that as a compliment.

"You're not expecting me to knit your socks? Are you? Because I don't know how to knit. I'd probably stab myself—"

His face fell. "I was teasing, Joelle."

"Oh. I'm sorry, I guess I didn't recognize . . ." She peered up at him. He'd never been known to joke about anything. Now how was she to determine what was a spiritual comment and what was supposed to be funny? "Never mind, I was just surprised. I mean, I was going to visit your house. Though, now that I think about it, maybe that wouldn't be proper, since we aren't married yet." And she was babbling. That was the thing about conversation. Either she couldn't think of anything to say, or she didn't know when to stop.

"You were coming to visit me?" Now he looked happy again. "We can go to the parsonage if you like. Bring Aurora along for a chaperone, and we'll all have tea."

"Aurora is not finished shopping yet," Aurora said from the other side of a stack of wooden crates. They were all stamped with the label "Limburger," and they smelled like feet.

No wonder Joelle's eyes were watering. She'd thought it was Gil. Relieved that she wasn't going to be sleeping with the most odiferous human in Mississippi, she looked over the crates and found her petite little sister frowning at a row of fabric bolts. "You've been here for more than an hour. Are you in a coma from cheese fumes?"

"Ha, ha." Aurora snapped her fingers, indicating that Joelle should come immediately. It was a habit she'd developed as a very small child, reserved for the rare times when big golden brown eyes and dimples failed to get her her way.

Joelle sighed and sidled around the crates. Resistance was pointless. Gil followed like a puppy trailing a side of bacon.

"What do you think of this?" Aurora had selected a bolt

of silk taffeta in a rich sable brown with coppery satin and grosgrain stripes. She lifted it next to her cheek and petted its folds as if it were alive. "With frogged lace at the sleeves and in the—"she glanced at Gil, then shrugged—"bosom?"

"I don't know why you're asking me," Joelle said. "You know it would look nice on you. It's the same color as your hair."

"Not on *me*! It's for you!" Aurora walked over and draped the cloth over Joelle's shoulder. "Look, Gil. Isn't this beautiful?"

His gaze locked on Joelle's face. "It sure is."

Joelle rolled her eyes. "How much does it cost?"

"Don't worry about it. I told you Grandmama—"

"Grandmama is not buying my clothes. How much?"

"Eighty-nine cents a yard," Aurora mumbled.

Joelle sucked in a breath. That would absorb most of what she'd just put into her purse. On the other hand, she would be traveling to Mobile tomorrow, and she could write something while she was on the train, to earn its replacement. Too bad she couldn't wear the new dress to the funeral, but even Charmion, the hotel seamstress, wouldn't have time to construct a new garment overnight. "All right," she said recklessly, "figure out how much yardage we need, and I'll pay for it."

Aurora blinked. "Really?"

"Yes. Hurry before I change my mind."

While Aurora scrabbled in her reticule for a notebook and pencil, Joelle remembered her second purpose for this trip to town—coaxing her fiancé to support a Negro politician. She smiled at Gil. He was already in a stupor of whatever substituted for lust in a Methodist preacher, so it shouldn't be *that* difficult.

She linked her fingers loosely at her waist. "Gil, how well do you know Reverend Boykin of the Methodist Episcopal Church?"

"Who?"

"The Negro Methodist pastor. The church is over in Shake Rag."

"I suppose I've seen him a time or two. I'm not sure I'd be able to pick him out of a crowd. Why?"

That did not sound promising. "I'll have to introduce you. He's a very nice man."

"How do you—Oh. Is he one of those colored men who have been coming to you for lessons?"

She didn't care for his dismissive tone. "As a matter of fact, he already knew how to read. But I've been loaning him some of Papa's books on history and theology. I was thinking he would make a fine person to represent our district in the state legislature in the next election."

If she had just announced that she thought bumblebees might make a perfect course for dinner, he couldn't have looked more revolted. "My dear, you shouldn't bother your head about such matters. You can't even—"

"If one more person reminds me that I can't vote, I may jump in front of a train. That may technically be true, but it doesn't mean I have no opinion on decisions affecting my government."

Gil gulped, apparently realizing that he had stepped wrong. "Your, er, concern is admirable. But perhaps you should look beyond your little world of local charity when championing candidates for such important offices. I'm sure Reverend Boykin is a fine man, but I hardly think he could hold his own with college-educated white businessmen."

She stared at him for a moment. Gil had a spot of pride with respect to education. He had worked his way through Northwestern University near Chicago, then struggled through its sister institution, Garrett Biblical Institute, before returning to Tupelo. A college diploma was rare in rural Mississippi, let alone a postgraduate degree. However, she told herself, if some enterprising soul cobbled together the mountain of books Joelle had read, along with the reams of pages of professionally edited manuscripts she had produced over the past five years, he would probably come up with at least three PhDs in as many subjects.

Pride could only take one so far.

"I won't argue with you, Gil," she said sweetly, "but it would mean a lot to me if you'd come by the schoolroom sometime to meet Reverend Boykin. I told him what a generous man you are, and I'd hate to disappoint him."

Gil gave her a troubled look. "I don't know if you know this—I don't see how you would, since you can't be a deacon—but the Methodist church is about to split off the colored churches into their own denomination. It might not be a good idea to cloud the issue." He paused, as if arriving at some monumental concession. "But I'll think about it."

Joelle supposed she would have to be satisfied, for the moment at least. But if Gil thought he'd placated her into giving up on her promise to Shug, he'd tangled with the wrong Southern belle. She looked around and found Aurora haggling with Mr. Whitmore, who clearly didn't stand a chance of making a profit on the brown taffeta. Wasn't there something she had come in here to tell her?

Oh yes! Selah.

"Thank you, Gil," she said with a smile. "That's very

generous of you." Giving Aurora's finger-snap tactic a whirl, she headed for the front counter.

"Quit asking me if I'm all right." On the way back to the Tavern from the coroner's office, Schuyler had done his best to hide his shaken feelings from Levi. The sun had fallen behind the buildings lining the street, casting welcome late-afternoon shadows. Anxious to reach the end of this miserable day, he walked faster. "I'm fine."

Judging by Levi's skeptical look, he was a terrible actor. "I can't imagine what would be going through my head if that was my father back there on that table," Levi said. "There's nothing good about this situation, except for the fact that you had him this long, to teach you right and wrong and to give you something to live for. You and I have more than a lot of men our age."

Schuyler thought about that for a silent moment. It was true. The male population of both North and South had been decimated by violence, families torn apart, churches destroyed, children left fatherless and adrift. Maddening that the sort of disruption that had killed his father kept the bitterness alive rather than bringing it to an end. It was so hard to think beyond the visceral need to find the man who had killed his father, to *eliminate* him.

He looked at Levi, demonstrably a good man, one whose principles seemed to moor him in every decision he made. Yet he was young, barely five years Schuyler's senior. "You did have a lot to live for. Why did you sign on for service? Was it patriotism? Hatred of slavery? Sheer adventurism?"

Levi hesitated. "My family were immigrants who worked

hard, grateful to be in a nation where you could make your own way. Nobody I knew considered the idea of owning another human being as something necessary or admirable. I heard Lincoln speak once, when I was young. He was funny and awkward and brilliant, and my father admired him—so I did too. Then as I got older, I had a teacher who helped me get admitted to West Point. I met a lot of Southern boys there. Debates were . . . interesting." Levi grinned, shaking his head.

"I can imagine."

"We were brothers in arms. But you know, upbringing matters. When hostilities broke out into war, we each had to make a choice as to where we stood." Levi sighed. "I stood on the side of union in every sense of the word."

"I was only fourteen at the time. I just wanted to take a gun and go Yankee hunting. When my pa wouldn't let me, I did the next available thing and volunteered to drown myself."

Levi laughed, then saw he wasn't joking. "What do you mean?"

"Early in the war, my father financed the engineering and construction of an underwater boat. Jamie nearly died in one of its test runs in Mobile Bay. They managed to raise it and move it to Charleston, where they repaired it. Because I was familiar with it—also because I was slightly war-crazed and young enough to think I was immortal—I volunteered to crew the infernal thing." Schuyler paused, astonished all over again that he had lived to tell this insane tale. "At the last minute, I came down with a kidney stone and couldn't go. The fish boat torpedoed a Union gunboat, but the entire crew blew up with it."

"That sounds like the plot of a penny novel."

"It's true, though not very heroic on my part." Schuyler sighed. "To make up for it, I joined my brother in blockade running. But after Camilla turned Union and escaped to New Orleans, none of us had much heart for the fight anymore. When Farragut took Mobile, we knew it was over. I think my father was secretly relieved."

"Is that when you started college?"

"Yes. I finally matriculated with a degree in engineering." By this time they had reached the front porch of the tavern. Schuyler stopped, hands in the pockets of his trousers. He didn't want to go to his room and brood, but he was tired of talking about himself. "The coroner won't release Pa's body until tomorrow morning. Why don't we split up and talk to some of the witnesses the sheriff mentioned?"

Levi nodded. "I was about to suggest that."

It occurred to Schuyler that he could barely distinguish Levi's features in the long evening shadows, and his friend had had a long, wearing day. "Go ahead and eat, if you want. I'm not hungry. I'll see you in the morning at breakfast."

Levi whacked him on the shoulder. "Fine, but don't starve yourself. The next few days are going to be taxing."

Schuyler didn't doubt that. He almost welcomed the distraction of traveling back to Mobile and blending into the chaos of family. He had only twelve or so more hours to get through before daylight.

A major conflict ensued over who was going to take the new carriage back to Tupelo to pick up Selah at the station. In the end, they all went, crowding in like pioneers in a Conestoga wagon. Wyatt handled the horses, allowing the three sisters and ThomasAnne to jabber all the way home, Selah's trunk thrown on top, rattling with every bump in the dark road.

When they got inside the manager's cottage, recently renovated to accommodate the whole family, Joelle pushed Selah into the corner rocker in the little kitchen, then settled on the hassock at her sister's feet. ThomasAnne puttered about collecting tea things, while Aurora fetched cookies from the larder.

Kissing Selah on the cheek, Wyatt said, "Welcome home and good night," then retired to his room to study for a Latin test. "Doc's a bear about this stuff," he said over his shoulder before disappearing.

"He's doing well, isn't he?" Selah touched her cheek.

Earlier in the year, Selah had more or less rescued the teenager after a train wreck—the same one in which she'd met Levi. Fostering him had been a good thing for all concerned. Wyatt worked hard, played hard, and studied hard. He had every intention of becoming a physician like his hero, Dr. Kidd, thereby contributing to the financial well-being of the family. He might be a Priester in name, but he considered himself a Daughtry of the heart.

"He's a good boy," ThomasAnne agreed, "if we could just convince him to make up his bed."

"I've missed him." Selah squeezed Joelle's fingers. "I've missed you all."

"You look tired," Joelle said. "We'll let you go to bed, and we can talk in the morning."

"I'm not sleepy, though it *has* been a long day." Selah stretched her neck to one side and then the other. "The leg from Meridian to Tupelo is the longest, especially without Levi."

Joelle stared at her sister, considering a range of awkward, nosy questions she wanted to ask.

What is it like to live with a man?

Are you ever coming back to Daughtry House to live?

Do you still feel like a Daughtry?

Are you sorry you lost your independence?

Are you less lonely?

"Did they tell you Gil asked me to marry him?" she blurted.

Selah laughed. "Again? How many times does that make?"

"The last, I presume," Joelle said glumly. "I said yes."

Selah's dark eyes opened wide. "Oh, Joelle. You didn't."

"She's blaming it on Schuyler." Aurora plunked a plate of cookies on the table. "They were arguing over a billiards game, and Gil caught her in a weak moment."

Selah started to giggle. "That's the—the funniest—" She burst into full-scale laughter.

Joelle had to grin. "It is *not* funny!"

But they were all laughing, bent double with pent-up nostalgia and relief in being together in one room, with mutual recognition that life moved on and changed, and they could never go back to days of dolls and lemonade and swimming in the pool across the road.

Finally Selah dabbed her eyes with her handkerchief. "Seriously though. You're not going through with it, are you?" She took a cup of tea from ThomasAnne, sipped it, and closed her eyes in pleasure. "Just tell him you made a mistake."

"Selah, I could never jilt him. Besides, think of the good I can do as the preacher's wife. I could have a lot of influence." Saying it out loud was a way of reassuring herself she'd not actually done something monumentally stupid. "I promised."

"A promise is important," ThomasAnne said, passing around the plate of cookies. She sat down at the table with her tea.

"Of course it is." Selah's brown eyes were troubled. "All that sounds noble, Jo, but this is a decision that will affect the rest of your life. Just think carefully before you commit yourself."

"I already did." Joelle's head ached from thinking. "Which reminds me, I promised Schuyler I'd go to Mobile for his father's funeral."

"Remember that telegram you gave me at the station? Levi decided to go to Mobile too, and said I should come down with you. The burial will be on Friday, so we'll have to travel tomorrow." Selah turned to Aurora and ThomasAnne, sitting together at the table. "Pete, ThomasAnne, I hate to abandon y'all so quickly, but I feel like I should be with Camilla and her family. We all know how hard this is."

Just six weeks ago, they'd buried their own father, a cathartic end to a traumatic series of events, most of them engendered by Jonathan Daughtry's descent into madness. It had indeed been a difficult spring, and Joelle was glad it was over. "Schuyler suggested putting off the opening of the hotel," she said. "That might not be a bad idea."

Aurora stuck out her dimpled chin. "But we've had reservations coming in. Horatia's been ordering food and other supplies. Mose has the grounds and general operations under control. Charmion and Nathan are a big help. We can take it on, can't we, ThomasAnne?"

ThomasAnne clutched her tea cup, large gray eyes wide. "Oh dear, I don't know. I've just had an awful feeling something bad is going to happen."

Aurora made a rude noise. "You always have a feeling something bad is going to happen. It will be fine."

"We'll get back as quickly as we can," Joelle said as a compromise between the Eternal Pessimist and the Princess of Rainbows, as Schuyler liked to call ThomasAnne and Aurora. "But I do have a suggestion. Perhaps we could join hands and pray before we go to bed. Then we'd all feel better about this situation."

With Selah holding one hand and ThomasAnne's fragile grasp in the other, Joelle felt her clenched stomach relax. She bowed her head and let out a breath. "Dear God, we thank you for your presence amongst us . . ."

Nine

BEAUMONT HOUSE, MOBILE, ALABAMA, had been Schuyler's home since the day he was born. But walking up the front steps with Levi, he felt as if he were entering some strange, crowded museum—a place that he'd visited before, but which moldered, old and faintly crumbly with disuse. His grandmother, fondly known as Lady, had been dead for two years, and now with Pa gone . . .

But that was nonsense, since Jamie and his family still lived here. Schuyler spotted a wooden train set under the white swing at the far end of the front porch. His heart pricked a little at the thought of his three-year-old nephew, Pierce. He hadn't seen the little fellow since Christmas, when the family had been together here. It was the last time he'd seen his father as well.

"What a grand old house!" Levi stopped to admire the wide front door with its brass lion's head knocker, flanked by a row of long windows open to the spring breeze. "Reminds me just a bit of Daughtry House."

"Greek Revival was popular before the war." Schuyler opened the door and stuck his head inside. "Anybody home?"

Light footsteps from the breezeway brought his sister-in-law, Bronwyn, into the foyer. Her face lit. "Sky! Oh, you're here! Jamie will be so glad!" She flung herself at him.

"Of course I'm here. I've brought Pa's body home." He hugged Bron fiercely, then set her back, searching her gentle face. Grief still shadowed her fine hazel eyes. "I'm so sorry, I know how much you loved him."

She blinked and sniffed. "It's going to be so strange without him hollering for Pierce the minute he walks in the door. And stuffing him full of peppermint. And keeping him out from under my feet!" She shook her head. "Pierce is like a lost puppy without his Papa-Z. He keeps asking when he's coming home and won't believe us when we tell him—" Her voice broke as she shook her head.

Helpless, Schuyler watched Bron dab at her eyes. Finally he put a hand on her shoulder and turned to Levi, waiting quietly by the door. "Bronwyn, I want you to meet my good friend, Levi Riggins. He's Selah's—"

"Levi! Oh, I feel as if I already know you! Camilla has mentioned you in her letters." Bron stuffed her handkerchief into her sleeve and offered a hand to Levi. "Welcome to Mobile. I'm sorry it's under such sad circumstances, but . . ." She looked around, as if she'd just remembered where she was. "Please forgive the disarray. We've had so many visitors since that awful . . . But y'all come on in, sit down, and I'll find us something to eat."

Levi murmured something polite, but Schuyler had no desire to pin himself to a chair in the parlor. "No thanks, we ate on the train. The . . . body will arrive shortly, and there's lots to do, to get ready for the service in the morning. Bron, where's Jamie?"

"At the shipping office. He's there all the time now. Since your father took on the campaign for office, Jamie's overwhelmed with the business." She sighed. "For the last six months Pierce and I have hardly seen him, and now that he's shouldered the entire thing . . ."

It crossed Schuyler's mind that Bronwyn seemed to rarely finish a sentence, but perhaps he was being too critical. "I'm sure he's handling things the best he can. And I'm here to help." He turned to Levi. "Would you like to walk downtown with me and see the offices of Beaumont Shipping?"

Schuyler found his brother seated at his desk, head in hands. Jamie had just turned thirty, but he looked at least a decade older—brown hair graying at the temples, furrows of care between the thick brows, the skin around his blue eyes puffy. Even his beard, always his most swashbuckling feature, had collected a sprinkling of frost.

Jamie looked up as Schuyler's shadow fell across the desk, his expression instantly lightening. He leaped to his feet. "Little brother!"

Suffocated in a bear hug, which he heartily returned, Schuyler realized that he had been missed. He'd always considered himself fairly expendable. "Hey, ouch, let go, you bully." He laughed and pulled back. Another thing that suddenly dawned on him was how physically slight his older brother was, belying his strength. Jamie was actually looking *up* at Schuyler, who topped him by several inches.

Huh. Guess I've grown.

"What are you doing here? I was about to go home for the day." Jamie might have looked a tad guilty.

"I came to make sure you weren't letting the business go to wrack and ruin," Schuyler said easily. "And I brought a friend to meet you and see the place. This is Levi Riggins, Selah's—"

"Selah's husband," Jamie finished with him, grinning and shaking hands with Levi. "Glad to meet you, brother. Or I feel like you must be. Selah has always seemed a part of the family."

"And Joelle," Schuyler blurted before he could stop himself. When Jamie gave him a funny look, he added, "And Aurora, of course."

"Of course." Jamie gestured toward a couple of chairs against the wall. "Have a seat, gentlemen, while I wrap things up here, sign a couple of papers, then I'll give Levi the grand tour."

Schuyler hadn't been in the office in quite some time. It had been their father's refuge, visits from the family discouraged, until a couple of years ago when Jamie began to be groomed to take over. Schuyler considered himself an outcast of sorts, mainly good for sales and free-ranging projects outside the state. He loved the water, loved machines and trains and engineering things, but sitting in an office held no appeal. He was happy to abdicate in Jamie's favor.

Levi sat in his usual relaxed manner, one ankle crossed over the other knee, taking in his surroundings. Jamie had done little to change the second-story office, though he had straightened the account books Pa had always kept in a towering pile on the credenza. The big picture window above the credenza was still curtainless, allowing an unobstructed view of the Alabama River sweeping by on the other side of the Water Street levee. Masts, sails, and steamboat smokestacks perforated the distant sky, with seagulls wheeling noisily in the foreground.

It was all a normal part of a Gulf Coast afternoon, and Schuyler wondered if Levi found it somewhat alien—an Illinois native who'd spent most of his life on horseback or aboard a train, with little access to the exotic coastal parts of the country.

As if he'd read Schuyler's thoughts, Levi steepled his fingers and smiled. "I think I could enjoy living in a place like this. Seems like it's got a little more culture than New Orleans."

"New Orleans is a steamy, alligator-infested swamp," Jamie said. "No idea why Camilla and Gabriel insisted on staying there after he finished medical college."

"Just wait until the temperature starts getting upwards of a hundred in the summer," Schuyler said. "You'll be ready to head back to Illinois."

"It's not much cooler here." Jamie scrawled his signature one more time and shoved aside the stack of papers he'd been working on. "Come down to the dock and I'll show you the improvements we've made to the warehouses." They all trooped down the stairs to the ground floor, where a carpeted reception area and handsome meeting room took up most of the space. "We're clearing up the storage areas here," Jamie said. "Pa never could throw anything away." He faced Schuyler, chin up. "How long are you going to stay?"

"Long enough." For once, Schuyler curated his words. "I'm surprised you're not taking some time off. Bron seems to be taking this pretty hard." He paused, glanced at Levi for support. "Jamie, our father just died."

"Yes, he did. Which leaves me with an unbelievable amount of work. You're just like him, you know. Getting bored with the monotony of daily desk work—taking off for more exciting places and events, hobnobbing with important people." A dry smile curved Jamie's lips, but his voice was brittle. "Don't misunderstand, I'm glad you're able to sow your wild oats while you're young and unmarried. It's a big responsibility, having a family."

Schuyler felt his pulse rattle. Of course Jamie had responsibilities here, but was he blaming that on Schuyler?

Feeling Levi quietly tap his elbow, he looked at his friend. Levi gave an imperceptible shake of his head.

Right. *Grow up, young man. Let the poor fellow blow off some steam, no skin off your nose.*

He deliberately relaxed his shoulders, uncurled his fists. "I'll stay as long as you need me to. Come on, let's go down to the wharf and look around."

Whatever his emotions, Jamie's manners were good enough that he wouldn't engage in a brawl in front of a guest. With a shrug, he opened the front door and gestured for Schuyler and Levi to precede him out to the street.

They spent the next hour wandering up and down the wharf, examining goods coming down the river on barges and steamboats, and sampling seafood from the bay, cooked right on the piers.

As they poked through one of the Beaumont warehouses, Levi admired the orderliness of Jamie's management. "So the business involves storage, movement of products and supplies, staffing, maintenance of ships and rail cars." Levi whistled. "That's a huge enterprise. What made your father turn his attention to political office?"

Jamie shrugged. "Pa was never satisfied with 'big' if 'gigantic' was on the table. I think he saw ways to increase his reach into the upper parts of the state—shoot, all over the southeast. He's always fostered relationships with people in government. The next step seemed to be sticking a leg over into it himself."

"It wasn't just commercial greed, though," Schuyler put in, alarmed at the way Jamie's assessment sounded. "He saw this critical period after the war as a chance to give Southerners a voice in developing fair policy."

Levi nodded. "I'm trying to draw a bead on some ideas that might have made enemies. In a city this big, a port this busy, I assume there's competition. Who would that be?"

"There's Lanier Maritime over on the eastern shore." Jamie moved down an aisle of stacked crates, periodically pausing to straighten one. "They were based in Mobile until shortly before the war, then moved across the bay to Point Clear when a large chunk of property opened up."

"Any hard feelings there?" Levi put his hand to the pocket where his notebook rested but seemed to think better of pulling it out in this informal setting.

Schuyler approved. His brother wouldn't take kindly to being grilled for information.

"Hard feelings?" Jamie grinned. "Not that I'm aware of. My wife is a Lanier descendent. If you want to know the truth, it was a little like a royal merger when we married. Also, Camilla's husband is some kind of wrong-side-of-the-blanket kin. In any event, the rail industry isn't their milieu."

"All right, what about your father's railroad activity?

Schuyler mentioned a merger with the Mississippi Central. How would that work with the crossing of state lines?"

Jamie looked at Schuyler. "That's top secret information."

"No, it's not." Schuyler folded his arms. "It's all over the state of Mississippi. Don't you read the paper? People are agitated about the idea of the government sticking its nose into interstate commerce with federal funding of new rails. Pa was on board with it." He looked at Levi. "It was one of the planks he was running on."

Levi put up a conciliatory hand. "All right. Could be enough of a bone of contention to upset somebody. What I don't know, Jamie—and Schuyler says he doesn't have information on either—is how far the negotiations have gone with regard to that merger. And how it would affect the extension of the M&O into Ohio. I've heard talk that's a strong possibility."

"Pa was lobbying for that," Jamie said carefully. "Our creditors are being patient, but who knows how long they'll hold out? At the end of the war, the rails were in terrible condition—due to you Yanks tearing things up every chance you got—and the Confederacy owed us over five million dollars. That doesn't even touch unpaid state bonds." He sighed.

"A new connection to Aberdeen will be finished this summer," Schuyler put in, to deflect from his brother's uncomfortable dig at Levi's Union service. "And for the last six months I've been negotiating for lines to Starkville and Oxford. That may increase revenue."

Levi smiled, apparently unoffended. "Clearly your father had a finger in a lot of complicated pies. At least now I have some concrete leads to follow up on. I'll write to Pinkerton tonight and see what he suggests."

"Good." Jamie nodded. "Meanwhile . . . I suggest we collect some of that shrimp from the wharf and take it home for Bron to boil up with some grits for dinner. I swear I could eat a pound or two all by myself."

"Shrimp and grits?" Levi made a face.

Schuyler laughed. "You have no idea what a South Alabama cook can do with those two ingredients, plus some cheese and Cajun sausage." He swung toward the open doorway and tossed over his shoulder, "On the other hand, Yankee Jack, you can just pass your helping on to me. I'll be happy to take care of it for you."

Why on earth did I think this was a good idea to come here? Joelle asked herself.

By the time she and Selah stepped off the platform at the Mobile train station, Camilla and her family had also arrived from New Orleans. The reunion scene when everyone gathered in the Beaumonts' parlor instantly made Joelle's head pound. The baby cried, adults shouted to be heard above the children shrieking as they dashed up and down the stairs chasing the dog, the doorbell chimed with the arrival of the mortician asking where he was to deliver the body in the morning, and three different neighbors came by with food for the grieving family.

In an effort not to get in the way, Joelle sat in a corner, fingers clenched in her lap. The headache was turning into a migraine.

She had not seen Beaumont House since Lady passed away. Camilla, Jamie, and Schuyler's grandmother had been, for all intents and purposes, their mother—the grande dame of the household, ruling her son-in-law with the same sort of velvet-gloved iron will wielded by Joelle's own grandmother. That funeral had been a somber occasion indeed, the space left by the removal of Lady's vital personality a palpable thing. Still, she had been elderly, frail, unavoidably approaching the end of her life. This violent wrenching of Mr. Zeke from the family fabric could only be described as tragic.

She searched for Schuyler and found him sitting at the foot of the stairs, petting the hairy black-brown-and-gray mutt that charitable persons might call a dog. It lay across Schuyler's feet, belly up and panting with the bliss of having its belly rubbed. Schuyler's expression was uncharacteristically contemplative and sad. When she'd walked into the house behind Selah, he'd plucked Joelle out of the crowd, squashed her in a brief hug, then let her go. She'd lost track of him until now.

Suddenly he looked up and met her gaze across the room. One finger crook and she was walking toward him, stepping over toys, children, and luggage. She sat down beside him, nudging the animal out of the way with her foot. It—she, apparently—gave her an injured look and flopped onto her stomach.

"You are a cold, cruel woman," Schuyler said, a welcome smile curling his mouth.

Joelle bent to scratch the dog behind its large pointed, shaggy ears. "Sorry, beast. What's your name?"

"Schuyler." He stuck out his hand. "I thought I'd introduced myself."

She laughed and took his hand, surprised when he didn't let go. After a brief tug-of-war, she gave in and let him hold it. "The dog. What's she called?"

"Hilo. Somebody saw an atlas picture of Hawaii." He snorted. "Does this dog look Hawaiian to you?"

"Well." She watched Hilo give Schuyler's wrist an adoring lick. "Maybe if you squint."

They sat together for a minute or so, Schuyler absently playing with her fingers. He was so unlike himself that she squelched the fluttery sensation of guilt in her stomach. He needed a friend. He was just missing his father.

Finally he said, "I've been thinking."

"That's a novel pastime. What brought that on?"

"I'm serious." He brought her hand to the top of his thigh and clasped it with both hands. "I've got a decision to make, and I need you to pray about it with me."

"A-all right." She didn't know whether to feel relieved or disappointed. There was nothing romantic about praying. Was there? Though there was a certain amount of intimacy in the way he had said that. Then again, everybody always said she overthought things. "What exactly is the problem?"

"It's this. For the last two days, I've listened to Levi ask questions about my father. 'Why did Ezekiel Beaumont do this? Why did he do that? Who were his friends and business associates? Where was he planning to go after the speech? Where had he been, the previous couple of weeks?'"

"That must've been hard."

"Some." His golden head was bent, and her gaze traced the familiar swirl toward the back of his head where some of his hair curled down, some went sideways, but none lay straight. He turned his face and looked up at her from beneath that messy, glorious lion's mane. "But like I said, it made me think. You know, about the way he worked so hard to take care of all of us. And I've watched Jamie today, taking on everything my father used to do—except he's so young, and this thing my father built is like a complicated machine that is going to take more than one man to run now. I've got to step up and do my part."

She didn't know what to say. She had so little wisdom herself. So she nodded, letting him know she was listening.

"The problem is," Schuyler continued with a sigh, "I'm not sure what my part is. I don't know much about the shipping and storage business. I understand rail transport a little better, but supervising a board of stockholders? Managing people?" He laughed. "I can barely manage myself!"

"But Schuyler, you're so smart! You finished at the top of your class at Ole Miss."

"Physics and geometry, Latin and Greek? Oh, yes, I'm quite the clever fellow. But practicalities like finding out why my father was murdered and who did it—" He blew out another disgusted breath. "I'm about as useless as this Hawaiian dust mop!"

"Well. Well, I think you're wrong. There are plenty of people who depend on you."

"Oh yeah? Who?"

"Hixon and Jefcoat, for two. They'd both be in jail by now if not for you. No, don't laugh. It's true. And Daughtry House wouldn't have happened without you."

His eyes lit with laughter. "Y'all just needed my money. Selah and Levi have got that place under control."

"You'll be rich when it gets going. That's an accomplishment."

"Rich. I used to believe that was what I wanted. Most people considered my father to be wealthy. But I don't think that's what made him get up in the morning, at least over the last few years. And I don't want that to be what drives me—you know what I mean?" His eyes narrowed, intensely staring at her. "I'm tired of wasting time on things that don't matter."

There was something exhilarating about being trusted with his thoughts. Something vaguely dangerous. Gil had never, ever talked to her this way. The thought of Gil brought her up short. She had been leaning in to Schuyler, their faces mere inches apart.

She sat up and snatched her hand away, tucking it into the folds of her skirt. "You've changed in the last couple of days," she said primly. "Have you noticed we haven't argued about anything since I got here?"

"That's because you haven't said anything ridiculous." He grinned.

"Just give me time."

"Why didn't you bring your fiancé with you?"

The non sequitur told her he'd noted her withdrawal. "He has to preach on Sunday and has other duties in between. Besides, he doesn't really know your family."

Clearly he didn't buy the explanation. "You don't have to go through with it if you don't want to, Jo. You and I both know that whole scene at the Peabody was about the two of us."

The words sat there between them, twisting with meaning. Schuyler, her lifelong enemy, her friend, the boy who had given her her first kiss, had somehow turned into this complicated, passionate, courageous man. And it was too late. "Yes, I was angry with you, Schuyler," she said, deliberately misunderstanding him. "That's how it always goes with us. Gil doesn't back me into corners."

If the expression on his face was anything to go by, he wanted to back her into a corner right now. And she couldn't have guaranteed she wouldn't go willingly. As a demonstration of his new maturity, however, he said evenly, "Then he apparently doesn't care to know you. Not really. Cracking you open is like getting the sweets out of a pecan. It's a lot of work, but the result is pretty tasty." He rose, dusted the seat of his pants, and snapped his fingers for the dog. "Come on, Hilo, I think we can find you something to eat around here. I'm hungry too."

He left her to wonder what in the world he meant.

Ten

HE'D DONE IT TO HIMSELF, bringing marriage proposals out into the open. Joelle might be painfully inattentive, but she wasn't stupid. She knew what he'd been getting at.

During the funeral, conducted by the open grave, she stood behind the family with her sister and other close friends. Even the physical act of lifting his father's coffin—his brother, brother-in-law, and an uncle at the other three corners—and lowering it into the grave, couldn't overcome his relief that she'd come all this way to be with him. Oh, she loved Camilla and had an affection for "Mr. Zeke," but she'd traveled two hundred seventy-five miles for *him*.

And if she hadn't pulled away last night, he might have kissed her, no matter how many family members cluttered the house. It wasn't just because she had the face of a Rossetti saint and a husky chuckle that knotted his insides. It was the fact that she understood him in ways no one else ever had. That she stood up to him and challenged him, emotionally and spiritually. That she could outthink him with half her brain tied behind her back.

But she *had* pulled away. There was Distance with a capital *D* between them now, and it was just as well. He should never have said it.

With a mental shake, he picked up a handful of red clay from the pile near the grave and tossed it onto the coffin. He and the other men—Jamie, Gabriel, and Levi—picked up shovels to finish filling the grave, while Uncle Goldon escorted the women back to the house.

Pa was gone.

Schuyler had lain awake all night, thinking about what he was going to do to help Levi find the killer. The problem was, they didn't know enough about the Tuscaloosa riot. Somebody had deliberately stirred it up. No surprises as to why. The Ku Klux Klan had been active in Alabama and Mississippi, heating up toward the elections in November. Liberals, heavily supported by freedmen, had won seats in the state legislatures, and Mississippi had even elected a black US senator. By all accounts, Hiram Revels was a good man, a patient and godly man, capable of navigating the tinder of political conflict with goodwill and common sense.

Instead of allaying the anger of displaced planters, Revels's popularity seemed to further enrage conservatives who wanted to maintain white power. As far as Schuyler knew, his father had been alarmed by his party's bigotry and radicalism. A man of his times, Ezekiel Beaumont had only gradually and reluctantly bent toward a moderate platform, never to the point of jumping parties. But Schuyler would have wagered his soul his pa never donned a hood and cape to terrorize innocent people.

Somebody had. That riot had been in the open, no costumed marauders visible, but an underground tremor of violence rumbled through the events of the day. Maybe the two Negro speakers had been the target, and his father had simply been collateral damage. He had to know. There had to be a way of finding out who had fired that gun and why.

According to the sheriff, there had been several armed white men in the crowd. At least three were the sheriff's own men, but that didn't mean they hadn't taken advantage of the chaos to fire at the balcony.

Sweat rolling down his back, Schuyler jammed the shovel into the dirt pile, relishing the expenditure of angry energy. They just didn't have enough information. The Klan had been fairly open in its activities of late, now that federal troops had been withdrawn and Southern states readmitted to the Union, but identities were kept within the organization. Schuyler had heard talk in billiards parlors and saloons, though he'd paid little attention. Toward the end of their last year of college, Hixon had tried to get him to don a hood and costume for a drunken lark, but Schuyler had refused on the grounds that he had finals to study for.

Now he was glad he hadn't gotten mixed up in that ugly tangle. Doubtful that Hixon was an active member of the Klan; still, maybe Schuyler could ask him for his connection. Rumor had it that General Forrest was some kind of Grand Wizard. Seemed a little undignified for such a decorated military hero, but who knew?

"All right, men. That's it." Jamie rested his shovel against the earth and leaned on the handle.

Schuyler threw on one last shovelful, then stepped back beside his brother. He watched Gabriel smooth the dirt across the grave, as always meticulous with details, his black eyes somber, mouth grim. In spite of their political differences,

Camilla's husband had gotten along well with their blustery father. When he finished, the four of them stood there staring at the grave, avoiding each other's eyes.

Finally Schuyler couldn't take it anymore. "What are we going to do about this?" he burst out.

Jamie looked at him as if he were crazy. "What do you mean? You said Pinkerton is running the investigation. Isn't that what he's here for?" He angled his head toward Levi.

Schuyler gripped the handle of his shovel. "Levi is here to help. But I'm not going to sit on my hands either."

Jamie laughed. "What are you going to do, *dig* for information?"

In his frustration, Schuyler might have launched himself at his hardheaded brother, but Levi put a hand on his shoulder.

"Someone's got to," Levi said. "If not literally, then figuratively. Yesterday I interviewed several black men who'd been in the crowd during the riot. We weren't allowed to talk to the prisoners, but we've got to figure out a way to do that."

"How do you know they'll tell you the truth?" Jamie sounded tired—which he probably was. Schuyler had risen at dawn and found his brother drinking coffee on the back porch. "What were they arrested for?"

"Probably nothing more than standing there covered in dark skin," Gabriel said.

Jamie flinched. "You know I didn't mean anything like that." Gabriel's half–Creek Indian descent left him open to the occasional snide remark here in the cradle of the Confederacy.

"It's implied by the question." Gabriel's tone was reasonable but relentless. "Go on, Riggins. What are you thinking?"

Levi held Schuyler's gaze. "Sky and I talked about this on

the trip down here, but the more I think about it, the more I'm convinced I missed something yesterday. I've got to go back to Tuscaloosa. Anyway, none of the freedmen in the crowd that morning were armed—it's against the law for them to own guns. But an unidentified witness reported that shortly before the fire they'd seen Thomas and Perkins, the two black rally spokesmen, scuffling in the dark for a rifle in the hands of a third Negro going by the name of Harold Moore. Moore claims this white schoolteacher, Lemuel Frye, had attacked him. Nobody seems to know where Moore came from, let alone how he tangled with Frye."

"Lemuel Frye runs a school for black children outside Tuscaloosa," Schuyler explained for Jamie and Gabriel's benefit. "He's a liberal agitator, and the sheriff jailed him along with the Reverend and the militiaman."

Gabriel tapped his lip, frowning. "None of that makes sense."

Levi nodded. "One thing that's obvious to me is there's some broader organization behind this. Even if Mr. Beaumont wasn't the target, those shots up into the balcony were not random. President Grant pulled federal troops out, but he's got his justice department looking into violence down here."

"The Klan isn't the only group," Schuyler said. "But they're the biggest and most influential. They'd be the first culprit to look at."

"Agreed." Levi shook his head. "Problem is, they're loosely organized, and though there are rumors of who the leaders are, identifying them for sure is nearly impossible."

"You need someone to infiltrate." Gabriel grinned. "But don't look at me—my spying days are over."

"Mine too," Levi said. "My accent would be a dead give-away, and this culture—"

"I'll do it." Schuyler said.

The other three stared at him.

Jamie was scowling. "You're out of your mind, little brother."

"No, he's perfect for it," Levi said slowly. "Confederate war service, Ole Miss grad, wild reputation, spoiled rich kid with too much time on his hands."

Schuyler tried not to wince as his character went under scrutiny, indictment, conviction. He had only himself to blame, even if the details were a bit blown out of proportion.

"You can't just walk in and join the Ku Klux Klan," Jamie insisted. "There are background investigations and initiation rituals."

"I hate to remind you of this," Schuyler said, "but no one is going to discover much political conviction on my part, in either direction. It should be fairly easy to convince them I'm interested in stepping into our father's shoes, but without his nasty moral complications. I can be seen to curry political favor, solicit campaign funds, whatever I need to do to work my way in."

Jamie seemed about to argue, but Gabriel held up a hand. "There's another problem. Most Klan activity seems to originate in Mississippi. Running for the Alabama gubernatorial spot won't help us much."

"Then I'll run in Mississippi's state congressional race. I've already established residency there with the hotel and Oxford-to-Tupelo rail venture."

Levi regarded him with respect, and Schuyler realized his and Joelle's prayer had been answered. If things went sideways, he might be throwing away his reputation and possibly even his life. But he knew without a shadow of a doubt that he had been born for this moment.

Then Levi said, "But you know you can't tell anyone what you're doing. Not even Joelle."

The women had taken over the front porch. Camilla, holding the sleeping baby, shared the swing with Selah, while Joelle and Bronwyn occupied the two rocking chairs. The three older children had been put down for a nap upstairs. Lazily plying a silk fan, Joelle pushed her toe against the floor to move the rocker. The story was, Mr. Zeke had imported the fan, along with a beautiful, gaudy kimono, from Japan for Camilla's sixteenth birthday. That was before she'd gotten caught smuggling escaped slaves up the Alabama River in whiskey barrels, then run off to New Orleans to marry a half–Creek Indian Union spy.

Camilla never talked about her wartime exploits when she was at home. Selah said that was because Camilla didn't want to embarrass her family by reviving the scandal. Joelle personally thought the Beaumonts should all be proud of a young woman who had repeatedly risked her life to help others. And she could certainly understand why Camilla would fall in love with exotic Dr. Laniere.

One day she might write Camilla's story and become as famous as Mrs. Alcott or Mrs. Stowe. Right now, however, she must listen to the three married women discuss prosaic topics like colicky babies and removing urine odor from upholstery. Why couldn't the conversation drift toward something more interesting like marital intimacy or—

"Joelle? Did you hear me?"

She blinked and focused on Camilla. "I'm sorry. What?"

Selah snorted. "I told you, there's some story in her head all the time. She's going to be standing at the altar with a blank look on her face while everyone waits for her to say 'I will.'"

"No I won't! Did you ask me something, Milla?"

"I just asked when you're planning the wedding. Gabriel and I were married on the run from Mobile to New Orleans." Camilla giggled. "Found a pastor as soon as we got to Union territory."

Joelle dropped the fan. Now, this was interesting. "Why? Didn't you want your family there?"

"We had no chaperone during the trip, and Gabriel was concerned for my reputation." Camilla patted the baby's bottom, a small smile on her heart-shaped face. "He is a very decisive man, and he doesn't like to wait for anything."

Joelle glanced at Selah. "Gil has been waiting for me for well over a year. He's very . . . patient."

Selah huffed. Joelle knew what her sister thought about Gil's patience.

"Do you love him?" Bronwyn asked.

Joelle bit her lip. She did love Gil, in a Christian brother sort of way. She admired him too, as the leader of their congregation.

Before she could reply, Bronwyn shook her neatly coifed head. "Never mind, that was impertinent. Obviously you do, or you wouldn't have agreed to marry him."

Selah cleared her throat. "Look, there come the men. We should put the food on the table. I'm sure they'll be hungry."

In the general confusion of preparing and eating a post-funeral meal with three little people and a shaggy dog

135

underfoot, Joelle managed to shrug off the sense of impending disaster that had hovered over her head all day. The three Beaumont siblings seemed to be taking the loss of their father remarkably well. Young mother Camilla, always an even-keeled sort of girl, clearly had too much to do, caring for her demanding little ones, to wallow in grief. Jamie took his feelings deep inside, to a private place not even his wife seemed able to penetrate. He ate with stoic duty, as if cleaning his plate gave him control over out-of-control circumstances.

Schuyler looked . . . odd, some pent-up engine propelling every movement. He pushed his food around his plate, then slipped it under the table for the dog. He tapped a maddening tattoo against the table with his spoon until Camilla took it away from him. He sloshed tea out of his glass, mopped it up, and went to the butlery for more. He said something in an undertone to Levi, who responded with a laugh, then fell into a morose silence that worried Joelle most of all.

Finally, he shoved his chair away from the table and announced, "I'm going for a walk."

"I'll go with you." Ignoring the stares of the other four adults, Joelle laid her napkin on her plate. "I'll clear the table when I get back," she told Bronwyn and hurried after Schuyler.

He was already out the front door and halfway down the block, headed downtown. She caught up to him by running at a most undignified pace.

Without slowing down, he glanced at her, frowning. "They're going to think . . . Never mind."

"I don't care what anybody thinks."

"Yes, you do." His lips tightened. "You've got to."

"Schuyler, stop." She grabbed his arm. "What's the matter?"

He pulled away. "Go back to the house. I need some time to think."

"It's a free country. I can walk and think just as well as you can."

He laughed, a rusty sound that broke her heart. "Leave it to you to turn a stroll down the street into an argument."

"We are not strolling. We're running an Olympic race."

He turned and stepped in front of her so suddenly that she plowed into him full-on. His face was a study in frustration, fists clenched, and she put her hands on his chest to keep her balance. Or so she told herself.

"What do you want, Joelle?" he said. "What do you want from me? We can't be confidants anymore. We can't even be—argument mates anymore."

"I know that. I do." She looked up at him, longing to slide her hands up around his neck, restrained by the fact that they were on a public street. Thank the Lord for that. "But this is a hard time for you and your family. I just don't think it's good for you to bottle everything up and pretend it's all right. I don't think there's anything wrong with me listening to your heart."

He closed his eyes, as though she'd just hit him. "Jesus, have mercy."

She knew that was a prayer, because Schuyler never swore in front of women. He was still and silent so long, she finally said, "Schuyler?"

With a long sigh, he opened his eyes and looked down at her. What she saw there for a split second buckled her knees, but it was gone so fast she couldn't be sure it wasn't just a flash of light flickering through the mossy oak limb draped over the road. Methodically he took her hands, squeezed them briefly, and dropped them as if picking lint off his suit. "Listen to me, Joelle. I'm going to say this as kindly and clearly as I can. Are you listening? Sometimes you go off into a daydream with your eyes wide open."

"I'm listening." Her heart thudded. What was she afraid of? This was just Schuyler.

"Good. This is hard, because we've been friends for a long time. I know you're used to telling me exactly what you think, and demanding your way, and putting up with my nonsense. But we are adults now, and it's got to stop. You chose another man, and I've got work to do, so I'm moving on with my life. Without you. We're going to see a good bit of each other, since the hotel will bring me to Tupelo occasionally, but that will be business."

You chose another man. You chose another man. The words banged about in her head like his spoon hitting the table earlier. Stop. Stop. Stop.

"Business," she repeated stupidly.

"Yes." He nodded, clearly relieved that she didn't argue. "Just so you'll know, I've decided to run for the Mississippi state legislature, which means I'll be traveling over the next few months. I'd appreciate it if you'd keep me in your prayers."

Her lips felt numb, but she managed to say, "Of course I will."

"Thank you. Now please, go back to the house and help the other girls clear the table. I've got a lot to think about right now. Trust me. I'm fine." He turned and walked away from her with his athletic Schuyler-stride, turned a corner, and disappeared.

Well. She'd tried to help him, but pray for him? She wasn't sure she could do that without falling apart. Best not to think about him at all.

Ten minutes later she walked into the kitchen without any concept how she'd gotten there.

Bronwyn, standing at the sink in an apron, dish towel in hand, turned to look at her. "Joelle? Are you all right? Is Schuyler—"

"He's fine. I'm fine." She picked up a hot pad and took the kettle off the stove. "Here. I'll rinse."

You chose another man. Bang. Bang. Bang.

Eleven

"I STILL THINK YOU SHOULD HAVE STAYED to go to church with your family," Levi said, giving Schuyler that concerned look that was beginning to rub his nerves raw.

On Saturday evening, the two of them sat at the same table they'd shared on Wednesday, each with a pint of ale and a plate of beef with mashed potatoes and tomato gravy.

"Pa wouldn't want me sitting around doing nothing, feeling sorry for myself." Schuyler shoveled beef into his mouth, though he was no more hungry now than he'd been for the last two days. Still, common sense told him he needed to eat. His breeches were starting to get loose.

"Not so much for you, as for your sister and brother. Did you see the way Camilla looked when you came downstairs with your bag this morning?"

He hadn't, because he'd been looking at Joelle—though he hoped he'd kept her from knowing that. He picked up his tankard. "Milla's used to me coming and going without warning." Levi was silent for so long that Schuyler thunked the tankard on the table hard. "What is it, Riggins? I know you want to lecture me about something."

"It's not my place to 'lecture' you, brother, but I'm worried that you've gotten . . . unmoored by losing your father this way. You know I admire your willingness to take on this new role. I've done it, and I know how hard it is. You won't be able to relax for one minute—in fact, you'll probably not sleep soundly until this thing is over. And who knows how long it will take."

Schuyler ate another bite. "I'm not afraid of it. Like you said, I've played the fool for years, so this is just one more monkey in the circus."

"All right. I know you can do this. I just wanted to say that you can always come to me. In fact, I'll be monitoring you as closely as I can without giving you away."

"That's fine. I expected that."

"One more thing." Levi hesitated.

"Riggins, you're worse than my grandmother used to be."

"From what I've heard, your grandmother was the original spymaster, so I'll take that as a compliment. What's going on between you and Joelle? Last night she came back looking like she'd eaten glass."

Schuyler looked away. "Nothing. Absolutely nothing. Which I made very clear to her."

"Oh. I have to say, I'm surprised. I'd thought you might fight for her."

"*What?*" Schuyler jerked his gaze back to Levi and found his friend's expression perplexed. "She's betrothed. I wouldn't betray that commitment. Besides, the charade I'm fixing to play . . . she shouldn't be anywhere near those people. Riggins, you *told me not to tell her.*"

Levi looked sheepish. "I didn't think you'd take me seriously."

"Well, I did. Because you're right. She blurts out things without thinking, and I can't take the risk." He shook his head. "I have to keep her at arm's length until all this is over. By then . . . she'll be a married woman." And there was a good chance he'd be dead. Time to change the subject. "You never did clarify your and Selah's plans. The honeymoon's over. Are you going to stay in New Orleans, launch the new Pinkerton office? Or quit the agency and stay in Tupelo?"

"As I told you, for now I'm here on assignment. That's all I'm at liberty to say. Selah and I discussed it and decided she'll stay in Tupelo. I'd like to travel with you, as your attorney—which makes sense, as we're established as partners in the hotel business."

A heavy weight of anxiety—which he hadn't realized had been clamped upon his chest—dropped away at the thought of Levi's support. For the first time in days, he smiled. "Just in time to escape mosquito season. Smart man."

Levi's answering smile was wry. "If I remember correctly from my days in Mississippi during the war, you folks grow them the size of small birds as well."

Schuyler laughed. "Fair enough. But at least you'll be able to kiss your wife occasionally."

"I'd brave any number of mosquitoes for that," Levi said with a grin. He pulled his notebook and pencil from his pocket. "I've been making some notes of where we might start your campaign. Look here . . ."

Pushing away the thought of a certain pair of bowed red lips he wouldn't mind kissing, Schuyler focused on the serious nature of what he had to do. He'd stand a much better chance of staying alive.

"Everyone turn over in your hymnal to hymn ninety-nine," Gil instructed the congregation. "We're going to sing of repentance. And isn't it interesting, how the number ninety-nine refers to those the Savior would leave behind whilst he goes looking for the one lost lamb? Who repented, I'm sure."

Joelle obediently flipped pages to the correct hymn, though she wished Gil would be more careful of his syntax. Imagining herself lying down on her open hymnal and rolling over made her want to giggle.

She also wished he would let someone else lead the singing. Ah well, Mr. Wesley had written some beautiful words, and she could enjoy singing them. "Since by thy light myself I see naked, and poor, and void of thee, thy eyes must all my thoughts survey . . ."

How uncomfortable to imagine God poking around in her rebellious mind.

Truthfully, she would have preferred to stay home from church and avoid the effort of smiling and making conversation, of pretending to be pious. But one couldn't wallow in misery for the rest of one's life. Well—she *could*, she supposed. But misery, as the saying went, loved company, and there was no one to whom she could confide her melancholy conviction that she had stepped off in the wrong direction.

Selah had tried to get her to talk, all the way home from Mobile yesterday, but Joelle refused to dump her puny troubles on her sister, who was clearly hiding her own sadness at leaving her husband at the station. So Joelle managed to turn the conversation to the oddities of life in New Orleans and the pleasure of living in the same city with her dearest friend. If Selah noticed that Joelle winced at the mention of Camilla's younger brother, she was kind enough not to mention it.

She made herself focus on the hymnal she shared with ThomasAnne—the only person in the pew tall enough to jointly hold a book with Joelle the Giantess.

"'Thou know'st the baseness of my mind,'" she sang, marveling at the verse's piercing truth, "'wayward, and impotent, and blind; thou know'st how unsubdued my will, averse from good and prone to ill; thou know'st how wide my passions rove, nor checked by fear, nor charmed by love!'" She handed the book to ThomasAnne and fumbled for her handkerchief. This was just silly. Music always made her happy.

She would go home and play the piano all afternoon. Or write a story, one of those melodramatic, romantic tales about a girl who comes upon a prince in the woods, a prince who recognizes her innate royalty and sweeps her away to life in a castle. A prince who never argued or teased, who played the lute and fed her sweetmeats, and rode her about on horseback.

Except that would be dull as dishwater, and she would end up weighing two hundred pounds, and where would she put her piano?

She must have laughed aloud as the hymn ended, for ThomasAnne gave her a very odd look.

"Are you all right, honey-pie?" her cousin asked as they sat down. "Selah told Aurora to let you be, but if you want to go home—"

"Of course not." Joelle hastily folded her handkerchief. "I

want to hear the message." Before church, she had reminded Gil about speaking for Reverend Boykin, and he'd promised that he was still thinking about it.

Gil stood behind the lectern in his severe black suit. His string tie was black, his vest was black, his thick, straight hair was black. When he officiated over funerals, this habitual attire was entirely appropriate. But on a bright May morning with sunlight streaming through the new church building's tall, narrow windows, lighting the women's pale spring dresses and hats, he looked like a raven cawing over a field of daisies. In ten or twenty years, he would undoubtedly be a handsome man—when he had had time to grow into his nose.

She fixed her eyes on his face, waiting for him to speak. He looked at her and smiled. At least he had good teeth.

"Reverend Boykin," she mouthed at him.

His brow furrowed. "What?" he mouthed back.

"Reverend Boykin," she repeated soundlessly.

He scratched his head and took his gaze across his flock, most of whom were old enough to be his parents or grandparents. Joelle and her family were the only young people in the congregation. "I think," Gil said, "a certain young lady wants me to mention something."

She beamed at him to encourage him. *Reverend Boykin.*

He smiled back at her. "This is the first opportunity I've had to publicly announce that your pastor has recently become betrothed. Before the year is out, Miss Joelle Daughtry will become Mrs. Gilbert Reese!"

Joelle suffered through the delighted "Ahs" that sighed through the sanctuary, endured the looks of curiosity and Mrs. Whitmore loudly whispering, "It's about time!" But when Gil placidly launched into his sermon on God's merciful redemption of those who least deserved it, without the slightest recognition of her one request, red waves of outrage blocked her hearing. She sat quivering with the restraint it took not to launch herself at the altar.

He said he would think about it. What would it hurt to say one kind word about a fellow minister, to aid him in pursuit of an office that would help untold numbers of worthy, formerly mistreated individuals gain a voice in their government? He *knew* it would make her happy and proud—when she had done her best to spare his feelings, to the point of giving up her own independence and *marrying* an oblivious, selfish . . .

Man. Well, what did she expect? She'd met very few men who attained anything like the hero status of the fairy-tale princes of her imagination. As far as she was concerned, even her own father had been the epitome of self-centeredness, no matter how Selah tried to explain away his crimes.

Well, Levi might perhaps have several redeeming qualities, but he was clearly an anomaly.

All right. So Gil was a man, the one she was doomed to spend her life with—no better, no worse than any of the rest of them. She'd best set about helping him become someone she could live with.

She stewed and fumed throughout the rest of the sermon, hearing little that she could absorb into her Christian walk. But by the time it was over, she knew what she was going to do.

After the last "amen," the women swarmed her. All she wanted to do was crawl under the porch. Instead, she found her smile and answered randomly.

"Thank you. Yes, I was surprised when it happened. I don't know. Maybe this summer? I suppose we'll live in the parsonage. I haven't seen it yet. Wait a minute. What do you mean, the bishop could move us?" She stared blankly at Mrs. Whitmore, who had asked what she would do if Gil were moved away from Tupelo.

"Well, sugar, you realize Methodist preachers are subject to the whim of the appointment cabinet. I just wondered how you would manage that *hotel*"—a word spat out with the same disgust as if the woman had said *brothel*—"when you're living in another town, or even another state." Mrs. Whitmore clasped her gloved fingers together at her thick waist, a sympathetic smile on her inversely proportionate thin lips. The eyes were snake dead.

"I—of course I knew that. We haven't had time to discuss management of the hotel—"

"Mrs. Whitmore, my wife will have nothing to do with managing a hotel," Gil said from behind her. "You can rest assured, she will be quite busy with the duties of church and home."

Joelle looked up at him, speechless. Of course, she was speechless most of the time, but in this case a series of realizations crashed down upon her. *This* was why she'd deflected Gil's marriage proposals for an entire year (besides the fact that she found him about as amusing as a stack of bookkeeping ledgers). She would literally have no right to determine where she lived, when she moved, or how she would spend her time. The man who stood behind her would not only protect her—he would own her. In the deepest, most secret pages of her journal, she had admitted to herself the relief she'd felt at her father's death. In a few short weeks she would voluntarily place her hands into manacles chaining her to another man.

A kinder man who seemed to genuinely admire her, but nonetheless a man who held the legal authority (and apparently no aversion) to yank her willy-nilly into another state.

It was at that moment that all common sense, patience, and feminine guile deserted her. She turned, smiled up at her intended, and said, "Gil, dear, I believe you forgot to mention one of my chief duties, which I shall certainly carry with me into marriage, and that is charitable missionary work." She turned to Mrs. Whitmore, which involved bending her head to focus on the pasty face. Should she stoop and chuck the woman under her chin? Too much, perhaps. "Reverend Reese and I have been discussing for some time our concern over our recently freed neighbors' well-being. After all, the Bible instructs us to 'Open thy mouth, judge righteously, and plead the cause of the poor and needy.' So many of them are unable to find employment—and when they do, they are often cheated because of the inability to read and reconcile labor and merchandise contracts. I've tried to remedy that as best I can by educating my own employees. However, I feel that there is much that can be done at the local, state, and federal levels to give freedmen a chance to improve their lot in life."

"Joelle." Gil was tapping on her shoulder.

"Specifically," she plowed on, ignoring him, "we must encourage our brothers of color to participate in government so that decisions which affect them will take them into the next century, fully prepared to flourish—"

"Miss Daughtry—"

"—and with that end in mind, Gil and I would like to encourage each of you ladies to exert your influence with your husbands, who will be voting in the upcoming elections. The pastor of our sister church on the other side of town is planning to run for the Mississippi state legislature, and we both think he would make a fine representative for our district. Don't you—"

"*Joelle!*" Gil fairly roared.

"—agree with me?" she finished in a rush, then stood there with her back to her betrothed, shaking with victory and righteous indignation. She had said it, and no one could unsay it. She looked around at the scandalized faces of the women around her. Most of them had known her since she was a baby. They knew she was the quiet one, the odd one, the one prone to migraines. Some people thought she had a stammer because she so rarely opened her mouth in public. Then she looked past the inner circle of neighbors and found her sisters and ThomasAnne, regarding her with utter astonishment. It was as if a parakeet had turned into a phoenix, burst into flames, and proceeded to burn down its cage, the room, and the entire building.

After fifteen seconds of silence, which seemed to Joelle to last a year, she dragged in a breath. Might as well be hanged for a sheep as a lamb. "Who knows—maybe we'll eventually get the right to vote ourselves."

Twelve

MONDAY MORNING SCHUYLER AND LEVI met downstairs for a breakfast of fried eggs, slabs of bacon, and crusty bread, all washed down by the Tavern's ubiquitous bitter coffee. They'd gone to church together yesterday, met a few people, asked some questions, and then spent the afternoon resting and planning a strategy for the coming week.

Turned out it was a good thing they did. Just as Schuyler was pushing away his plate, full as the proverbial tick, a snow-haired gentleman, sporting a matching venerable mustache, rolled through the front door.

"Morning, Judge Teague!" called out a couple of diners. They wandered over to shake hands, slap the judge's back, and linger for a few moments' conversation. But most of the patrons turned their backs and pretended not to notice his entrance.

Interesting. Schuyler took himself to the bar, according to previous plan, and pretended to nurse a pint of ale. Levi waited until the judge was alone, then approached him.

Schuyler had spent three years of college watching his

fraternity mates imbibe copious amounts of alcohol, then try to carry on a conversation. By graduation, he had become quite adept at mimicking the sloshy diction and convoluted syntax of the chronic drunkard while maintaining a sober head, a talent which had come in handy on more than one occasion.

Remembering Levi's favorite Pinkerton quote, that the human mind could not maintain a secret, he propped his elbows on the bar. "Pssst." He beckoned the bartender over. "Who's the gent with the mustache?"

The bartender's lip curled. "That's the Honorable S. Marmaduke Teague, circuit court judge for Tuscaloosa County."

Schuyler looked over his shoulder at Levi hobnobbing with the judge. "Huh. Seems to be getting along well with my Yankee friend."

"Not surprised. Teague was federally appointed under Reconstruction laws. Liberal." The disdain coating that last word told Schuyler all he needed to know about the barkeep's opinion.

Schuyler attempted to look both wise and soused. "The Yank is my lawyer. He's a liberal too."

"This county's crawling with scalawags and carpetbaggers." The barkeep leaned in, the classic gossip. "You heard about that dustup last week? Right outside my door."

His father's murder a "dustup"? Schuyler wanted to leap over the bar and throttle the man. He grinned instead. "I heard it was one of those scalawags you mentioned, got himself put six feet under by a stray bullet."

Barkeep nodded. "A politician from Mobile. Mayor Samuel's idea was to get federal troops down here to control the Klan. But he just wound up stirring up more trouble." He made a disgusted noise and called Ezekiel Beaumont an ugly name related to his relationship with Negroes.

Schuyler decided he'd better turn the conversation a bit, or he would not be responsible for the state of the barkeep's nose. He hiccuped. "Yessir, my sentiments ezzackly. Can't understand why rich white men wanna waste time with uppity coloreds like that preacher and the militiaman that was up on the balcony with him. Whoever did the shootin' didn't aim too good!"

The barkeep laughed. "Now, now, son. Reverend Thomas ain't a bad man. I see him in town on occasion, and he's always nice and polite. Even seems to be somewhat educated. Don't know the one called Perkins." He slopped his towel onto the bar and wiped. "Now that you mention it, though, it does seem odd that Beaumont was the one directly hit."

Schuyler put his finger beside his nose. "I'd be willing to bet somebody decided to put a stop to his interference. Heard there was a lot of armed men out there."

"Well, if you want to know who did it, I'd attend the hearing this morning. That's why Judge Teague is in town." Barkeep glanced over at the table where Levi sat engaged in conversation with the judge. "You mind me asking what *you're* doing here—and what you need with a Yank for your lawyer?"

"That's personal, but you seem to be a man who can keep a secret." Inwardly cringing at the inanity of that statement, considering the dump of information he'd just pulled from the garrulous bartender, he lowered his voice to a mild roar. "I'm in a little trouble with the federals myself. Just a little . . . 'dustup,' as you say, over a lark with my fraternity brothers over in the colored part of town."

Barkeep chuckled. "Oh, a 'Bama boy, huh? I think this is only the second time I've seen you in here. New student?"

"No, sir." Schuyler listed to the left on his stool. "I go to Ole Miss. But things got a little hot, shall we say, over in Oxford. My pa said I'd better get across the state line until things calm down."

"I'd tell my boy the same thing. And I'd also tell him to go easy on the ale before noon." With a wink the barkeep responded to a request for service at the other end of the bar, leaving Schuyler to reflect that what he'd just heard served to confirm the sheriff's account. And to congratulate himself that he'd established his relationship with Levi as business underlaid by mutual contempt.

He'd wasted quite enough time here. Jerking his tie and collar into a semblance of Hixon's state of perpetual disarray, he left a two-bit piece on the bar and meandered out to the street. Levi could follow at his leisure.

Schuyler stopped to look up at the clock tower on the west end of the courthouse, located on Sixth Street just south of the old capitol. He should have time to talk to the accused before Judge Teague started the hearings at nine. A short walk took him to the two-story jail next door to the courthouse. As the door was ajar, he knocked and pushed on it.

"Hello? Anybody here?" Poking his head in, he found a scruffy bejowled deputy reading a newspaper behind a battered oak desk.

Looking like a hound dog who'd been awakened from a nap, the deputy scowled over the top of the paper. "You're in the wrong building, son. Saloon's down the street."

Was there something on his forehead that said "Intoxicated college boy below"?

Schuyler gave the deputy an amiable, sloppy salute. "Yes, sir. I found it. But one of my professors back in Oxford is related to Mr. Frye, and I promised to check on him before his hearing." He reached into his pocket for another two-bit coin, flicked it upward with his thumb, and caught it. "With your permission, I'd like to talk to him."

"Frye is one of those Negro-lovin' Lincolnites. I doubt he's got any friends."

"Didn't say 'friend,' I said 'relative.' You don't choose your kin, know what I mean?" Schuyler flipped the coin again, and it landed on the desk. "Oops." He let it spin there as he stumbled toward the stairs. "Kindness is kindness, and I really want an A in that class."

The deputy shrugged and went back to his newspaper. "First cell on the left."

At the top of the stairs, Schuyler found two rows of cells lining the barnlike building. Two of the cells on the right contained well-dressed Negro men, and on the left he found a squirrelly white man with thinning brown hair and large, innocent brown eyes behind a pair of rimless spectacles. Seated on his bare cot with a Bible on his lap, he wore an ill-fitting suit of brown worsted and boots that looked like they might have been cobbled during the War of 1812.

Schuyler walked right up to the white man's cell. "Mr. Frye?"

The man stared at him with myopic disinterest. "Yes. I'm Frye. Do I know you?"

"No. I'm Schuyler Beaumont. But if the deputy asks you, you have a cousin teaching physics at the University of Mississippi. He sent me to see to your needs."

"That would be a lie."

Schuyler nodded. "Yes, but it's my lie, not yours. Besides, I *am* going to send over a meal from the tavern after the hearing. Do you mind if I ask you a few questions?"

"They're taking care of our meals, so there's no need to do that."

Schuyler sighed. Some people were entirely too legalistic for their own good. "Fine. No food—"

"Better send some, young boss," interrupted the elder of the two black men. "Schoolmaster's been giving us his meals, since they barely fed me and Perkins after they threw us in here last week."

Schuyler stared at Frye. Scrupled and legalistic. "I'm sorry to hear that. All right. I will. Now, Mr. Frye, I'm going to tell you the truth here, since you seem to be fond of that commodity. My father was the one killed in that riot last week. I don't think you did it, and I don't think you beat up that third colored man—what does he call himself?"

"Moore," said the Negro who'd asked for the food. "Harold Moore."

"Thank you," Schuyler said. "And what's your name, sir?"

"Josiah Thomas."

Thomas. The minister who'd been on the balcony with Schuyler's father. "Reverend Thomas, what are you and Perkins accused of?"

"Arson and disorderly conduct. They said we set fire to the livery stable."

"But they let Moore go and kept you two? That doesn't make any sense."

"No sir, it sure don't," Perkins said. "None of us ever saw Moore before that day. Just showed up here in town, apparently for the rally. Then when he got rounded up with us two after the fire, he goes to screamin' that Mr. Frye had beat him up. All Mr. Frye ever done was teach our children how to read and write."

Schuyler gave the schoolteacher a thoughtful look. "That true, Frye? Did you lay a hand on Moore?"

Frye laid his Bible on the cot and folded his arms. "I'm not sure I'd recognize him if he walked in here."

"Why would he accuse you of such a thing?"

"There are a lot of folks around here who want me to go away, Mr. Beaumont. They say educating Negroes is equivalent to handing them a club to wield over white people." He shrugged. "I disagree, and I'm not going away."

Schuyler knew a certain red-haired young lady who felt the same way. Looking through the bars at Frye's pale, hungry face, marred by a swollen welt running from his cheekbone into his hairline, Schuyler felt a chill of foreboding shiver through him. What if Joelle drew this sort of censure from her Tupelo neighbors? Because of her femininity and stature in the community, no one would get violent—he thought—but there had certainly been gossip about the "odd" Daughtry women.

"Hey, you three," came a voice from the stairway. "Time to go." The deputy appeared in the doorway, a hand on the pistol at his belt. "You'd best get out of here, boy, so I can take my prisoners over to the courthouse."

"Yessir, I was just leaving." Schuyler peered through the bars of Frye's cell. "I meant what I said, Mr. Frye. I'll be at the hearing, and I'll be by to check on you afterward. Godspeed, sir." He stepped around the deputy and clattered down the stairs.

Joelle rubbed her scratchy eyes with cramped fists. Since Selah was checking linens in the big house with Horatia, Joelle had taken over the desk in the office of the manager's cottage. Usually she wrote piled up in bed in the little bedroom she shared with Aurora, blocking her sister's chatter with wads of cotton stuffed into her ears. But today she'd felt she needed a more concentrated work space and access to her father's library. Papa had been a coldhearted blackguard, but he had good taste in literature.

She had worked on the article all afternoon on Sunday and late into the night, then she'd risen with the first cry of the rooster and dressed in the dark. Leaving Aurora sound asleep, she visited the privy, then tiptoed over to the kitchen to wash her hands and face. Horatia and Mose hadn't arrived for the day, so she found a loaf of bread in the larder, spread it with butter and fig preserves, and headed back to the cottage, munching. Then she'd settled in to write.

Waving her notebook to dry the ink, she glanced out the window, open to the breeze. Her story still wasn't finished; in fact, there were a few more people she wanted to interview before "T. M. Hanson" turned his masterpiece in to Mr. McCanless. But it was nearly noon, she was hungry, and if she didn't get up out of this chair, she was going to atrophy. Yawning, she went to the bedroom to stuff the notebook under the mattress in the center of the bed. Should be safe there. She'd been hiding manuscripts in the attic of the big house since she was little, but lately there had been too much renovation activity to make that a viable choice.

She ought to find out if Selah or Horatia needed her for anything, but it occurred to her to wonder about Charmion's progress on her new dress. Grabbing a sun hat off the hook by the door, she headed for the Vincents' new cottage over by the blacksmith shop. Daughtry House was fortunate to have secured the ablest blacksmith in the county and his wife, a gifted dress designer and seamstress.

Through the open screened windows, Joelle could hear Charmion singing a hymn. She stood on the little porch listening for a moment, enjoying the rich alto, but as Charmion reached the end of the verse, Joelle knocked. "Hello, Char, it's Joelle!"

"Coming!" Slow, heavy footsteps approached, and the door opened. Charmion, a hand supporting her large belly, greeted Joelle with her big white smile. "Oh, I'm glad to see you! I'm working on your dress, and I wanted to try something on you."

Joelle couldn't help staring at the round shape under Charmion's gingham housedress. "How much longer before the baby comes? You look like you're about to explode!"

Charmion laughed and backed up to let Joelle in. "Maybe another month. Nathan swears I'm taking up enough room in the bed for three people!"

"Well, that's rude." Joelle laughed at herself. "I guess I was rude too. I'm sorry!"

Charmion sighed as she cleared a pile of scraps off a chair for Joelle. "Don't matter. It's true. I'll be glad when this little mite gets here so I can put him down occasionally, 'stead of lugging him around twenty-four hours a day."

"I can imagine. Well, not really, but you know what I mean."

Charmion grinned, used to Joelle's meandering style of conversation. "Yes'm. Now let me show you what I've been putting together. This is the prettiest material! You have such good taste!"

"Aurora picked it out," Joelle said, watching Charmion handle long swaths of the shimmery brown fabric. "I don't know voile from sateen."

"You should learn," Charmion said. "Girl with your coloring could wear just about anything except pink."

"Even I know not to do that!" Joelle laughed. "I'd look like a flamingo!"

Charmion snorted. "Come on, stand up, let me slip this over your head."

"Over my clothes?"

"Yes, we measured before I began, remember? I just want you to get an idea of what I'm doing here."

Joelle submitted to being draped, reflecting that the dress she had on was so thin from washing that it was close to being underwear anyway. Charmion pinned and hummed and twitched and muttered to herself, and after a few minutes she stood back to survey her handiwork.

Charmion sucked in a breath. "Oh, Miss Jo. You gonna turn a head or two."

Joelle did not want to turn heads. Generally she wanted to fade into the curtains and hope nobody noticed her. But if she was going to take on some of the responsibility from Selah, she had to look more like a professional hotelier than the second upstairs maid. And she had noticed that when she made an effort with her appearance, certain people took her more seriously.

She didn't see a mirror, which was just as well. Her hair was probably a rat's nest of red curls, which she had wadded in a net at the back of her head in the dark. She looked down at the rows of tiny pintucks cinching the waist of the princess-style dress, the elegant gores of the skirt sweeping to her feet. Gleaming copper fabric puddled on the floor around her. She lifted her arms to admire the medieval bell sleeves, falling under the arm to a graceful point.

"There will be some simple tatted lace edging on the sleeves," Charmion said, "and a little bit along the neckline. I didn't want to take away from the beauty of the fabric."

Joelle blinked at the Negro girl, once her slave and now her friend. "You are an artist," she breathed. "I don't know what to say."

"Say you'll tell everybody who made it." Charmion laughed.

"Of course I will. Where did you get this idea? I haven't seen anything like this outside of my fairy-tale book."

"That's what made me think of it. When we were girls, I'd sneak in your room after everybody was asleep and get that book and find a patch of moonlight and just stare for hours at the pictures."

Joelle swallowed, crushed by guilt. She tried to speak, but Charmion put out a hand to brush the sleeve of the dress.

"You don't know what you don't know, Joelle. I'm so happy now, Nathan and me, and you and your sisters gave us this chance."

"I'm glad you're happy. But you know, if I could crawl inside your skin and feel what you feel, I'm sure I'd do things differently every day."

Charmion cupped her hands under her belly. "If you could crawl in my skin, you'd be looking for the privy every five minutes. But I appreciate the thought."

They laughed together, and Charmion began to unpin the dress so that Joelle could slip out of it. "This is so exquisite, I'm not sure I'll want to wear this for daily—"

"Charmion!"

Joelle, back to the door, turned to find big, muscle-bound Nathan Vincent leaning in. Sweat poured off him and his face was grim.

Charmion dropped the material in her hands. "What's the matter?"

"I got to go out to Shake Rag. The church has burned down."

Thirteen

THE SECOND-FLOOR TUSCALOOSA COURTROOM, like a hundred others scattered across the South, provided the circuit court judge with a lofty perch from which to view his minions below. The jury box to one side of the raised bench and witness stand to the other were faced by rows of wooden pews designed for maximum discomfort, with tables for the litigating parties center front.

Positioned halfway back and to the right of the defense, Schuyler scanned the packed room from beneath drooping lids. Fortunately, as a seasoned church sloucher, he had developed a spinal column flexible enough to find comfort in the most rigid of seats. His thoughts were not as sanguine as his posture would indicate. He could see Levi sitting toward the front, three rows behind the accused. The two Negroes, Thomas and Perkins, both flinched at every sudden noise, while their white codefendant sat beside them in stoic silence. If Frye was nervous, he hid it well.

Schuyler couldn't think of anything practical he could do to help. And he found, to his surprise, that he did want to help. He kept picturing Mose or Reverend Boykin or Nathan seated at that table, with no one to speak for them. But he must sit here pretending lazy interest, as if he were a bored student with nothing better to occupy him. Levi had to be worried too. Though he pretended to be an attorney, he had no authority to affect the outcome for the defendants.

At the plaintiff's table sat a light-skinned Negro of about thirty years who bore livid marks of a beating. He had to be Moore. Every so often he would turn his head and glare at Frye. Bad blood evidently flowed there.

Schuyler wished he'd had a chance to confer with Levi before the hearing. Doubtful the judge would have shared his thoughts about the case, particularly with a Yankee lawyer. But Levi would have at the least developed a general impression as to what to expect from the proceedings.

Before he could jeopardize his lackadaisical cover by moving down front to speak to Levi, an elderly court officer shuffled in from a side door. "All rise for His Honor, Judge S. Marmaduke Teague," the man intoned as he positioned himself near the bailiff's chair.

Schuyler unfolded himself and stood along with the large crowd of spectators. He recognized the tall, burly sheriff, the deputy from the jail, plus a second deputy, and a well-dressed unidentified white man, all seated on the front row. Undoubtedly they would be called as witnesses.

As the judge dropped into his chair, the assemblage also settled, with a sigh and shuffle of feet. Teague laced his fingers together atop the desk and surveyed the courtroom, his expression bland with a soupçon of cynicism under the magnificent mustache. "Now, let's see if we can get to the bottom of this mess." His gaze lingered on the plaintiff. "Are you Mr. Moore?"

The small Negro man's scowl relaxed into an expression of deference. "Yes, sir."

"Good. I realize some of the information I'm looking for has already come out in the preliminary hearing before the justice of the peace, but since he had to leave town for a family emergency, we'll need it again for our records today. Will you please stand and state your full name and place of residence."

Moore rose. "I be Harold Moore of Tremont, Mississippi, in Itawamba County just across the state line."

"All right, Mr. Moore, what is your business here in Tuscaloosa?" The judge's tone was polite but firm.

Moore seemed reluctant to answer for a moment. He finally said, "I been deputized to bring back some field hands what took off a month or so ago."

"And did you find your quarry?"

"Sir?"

"Did you find the men you were looking for?"

"Yessir. I mean nossir. They was ten of 'em sign a contract and run out on it. Took me a couple of tries, but I founds all but two and brung 'em back."

"Your Honor." Lemuel Frye stood. "May I interject a pertinent point here?"

The judge frowned at the interruption. "You'll have your turn to speak momentarily, Mr. Frye."

"But—"

"Sit *down*, Mr. Frye."

Frye sat.

"Please continue, Mr. Moore. I'd like to hear your complaint against the defendants."

"Yes, Your Honor," said Moore. "So when I come back for the last two men, Mr. Frye here and some colored men was waiting for me. They drug me off my wagon and out in the woods, and beat the tar outta me. This was a week ago, and the cuts is just now healing." He lifted the back of his shirt and turned so the judge could see the raised red welts across the dark-skinned back.

There was a ruffle of reaction from the audience. Schuyler couldn't help a silent whistle. No denying that *somebody* had beat the man.

Judge Teague pinched the end of his mustache, maybe in an attempt to hide his own dismay. "Mr. Moore, I'm sorry for your injury. Do you have the names of the men who were with your attacker? And is there anyone who can verify your account?"

Adjusting his clothing, Moore turned to face the judge again. He shook his head. "It were near dark when they got me. The white man held the lantern and the whip while the coloreds tied me up and stripped me. Then he give them the whip, and they took turns whaling on me." He turned to stare at Frye with clear hatred singeing his face. "It's a miracle I didn't die where they left me, but I crawled to a house nearby, where a kindly granny took care of me until I was well enough to walk to town. I reported what happened to the sheriff, but he didn't arrest nobody."

"Who is this granny? Did she witness the incident?"

"I don't know her name, Your Honor. Didn't think it mattered, 'cause she didn't see nothing."

"Hmm." Looking skeptical, the judge addressed the sheriff. "Sheriff Stevens, I will get your take on the situation in a moment."

"Yes, sir," said Stevens. Schuyler could see the sweat dampening the entire back of the lawman's shirt.

"All right, Mr. Moore. Let's wrap this thing up now. What happened after you left the sheriff?"

"I went to the justice of the peace, Mr. Ashby. He questioned Mr. Frye, but let him go. Said they wasn't enough evidence to charge him."

"I can see why," muttered Teague, looking perplexed. "So what were you doing back in Tuscaloosa last Monday?"

"I heard about the rally. Wanted to get them last two men and figured they might be in the crowd. They was. When I tries to round 'em up that night, these three men here try to take my gun away and set fire to the livery. The deputy will vouch for that."

The judge sighed. "Do you have anything else to add to your testimony?"

Moore folded his arms. "I want the five-thousand-dollar reward for turning in this blackhearted villain what lays in wait to attack and try to murder a poor innocent Negro. I was just tryin' to do my job!"

A chorus of shouts rose from the back of the room and the balcony. "Hang Frye, Judge! Throw him in jail for the rest of his life!"

Schuyler looked around and found several white men on their feet. Of course he didn't know any of them, but all had a similar look of well-fed violence.

Before the crowd could get thoroughly out of control, the judge brought down his gavel. "Order!" He pounded it twice more, louder this time. "Desist in this nonsense immediately," he roared, "or I'll have every one of you thrown out of the courthouse!" As the noise subsided, the judge speared

Harold Moore with an ironic glare. "You may sit down, Mr. Moore. I'll let you know about the five thousand dollars." As Moore obeyed, Teague addressed Lemuel Frye. "I suppose we'd better hear from you, Mr. Frye. Please stand and state your full name, occupation, and place of residence."

"I'm Lemuel Frye, Your Honor. I'm a schoolteacher. I've lived right here in Tuscaloosa for the past five years."

"Fine. What is your connection to Mr. Moore?"

"Last Monday was the first time I've laid eyes on him."

The judge looked stumped. "Then why has he accused you of attacking him?"

Frye's thin, bruised face closed. "I suspect it's because I don't ask where the men I teach come from. What I was going to say earlier is that Moore didn't come across the state line alone. He brought a posse of white men with him, riding under the aegis of the Ku Klux Klan. They are bent on sustaining the cotton empire they're in danger of losing to freed slaves—men who want to farm their own land, feed their own families. You can understand why freedmen resist enforced servitude under lopsided contracts to their old—"

The courtroom erupted in shouts and jeers, drowning the rest of Frye's sentence.

"Order!" *Bang, bang* went the gavel. "Bailiff! Sheriff!"

Sheriff Stevens rose, a hand on his gun. He slowly turned to face the crowd, his beefy face stern. The noise simmered to angry mutters.

The gavel slammed again. "The next person who utters one syllable out of order," the judge ground out, "will be escorted from the room. Am I understood?" The courtroom went silent as Stevens dropped back onto the pew. "Now.

Mr. Frye, you will please stick to the facts and resist the temptation to preach. We are not making law here, we are simply trying to determine whether or not Mr. Moore can provide enough evidence to bring you to trial. Can you prove your whereabouts on the evenings in question?"

"I was at home, reading a book."

"Did anyone see you there?"

Frye's expression tightened. "No."

Even Schuyler could see the man was hiding something. Judge Teague peered at the defendant as if trying to read his soul. "Are there any witnesses you'd like to provide?"

"None that you would believe," Frye said.

"You'd be best served not to ascribe motive to your adjudicator, Mr. Frye," said the judge dryly. "All right. You may be seated."

"Your Honor, I'd like to speak on behalf of Mr. Frye."

The judge's attention swung to the gentleman on the front row whose white summer suit, frilled shirt, and shallow-crowned straw hat proclaimed the Southern gentleman of means. "Mr. Samuel, I'd be happy to hear what you have to say."

"Who is that?" Schuyler whispered to the man seated next to him.

"The mayor," the man whispered back, looking at Schuyler as if he'd just dropped from the moon.

Schuyler leaned a little to one side so he could see around the hat of the lady in front of him. The sheriff's earlier account to Levi and himself had characterized Samuel as a moderate man, perhaps along the same political lines as his father.

Meanwhile, Samuel had stepped to the witness box and sat down. "Thank you, Your Honor. For those that don't know,

I'm Thad Samuel, mayor of this great city. I was the sheriff a few years back, so I'm used to assessing a man's character according to his actions, not necessarily the hot air he expels." When laughter ruffled through the crowd, Samuel smiled a little. "I been watching Mr. Frye since he come here after the war to help out the freedmen in the area. He's paid by the Bureau, but he can't be making much. I never seen such a skinny, hungry soul in my life. And he don't take a penny from none of his students. Occasionally one will bring him a chicken or a dozen eggs, but I've even seen him turn that down."

Schuyler glanced at Frye, who had hunched down into his shoulders.

The mayor went on. "And it is true that the Klan has been moving across the state line—in both directions, I might add—to intimidate freedmen into signing labor contracts and staying away from the polls. Of course they don't like teachers like Mr. Frye, because men who can read are less likely to be duped. Frankly they don't like me either. But I'm not a pushover. When they tried to oust me, I sent Mr. Frye and Mr. Beaumont, a respected board member on the M&O, to Montgomery to appeal to Governor Smith on my behalf. The governor denied my request for troops to repel our uninvited Mississippi guests"—a titter of laughter responded to this sally, along with a couple of muffled hoots from the balcony—"and sent my emissaries home with a flea in their ear." Samuel paused, surveying the courtroom.

The judge leaned forward, clearly intrigued. "Go on."

"I'll be honest with you, Judge Teague. When we planned that rally, I knew there might be some resistance. But I never thought anybody would resort to murder in broad daylight and torching a public servant's property by night."

An incipient surge of protest was quelled by the judge's beetled brow and a tap of the gavel. "I'll remind the court that disorder will not be tolerated. Mayor Samuel, do you have anything else to add?"

"No, sir, I believe I've done all the damage I can do."

"Fine, you're dismissed."

The mayor rose and sauntered back to his seat on the front row.

"All right. I'd better hear from law enforcement. Deputy Foster, will you come to the stand?" The judge circled a hand. "Tell the court who you are."

One hand on his weapon, the other grasping a mahogany cane, Foster swaggered to the witness box and stood there surveying the crowd. His gaze lingered on the balcony, and he acknowledged the spectators there with a nod of the head. "My name is Deputy Sheriff Newborn Foster. I was born and raised right here in Tuscaloosa County—shoot, everybody knows me."

"Thank you, Deputy. Please give us the facts of what happened on May 5."

Foster squinted at the judge.

"The day of the riot," Teague prompted patiently.

"Oh yeah. Like Mr. Moore said, Your Honor, the situation commenced way before that day. Started with these runaway Miss'ippi slaves, uh, freedmen, hiding out on the colored side of town. We'd of sent 'em back if we coulda caught 'em. Sheriff Stevens and Deputy Dent and me was glad to get a little help from across the state line, wasn't we, Sheriff?"

Deputy Dent nodded vehemently. Stevens shifted on the pew but didn't deny it.

Foster thumped the cane against the floor as if to emphasize his point. "We let 'em go after their property, just keeping an eye out to make sure things didn't get out of hand, you understand." When the judge merely stared at him, Foster shrugged and went on. "Maybe it did get out of hand, but we's just two men, and like the mayor said, the governor didn't want to interfere in local business." That seemed to Schuyler to be the opposite of what the mayor had meant, but the judge let it go. "But when Mr. Frye took to beating up this poor colored man, Mr. Moore, we couldn't let that go. Which is why we brung him in—"

"I did not beat up Mr. Moore!" shouted Frye, apparently goaded beyond restraint.

"Mr. Frye," growled the judge. "You've been warned."

"Yes, sir. I'm sorry, Your Honor."

"Evidently the justice of the peace saw no reason to keep Mr. Frye in custody," Judge Teague observed, "so let's skip to the night in question. Deputy Foster, can you explain to me why you alone witnessed this confrontation between Mr. Moore and the three defendants? Where was the sheriff?"

"He was dealing with the fire. I had run back behind the livery to see could I break some of the horses out, and I saw Mr. Moore had the same idea. Looked like he'd just pried one of the boards loose, when these three come skulking 'round the opposite corner of the building."

"These three, meaning Frye, Perkins, and Thomas?" the judge clarified. "Mr. Moore said earlier they attacked him, and *then* set fire to the livery. Which was it?"

Foster looked confused. "Well, I guess it could have been before. I disremember. Anyway, before I could reach him, they'd took his gun and commenced to whaling on him, looked like they was gonna kill him—"

"That is a bald-faced lie!" Lemuel Frye jumped to his feet, shaking off Reverend Thomas's restraining hand. "You are a despicable liar, curse you!"

Deputy Foster leapt over the witness box railing, cane upraised, to rush the livid schoolteacher, who was being held back by Reverend Thomas and Perkins.

The courtroom erupted in noise and wild motion. Judge Teague banged the gavel in utter futility, spectators gawked and squawked and dodged about like geese. Then gunfire exploded.

Schuyler dropped to the floor and rolled under a pew. Deafened by shots crashing about on all sides of the room, he expected each moment to be his last. He'd never gotten into the habit of carrying a gun, though he knew Levi went armed at all times. He prayed his friend had reached safety.

Since nothing could be more stupid than staying in one place, a sitting duck for the gunmen, he crawled under pews in the direction of the door, dodging feet and fallen bodies along the way. Blood dripped from the seats overhead. The smell of sulfur and smoke set him to coughing, and his eyes watered and stung unbearably.

He was almost in the clear, he thought, when he rolled over something hard, bruising his ribs. A pistol. He grabbed it, rubbed his eyes clear, saw that it was loaded. *Thank you, Lord.* Some poor soul had his gun shot out of his hand, but it was Schuyler's salvation. At least he could defend himself now.

Cautiously he peered out from under the pew, saw that he was near the door. Though his ears still rang, the gunfire in the courtroom had stopped, and he could hear the *pop-pop-pop* of shots in the street. He got to his feet, holding the gun cocked and ready, but his knees were so wobbly he had to lean against the nearest wall. As the smoke moved out the window and cleared, what he saw brought sick bile to his throat.

The judge sat pitched back in his chair, a gunshot hole through his forehead, gore marring the wall behind him. Several black spectators seemed to be dead as well, many others injured, moving slowly and moaning in pain. White men in the crowd still cowered under the pews or hunkered against walls. One or two of them might be injured as well.

"Riggins!" he shouted. "Where are you?"

No answer.

Holding the gun up in a shaking hand, Schuyler scoped out the balcony at the back of the courtroom, where smoke still drifted in evil clouds. There might be a couple of people still there, but the action seemed to have moved outside. He walked over to the judge and, out of respect, closed his eyes.

He would have to get help for the injured people in the courtroom, but where had Levi gone?

Suddenly violently ill, Schuyler rushed to the window and hung his head out.

Below him lay militiaman Sion Perkins, sprawled on the gravel road two stories below, his throat cut from ear to ear.

Joelle, seated beside Nathan in the loaded wagon, rode past rows and rows of sheets and dresses and work shirts hanging on ropes strung from gum tree to gum tree. Shake Rag. The name apparently came from the laundry business that kept the families of this dreary little community from starving.

She glanced at Nathan's set face. He had left the Ithaca

plantation and moved here after the Northern victory made him a free man. He'd used the skills learned as an enslaved blacksmith to slowly and painfully build a business of his own. He'd wooed and married Charmion Lawrence against her parents' wishes. Then, apparently seeing someone trustworthy in Levi Riggins, he'd agreed to come back to Ithaca to work as a freedman upon the creation of Daughtry House Hotel. In the process, as part of his employment contract, he'd negotiated the purchase price of a piece of property and built the snug little cabin for his bride and unborn baby— leaving Shake Rag behind.

But it was clear to Joelle that Shake Rag would forever remain part of Nathan's identity.

As he guided the wagon onto the church grounds and stopped in front of its burnt-out hull, his strong jaw clenched, a muscle twitching in his cheek as if he fought the urge to scream in rage.

She wasn't afraid of him. Never. He was one of the most gentle, controlled men she'd ever met. He'd insisted that Charmion not be allowed to come, for fear of harm to her or the baby. Still, Joelle couldn't predict what he would do. They'd driven all the way out here from the hotel in taut silence. Even Wyatt, sitting in the back with the supplies— food, water, and as many different things as she could think of to throw in for people who had lost so much—had stifled his usual random chatter.

There were no words for this level of evil. Who would burn down a church?

"Are you sure it wasn't an accident?" Joelle sat looking at the charred timbers, fallen in on themselves, the simple pews mostly in ashes.

"Look at that word on the pulpit." His deep voice, with

its fading African accent—*that* sounded like *dat*—came slow and harsh. "It's no accident."

She stared at the lectern, bizarrely the only intact piece of furniture in the center of the destruction. Someone had taken the time and trouble to remove it, carve out that ugly word, and put it back after the fire. Oh yes, she saw it, a word she winced at, a word she never used herself.

"Nathan, I'm sorry," she said for the hundredth time.

Nathan tied off the reins and came around to help her down from the high wagon seat. "Me too, Miss Jo."

Wyatt hopped out on his own. "Here come Shug and Tee-Toc. Where you want this stuff, Nathan?"

"Leave it for now. Mose and Horatia comin' with another load. We'll let her and Miss Selah manage distribution." Nathan stood staring at the black-and-gray mess of charred boards, broken windows. "Good thing it rained last night, or we'd have the whole community in ruins."

As it was, three shacks to each side of the church had caught fire and burned to the ground. It was bad enough. Joelle swallowed. It was just plain bad.

The ground was marshy, poor, here at the edge of the gum swamp, and Joelle stepped over puddles to get to the church entrance. A set of brick steps remained intact, and she walked up them, absurdly, because she could have simply stepped over the remains of the wooden walls. She stood there looking at piles of ash that had been wooden pews, lovingly made by local carpenters. In a corner she saw a scrap of fabric peeking from underneath a couple of soggy blackened boards and walked over to twitch it free.

She held the brown calico rag doll in both hands and examined the black shoe-button eyes and sooty gingham dress.

Its yarn hair had been neatly sewn onto its head and plaited into pigtails. Some little girl's church dolly, left behind by mistake, had miraculously survived.

What if its owner had been in the building?

Joelle felt something crack inside her.

God, oh God. Why? Who hates to this degree?

Her thoughts flashed to Mrs. Whitmore, needling her in church on Sunday, the day she'd espoused Reverend Boykin's candidacy for Congress. The implication was sickening. Impossible.

But she couldn't shake the notion that she bore some responsibility for what had happened here last night.

Schuyler made it out to the street somehow. He had to find Levi, the only sane person he knew in this crazy town. As he slid along with his back close to the courthouse wall, gun drawn but not raised, sounds came and went as if he were sticking his head in and out of a barrel. He came upon the crowd gathered around Perkins's dead body—something he had no desire to see again.

But he had to know what had developed during and after the gunfight in the courtroom upstairs.

Edging closer, he elbowed a tall man in a coonskin hat. "Hey, what's everybody looking at?"

The man's eyes cut to Schuyler. "A colored prisoner fell out the window, then a gang of white men run out of the courthouse and found him alive. One of them slit his throat. That's what I heard, anyway." His gaze went back to the body on the street. "Sheriff come out, saw what happened, then went tearing after them."

"Anybody else? Tall young fellow in a military-style hat and coat?"

"Man, it's been a regular parade out here. You up there when the guns started popping?"

"Yes." Schuyler started moving away. "Has somebody gone after the coroner?"

"Don't know." Coonskin Hat shrugged. "Guess I could do that."

"Good man. I'm going to see if I can help the sheriff."

He moved toward the sounds of yelling down the street, possibly inside a shop close to the tavern. He had no idea how much time had passed since the first gunshot in the courtroom, but he guessed five or ten minutes, maybe less. Events had unfolded quickly. As he passed an alley between two buildings halfway down the block, he felt something hit his back.

He whirled, lifting the gun.

"Beaumont." It was a whisper, but he recognized Levi's voice. "Over here."

Retracing his steps, he stepped into the alley he'd just passed. Levi crouched there, the bulk of his shoulders and coat shielding a smaller man behind him.

"What are you doing?" Schuyler whispered.

"Quiet. Come this way." Levi turned, shoved his companion farther into the alley.

Schuyler followed. They came out at the back of the building into another alley, where a warehouse took up half the block behind the courthouse. Levi seemed hale and hearty, though out of breath. The second man, none other than schoolteacher Lemuel Frye, had added a bloody lower arm to his other injuries.

"Have you lost your mind?" Schuyler stared at Levi.

"We've got to get him out of here before they kill him," Levi said grimly. "Have you got a clean handkerchief?"

"Yes, but—"

"Give it here."

"You have a sudden desire to blow your nose when people are shooting at you?"

"For his arm, Beaumont."

"Oh. Right." Schuyler handed over the required article, which Levi proceeded to bind around Frye's arm. "Where's the sheriff?"

"Down the street, I suppose. He and the two deputies went after the gunmen—who think they're after Mr. Frye and Reverend Thomas."

"Thank you," Frye muttered as Levi dropped his arm.

"'Think'?" Schuyler asked. "Where is the Reverend?"

"On his way to Montgomery."

"And you know this how?"

"One of my agents has him. We didn't make it out fast enough."

Shoving his co-opted gun into the back of his pants, Schuyler eyed Levi. "Neither did Perkins."

"I know." Levi grimaced. "I saw a couple of ruffians push him out the window. We went down a back stair the judge had shown me earlier and came out the alley."

"Wait. You know—knew the judge?"

"That's why I'm here. Look, Beaumont, we've got to get this man out of here."

"Of course. But, Riggins, they didn't just kill a federal judge and push Perkins out the window. They *slit his throat* to make sure he was dead." He stared at the small, unassuming man who had apparently precipitated the day's excitement. "Who *are* you?"

Frye looked away. "I'm nobody."

Schuyler whistled through his teeth and looked at Levi. "All right. I assume we're going back to Mississippi on horseback. I wouldn't want to be waiting around in a train station when Frye's friends come looking for us."

"Not 'we,'" Levi said. "You're going on without us by train. I'll bring him—"

"And my wife," put in Frye. "I'm not leaving her."

Levi nodded. "We'll come the slow way and tuck you both someplace safe across the state line."

"I'm going by train?" Schuyler fought the sensation of making his way in the dark. "Why?"

"Because I need to unearth this cabal of supremacists as fast as humanly possible. They're dangerous, and the president wants them destroyed."

"The president? Of the United States?" Now the breath was knocked out of him. What on earth had he gotten himself into?

Fourteen

ON FRIDAY AFTERNOON Joelle sat on a stump in the middle of Shake Rag, surrounded by laundry and children. She couldn't think when she'd been much happier. "And that's why the king never ever again, in all his born days, ate dandelion soup!" Flicking imaginary fluff over her shoulders, she smiled at her rapt audience. "The end."

Olivia Pogue, mama to the church dolly found hiding in the corner after the fire, leaned forward, big brown eyes wide. Her full lips parted to display a generous gap where her teeth had recently resided. "Mith Joelle, you made that up."

"I surely did," Joelle admitted. "Did Polly like it?"

Olivia held the doll to her ear and reported, "She wanth to hear it again."

"Olivia, that's the third time Miss Joelle has told that story. She's got better things to do." India Pogue, boiling a mess of collard greens in a large iron pot over a fire nearby, gave her daughter a censuring look.

Uncowed, Olivia grinned at Joelle. "Pleath?"

Joelle was saved from having to deny that adorable lisp by

the arrival of a wagon coming from the direction of town. "I'll tell it again later, honey-pie. Let's see what Wyatt brought, okay?" She held out her hand, the little girl took it, and they skipped toward the road.

Wyatt pulled up the mule and wagon with a big grin on his freckled face. "Want a ride on my chariot, ladies?"

Joelle curtseyed, then boosted Olivia onto the back of the wagon and hopped on herself. They rode the remaining few yards to the church on top of a pile of sawn lumber brought over from the mill at Daughtry House. The Shake Rag men had been working from dawn to dusk in an effort to rebuild the church before Sunday. They just might make it.

The first two days after the fire had been spent clearing away the mess, sorting what could be salvaged from the ruins, and drawing a design for the resurrection. The Daughtry sisters pitched in to provide supplies, purchasing with their own funds what could not be built locally. Shug and Nathan shared the responsibility for bossing the project. More than once, Selah wished for Levi's engineering skills, but Joelle thought they were managing just fine. The roof was on, the building framed, and this load of lumber would go a long way to finishing the walls.

When Wyatt stopped the wagon again, Joelle and Olivia jumped off and moved out of the way so that the men could unload the lumber. Old Reverend Boykin sat on a salvaged pew under a tree, fanning himself with his hat. Leaving Olivia to make mud cakes near a convenient puddle, Joelle walked over to the pastor and sat down beside him.

He had risen respectfully as she approached, but she waved him back to his seat. "Sit still, Reverend," she said. "You've been at it since sunup. India's close to having dinner ready. I imagine we'll eat after they empty the wagon."

He laid the hat on one knee and smiled at her. "You girls been working just as hard as the men, keeping everybody fed."

"We want to help." She picked at her skirt, frayed from the hours she'd spent sanding that ugly word off the pulpit. "Reverend, I've never been much good with practical things, but I want to learn. Your wife has been good to let me sit with her and listen while the women cook and quilt. You know I'm going to marry our preacher?"

"I heard that," he said cautiously.

"Yes, well, I need to tell you something. I think it's my fault this happened."

"It's your fault you got engaged?"

"Well, that too." She laughed, then sobered. "No, I meant this." She gestured toward the skeleton of the church.

The minister gave her a long, silent look. "I think you're gon' have to tell me what you mean."

She took a deep breath. "Last Sunday—the day of the fire—I tried to get my—my fiancé to speak to our congregation on your behalf. For the congressional campaign. He said he'd think about it, but he didn't do it." She looked at the old man, noting the grizzled wiry hair, the smile wrinkles around his deep brown eyes. There was wisdom in that face, and grace. She felt ashamed but somehow took courage in confession. "It made me so angry, Reverend. I didn't want to be led by him. I wanted him to do the right thing, and when he wouldn't, I took it in my own hands. I started talking to the ladies about how they should influence their husbands to vote for a good man like you."

After a short silence, Reverend Boykin said, "And you think instead they went home and told their husbands to burn down my church?"

"I don't know." She twisted her skirt in her hands. "I hope not, but I'm afraid—"

"Sugar, there's two things tangled up in what you just told me, so let's separate them out. First of all, you right that anger will sometimes lead us to improvidence." He grinned. "That's a word I learned from one of those books you loaned me last week. But seems to me the kind of anger you felt in that situation might be closer to what Jesus would call 'righteous anger.' The kind where the Savior took a whip to the money changers in the Temple. Now you can probably ask my wife about a wiser way to manage your man than embarrassing him in front of his congregation, but we all got to learn things the hard way sometimes."

She laughed at the twinkle in his eyes. "Yes, sir. That's true."

"Now the other thing you're worried about is, I'm both glad and sorry to say, completely out of your control. It's rooted in a man's fear of what he don't know. And, frankly, selfishness and pride." He turned his head to look at the burn pile made of the remnants of pews and holy walls. "The men who did that will reap what they sow, 'cause the good Lord is a God of justice. Psalm 94 says, 'He shall bring upon them their own iniquity, and shall cut them off in their own wickedness; yea, the Lord our God shall cut them off.'" When his gaze returned to Joelle, it was full of sorrow. "May not be soon, may not be in fire. But hatred creates its own hell, you know, child?"

Joelle thought about her father's mind and heart, ravaged by rage. Yes, by pride and selfishness too. It had been horrible to witness his fall at the end. "Yes, sir," she said, drinking in this man's love and mercy. "I just don't know what to do, going forward from here. I don't know that I can respect or trust Gil Reese anymore. And I don't trust the women in my church. Even if it wasn't my fault, I hate that somebody did this. I don't want to worship with them anymore."

He was quiet for a moment, his lips moving as if in prayer. Finally he said, "Stay as long as you can, without damaging your spirit, child. They need truth-speakers, but you got to speak in love, not disgust or contempt. Somebody got to be a go-between. As to your preacher-man . . . you take that to the Lord. He'll let you know when or if it's time to part ways. But I'll tell you one thing. There ain't no perfect man out there. Least of all this one." He tapped his own chest.

Joelle sighed. She wanted a man she could talk to like this. Or none at all. "Are you going to pull out of the election?"

"The Lord hasn't told me to do that yet."

"How will you know? How will I know when it's time to break with Gil?"

"God has a way of using Scripture and events and his prophets to guide us. You be sure you stay in his Word and on your knees every day."

"I can do that. I have been."

He nodded. "Then stop worrying. Walk in one step of light at a time."

Joelle tucked that bit of advice deep into her heart where she wouldn't forget it. She had a feeling she was going to need it.

"Miss Joelle, I forgot to give you this!"

She looked up to find Wyatt approaching, waving an envelope overhead. A letter? Maybe it was from Schuyler. She hadn't heard from him since she and Selah left Mobile last Saturday morning. He hadn't even gone to the station with them. He'd just waved goodbye, seated at the breakfast table, with his eyes on the newspaper in his hand.

On the other hand, she couldn't think of any reason for Schuyler to write. More likely it was Levi, communicating with Selah. He'd wired yesterday to say he'd be in Tupelo by this evening.

Wyatt flicked the envelope into her lap and went right back to hauling supplies. She picked it up and saw that it was indeed a telegram. Addressed to her. She glanced at Reverend Boykin, who politely looked away from the envelope. "Telegrams usually bring bad news," she said with a nervous laugh. "Do I have to open it?"

He gave her a wry smile. "News don't go away if you don't hear it."

Well, that was true. She slipped her thumb under the flap and pulled out the paper inside.

ARRIVING SATURDAY AFTERNOON ON 2 PM TRAIN. WILL STAY ONE WEEK. LOOKING FWD TO SEEING YOU AGAIN.

It was signed "Delfina Fabio."

Schuyler dismounted his hired horse in front of Daughtry House and tied it to the hitching post. He wanted a meal, a bath, and a long sleep, in that order, and he was not going to camp in that fleabag Gum Tree Hotel in Tupelo. For crying out loud, he was half owner of a resort inn, and why shouldn't he take advantage of it?

Putting two fingers to his lips, he produced a long, shrill

whistle for service. He could have taken the horse around to the stable himself, but Tee-Toc lived and breathed horse-flesh. The boy would appreciate the chance to cool down and water this nag.

When Tee-Toc hadn't come running around the corner by the time Schuyler had unstrapped his travel bag from the saddle, he walked around the side of the house to go looking for him. Where was everybody?

The backyard seemed equally deserted. The porch, the pagoda, the icehouse, the kitchen, the office—everything was shut tight. Then he saw a thin stream of smoke in the distance, coming from Nathan and Charmion's little house. Char's baby was due soon, he was pretty sure, so she would be staying close to home. The Daughtry girls could be any-where on a Friday afternoon. But Horatia and Mose were generally at work in the kitchen and the garden respectively.

The place looked like someone had come and dismissed the entire staff.

Grumbling, he retraced his steps, tied his bag back onto the saddle, and gathered the reins. *Nice welcome home*, he thought as he swung into the saddle. *Where is Joelle?*

The short ride to the Vincents' house took less than five minutes, though it seemed longer. Ground-tying the horse, he halloed for Charmion. "Anybody home?"

The door opened as he reached the porch. "Mr. Beau-mont!" Charmion gaped at him. "What you doing here?"

"Looking for the Daughtry girls." His gaze of its own volition went to her bulging belly. "Are you all right? Maybe you shouldn't be up walking around."

"I'm perfectly fine," she said wearily, stepping back. "The family ain't here. Come in, I'll fix you something to drink."

She moved a pile of slithery brown fabric off a chair and gestured with her head for him to sit down. "Sorry for the mess. I'm working."

He hovered near the door. "I see that, and I'm sorry for intruding. Don't bother with a drink, I'm not staying." He looked around the small sitting room. It was the neatest "mess" he'd ever seen. There was a big, heavy freestanding mirror and a wrought-iron table by the fireplace. Gauzy curtains fluttered in the open windows, and a couple of charming pictures decorated the wall behind a simple brown horsehair sofa. "Did you do those?" He'd heard Joelle comment on Charmion's artistic talent.

"Yes, sir. They not my best work, but I like 'em." She stood there with the fabric across her arms. Come to think of it, it looked like a dress.

"I think they're very pretty. What are you making?" He should leave, but he'd traveled all the way from Memphis by himself, and he was lonely.

A grin curled her lips. "A dress. For Miss Joelle. Look." She unfurled the dress, held it in front of her.

He imagined Joelle's tall, womanly figure filling out the deep bodice and curved hips. Then he imagined undoing the self-covered buttons that walked up the front, then sliding it off her shoulders. Then he realized where his thoughts had gone, and reined them in with a jerk. "It's very nice," he mumbled. "Do you know where she is? Joelle, I mean?"

There was something uncomfortably knowing in Charmion's dark eyes, but she said mildly, "They all out to Shake Rag, where they been all week. Guess you don't know about the fire."

"Fire? What fire?"

187

Charmion folded the dress, then laid it carefully down in the chair. "Sunday night somebody burned down the Shake Rag church. Everybody here's out there rebuilding it so we can have services on Sunday."

"Somebody? Somebody who? Are you sure it wasn't an accident?"

"Oh, it wasn't any accident. They made sure we knew that. As to who . . ." She shrugged. "Plenty white people around here don't like us in possession of anything good or nice."

That was all too true. And there was no sense asking why. Considering the events he'd left behind in Tuscaloosa, motive could be in little doubt. But he resented her use of the word "us," as if there were some impenetrable divide right here in this room. He considered her lovely, coffee-with-cream-colored face, its oddly pitying expression. "I hope you won't put me in that camp, Charmion. No matter what happens in the next month or so." Giving her a grave bow, he stepped back onto the porch and replaced his hat.

He hoped it wouldn't take any longer than a month to root out his father's killer and bring him to justice.

There was something different about him.

Caught in the act of biting off a thread she had just knotted in Charmion's baby quilt, Joelle jabbed the needle attached to it into her thumb. "Ow!" Sticking the injured digit in her mouth, she jumped to her feet, jarring the frame, and stared at Schuyler, who stood in the doorway of India and Shug's two-room house.

"Don't bleed on the quilt!" Aurora fixed Schuyler with

a look equally annoyed as the one she'd given Joelle. "And you. You're blocking the light."

Removing his hat, Schuyler sauntered in and looked around. In fact, he looked at everything in the room except Joelle. She could have been a tall, red-haired gnat for all the attention he paid her. "Would have been nice if you folks had left a note on the door, to let people know where you are."

"Clearly you figured it out," Joelle said around her thumb. "Because here you are, like a—a mosquito one can't escape."

He looked at her then, and his lips tightened.

Hit! She'd gotten a reaction.

He shook his head. "Mosquito? Miss Wordsmith, I would have thought you could come up with something a little more creative than that."

"I'm just surprised to see you. We assumed you'd gone off on one of your drinking binges with Hifcoat and Jexon."

His cheeks tinged red. "Hixon and Jefcoat. And I haven't seen either of them since the opera."

"I stand corrected."

"Would the two of you please sit down?" demanded Aurora. "The rest of us are getting a crick in our necks. Here, stop the bleeding."

Accepting Aurora's proffered handkerchief, Joelle reluctantly resumed her seat. "Thank you." She busied herself with binding her thumb, then jumped when Schuyler plucked the handkerchief away from her.

"Here, let me," he growled, kneeling beside her. "You can't do that with one hand."

"I know that, I was just . . ." She couldn't finish the sentence because her hand was engulfed in both of his, and they were gentle and deft, and all her blood had rushed to places in her body she hadn't known were there. It wasn't fair that he should arrive here with no warning, after she'd made up her mind that she never wanted to see him again. Despite the fact that she dreamed about him nearly every night. In full color.

He dropped her hand and rose, brushing at the knees of his breeches. "I smell food." He sniffed. "Collards."

Selah jumped to her feet. "I'll fix you some. We already ate. Did you stop by the church to see the work? It's going to be so beautiful."

"Yes, I went and poked my head in. I'll go help after I eat. Haven't had anything all day." He followed Selah to the table in the corner and watched her ladle greens into a bowl. "I don't suppose there's any ham and cornbread to go with that?"

"Where have you been?" Joelle blurted, then wanted to bite out her tongue. She hadn't meant to let him know how much he'd been missed.

He glanced over his shoulder, eyebrows raised, collards dripping off his fork. "I went to visit your grandmother."

"What on earth for?"

"She promised me snickerdoodles."

Aurora snorted a laugh. "Grandmama loves you a lot if she shared her snickerdoodles."

Schuyler looked smug. "Women like me."

"Some do," Joelle muttered. "Apparently he bamboozled an opera star."

"What does that mean?" he asked.

"Look at this." She reached into her pocket and tossed the telegram at him.

He set down his bowl—with great reluctance—and picked

up the envelope, which had fallen to the floor. He read the telegram and whistled. *"Tomorrow?"*

"It seems her performances for the next week had to be canceled because of an attack of laryngitis. She needs a place to rest and recuperate."

Schuyler turned the brief message over and back again. "How do you know that?"

"There was an article in the paper this morning. I didn't think anything about it until Wyatt brought this telegram from town a little while ago." Joelle folded her arms. "This is your fault. Now what are we going to do? We aren't ready for guests."

"*My* fault—"

"She could have laryngitis just as easily at the Peabody, but noooo . . . She has to travel all the way to Tupelo, chasing the 'beautiful *pazzo* boy who make you so angry.'" Joelle mimicked Delfina's sultry Italian accent.

"Holy cats, did she really say that?" Aurora burst into laughter. "I've got to meet this woman."

Blushing, Schuyler dropped the telegram as if it contained some communicable disease and took refuge in his collards.

Joelle was in no mood to rescue him. "She's the one who kept me from crying in a closet after this bully insulted me in front of the entire opera board."

"Because you tried to shark my best friend out of forty-five dollars," Schuyler reminded her.

Joelle came off her chair again. "Why, you—"

"Children, children," Selah said mildly. "Instead of casting blame all over the county, perhaps we'd better decide how we're going to make the most of such a celebrated guest."

"Guests," mumbled Schuyler through a mouthful of cornbread.

All four women stared at him.

"What. Do. You. Mean?" asked Selah.

Schuyler swallowed and wiped crumbs off his vest. "General Forrest and his wife are coming too. Tomorrow," he added, as if that would somehow make it better. "They were at your grandparents' musicale Wednesday evening. Mrs. Forrest mentioned the hotel, so I, uh, invited them to come."

"Without checking with us?" Even Aurora, who generally gave Schuyler the benefit of the doubt, looked annoyed.

"It seemed like a good idea. We pulled off a ball last month. Surely we can put up a couple of guests for a few days." His expression was defensive. "We *are* a hotel, are we not?"

"Which is not set to open for at least another month." Selah's brown eyes narrowed. "Schuyler, we've had funerals and burned-down churches and all sorts of delays."

"And if I'm counting correctly," Joelle added, "this will be more than a 'couple' of people involved. Delfina and her manager. General Forrest and Mrs. Forrest, and probably their servants. We'll need to entertain them. We'll need to feed them."

"It's too late now," Schuyler said. "They're on their way."

Before Joelle could throttle him, Aurora clapped her hands. "I have an idea."

Joelle could hear the capital *I* on that last word. "It had better be a good one."

"We'll have a barn dance." When her Idea was met with blank silence, Aurora raised her chin. "In a barn."

"You're going to subject a world-renowned classical musician to a country hoedown?" Selah's voice was soft but incredulous. "I don't think so."

"I agree," Joelle said. "That's ridiculous. But it gives me

a better idea. India—" She addressed their hostess, who had continued quietly stitching, listening and smiling as the conversation bounced about in increasing absurdity.

India put down her needle with a smile. "Yes, Miss Jo?"

"I have heard some incredible music in this community while we've been working on the church. Would y'all consider coming to sing and play for our guests one evening while they're here?"

Fifteen

On Saturday morning Schuyler sat at a table in the Gum Tree Hotel dining room, struggling to sip coffee as he watched Doc wolf down a giant plate of hotcakes and ham.

He'd tried to keep his hands off Joelle, but then she had to poke her finger with a needle and look offended, as if it were his fault. So what was a man to do but prove his courage by throwing himself straight into the fire of those blue eyes?

Only it turned out he was a coward after all. He *did* care. He'd muttered an excuse and left Shake Rag to repair to the closest saloon. Without Hixon and Jefcoat to distract him, forgetting the disappointment that twisted Joelle's lips when he'd laughed at her suggestion only came at the bottom of his third tankard.

And it wasn't worth the hangover. Never again.

"Have you seen this?" Doc threw the newspaper at him and shoveled in another bite of ham. "This T. M. Hanson, whoever he is, is courting trouble."

Schuyler straightened the *Tupelo Journal* and searched for the appropriate byline. Above it, the title ran "Push for Negro

Education Law Intensifies in Every State." He skimmed the article, found it tightly written, factually supported by quotes from high-profile sources, and sympathetic to the liberal viewpoint without inflammatory language. After reading it again, more carefully, he looked up at Doc. "I've read this writer's work before, I think. You've lived here most of your life. Do you know Hanson?"

Doc shook his head. "Not that I know of," he said, pouring cane syrup on his pancakes. "I think he lives in another county."

"What do you think about it?"

"Educating Negroes?" Doc shrugged. "We're moving into a new decade, essentially a new era. I see no sense in fighting the inevitable. Besides, Hanson is right. We're all better off with a more educated electorate."

Schuyler's head hurt, and he didn't feel like talking about Negroes and education, but Doc had brought this up. Perfect opportunity to establish himself as the sort of jackweed who couldn't think past his own nose. "There are folks who'd like to stifle the new electorate's influence."

Doc put down his fork. "Yes. Shortsighted fools. Do you know anyone like that?"

"Maybe you can afford to offend whoever you want, Doc, but I've got money to raise. Expectations to meet."

"What are you talking about? You haven't embroiled the Daughtry ladies in anything illegal, have you?"

"What? No! I'm just saying a man has to be careful which crazy liberal causes he takes up."

"You've been drinking this morning already?"

"Why do you say that?" Schuyler gulped his coffee, burned his mouth, and spit it back into the cup. "Ow!"

"There's something off about you, Beaumont. More than usual." Doc's pale blue eyes penetrated past Schuyler's skull, seemingly into his very brain.

Couldn't a fellow have a private thought without some Puritan trying to yank him back onto the mental straight and narrow?

"I have not been drinking anything but this coal oil that passes for coffee in here. I'm merely shoring up my nerve before I go to the station to collect Joelle's opera star and deliver her to the hotel. You asked me what I thought of that article, and I answered you as diplomatically as possible."

Doc's dry smile appeared. "I'm not known for diplomacy. You're serious about this run for Congress?"

"I am. I've been launching my career beyond the family boundaries, with moderate success. I'm hopeful the hotel will eventually prove profitable. In the meantime, I want to try my hand at the political arena. Connections, you know." Schuyler paused. He must be careful. It would be tricky to get information out of Doc without raising his suspicions. *You are an insouciant noodlehead, Beaumont. You've done this before.* "In fact, you are one of the best connections I have hereabouts, Doc, and I know you've lived here most of your life. You've built a successful practice seemingly from nothing. Perhaps you could give me some advice on how to proceed. You know, who to court for favor."

Doc didn't answer for a moment, simply stared at Schuyler while thoughtfully chewing ham. Finally he laid down his fork and knife, put his elbows on the table, and steepled his long, clever fingers under his chin. "I could tell you, but you won't like it."

"I'm no baby to cry at hard words."

"No, but you're used to indulging yourself, and you seem to be happy letting events happen to you. It's not a matter of 'courting favor,' but of courting action."

Stung, Schuyler sat back. "Go on."

"Yes, all right. Second, you find what you're good at and run for it full-out. This scatter-shot business of playing at four or five things won't do. I took on young Wyatt, for example, because his thirst for scientific knowledge so impressed me."

He had just been negatively compared to a fifteen-year-old stripling. Well, all right then. He nodded.

"Third, you keep going when no one is watching. Discipline yourself when things are boring and tedious. Medical breakthroughs only come along in the wake of failure after failure. I should imagine it's the same with the rail business—or whatever you decide to take up."

Was he too easily discouraged? He didn't want to think so. "Thank you, Doc. I appreciate your—"

"I'm not done. You're going to be successful, Beaumont. I believe you can do those things, even though the evidence has certainly been spare." When Schuyler laughed, Doc held up a hand. "So I want to go ahead and say this, let you tuck it away in preparation. You can bring enormous ruin on your own head if you don't mark this well. Do you hear me?"

"I hear you." Fully electrified, Schuyler leaned in. His brother had said some of these same things, though he'd admittedly barely listened. Somehow it was different coming from this physician, whom he admired and genuinely desired to emulate.

"Good. So when you *are* successful, got your wagon rolling downhill, so to speak, you *must* stay in control. Temptation to abandon principle will hunt you down." Doc glanced at the bar, where a row of soused men of various ages lined the counter, even at this early hour. "Drunkenness and loose women will pull you under, tie you up, and refuse to let go."

Schuyler had never been overly fond of strong drink, preferring to keep his wits about him. And he possessed a well-hidden selfish streak that kept him away from the sort of fleshly entertainment his cohorts found so alluring. Why would he desire a woman who had given herself indiscriminately to other men? But proclaiming himself a Methodist would do him no favors at this juncture.

He grinned. "Oh happy demise! Have done with your preaching, Doc. I don't see why a fellow can't let his wagon roll down an occasional side trail in the pursuit of excellence. Life's too short to refuse a little sip of eau-de-vie!"

Doc's expression was a peculiar mixture of contempt and disappointment. "It's your funeral. But if you think Joelle is going to abandon her preacher for that sort of slipshod nonsense, you don't know her very well." He went back to his paper.

Joelle? Who'd said anything about Joelle? Was he an open, curtainless window that everyone so easily read his feelings? He'd best dispatch that assumption *instanter*. He made a rude noise. "The preacher is in for a rude awakening with our beautiful bluestocking, and I wish him well." He looked at his watch and got to his feet. "I find well-seasoned Italian opera stars more to my taste. It's time to meet the Fabio's train. You coming?"

"My office opens at nine. I've patients to attend." Without looking up, Doc gave Schuyler a dismissive wave. "I'll be out later to check on Charmion's baby."

"Is there something wrong? She looked well yesterday."

Doc glanced up, a surprising flush rising to his cheeks. "It's her first, and I want to keep an eye on her."

"Huh. All right, then. I'll see you later." When there was no further comment from Kidd, Schuyler shrugged and left the dining room.

A short stroll down the street took him to the station, where he'd left the carriage tied to a hitching post in a tree-lined lot reserved for that purpose. After checking on the two sorrels, he entered the station, thrumming with a crowd of citizens gathered to meet the midmorning train from Memphis via Holly Springs—one of the last two scheduled to arrive for the weekend.

Cooling his heels in a sunny spot on the boardwalk near the tracks, he allowed his thoughts to rove to that serendipitous trip to Oxford in late February, when he'd fallen into company with Levi Riggins. Inescapable, the idea that some higher power had arranged that meeting. Levi—claiming to be a hotel agent as cover for his true assignment of investigating a spate of railroad robberies and murders for the Pinkerton agency—had reconnected Schuyler with the Daughtry sisters. In order to complete his vision of establishing a new rail link between Oxford and Tupelo, supported by a luxury hotel, Schuyler had been attempting for some time to purchase Ithaca plantation from the impoverished young women. For some reason, though he'd known the family for decades, his offer of cash for their moldering ancestral home had been met with every shade of resentful resistance.

Levi had somehow managed to smooth the negotiation and turn Selah's smoldering refusal toward compromise. Once he heard the tale of Levi and Selah's dramatic and frankly romantic meeting in a train wreck rescue, Schuyler better understood her shift in stance. Practical and outspoken Selah would never be Schuyler's cup of tea, but Levi had been besotted from the outset. And, it seemed, vice versa. They were a cloying pair of lovebirds, for sure.

Joelle's capitulation to his scheme was a bit more puzzling. From something Selah had mentioned, Joelle's opinion had tipped her agreement to the joint venture Levi proposed. Every time Schuyler tried to bring up the subject with Joelle, though, she'd give him one of those dreamy stares involving not a whit of mental engagement and start rattling about some antiquarian topic in which he had no interest whatsoever—until she said something contrarian and ridiculous, forcing him to disagree. And then they'd be off on a perverse and mentally stimulating discussion which he could barely keep up with, but which inevitably took at least an hour of his valuable time.

He shook his head. Joelle and her ten-dollar words and convoluted sentences.

Aurora, living in Memphis with her grandparents at the time and apparently not a voting party in the deal he'd struck with Selah, had at first seemed a nonentity. But Grandmama. Oh yes, Mrs. Winnie McGowan, matriarch of the family, had determined to interject herself in the project, presumably with the idea of stopping it.

Miss Winnie and Aurora had made the trip by train from Memphis, and Schuyler, coming from Oxford, just happened to arrive at the Tupelo station at the same time. Aware of the old lady's soft spot for him, he'd offered the use of his hired carriage, and by the time they'd arrived at Ithaca, he'd used every ounce of charm he possessed to outflank her opposition to Daughtry House Hotel. Aurora, whom he'd last met as a dimpled, chubby preteen, had turned into quite a lovely and fashionable Titian-haired belle. Too young and giggly for Schuyler's personal taste, but a useful advocate in skirmishes with the older, more prickly and suspicious sisters.

This balancing act of playing the foolish young entrepreneur and hopeful politician had become quite the challenge. He risked not only his business reputation but the regard of people like Doc, whose opinion mattered. Despite Levi and Jamie's warnings, he had no real fear for his life. The fact that he'd managed to escape all manner of hair-raising adventures during the war implied that God was on his side.

Wasn't that the way it worked? He called himself a Christian, gave the occasional offering at church, made an appearance at services when it was convenient. Of course no one lived forever, but he saw no reason to expect his life to be cut short anytime soon.

Before he could mentally delve further into the conundrum that was his father's sudden and violent demise, he heard the rumble of wheels on tracks. The approaching train released an earsplitting whistle and chugged into view.

Charm on, Beaumont, he told himself, straightening away from the post he'd been slouched against. *One thing at a time. Do what you do best.* He took off his hat, smoothed his rumpled hair, and put it back on. The opera star's presence could be a valuable advertisement for the hotel.

Joelle stood in an open window of the cupola, looking out toward the front yard and down the drive path to the gate. Any moment now, Schuyler would be arriving with their first wave of guests.

There was so much to do, getting ready for company. She and Selah and Aurora had risen at dawn to help the maids finish putting fresh linens on all the beds, dust the furniture, sweep the floors, and clean windows. Horatia and Mose had arrived shortly thereafter to work in the kitchen and garden. Food would be a critical part of the success of this party.

Now it was nearly noon, and Selah said they were as ready as it was possible to be at this short notice.

Maybe so, but Joelle would never feel prepared for the strain of entertaining. What if Delfina, who had traveled all over the world and was used to the best, didn't like her accommodations? What if she was bored? What if she went away telling everyone she met that Daughtry House was just a provincial monstrosity of a place in the middle of nowhere? Why on earth had Joelle thought it would be a good idea to present Negro former slaves as entertainment for a visiting opera singer?

She leaned out the window, relishing the breeze and the dizzying drop to the ground three stories below. Usually she could come up here and find a little solitude. Selah had always been afraid of heights and truly hated the place since their father's death. Aurora had somehow got it into her head that the honeybees they'd once found here might come back.

Joelle preferred to think of it as her personal tower, her place of refuge. As a little girl, she'd pretended to be Rapunzel tossing her golden locks down to the prince below. Now, of course, she was long past such nonsense. A man was a man—one no better than another—and princes only existed inside books. No one was going to rescue her.

A faint cloud of dust kicked up in her peripheral vision, from the direction of town, and she sighed. Her moment of reflection had come to an end. She had started to turn for the stairs leading through the attic and down to the second floor, when she saw that the arrival was a lone horseman. That couldn't be Schuyler with the carriage. Intrigued, she stayed at the window, watching the rider approach. As he got to the gate, she recognized the military posture, the erect carriage of his head.

"Levi!" She ran for the stairs.

By the time she made it to the ground floor, Levi had dismounted and Selah had launched herself at her husband, making Joelle witness to an extravagant and unbridled display of affection between her sister and brother-in-law. She stood there on the porch, unashamedly gawking. Rather than making her uncomfortable, the embrace left her aching with emptiness. She couldn't imagine feeling that glad to see Gil Reese.

"All right, all right," she said, descending the porch steps. "It's only been a week!"

Levi reluctantly let Selah drop to the ground, his grin creasing one lean cheek. "A very long week." He kissed Selah's forehead and released her. "Is Wyatt somewhere around here to water this nag?"

"I'll take him." Aurora had come out of the house behind Joelle and pushed past to run her hand over the black gelding's glossy neck. "Is he yours?" she asked Levi. "Good-looking horse for a hired mount."

"Yes, I bought him in Meridian. His name is Amadeus."

Aurora rolled her eyes. "Only you would name your horse after a crazy Austrian piano-plinker." Taking the reins, she led the horse away toward the rear of the house, cooing to her charge as they went out of earshot.

Levi picked up the hat Selah had knocked to the ground in her enthusiasm, batting it against his leg to remove the dust. "Hello, little sister," he said to Joelle. "I was hoping you'd be around."

Levi was one of the few people of Joelle's acquaintance to call her "little" anything. Laughing, she gave him a quick hug, then followed the newlyweds into the house. "You two would probably like some time to yourselves," she said fondly. "Why don't you go into the parlor while I fix us something to drink?"

"I'm much more in need of a bath, I'm afraid," Levi said, giving Selah an apologetic look, "but coffee would be welcome."

Joelle took her time brewing coffee and collecting a tray for the dishes. Deliberately rattling cups against saucers to announce her presence, she entered the parlor. She found her sister seated primly beside her husband, smoothing her skirts.

"There you are!" Selah said, blushing.

"Indeed. Here I am." Joelle set the tray on a table. "I trust I allowed enough time for everyone to get properly reacquainted."

Levi's and Selah's eyes met with a look that made Joelle feel both left out and full of joy for her sister's happiness. Levi picked up Selah's hand with casual intimacy. "We'll get to that later. Sit down, Jo. I need to talk to you."

Uh-oh. A request to *talk* to her generally indicated something unpleasant on the horizon. "What about?"

Selah laughed. "Don't worry, you haven't forgotten anything or burned anything." She tilted her head. "At least, have you?"

"Not that I know of." Joelle sat on the edge of a chair, prepared to bolt. "At least not today. What's the matter?"

Levi's gaze was level. "I've discussed this with Selah, and she believes you can be trusted with . . . delicate information."

Unsure what was expected of her, Joelle nodded. "Of course I can. Go on."

"Very well, then. If you're interested in a little assignment, I'm in need of your writing skills."

"What kind of assignment?" She frowned at Levi. "Did you tell her—"

"Joelle, I've known for some time you've been writing for the newspaper." Selah wrinkled her nose. "You start purchasing things like dress fabric without asking for money. It has to come from somewhere, and I know you're not a thief. How else are you earning it, if not by writing?"

"Well, I—well, I—" Joelle gulped her coffee and winced. She'd forgotten to put any sugar in it. "Maybe I did. It's not a crime. But I asked him not to tell anybody."

"We don't keep things from each other, Jo," Selah said soothingly. "I promise, it's just between us."

Joelle looked from Selah to Levi. It was rather flattering that her clever brother-in-law needed her help. Finally curiosity won. "What sort of assignment?" she repeated. "Is it related to a case you're working on?"

"Not directly." Levi leaned back against the sofa and crossed one ankle over the other knee. "I want you to write an article announcing Schuyler's campaign for Congress."

Write a whole article about Schuyler Beaumont? "Why? Is he involved in some illegal scheme?" She wouldn't have thought so, but his whole demeanor had been decidedly odd ever since his father's funeral. Yesterday at Shug and India's cabin, he'd been his normal argumentative self, but there'd been a sort of frenetic energy to his movements and tone of voice. A lot like during the meal just before he'd pushed her away.

"Of course not," Levi said, chuckling. "But his candidacy has a good chance of helping me unearth some information I want, and I'd appreciate any support you can drive his way."

She'd promised Reverend Boykin she'd be a truth speaker. "Levi, I am a reporter. I have to write the facts."

"That goes without saying."

"I would have to interview him."

Levi's dimple appeared briefly. "Yes, I imagine you will. The two of you usually don't lack for anything to talk about."

"It's not that." Joelle didn't know how to explain her reluctance to solicit information from a man who had told her, in no uncertain terms, he wanted nothing else to do with her. She sighed. "I suppose you want me to make him sound like an upstanding candidate."

"That would be helpful—but as you say, within the bounds of truth."

Could he be any more cryptic? "Levi, what is going on? I don't like working blind."

Levi shrugged. "For now you're going to have to trust me."

Levi she trusted. But Schuyler was another story entirely.

Sixteen

SHOULDERING THE LAST OF DELFINA'S LARGE TRUNKS, Schuyler started the trek from the front of the house—currently a beehive of noise and activity, due to Daughtry House's sudden explosion of paying customers—up the marble porch steps and into the rotunda. Shifting his load to a more comfortable position, he heaved a breath and took on the grand spiral staircase. Transportation from the station out to the hotel had been a challenge, since General and Mrs. Forrest and her maid, plus the Fabio and her retinue, had all arrived on the same train. To no one's particular surprise, Jefcoat and Hixon had also appeared as if by magic—probably drawn, Schuyler thought cynically, by the word "party," like flies to an open bowl of fruit.

He'd had to foot the bill for an extra carriage, which was going to seriously cut into profits. Selah wasn't going to like that, but what choice did he have? And the Italian songbird had insisted on sitting beside him the whole way, clinging to his arm and seriously hampering his ability to control the horses. General Forrest had driven the second carriage, with Hixon and Jefcoat bouncing on the rear seat, singing a bawdy song that undoubtedly scandalized Mrs. Forrest. Her lips were certainly drawn into a straight line by the time they pulled up at Daughtry House—and not a moment too soon.

Schuyler found Selah on the second-story landing, scowling at one of her ubiquitous lists. He set down the trunk and moved to peer over her shoulder. "What's the matter?"

"Two extra men," she muttered. "This is a disaster."

"Let me see." He took the paper, which turned out to be a sketched map of the hotel's room layout.

She had put the Forrests in the downstairs master suite, Delfina and her maid in the first bedroom on the second floor. Manager Poldi Volker took the second, with Hixon and Jefcoat sharing the third. Selah and Levi, current resident managers, had the remaining room, leaving the rest of the family in their quarters in the remodeled outbuildings—the unmarried women in the manager's cottage and Wyatt in the old overseer's cabin.

Schuyler rattled the sketch. "I hesitate to mention this, but I'm the only person without a place to sleep. Are you banishing me to the stable?"

Selah put her hands on her hips, her warm brown eyes sparking with humor. "I had assumed you'd go back to your hotel room in town."

He gave her his best wounded look. "And miss all the fun?"

"Well, you could sleep in the schoolroom or roll up in a blanket on the porch if you like. Levi did that a time or two before we married."

"What you're telling me is that a man has to pay or marry into the family in order to rate a bedroom. Hmm. There are only two Daughtry girls left. Which one do you recommend?"

Selah rewarded him with a ferocious frown. "Joelle is

spoken for, and you'd best leave Aurora alone, if you know what's good for you, Schuyler Beaumont."

He stepped back, hands in the air. "I'm joking, for heaven's sake. Put away the teeth, Mama Bear."

She made a shooing motion. "Go find someone else to pester. Go charm the diva. I'm busy."

"The diva gives me a twitch." Having successfully gotten a rise out of the unflappable Selah, he realized there was one person missing from the usual welcoming committee. "Speaking of Joelle, perhaps I'll pester her. Where is she?"

Selah was clearly more concerned about housing assignments than Schuyler's boredom at the moment. "Writing somewhere, I think. Sometimes she hides in the cupola. Sometimes she locks herself in her bedroom. I don't know, Schuyler. If you're not going to be useful, go look for her."

"All right, all right." Sticking his hands in his pockets, he peered up the attic stairs. If Joelle was writing, she wouldn't want to be interrupted. Besides, as he belatedly remembered, he'd told her he wouldn't be seeking further tête-à-têtes with her. "On second thought, I'd better make sure Jefcoat and Hixon are staying out of trouble."

"Trouble?" Selah gave him a startled look. "What do you mean?"

He laughed and waved over his shoulder as he ran down the stairs.

Back in the rotunda, he could hear the women gabbling from the parlor—Aurora's light giggle, Delfina's sultry Italian accent, Mrs. Forrest's matronly voice, ThomasAnne's breathy gush, all accompanied by the musical chink of teacups in saucers. That way lay a trap into which no sane man would voluntarily stick his head.

Levi must have taken retreat as the better part of valor and hustled the men outdoors. Schuyler turned into the breezeway and out the back door.

On the porch, he let out a halloo.

Wyatt's curly brown mop poked through the barn's open door. "We're out here, Mr. Schuyler!" the boy called. "General Forrest asked for a tour of the grounds."

Schuyler waved and headed across the yard. He passed the pagoda, its columns and furniture freshened with paint and judicious placement of flowers, then the two-story icehouse. To his right lay the manager's cottage, where the family had lived since the end of the war—the main house being uninhabitable until Schuyler's money—well, technically his credit—pumped new life into the old place.

That was something he supposed he could be proud of. He'd given the Daughtry women a way to resurrect their self-respect by supporting themselves, and enabled them to hire nearly two dozen out-of-work former slaves. And in the process he'd made himself some friends. Levi and Doc had become mentors and comrades, Wyatt like a younger brother. The women, of course, had always been family—if, at times, of a distant and somewhat contentious variety. In fact, to his surprise, he realized that Daughtry House felt more like home than Beaumont House in Mobile. He might not own it outright, but he'd invested much more than his finances here. He suspected that his heart and purpose in life might actually be found in the soul of this place.

On that maudlin note, he passed from bright open sunlight into the barn. He found the tack room door open, with the four men—Levi, Forrest, Jefcoat, and Hixon—and Wyatt inside examining the hunting rifles kept in a case there. Most of the guns had belonged to old Colonel Daughtry, God rest his soul, but Schuyler saw his own Yellow Boy in General Forrest's hands.

Forrest looked around as Schuyler's shadow fell into the room. "This yours, boy?"

"Yes, sir. My father gave it to me a few years ago."

Forrest hefted the rifle, pulled it up against his shoulder. "It's a good old gun."

"It is." Schuyler took it from the general and swept his hand down its gunmetal receiver and smooth wooden stock. "We'll arrange a hunting party next week, if you like."

"Bear?" The general's face lit with interest.

"If you want," Wyatt said. "There's a mean one that took out a cow a couple days ago. I like to hunt coons at night too, though."

"We've some good hunting dogs out in the kennel," Levi said. "Wyatt's been training them."

"Where'd you get that accent, son?" the general asked Levi as the group left the barn and headed for the kennel. "You one of those doggone Yankees that tore up our Mississippi rail lines during the war?"

The tic that sometimes appeared in Levi's jaw when he was tweaked about his clipped speech pattern jumped violently. Forrest was more abrasive than most, but it seemed to Schuyler that Riggins had something of more substance against the general than just a friendly dig.

"I served in Grierson's unit, under Smith and Sturgis. And yes, sir, we tore up about ten miles of M&O rail after we thumped you Rebs at Old Town Creek."

"Which happened one day after we'd tricked y'all into the bottleneck retreat at the Tishomingo Bridge. If I hadn't been wounded out of commission that day, you'd never have come back at Old Town Creek."

"Well, we'll never know that, will we, sir?" Levi's tone was respectful, quiet. But Schuyler heard the flint underneath. Levi was angry.

Forrest stopped and peered into Levi's face. "You look familiar. Did I run into you personally somewhere?"

Alarmed, Schuyler gave Levi a warning look from behind the general's back.

"I doubt that," Levi said evenly. He suddenly grinned. "You wouldn't have recognized me anyway, I was so covered in mud during those three days of the engagement. Horses could hardly keep their feet under them."

Forrest laughed. "That's true. But they gave it a valiant try. I remember your boys and your animals being skinny, undernourished, tired from long marches away from provisions. Amazing you fared as well as you did, especially in unfamiliar territory with poor sources of intelligence."

"Sheer Yankee grit," Levi said, acknowledging the generosity of the compliment. "And good equipment."

"You still got one of those Yankee rifles that they load on Sunday and shoot all week?"

"Traded it in for a Winchester when I mustered out," Levi said. He looked around at Jefcoat, Hixon, and Wyatt, listening with avid interest to the veterans' conversation. "But enough war talk. It's over and done, and we're back to being fellow Americans, not enemies. Schuyler, I'm going to let you take over the tour from here. Selah asked me to stop at the blacksmith's to see about a set of knives she had Nathan working on." Giving Wyatt a friendly thump on the shoulder, Levi swung off toward the blacksmith shop, set a

212

hundred yards or so up on a hill, not far from the Vincents' cabin.

Schuyler was happy to gain the general's attention, but he could hardly address what he really wanted to discuss with Forrest in the presence of others. "How would you like to inspect our cotton fields, General Forrest? We're bringing them back on a different model than before the war."

As he could have predicted, Wyatt and Schuyler's two comrades quickly turned down this entertainment, but Forrest jumped at the chance to compare agricultural notes. The two parties went separate ways, the younger set to continue on toward the kennel, Schuyler and the general taking off in a meandering path toward the fields located just past a stand of trees to the west.

Before long they reached a slight rise, where the tilled fields, outlined by a creek on one side and a dirt road on the other, became visible as far as the eye could see. The general paused, legs planted wide, to take a deep, satisfied breath.

Schuyler found himself, to his own surprise, breathing an awkward prayer for guidance. There seemed something deeply problematic about asking the Almighty for help in dissemination. His whole life had been a direct blast toward fame and fortune—whatever that might turn out to look like. This detour into rooting out criminals, by virtue of pretending to be one, rather made his skin crawl.

Don't think about it so hard. This is the right thing to do.

"Beautiful piece of property," Forrest said. "Daughtry was proud of it. So proud that I'm afraid it destroyed his mind when he lost it. You've done a good job of bringing it back. How are you managing the labor? Sharecropping? Gang contracts?"

"I'm afraid you'd have to ask Selah about that," Schuyler said. "She's the manager. Though I believe she's turned over a good deal of the day-to-day land management to Mose Lawrence."

Forrest squinted at him. "Lawrence? The colored gardener?"

Schuyler wanted to say that Mose was much more than a gardener, but he nodded. "Unfortunately, I retained slightly less than half interest in the business, and she outvotes me."

"That's what's wrong with allowing women to own property. No idea how to keep control of an investment. First thing you know, freed slaves will overrun the agricultural economy, and we'll have chaos all over the South. No concept of profit and loss, planning for the future, care for the land. It's like asking a newborn baby to feed and clothe itself!" The general's tone wasn't so much angry as puzzled, disgusted. "They send Northern 'missionaries' down here to overeducate people who'd be better off working the crops, politicians who don't understand our culture to dictate our government . . . Someone's going to have to step in and put a stop to it."

Schuyler was very glad the headstrong Selah was safely in the house, nearly a mile away, or the general might have returned to dinner with a bloody nose. He hid his smile. "I know what you mean, sir. But I don't know that there's anything we can do about it. Now that the Negroes have been enfranchised, the horse is rather out of the barn."

Forrest's hawk-eyed stare focused on Schuyler's face. "No disrespect to the dead, but your father said something similar—indicated that he was willing to work with liberal extremists to find common ground." He spat on the ground.

"That for common ground. Some of us have taken a stand to push back. Make them come *our* way for a change."

Schuyler nodded. "I'd heard there's work to that effect going on in Alabama, Georgia, and Tennessee. I'm hoping to see it here too."

"Why do you think I came down here, son? Reports of your presence at that trial over in Tuscaloosa came back to me. You're obviously interested in slowing down this creeping liberal shadow trying to overtake us. You're educated, well connected, personable. I think you've got real leadership potential."

It was really horrifying, Schuyler thought, how close he had come to being drawn into the quagmire of evil he was looking in the face. Six months ago he might actually have been flattered by the general's assessment.

As it was, his stomach churned. He made himself smile and say, "I thought you'd never ask, sir. Tell me where and when, and I'll be there."

It was a big plantation, and finding a place to be alone shouldn't have been that hard. But Joelle had finally been forced to resort to scrubbing the bathhouse to get her thoughts in order. Now she stood looking at the gleaming tiles, smelled the eau de Javel on her hands—the miracle solution for which Mr. Whitmore had truthfully claimed the ability to bleach any surface clean of mold or stains—and considered jumping in the pool to bathe.

That would be decadent, wouldn't it? Taking a swim alone, before anyone else had a chance to enjoy the luxury. But she deserved it—after all, she'd done the work without any help.

She went to the doorway and peered across the road. No one knew where she was, because when she'd left Charmion's house two hours ago, she'd told Doc and ThomasAnne (who had arrived to check on the baby's progress) that she was going to the pagoda. Which she had done, but she'd kept getting distracted by the jays quarreling in the magnolia trees, and who could compose combative political questions outdoors on such a beautiful day? And then she'd wandered into the icehouse, which proved to be both creepy and confined, a combination she simply could not bear. Like Goldilocks seeking just the right chair, just the right bed, she'd gone around to the front porch, where she spotted the bathhouse through the front gate.

Eureka. Mindless tasks provided the perfect fallow field for deep thought.

And now the bathhouse was pristine. She had questions for Schuyler all lined up in her head, and there was no reason not to swim for a few minutes before subjecting herself to the torture of entertaining a houseful of strangers. She walked back over to the pool burbling through a pipe from the spring-fed creek in the woods behind the bathhouse. Almost she could see her thirteen-year-old self reading her book there, innocently unaware of the creature that was about to descend upon her unsuspecting head.

She was going to eliminate that memory, right here, right now—replace it with a sort of baptismal ceremony of independence. No more Schuyler, metaphorically jumping upon her without warning, inhabiting her mind and heart and refusing to leave. Of course, she still had to interview him for the story, but that was purely business. Literary commerce. Reporter and subject.

Catching her thoughts verging upon unhealthy obsession, she gave herself a mental shake. "You deserve a nice solitary bath," she told herself aloud.

Unfortunately, she hadn't thought to bring a bathing costume with her. In fact, she *had* no bathing costume. Probably Aurora did—Aurora owned every possible article of clothing invented since Eve started sewing with fig leaves—but it was too late to borrow, and besides, baby sister wasn't as big as a minute. Anyway, as she had already noted, no one would know if she simply took off her dress and swam in her chemise and drawers.

Before she could change her mind, she unhooked the waistband of her skirt and let it drop to the clean tile floor, then began to unbutton the sleeves of her blouse. Once free of the simple outer garments she habitually wore for housework— she'd never been fond of the rolls and pads fashionable for shaping the hips into fantastic shapes below the waist, in fact dispensed with them whenever she thought she could get away with it—she bent to take off her shoes and stockings. Feeling giddy with anticipation, she sat down on the edge of the pool and dunked her feet in.

She shrieked in shock at the icy temperature. She'd forgotten how *cold* creek water could be in the springtime. But she also remembered that the body had a way of adjusting, so she took a deep breath and jumped in. Submerged, she forced herself to stay under, shivering, until she could no longer hold her breath. At last she broke the surface, gasping, shuddering with cold, but delightfully refreshed and laughing with pleasure.

And found herself scooped into a pair of strong, muscular arms and held close to a broad chest.

"Joelle! Are you all right?" Schuyler stood up with her, fully clothed and sopping wet.

Dumbfounded, she looked up at his drenched face. "Have you gone stark raving mad? What are you doing?"

"I heard you scream. I thought you were drowning!" His eyes raked her from her dripping hair to her bare toes. "You seem to be all right."

"Of course I'm all right! I was just startled by the cold. Put me down! And stop looking at me!"

"You might have a little gratitude," he growled. "Here I've ruined my clothes—"

"Put me *down*!" She struggled against his arms, he lost his balance, and they both went under. Kicking and thrashing, she started to panic, until Schuyler shoved her up into fresh air once more. She swallowed water, choked and coughed. Schuyler grabbed her and turned her back to his chest. One arm hooked around her waist, he squeezed, gently pounding her between the shoulder blades with the heel of the other hand. "Let"—she coughed violently—"go—of me!"

The most awful part of this whole debacle was the terrifying surge of joy she felt in his sudden presence. She wanted him to hold her, she wanted to turn and fling her arms around his neck, but this was indecent. She'd had no business removing her clothes, and he certainly had no business pulling her closer.

Which he did.

Whereupon she lost control of her limbs and went utterly slack with his forearm under her ribs, floating in the water as she caught her breath. Her head went back against his shoulder, her face turned under his chin, he dipped his head, and his lips came for hers.

"Joelle," he muttered, his lips catching hers. A second later he drew back. "Salt."

"What?" She sniffed.

"You taste like salt. You're crying."

"Of course I'm crying. I've just lost every bit of dignity I ever possessed."

"But you're breathing."

"Yes. Barely."

"All right then. Can you stand up?"

"Yes."

"I'm going to let you go and turn my back. Get out and put your clothes back on. Then we're going to talk."

"You said no more—"

"I'm an idiot. Don't listen to me. Well, listen to me now. Just—" He heaved an exasperated breath. "We have to talk, Joelle. But with your clothes on." His arm slid away.

Bereft, she cast a quick look over her shoulder and found him launching himself out of the far side of the pool. True to his word, he stood with his back to her, dripping like a statue of Poseidon in a fountain. Hurriedly she dressed, hands shaking, fingers fumbling at closures. Looking down at herself, she realized she was only marginally more modest than she'd been a few minutes ago, since she didn't have a towel, and her wet undergarments soaked through her blouse. Her hair hung in sopping red waves about her shoulders.

She folded her arms across her chest. "I'm dressed," she mumbled. "You can turn around."

He did so, and to his credit, his eyes remained on her face. "I'm sorry to have scared you like that," he said humbly. "I really thought you were in trouble."

"I know."

"You're still shaking." He looked miserable. "Didn't you know creek water in May is like ice?"

"Yes, but I *was* enjoying it. I'd been cleaning, and I was hot and dirty, and I wanted a bath." She paused, suddenly suspicious. "How did you know I was here? Were you following me?"

"No! But I happened to be walking around the side of the house, and I saw you come to the door of the bathhouse and look out. I just wondered what you were up to."

"I'm not *up to* anything! I was going about my business, working like a—like a servant, which I am, trying to make this place habitable for our guests. I thought Delfina might like to go swimming later in the week, so I came over to clean it and have some thinking time. Then, like I said, I got all sweaty and needed a bath, and—What? Why are you looking at me like that?"

His mouth was grim, and there was a sort of smoky look to his eyes, an expression she could not interpret. Slowly he lifted his hand to rake water off one cheek. After an interminable minute, he exhaled, jerked his gaze away. "Ten. Nine. Eight. Seven. Six. Five—"

"Schuyler! What on earth is wrong with you?"

"Don't move!" he said, putting out a hand. "Stay over on that side of the pool and we'll be fine. In fact, sit down right where you are. We'll get this little conversation over with, I'll be on my way, and you can think to your heart's content."

Tired of arguing, tired of explaining herself, she shrugged and dropped to sit on the tile floor. Arms encircling her knees, which were drawn up under her skirt, she stared at Schuyler resentfully. All her carefully worded interview questions had flown to bits. Let *him* do the talking for once.

"This is not working," he finally said, taking a seat on the bench against the wall behind him. He leaned forward, elbows on his knees, hands clasped between them. "I thought I could come here and play host to our guests and ignore you. But it seems I can't. So I'm leaving. Today. After I change my clothes." He paused, as if waiting for her to add something. When she pinched her lips together and shrugged again, he sat up. "And don't tell me you don't care, because you obviously do! You know what almost happened as well as I do. I'm not a child anymore, Joelle. It's not fair for you to be sitting there looking like a mermaid out of a fairy tale, when I can't—when you—" He shoved both hands through his hair, looking at her with his eyes burning. "And while I'm at it, don't you ever go walking around by yourself anymore, especially if you're going to be taking off your clothes to go swimming. Bring one of the other girls or a servant, or *somebody* to watch out for you. What if it hadn't been me that came along? What if somebody—" He lurched to his feet. "I'd *kill* any man who touched you, Joelle, so don't put me to the test. Do you understand me?"

Her mouth fell open. He was so angry, so clearly frustrated, and she had no idea what she'd done to make him that way. He'd actually kissed her, that wasn't her imagination, but now he looked like a lit torpedo. She wasn't sure she wanted to know what was going on behind those steel-blue eyes. So she nodded. "Where are you going?" she whispered.

"I'm not sure. Come on. I'll walk you back to the house."

She got up without his help and followed him out the door. They crossed the road together, a pace or two apart, went through the main gate, and up the drive path. After walking her around the side of the main house to the manager's cottage, he gave her a stiff nod, then marched toward the stable, boots squishing with every step.

Joelle picked up her damp skirts and tiptoed inside to her bedroom. She got out of her clothes—just let them fall into a soggy pile on the floor—put on a dressing gown, and lay down on her bed, where she cried herself to sleep.

Seventeen

SCHUYLER WALKED DOWN MAIN STREET TUPELO, barely aware of the Saturday evening shutdown going on around him.

Tupelo or Oxford. He had a choice of where to begin this odyssey. Lots of connections in his college town. A comfortable place to hole up at the Thompson House. No Joelle within sixty miles.

He kicked a rock into the street. Yes, there was that—probably the most compelling reason to leave Tupelo on the next train. The sight of her coming up out of that pool, water sluicing over her shoulders and pasting her garments to her body, turning her hair into rivers of molten gold, would remain forever branded in his mind.

Dear God, how many ways can a man be tortured by his own stupidity? I vow, I'm trying to become the man you want me to be. I realize I brought that on myself. I walked across the road when I should have gotten on a horse and ridden myself into submission. But once she screamed, what else was I to do? I couldn't let her drown!

And around it went again. Until he came to the bottom

line, which was: *I want the best for her. I'm willing to let her go, Lord, if that's what you want. Just please wipe my mind clear of anything that will take me in unholy directions.*

With that plea ringing in his brain, he fetched up in front of the Emporium on one side of the street and the Rattlesnake Saloon on the other. Oliver Whitmore owned both. According to the conversation he'd had with General Forrest, Schuyler should start with Whitmore in his pursuit of Klan activity. No big surprise there. The merchant had made no secret of his disparagement of the Daughtry ladies' nasty habit of promoting and encouraging Negro suffrage and employment.

Thinking he'd more likely find loose tongues and volatile opinions inside the saloon than the mercantile, he dodged across the street.

He found the Rattlesnake thriving in anticipation of the next day's dry twenty-four hours. Every table was full, and a row of farmers lined up at the bar, elbows bent with the quaff of choice to hand. With a quick scan of the murky interior of the room, Schuyler located Whitmore himself, holding forth in a back corner, at a large round table surrounded by a motley variety of gentlemen. A few of them, including town barber JJ Fisher, Mr. Brown of the Gum Pond Hotel, and constable Alonzo Pickett, Schuyler recognized. As he approached the table and moved to a position that enabled him to see those with their backs to the door, he was surprised to find among the company his friend Hixon and Joelle's betrothed, Gil Reese.

Stiffening his resolve, he hailed Hixon with a loud "Halloo, old man! What are you doing here?"

"I'd ask you the same thing, Beaumont," Hixon said with a sloppy grin that proclaimed he'd already been sampling the

Rattlesnake's stock. "Pretty women back at the plantation, I'd not expect you to be anywhere else."

Schuyler glanced at Reese, whose stoic expression disguised whatever discomfort he felt in his surroundings. He seemed to be unaware of the full tankard of beer at his elbow.

"Beaumont," Reese said between his teeth, giving Schuyler a stiff nod.

Schuyler carelessly returned the greeting and dragged over a free chair, which he turned around and straddled backward. "Hixon, I expect you to alert me in the future of meetings that could be of interest to my campaign." He sent his friend a look intended to convey good-natured rebuke.

Hixon blinked. "You're serious about that? I thought you was just blowing smoke."

"Of course I'm serious. Time to make a bigger mark on the world."

"Well, but . . ." Hixon looked around at the older men at the table, shrugged, and retreated behind his tankard.

"Son, you can't just walk in on a private meeting," the constable spoke up, "no matter if you're acquainted with one or two of us."

Having anticipated some resistance, Schuyler cocked his head and grinned as if he'd just heard a great joke. "Mr. Pickett, you misunderstand. General Forrest is my guest at the hotel, and he assured me of my welcome with you gentlemen. In fact, he'd planned to accompany me and introduce me himself, but finds himself indisposed today by that little wound from the Crossroads." He paused and rubbed his own right thigh, as if experiencing a twinge of sympathetic pain. "The general bade me extend his regards and asked me to assure you all of his continuing support for the cause."

A muttering of appreciation for the war hero went up around the table, and everyone relaxed.

Everyone, that is, except Gil Reese, who gave Schuyler a hard stare. "Have you seen my betrothed today? Will she be at church tomorrow?"

"Miss Daughtry has not made me privy to her daily schedule. But if you are concerned that she might be forgetting who you are, I suggest a bit of attention in the form of flowers and poetry, to assure her of your continued devotion." Fully aware of Joelle's expressed opinion of maudlin sentimentality (despite a well-hidden romantic streak), Schuyler told himself that he was utterly wicked. *Frankly, sir, I do not care*, his wicked self replied. *Let the games begin.*

"Then she doesn't know where you are?" Reese pressed him.

"No. And she won't, unless you tell her." The hypocrite. The threat was clear. Beginning to understand his father's growing antipathy to the excesses and blindness of the Confederate status quo, he turned to Whitmore, as the most likely leader of the group. "I'm sorry I missed the fun last Sunday. Perhaps you'll fill me in on what progress has resulted from this more head-on attack on the problems we're facing."

Whitmore cut his eyes at Reese. "Sunday? Everyone here was in a place of worship that day."

"Not me," Hixon blurted. "I was asleep half the day, over at the Thompson in Oxford. At least until Jefcoat dragged me out of bed." He blinked owlishly. "I think that was Sunday. The days run together a bit. Is today Friday? Or Saturday?"

Ignoring both Hixon and Whitmore, Brown addressed Schuyler's question. "I believe we have seen a natural recoil in certain parties. My bootblacks and maids at the hotel seem convinced that their vote is not worth the cost of lives and property. Whoever did it, the loss of the church has made everyone think twice."

Schuyler glanced at Reese, who seemed to be the one member not entirely on board with the group's agenda. Expecting the preacher to protest, Schuyler braced himself to pronounce his own enthusiasm.

But Reese gave a rather sullen nod, folded his arms, and remained silent. He might not agree wholeheartedly, but he was going along with whatever had been cooked up at this roundtable.

"We've got to think long-term," Whitmore declared. "Nobody really wants to exert more harshness than is absolutely necessary. But sometimes one must cut a plant off at the root in order for it to grow healthy branches. Am I right?" He looked around, clearly daring anyone to disagree.

No one disagreed.

Brown cleared his throat. "Speaking of long-term, I'm wondering about the next step. Turning up the heat, so to speak."

Whitmore cast Brown a warning look. "Not here. We'll meet tonight in the usual place at midnight. Anybody squeamish stay home."

Schuyler knew he was about to get shut out. "Where—" He stopped when Hixon kicked him under the table. "Where will you gentlemen be next Friday evening?" he said smoothly. "Out at Daughtry House, we'll be hosting a hoopla for General Forrest and his wife—and there's an Italian singer here, took it into her head to slum it with us for a week or so. You might be interested in the spectacle. I don't recommend the caterwauling myself, but your wives might find it entertaining!" He laughed. "I can promise there'll be good food! Our Horatia knows what to do with a barbecue butt!"

Enthusiastic acceptance greeted the invitation, and Schuyler allowed the conversation to turn to general anticipation of food, music, and beautiful foreign women. It seemed he had passed a preliminary hurdle, and presumably Hixon would fill him in on the location of tonight's meeting.

He didn't look forward to it, and he'd have to be very, very careful not to be tripped up. But there was great satisfaction in having accomplished a step toward discovering his father's killer.

Joelle got up in time to dress for dinner. Her eyes felt bruised, her throat was sore from coughing, and there was a mark like a brand under her rib cage where Schuyler's arm had clasped her. He hadn't hurt her on purpose, but they'd crossed a line of no return. She stood in front of the mirror, trying to see what he saw. He'd said he couldn't even look at her anymore. A woman of such loose morals that she would undress, leaving herself vulnerable to the gaze of any passing man who wanted to see.

Shame nearly buried her. Oh, how she hoped he'd already left. She couldn't bear to face him now.

A scrounge through her wardrobe produced an out-of-date dress with a high neckline, long sleeves, and matching sash crisscrossing the bosom. Perfect. After putting on clean, dry undergarments, she managed to get herself laced into a corset, then realized the dress fastened in the back. She would have to beg for assistance.

Poking her head out the bedroom door, she looked at

ThomasAnne's closed door across the hall. Her cousin had moved into Selah's old room when Selah and Levi married, an arrangement that suited everyone better. ThomasAnne was the most private person Joelle knew, even more introverted than Joelle herself—and that was going some.

"ThomasAnne, are you still here?" she called in an embarrassed undertone. "I need some help."

The opposite door opened immediately, and Thomas-Anne's gentle, worn face appeared in the opening. "Of course, dearie. What's the matter?"

"My dress buttons in the back." She turned to show her cousin the gaping opening of her dress.

If ThomasAnne wondered at Joelle's choice, she kept it to herself. "Well, that's inconvenient," she said with a rare flash of humor. "Let me see what I can do." ThomasAnne crossed the hall, reached for the dress, and pulled it together, then paused. "Joelle, did you have an accident? What is this bruise?" Her fingertips gently brushed Joelle's upper back, where the heel of Schuyler's hand had bumped her in an attempt to push the water out of her lungs.

Joelle hadn't meant to cry, ever again. But she turned and folded into her older cousin's arms. ThomasAnne was a tall woman, nearly as tall as Joelle, and thin as a rail, but her arms took on a motherly cushion that Joelle hadn't even known she needed.

"He didn't mean to," she wailed. "I didn't mean to. It just happened. How am I going to be a preacher's wife if I can't—if I don't—"

ThomasAnne responded to this nonsense with nearly a full minute of silence before she released Joelle and took her by the upper arms. Giving her a little shake, she said sternly,

"Stop it. Joelle. Deep breath now." When Joelle obeyed with a loud hiccup and tried to wipe her face with her wrist, ThomasAnne grabbed her hand, pulled her into her own room, and shut the door. Pushing Joelle down to sit on the bed, she efficiently took a handkerchief from a drawer and handed it over. "Blow."

Joelle blew, then wiped her eyes. "I'm sorry."

"Don't be silly. I knew there was something wrong when we didn't see you all afternoon, and your opera singer here." ThomasAnne stood over her, hands clasped in ladylike fashion at her waist. "Can you talk and breathe at the same time now?"

Joelle thought of Schuyler asking if she could breathe and nearly burst into fresh tears. She heaved in air and slowly exhaled. "I think so."

"All right. Then start at the beginning and tell me what has you so upset."

"I'm so ashamed."

"Someday I'll tell you about real shame. But for now, I'm listening without judgment." ThomasAnne paused. "Look at me, Joelle."

Joelle looked up and saw genuine empathy in Thomas-Anne's faded blue eyes.

"No judgment." ThomasAnne pulled over Joelle's desk chair and sat knee to knee. "And I won't tell anybody."

Joelle knew that was truth. Relief washed over her. "Why am I so weird, ThomasAnne? I like people, but I don't like them in large batches, and I have to get away to be by myself, which is what I did today."

"If that's weird, then I'm beyond the pale. What else?"

"I scrubbed the bathhouse."

ThomasAnne blinked. "Very well. One of the maids could have done that, but I suppose that's not a hanging offense."

Joelle sighed. "Not until I took my dress off and went swimming."

"You took off . . . Do you want to explain that?"

"It was just an impulsive decision. I'm not sure I can explain it. I felt like I wanted to baptize myself, and we all know the bathhouse has been a ruin for years—I suppose I thought the likelihood of anyone coming in on me would be next to zero."

There was a long, silent pause. "But someone *did* come in? Joelle, did someone hurt you?" ThomasAnne's knuckles were white on the fists clenched in her lap.

"No, not like you mean. Schuyler heard me scream when the cold water hit my feet, so he came running and jumped in after me. I—we—he startled me so, and I swallowed some water, so he squeezed me and thumped me on the back." Joelle gulped. "That's where the bruise came from."

That was all she could get out, but as she looked into her cousin's face, she recognized understanding in the otherwise bland expression. As promised, no judgment—but wisdom of experience that beckoned confidence. Joelle had always thought ThomasAnne had had no life of her own, having been blown like a dandelion seed from one relative's home to another.

Joelle had always pitied her cousin. Now she wondered.

"Honey, I know you love Schuyler," ThomasAnne said.

"What? No! It was just—" The breath truly knocked out of her, Joelle all but reeled where she sat. "Why would you say that?"

ThomasAnne laughed. "Dr. Kidd and Wyatt are always

going on about electrical charges, until one wants to 'unplug' them both. There's that sort of pulsing energy when you and Schuyler are in a room together. It's a wonder you haven't set the house on fire in the last couple of days."

Joelle covered her face with both hands. "It's me. I loathe him and I need his attention, and he makes me blurt out things I have no business saying, but it's not his fault. Not entirely. Maybe I secretly wanted him to come to me in the bathhouse. Did I? ThomasAnne, I'm an engaged woman! How could I have encouraged him to . . . He said I knew it as well as he did, and he's right! Thank God he pushed me away and made me get dressed and . . ."

ThomasAnne gripped Joelle's hands and pulled them down. "Mercy goodness, what a Greek tragedy. Calm down. If I'm understanding you correctly, Schuyler yanked you out of the pool and kept you from drowning. He kissed you briefly, had the good sense to let you go, and he walked you back to the house, where he said goodbye and left for town. The end."

"Um, that about sums it up." Joelle stared at her cousin. "How did you know he walked me back to the house?"

"Benjamin and I were coming back from Charmion's and saw you coming around the house, looking like a cat and dog negotiating rug space in front of the fire. He went into the stable, so I assume he was taking a horse somewhere."

"Then he *is* gone." Joelle's shoulders slumped.

"Yes, and he'd best stay gone until you have the courage to end this ridiculous engagement with Gil Reese."

"I can't jilt Gil! He doesn't deserve—"

"He doesn't deserve marriage with a woman who loves another man."

"I don't love—"

"Joelle. That is utter claptrap."

Shocked to the core, speechless, Joelle stared at Thomas-Anne. "Oh no."

She was absolutely right.

Eighteen

THE MEETING TOOK PLACE AT MIDNIGHT in an abandoned smokehouse out in the middle of nowhere, and Schuyler marveled at the complete absence of light. Clouds blanketed the sky, blocking moon and stars, and no one seemed to think it prudent to light a lamp. If Hixon hadn't brought him here, both cloaked in dark clothing, faces blackened with soot, he might have wondered if he'd arrived by mistake at some devilish séance. As it was, he questioned the sanity of men so twisted by resentment, bitterness, and fear that they behaved more like vengeful little boys dressing up in costume than grown men with families and responsibilities to church and community.

He recognized some of the voices from the meeting at the saloon this afternoon. Others sounded familiar, but he couldn't have sworn to their identities. He wished he had Joelle's unerring ear for tone and inflection. As it was, he stood next to Hixon in the dark building, praying no one would realize he hadn't precisely been invited. Men had been silently gathering in the little brick building for close to an hour, by his best guess. He wondered when the meeting would start and what the agenda would entail. Hixon claimed not to know.

"Then why are you going?" Schuyler had asked him as they rode their horses down a deserted country road, shortly before their arrival at the defunct Saltillo plantation.

Hixon had snorted as if the question were ridiculous. "For the fun of it, of course. I rather like setting things on fire."

Schuyler barely repressed a shudder. The friend he'd always thought of as a harmless drunk just might be a madman.

Silence fell as a light flared in a lamp across the room, revealing a row of dark-costumed men. The top of each face was covered by a black mask, tied at the back of the head. A short, tubby man in the middle held the lamp, and Schuyler was sure he recognized the off-center toupee of Oliver Whitmore. He'd expected Forrest to be here, but Schuyler hadn't yet identified the general's distinctive tall frame and military carriage.

"Gentlemen," Whitmore intoned, "we are brothers here on a crusade for justice. Brothers whose individual and collective rights have been trampled to the point that we have been forced to fight back. As such, we must take every precaution to keep our identities secret and make sure that our activities proceed with the utmost loyalty and courage. It has come to the leadership's attention that besides our distinguished guests from our sister state of Alabama, two local newcomers have joined us tonight. And so our first order of business is to vet them to the satisfaction of all."

The hair on the back of Schuyler's neck stood on end. He was to be vetted? How did anyone even know he was here? He glanced at Hixon and found his friend slumped, chin tucked as if he were asleep. Apparently he had been sacrificed to Hixon's demons.

He doubted anyone would judge him if he acted upon the better part of valor and dove out the back door. But unbidden images flashed through his mind. Judge Teague presiding over a hostile courtroom and ending with a bullet through his head. Schoolteacher Lemuel Frye defending himself and his students' right to learn. The community of Shake Rag rebuilding their church and their faith. Most graphic of all, his father's body in a Tuscaloosa morgue.

Running away was no real option.

All right, then. God sees me. He knows my heart. I don't know why he led me here, but surely he'll be with me in the lion's den. Or the furnace. Or whatever torture device this turns out to be.

On that depressing thought, he stepped forward. "Good evening, gentlemen. I'm one of the newcomers."

Hixon yanked on the back of his coat and hissed, "Shut up, you fool!"

Schuyler ignored him. "I hope you'll let me do my part to maintain the civilized and educated American way of life we're in danger of losing. Just tell me what to do."

A muttering of approval, or maybe protest, ruffled through the company. Then a man standing off to Schuyler's left moved out of the shadow. "You'll prove you're not a Lincolnite plant is what you'll do first," the man growled. Tall, broad-shouldered, and brawny, he gestured with an unlit cigar in his hand. There was something familiar about his build and his voice. Schuyler would have sworn the man had been in that courtroom in Tuscaloosa. Possibly one of the two deputy sheriffs. What were their names? Benton or Denton? No, Dent. Foster was the other, *Newborn* Foster—Schuyler would never forget an oddball name like that.

The presence of people who had seen him in Alabama put him in even greater danger.

"I'm no Lincolnite," he said evenly. "I served on a Confederate naval vessel when I was still in my teens."

"Don't mean you're not a turncoat." The tall man turned to the smaller man beside him. "In Alabama we've got ways of finding out who's full-blooded and who's not."

"How do I know *you're* who you say you are?" Schuyler asked, casting a direct challenge.

Hixon tugged more violently. "Are you *trying* to get us killed?"

Schuyler jerked free and swaggered toward the front of the room. He wheeled to face the crowd. "I'll take whatever oath of loyalty you want. My father was killed by some federalist who didn't like conservatives of any stripe, and I want revenge."

That set up a responding whoop from several parts of the room. Schuyler lifted a fist high and let out his best Rebel yell.

Then somebody behind him threw a sack over his head. "I'm sorry, Sky," muttered Jefcoat from behind him just before pain exploded across the back of his head.

Joelle had been in a deep sleep for perhaps an hour when something woke her. She sat up in bed, rigid, disoriented, but wide-awake, and tugged down the nightgown that had tangled around her legs. Rain slopped in through the open window, so she got up to pull it shut. Standing there in the pitch-blackness, she considered lighting a lamp.

But she didn't want to chance waking ThomasAnne or Aurora. Instead, she fumbled for the softer light of a candle and set it on her dressing table. With the window closed, the room was damp and stuffy, and the flickering candle threw weird shadows over the wall. Sleep wasn't going to come back anytime soon.

She sat in her rocker, pulled her feet up under her nightdress, and wrapped her arms around her legs. She'd managed to make it through the evening—dinner with that tableful of strangers, listening to Levi entertain them at the piano afterward—without thinking of Schuyler more than once every ten minutes. Wondering where he'd gone. Denying her chaotic feelings. She'd laughed and deflected questions about her whereabouts that afternoon with the truth—she'd been scrubbing the bathhouse as a surprise for their guests. Wouldn't an old-fashioned swimming party be fun? Deliberately she'd avoided ThomasAnne's concerned gaze.

Now she wondered about her cousin's cryptic response to that spate of self-flagellation that afternoon. *Someday I'll tell you about real shame.* What did she mean? What could ThomasAnne, the most rigorously upright and rules-conscious person she knew, possibly have to be ashamed of?

And even more puzzling, she'd called Dr. Kidd "Benjamin," offhandedly, as if she thought of him that way in her most private thoughts. Come to think of it, they'd been spending an inordinate amount of time together of late. Doc claimed to be teaching ThomasAnne some nursing skills, so that he'd have an extra pair of hands when he came to treat the employees of the hotel. That might be true, but there also seemed to be a kindling friendship between them, growing stronger every day.

Was it, perhaps, more than friendship?

Imagination rolling as usual into places it ought not go,

Joelle tried to picture eccentric Benjamin Kidd and her strait-laced, middle-aged cousin involved in anything remotely as "charged"—as ThomasAnne herself had put it—as her own interactions with Schuyler.

Good gracious, she thought, putting her head on her knees. The mind positively recoiled.

Which brought her inevitably back to Schuyler himself.

God, I do not want to be rebellious. I am not wise or good enough to know what to do. But you are both wise and good. So I give you myself. I give you my feelings for Schuyler. Please take them away if they are displeasing to you. And I pray that you will protect him and guide him. While I'm at it, I'd better ask you to protect and guide Gil also. Sometimes I think he doesn't need as much guidance as I do. But that's silly. We all need you.

She lifted her head, looked at the candle now guttering in its saucer. Even as she watched, it went out, leaving her in darkness once more. Hoping that wasn't some divine omen, she sat there listening to the rain hit the roof of the cottage, splash against the windowpanes, shake the trees in the yard. She should go back to bed. They would all go to church in the morning, and she would look haggard if she didn't get some sleep.

But her spirit still felt unsettled, as if her prayer wasn't finished.

Search me, O God, and know my heart: try me and know my thoughts. And see if there be any wicked way in me, and lead me in the way everlasting.

Watch over Schuyler.

And Gil, she added guiltily. *Amen.*

The rain saved him. Or maybe it was Gil Reese's squeamishness—Schuyler would never know which.

In any case, wet and chilled to the bone, his back on fire where his shredded shirt touched the welts, he started the walk back to Tupelo. They'd taken his horse, and every step jarred his injuries with agonizing regularity. Still, he was grateful to be alive.

After the sack went over his head, someone tied his hands and then hauled him reeling through the crowd. Disoriented, he didn't know where they took him—and judging by the noise, everyone in the room had gone along—except somewhere outside the smokehouse, down a bumpy dirt road. No telling how far he'd walked before the road ended in a cornfield. Dead stalks grabbed his clothes as they shoved him along from behind.

He knew the Tuscaloosa deputy was the one who lashed him to a post, hands looped around it, with his chest against the rough wood. He could smell the tobacco on the man's breath as huge hands ripped Schuyler's shirt open in the back, tearing the fabric from bottom to top—the exposure and vulnerability doubly cruel because of the blanketing of his head. He could hardly breathe.

"Take the oath! Take the oath!" The chant went up from the mob behind him, rolling over him like thunder.

Or perhaps that *was* thunder. Schuyler could see vague flashes of light through the burlap over his face, could all but feel the electricity charging the humid blackness. Rain began to rattle the dead cornstalks, a chattering, eerie rustle.

And then the flogging started, some kind of leather strap that stung like a hundred wasps, at least an inch wide and long enough to wrap from one side of his back to the other, with stitching that dug into his flesh. He jerked and bore it, not sure what they wanted him to say. He'd already claimed loyalty, and he wouldn't beg for mercy.

The rain was coming down in sheets now, soaking the strap so that it stretched and slapped harder against already bruised muscle and broken skin. His boots slipped in the mud collecting at his feet, and his chin hit the top of the post, hard enough to jar his teeth.

Oh, God, he prayed, hoping he hadn't groaned aloud. *Bear me up.*

He regained his balance, dragged himself upright by bracing the ropes around his hands against the stake.

"Admit you're a Lincolnite scalawag!" demanded someone, maybe Whitmore.

The strap hit again, and Schuyler jerked with the pain. The sack over his head was now so wet that he couldn't take a full breath. Was he going to end up drowning? What if he fell again? This bunch was so insane now, they might just kill him to prove a point. Levi had been right to warn him.

Finally he decided he'd better say *something*. "I'm not a Lincolnite," he said. "I told you, I was raised a—"

"You're a liar," Dent said with cold certainty. "I saw you having breakfast with that Yankee lawyer. No amount of fast talking is gonna convince me you're not good friends. The preacher says you're in love with his wife's sister—and the whole town knows how much she loves her black—"

"Stop it!" That was Gil Reese's carrying voice. "Don't say another word about her!"

Schuyler barely heard him. A red haze of rage had consumed his every coherent thought. He was going to get his hands free and choke Dent, if he died in the attempt.

But two things happened simultaneously that shifted

events. The bottom fell out of the heavens, releasing a down-pour the likes of which north Mississippi hadn't seen since the days of Noah. Thunder crashed in concussive strikes that collided one upon another like cannon fire. Even as the storm released its fury, Schuyler felt more than heard someone grabbing at his attackers and tossing them out of the way like matchsticks. The beating ceased, the sack was yanked off his head, and through the driving rain he saw Gil Reese's tall, bony frame kneeling to work at the sodden knots of the ropes tying Schuyler's hands. A shotgun lay on the ground in the mud, and the mob had dispersed.

Thank God. But what an idiot.

"You're going to have to cut them off," Schuyler said. "Do you have a knife?"

Reese looked up at him, blinking against the rain pelting him in the face. "A knife? No."

"All right, then pull the post out of the ground."

Fortunately, the ground was soft enough now that three hard jerks pulled the post free. As Reese slanted it sideways, Schuyler worked his hands upward and over the top. Once free of the post, the ropes fell off his hands.

"I didn't mean this to happen." Giving Schuyler a look somewhere between relief and horror, Reese turned and ran.

Which was how Schuyler came to be walking back to town alone, in the wee hours of the night, wet to the skin for the second time in twenty-four hours, beaten to within an inch of his life.

And he could not have been more grateful. Something had saved his life. Some *One* had saved his life. And he was pretty sure it was neither the rain nor a jealous, miserable preacher named Gil Reese.

Nineteen

GIL'S SERMON THE NEXT MORNING featured a lot of gloom and doom. Of course, he'd never been a particularly jolly person anyway, so she shouldn't have been surprised. But when one happened to be suffering from an excess of anxiety and a dearth of sleep, the verbal tongue-lashing from the pulpit struck Joelle as not only unnecessary but tiresome.

Surely there were biblical passages of hope and encouragement he could occasionally offer up to his little flock? Did one need a constant diet of affliction and warning? Maybe it was just her personal guilt coloring her hearing. On the other hand, could hearing be colored? She really should have stayed in bed, if that was the best imagery she could construct.

Delfina, seated on her right, seemed engrossed in the dour message. Earlier, from her seat at the piano, Joelle had watched the singer enthusiastically join in the hymn singing, her voice much improved from last night's husky rasp. In fact, everyone else (except Gil, who thought he was required to sing at the top of his lungs) stopped singing to listen to

Delfina. Maybe she would be well enough to perform before the end of the week.

Joelle hoped so. Not that she wanted Delfina and her entourage to leave early. But the responsibility of seeing to their constant entertainment was beginning to take its toll. Fortunately, Aurora had taken on meals and transportation, so all Joelle had to do that morning was join everyone in the breakfast room before jumping into the carriages and heading to town for church. But she'd been late to rise, slow to dress—what did one wear to church on the day after she'd placed herself in the role of unintentional seductress?—and not at all in the mood for Italian-accented chatter while consuming grits and eggs.

Lord, what is wrong with me? Help me think past my own feelings for a change.

On the thought, she heard the door open at the rear of the church. The congregation turned its collective head, even Gil stopping midsentence to see who had come in at the end of the service. Everyone knew that Gil preached until 11:50 on the dot, prayed for another two minutes, led the congregation in a final hymn, then released everyone to go home for lunch. Anyone who came in this late must be visiting from out of town.

Schuyler. Perfectly turned out as usual in a buff-colored summer suit with dark blue tie, his golden-wheat hair the only unruly element of his sartorial magnificence. His hat was clamped under his arm at an odd, stiff angle. The entire gathering watched as he shuffled up the aisle at the pace of an octogenarian turtle and stopped beside Levi and Selah. The two of them smiled and moved over for him. As he sat down on the pew, he let out a little grunt, closed his eyes, and gingerly settled back.

Everyone else lost interest and turned back to look at Gil, but Joelle couldn't take her eyes off Schuyler's pale face. Strawberry-colored scrapes marred his cheekbones and a livid bruise traced the underside of his jaw. Something awful had happened to him, she knew it in her very bones, and what did that say about her prayer for him last night?

But what if he'd brought some beating on himself? Maybe he'd been drinking with his old college friends, gotten into a brawl of some sort. What if he had come here as an act of repentance?

There was no way to know. His expression was blank, the gray-blue eyes steady on Gil's face.

Gil himself flushed under that flinty gaze. "So, brothers and sisters, I commend you to the watch-care of the Holy Spirit. I charge you to depart from here ready to uphold and defend one another against the onslaught of the enemy who hates our souls. God is good, but God is just. We must live in sincere holiness, urging each other on toward faith and good works. Greet one another with a holy kiss. That is, hold on to what is good and pure and just and right, forgetting what lies behind and pressing on toward the mark of the high calling that is in—" Gil stood gripping the edges of the lectern, mouth open like a landed fish. He jerked his gaze from Schuyler to look at Joelle. "Amen. Go in peace."

There was no hymn, no prayer, just a long, awkward silence as Gil walked down the aisle and left the building without looking either right or left. Finally, when it seemed he didn't plan to come back, the congregation rose. Conversation began to ruffle through the room, someone laughed, and the strange moment was over. Joelle got to her feet.

Delfina reached out to grip Joelle's hand. "Oh, *cara*, what pleasing words your young minister preaches! I think I never hear anything so straight to my heart!"

Joelle blinked. "Really? I mean, yes, Gil does a very good job of putting words together. Usually he does, that is." Perhaps she shouldn't point out the vapidity of that last chunk of nonsense Gil had spouted. If Delfina hadn't noticed, how would it help to reduce Gil's stature in her eyes? "And usually he stands at the door to shake hands with everyone as they leave. I wonder where he went."

"I think he is so overcome with emotion that he can no longer to bear our critical gaze." Delfina's dark brown eyes sparkled with admiration. She clasped her hands at her bosom. "Your young man is such the fine shepherd of the flock. I would please to hear him speak every Sunday for the rest of my life!"

Joelle nearly blurted out that she would gladly trade places, giving Delfina her spot at Gil's breakfast table and in his bed without a qualm. Then she remembered that a spotlight on a stage, with thousands of people staring at her for a couple of hours while she tried to remember Italian song lyrics, would hardly be the ideal occupation for the Hermit of Ithaca Plantation.

"End this ridiculous engagement," ThomasAnne had advised.

Well, she would. As soon as she could catch Gil alone. When she had entered the church with her family, he'd barely said "good morning" to her before closeting himself in the prayer room with the deacons. The fact that Joelle had felt relieved rather than insulted told her a lot about the state of her heart. *Love is a decision*, she'd heard many times from well-meaning people. Undoubtedly that was true when one was already committed in marriage. But ordering her feelings to respond in one direction, when they insisted on shoving off toward the opposite pole, turned out to be a lot more difficult than she'd anticipated.

During these mental perambulations, Delfina had attracted quite a coterie of music enthusiasts who had heard about the star in their midst. Joelle found herself standing at the outside of a chattering gaggle of women.

"Miss Fabio, we are so honored to have you visit our little church! How did you come to be acquainted with the Daughtry girls?"

"You must tell us all about the great cathedrals and theaters in which you have performed!"

"I simply adore your dress—is it true that the modistes of Europe refuse to design for certain members of the nobility?"

To her credit, Delfina kindly answered as many impertinent questions as she understood, filling in the gaps with charming and unintelligible Italian observations. Bored, Joelle looked around and saw Selah and Levi, still seated and in deep conversation with Schuyler. With the first two there to buffer her against the likelihood of being either ignored or scorned by the third, she squared her shoulders and walked over.

At her approach, Selah gave her a false imitation of her usual bright smile. "Tell Schuyler he's coming to dinner, and we're not taking no for an answer."

Joelle gave Schuyler a hard look. "What's wrong with you? Why were you late? What have you done to your face? And why are you holding yourself so oddly?"

Releasing an exaggerated whistle, he stretched an arm across the back of the pew behind Selah. "Four questions in one breath. That's got to be a record. Let's see. The same thing that's always been wrong with me. I couldn't decide which tie to wear. Cut myself shaving. And I fell out of a window last night. Next?"

Joelle looked at Selah. "*Why* do you want him to come to dinner?"

Schuyler's laugh cheered her for some reason. It told her he wasn't in as much pain as she'd feared, and it drew her gaze back to him. The vertical lines between his eyebrows and the hitch in one shoulder still worried her, but at least his voice sounded normal. "Believe me, I would come," he said, winking at Levi, "but I have another engagement tonight."

Levi's hazel eyes were troubled. "Are you sure?"

"Wouldn't give it up for anything," Schuyler said easily. "Important for my campaign."

"You were so intent on impressing General Forrest," Joelle said, forgetting that she had vowed not to argue with him ever again. "You brought him all the way to Tupelo for that purpose. Now you're going out of your way to avoid him."

His expression was inscrutable. "Circumstances change."

"Indeed they do." Stung, she said to her sister, "Good luck convincing him to do anything remotely sensible. Would you mind collecting Delfina? I need to see what Gil is doing before we leave. Perhaps *he'd* like to come dine with us tonight."

Without stopping to see if the arrow had hit its mark, she wheeled and marched down the aisle toward the back door of the church. *Circumstances change indeed*. Pompous donkey. *Fell out a window indeed*. Ridiculous idiot.

She sighed. Dinner would be boring without him. Oh, how she missed him when he wasn't around.

Outside the church, she hesitated on the shallow front step, shading her eyes against a thin, watery sun peering through clouds left over from last night's storm. The trees dripped rainwater onto the wagons parked underneath them, and children played in the puddles along the road. Clusters of family groups stood talking about the service—particularly their cosmopolitan guest—about upcoming town events, about new babies and an old-timer who had passed away during the week.

She didn't see Gil's tall figure anywhere at first, until her reluctant gaze skimmed the Whitmore family. Joelle had avoided Mrs. Whitmore since the confrontation last Sunday. Had that only been a week ago? A lifetime of events seemed to have occurred in the meantime.

And there was Gil, comfortably engaged with the Emporium owners, Mrs. Whitmore patting him on the arm with motherly indulgence. Well, wasn't that just a fine howdy-do? As a general rule, when people indicated that they didn't want to talk to Joelle, she was secretly relieved and had no problem otherwise occupying herself. For the second time in the space of a few minutes, she found herself barging into a conversation to which she hadn't been invited.

Perhaps the apocalypse lurked over the horizon.

Joelle smiled up at Gil as she took his arm. "I wondered where you'd got to. Are you feeling all right, Gil?"

Mrs. Whitmore frowned. "Why would you ask that? We were having a perfectly congenial discussion about our grandson's baptism."

"Really?" Joelle tilted her head. "Don't your son and his family go to the Baptist church? Have they started baptizing infants?"

"No, and that is exactly what—" Mrs. Whitmore gave an

exasperated sigh. "Never mind. Reverend Reese has agreed to come to our home for lunch. Would you care to join us as well, Miss Daughtry?"

In the ranks of gracious invitations, that one rated right up there with "I suppose we have no choice but to let you come."

Joelle smiled at the old bag. "No thank you, as I'm already engaged with my family." Turning to Gil, she added, "But perhaps you would come to the hotel this afternoon for lemonade and then stay for dinner. Miss Fabio has expressed an interest in hearing more of the gospel." And, if she could screw up her courage, she would take the opportunity to break his heart.

Gil's expression brightened. "Did she? I must have done better than I—" He cleared his throat. "That is, I would be happy to come. Are you sure you won't join me and the Whitmores for lunch?" He patted her hand on his arm.

She looked down, then did a double take. Gil's knuckles were scored by deep, raw scratches, and she couldn't help thinking of the scrapes on Schuyler's cheeks and his obvious bodily injury. Coincidence—it had to be.

She didn't want to be betrothed to this man, but neither did she wish him any harm. Furthermore, she had been fully aware of his infatuation with her for quite some time, and the idea of even hurting his feelings curdled her stomach. Still, there was something deeply unsettling about his behavior this morning. Come to think of it, he hadn't looked her in the eye even once.

With a pang of dismay, she wondered if he had somehow found out about her encounter with Schuyler in the bathhouse. But the only person who knew about it—outside of herself and Schuyler—was ThomasAnne. ThomasAnne would never in a million years volunteer such information. Schuyler might, but—

She looked over her shoulder at the church building. He wouldn't. He *wouldn't* tell Gil about that.

Besides, she was only creating what the Bible called "vain imaginations," inventing trouble where there was none. Gil didn't know about it.

"What's the matter?" Gil asked, seeming to finally focus on her.

"Nothing." She clung to his arm. "Everything is just fine."

The crooked, muddy road to Shake Rag had been beaten into ruts over the last five years by innumerable sets of dark, mostly bare feet. Schuyler walked it all alone. He'd exchanged the fine new suit, purchased in Memphis, for faded breeches and a frayed shirt scrounged out of the bottom of his suitcase—items kept for working on the Daughtry House roofs, in the fields, wherever he'd been needed.

Sitting in church that morning, watching Gil Reese stumble over a sermon, had done something to his soul. He wasn't sure if he was softer or harder, but he was different. If he hadn't felt the lacerations on his back, if he hadn't been able to see with his own eyes the bruises and cuts on the preacher's shaking hands, he might have thought last night's events had been a very bad dream.

We're all broken. We all sit or stand in your presence, dressed in our best, pretending for one another that our lives are fine and dandy. But you see us. You know how we struggle to manage the weight of our guilt. Gil Reese—he's no better or worse than me. I can't begin to understand why he was in that place last night. Undoubtedly he wonders the same about me.

If I didn't believe in your love and goodwill for us all, God, I would lose all hope. If I didn't believe that you see me and know where I am right now, if I didn't trust that there is some purpose for this craziness . . .

What would he do? Move to Memphis or back to Mobile or out to California and start over? Ask Joelle to go with him? Take her out of this circus and make a new life together, without the overhanging darkness that plagued the modern South? She would go, he knew it in his bones.

The very idea was ludicrous. Dishonor upon dishonor.

They both had responsibilities and family here who depended upon them. They each had made promises that must be fulfilled.

And he *did* believe. He *did* trust. God *was* real, he *did* see Schuyler Beaumont and Joelle Daughtry, and there *was* a purpose he was traveling toward. Maybe he couldn't see it, maybe he'd have to wait until he was right on top of it before God showed him what to do. All he knew for now was that there were certain people he had to talk to before he climbed over the walls of Jericho without even a Caleb or a Rahab to watch his back.

He kept walking.

When he got to Shake Rag, he headed straight for the church, guided by the cross now affixed atop its steep roof. As he'd expected, the congregation was still there. People who had a lot to lose, he'd noticed, took more time to pray. They relied on each other, trusted one another, became vulnerable as brothers and sisters. There was something profound in that, something he wanted to sit down and think about when this was all over and he had the time.

He stood in the doorway, wondering. Not one soul sat in a pew. Most were on their knees facing the pews, with their elbows or foreheads on the seats. Many lay prostrate, facedown on the bare wooden floor. Schuyler absorbed the sounds, the smells of anguished intercession. A quiet, groaning rumble of prayer shook the little room and sent a shiver of longing through him.

His mission changed on the instant. He slipped in, edged along the wall, careful not to disturb anyone, and found a spot at the back near Tee-Toc and his family. Falling to his knees, he bowed to the floor and covered his head with his arms.

Sometime later, he became aware of the rumble fading to a sigh, a whisper, then silence. He sat up, wiping his face on his sleeve. Tee-Toc was staring at him as if an albatross had flown into the building and decided to nest on a pew.

"Mr. Schuyler? What you doing here?" The boy got to his feet. "Pastor, you better come. Mr. Schuyler's here."

Schuyler sat on his heels, looking around at the dark faces encircling him. Of course he recognized Mose and Horatia, Nathan and Charmion, Shug and India. Others he knew because they had worked at the hotel; some still did, and he saw them every day without really seeing them. Deeply humbled by that thought, he took in each one now, noting gradations of skin color, texture and design of hairline, nose and eye socket shape, curve of lips. Alien, frankly suspicious of him, but human in a way he'd not been consciously aware of. It was a little bit like watching a beautiful painting one had walked past every day suddenly coming to life.

He smiled at the thought. To his surprise, his startled

audience smiled back at him. A couple of children giggled, their parents shushed them, and then a different rumble filled the little building. Laughter. Joy.

Schuyler got to his feet and met Pastor Boykin in the middle of the room. "Apologies for intruding on your meeting, Reverend. I didn't know I needed it, but I did. I hope you don't mind."

The old man reached out to grip Schuyler's shoulder, his dark, rheumy eyes boring into Schuyler's with neither pretense nor deference. "You're welcome to pray with us, son, anytime you want—and you don't have to ask. But I think you came for another reason."

Schuyler nodded. "You might want to come aside. There are children here, and what I have to say—" He broke off, swallowed.

The minister looked around. "India, you and Char take the little ones out to play, would you? We'll tell you about it later." After the two young mothers, with little fuss, had shepherded a clutch of youngsters under six or so out of the church, Boykin instructed the remaining congregation to return to their seats. "Come with me," he told Schuyler quietly and returned to the pulpit. "Listen to our brother," he said simply, then stood aside to give Schuyler the floor.

Schuyler didn't know how to phrase his message without exposing his part in events, so he just blurted it out. "There are people in this community who resent you all because they're afraid the little they have will be taken away and given to you by the government. They might not have the courage to do anything about their resentment, except there are others with evil intent who will use those fears to their own ends. There are still others who will stand by and let wrong prevail because they're too lazy or indifferent to intervene. I'm ashamed to say I was in that third group until my own father's life was taken by one or more of the evildoers—and I'm still not sure I know why. In any case, I took on the task of finding my father's killer and handing him over to law enforcement, along with his leaders and minions." Schuyler scanned his audience. There was concern here, certainly, and some anger, but none of the terror he'd expected. Indeed, there was a level of weary acceptance that was more telling than Schuyler was quite ready for.

He took a deep breath and continued. "You're going to hear things about me, about my presence at meetings, my participation in demonstrations of power and force. I want you to know that I'm going to stay out of as much as I can without giving myself away. I've got to have information, and that comes at a certain cost." Would they believe him? Would they ever forgive him if events took him down irreversible trails? "In fact, I really shouldn't be here. If someone saw me come in here—"

"Nobody gon' hear it from us, so don't you fret," Reverend Boykin said. "Finish your piece and we'll decide what to do."

Schuyler looked at the old man, nodded, then refocused on the congregation. "All right then. All I have is a warning. I've seen and heard plans for a series of nighttime attacks to come against every black church of any size, all across the state, and over into Alabama and Georgia. They're going to burn and terrorize, and they might even lynch anybody found alone. Businesses could be targeted too, I'm not sure—but destroying the churches is the main goal, because they know that's where the root of your strength is."

There was a groan of understanding from the pews, a few muted "amens" and "What we gon' do, Reverend?"

Schuyler hesitated, aware of Boykin's quiet, intent prayerfulness at his shoulder. The Reverend would speak, and he should, but as Schuyler looked at the old man, respect and love flooding his heart, he added, "Reverend, can I say one more thing before I step down? You didn't really need me to come here today. You are God's people, and he could have brought you a warning in any way he saw fit. I guess I'm a little bit of Balaam's ass in this situation!" He grinned at the laughter that rumbled through the room. "I know you don't need me to rescue you—*he* fights for you. But I'd be honored if you'd allow me to stand with you."

Twenty

Seated in the pagoda swing beside Mrs. Forrest, Joelle enjoyed the warmth of the waning afternoon sun on her back and the chilled glass of lemonade in her hand. After supper the men had taken fishing poles and bait to the creek, leaving the women to their hen party. Her two sisters and ThomasAnne carried the burden of the conversation floating around her, leaving her free to listen, watch faces, smile when something funny was said, and mentally record interesting turns of phrase.

But when Gil rounded the side of the house with Elberta Whitmore and her daughter Sophronia—mother to the unbaptized infant Roman—she knew there was something wrong. Even more wrong than there had been this morning during that awful sermon. The second and perhaps most obvious indication that she should have pretended to migraine and retired to her room was the folded newspaper tucked under Gil's arm.

She got up out of the swing fast enough to slosh Mrs. Forrest's lemonade. "Excuse me," she mumbled and hurried to meet the new arrivals halfway. "Hello, Gil! I see you decided to come by after all." With considerable trepidation, she eyed the newspaper, which he now brandished as if it were the sword of Damocles ready to drop and slice her in twain. "And you've brought guests. How enterprising of you."

Gil frowned. "Enterprising? I should rather call it obedience to biblical exhortation. These ladies have accompanied me as witnesses."

"Witnesses to what? Has someone stolen something from you or attacked you?" She looked at his bruised knuckles. "I knew there was something wrong this morning! What happened?"

He flushed. "Nobody attacked me. I'm talking about this article in yesterday's paper. Mrs. Whitmore says you wrote it!"

The sword had fallen.

Joelle glanced over her shoulder at her family and guests in the pagoda. She could hear Selah's husky alto chuckle, Aurora's lighter voice, and Delfina answering in her butchered but charming Italio-English. Joelle was not going to subject them to this disaster that *she* had created.

Neither was she going to back down. All right then, here and now it was. "I realize that you are the acknowledged biblical scholar of the two of us, Gil, but you seem to have skipped over a very important part of this 'exhortation' to which you refer. If one has an offense against one's brother—or sister, as the case may be—he is first to privately approach that person."

Gil's face grew even redder. "How dare you instruct me regarding scriptural protocol! You know very well you have lied to me, and to the community at large, by writing these articles under a false name! This is beyond the pale! It is unladylike. It is unchristian. It is embarrassing!"

258

"I'm sure you are embarrassed, and with good reason—if your accusation were true. What on earth makes you think that I am the same person as Mr. Hanson?" Lips tight, she looked at Mrs. Whitmore. "Who told you such nonsense?"

Elberta Whitmore folded her arms. "You are not the only intelligent woman in this town, Miss Daughtry! I was coming out of the bookstore next to the newspaper office one afternoon and saw you arrive. Naturally I was curious—a married man like Mr. McCanless in conference with a beautiful young woman for an extended period of time could not but strike me as odd!—so I waited until you left, then paid him a visit. To my surprise, he did not even mention your recent arrival and departure! Even more suspicious, I casually looked around and saw the manuscript Mr. McCanless had been reading upon his desk."

"And you immediately connected that manuscript with me?" Careful not to deny anything outright, Joelle probed for information. "Why would you make that leap? And even if it were true, perhaps you could help me understand why that should offend *you*."

"Don't you address my mama in that sassy tone, Joelle Daughtry!" Sophronia drew herself up to her full five foot two, looking remarkably like her mother.

"If it were any of your business, Sophie—and it's not—I'd remind you that we are not five years old anymore. I am a businesswoman with guests to entertain, and I'd appreciate it if someone would get to the point so I can return to them." Joelle stared down her nose. Sometimes an extra inch or two came in very handy.

"The *point*," Mrs. Whitmore said, "is that Reverend Reese has every reason to be embarrassed and outdone, for you have undermined his integrity at every turn. No young woman of modest upbringing would usurp God's sanctuary to encourage Christian ladies to override their husbands' political opinions. Neither would she demean herself with employment outside the home *or* turn her home into a public wayside inn, for every foreign tumbleweed and whiskey-sodden vagrant to find a place to lay his or her head." She paused for breath, eyes protruding in her righteous zeal. "Can you deny any of the aforementioned *facts*?"

"I'm not denying or confirming anything—to you!" Joelle said. "But I will address my betrothed, since he insists on confronting me in front of outside parties. The only thing I'm sorry about is that my disquisition in church last Sunday seems to have resulted in a retaliatory attack on my friends' and students' church. I can hardly believe that the inhabitants of our community are vindictive enough to have engaged in that *evil, evil* deed."

Sophronia put her hands on her hips. "We know you went to a fancy boarding school, Joelle, but can you *try* not to talk as if you swallowed a dictionary?"

Joelle sighed. "Ignorance on your part, Sophronia, does not constitute pretentiousness on my part." She propped her hands on her hips. "I swear, Gil, can't you say what you want to say without hiding behind a couple of women?" Ignoring the gasps behind her, she stared at her fiancé, eyeball-to-eyeball. "I'll try not to humiliate you in public again, but if you want to marry someone who will never disagree with you, you've got the wrong girl. It is true that my sisters and I started a business to feed ourselves and others. But you knew that before you asked me to marry you—at least before the *last* time you asked! I'm sorry if that offends you, but you shouldn't have assumed I'd abandon my sisters in our venture. Lastly, of *course* we open our hotel to anyone who wants to stay here! How else can we practice hospitality, as the Bible tells us over and over to do?"

Gil straightened, rigid as a scarecrow on a pole. "I notice you did not deny the original charge. Did you or did you not write this disgusting article?"

"Disgusting? I beg you to explain to me what is disgusting about teaching people to read and write, so that they may participate in and contribute to a society that has, for the bulk of their lives, demanded everything of them and returned nothing!" Hurt past restraint, Joelle snatched the newspaper out of his hand. "*Yes*, I wrote it! I penned every blessed word, I'm proud of it, and I won't take it back!"

"You are T. M. Hanson," Gil clarified.

"That is my pseudonym." She could add that Mr. McCanless had been the one to insist on the pen name, but she had agreed to it. It was her own responsibility. "I took it on because I was afraid you and other people would react this way to my unvarnished beliefs."

Gil's face was now dead white. "You are not the woman I thought you were."

"I tried to tell you that," she said in as reasonable a tone as she could manage. "You just wouldn't listen."

"But you are so beautiful," he said helplessly.

She stared at him for a moment or two, before laughter bubbled. "My mama always said, 'Pretty is as pretty does.'"

"Your mother was a godly woman," Mrs. Whitmore said. "She would have been horrified to have seen you come to this."

"Don't." Joelle wheeled on her, all amusement vanquished.

"Don't you tell me what my mama would have said or felt about me. She loved me and my sisters and was proud of each of us, no matter what." When Mrs. Whitmore huffed but for once held her peace, Joelle turned back to Gil. "Gil, I'm going to let you off the hook. Right now. We are not a good match—you know it and I know it. I truly hope you find someone who will love you the way you ought to be loved." She fluttered her fingers as if shooing away a bird. "You're free now."

Gil shifted his feet, clearly uncomfortable with his freedom. "You're never going to find anyone to marry you now."

"Thank you for your concern," she said dryly, "but I'm not so sure marriage would be good for me anyway. Or that I would be good for any man. As it turns out, I'm pretty fond of doing things my way, and God gave me the gift of communicating things in writing. If I can't do that and be married too . . . well, I'd rather be pleasing to him and go *his* way."

He stared at her, a flash of something that looked like envy in his eyes. It quickly hardened into resentment. "Even Schuyler Beaumont won't take you when he finds out you're dead-set on making the government pay for Negro education. He's joined the local Klan, and you know they're targeting those people you love so much."

If Schuyler had met Lemuel Frye six months earlier, he probably would have dismissed the man as a fringe-element lunatic. But when the skinny, stoop-shouldered man in the center of the room rose and removed his dilapidated straw hat, Schuyler realized he had rarely, if ever, been so glad to see someone.

Of course Levi would put Frye right here in Shake Rag, hiding in plain sight.

The schoolteacher's face and hands had been darkened with walnut juice, or some other dying agent, and the hat had covered his thin, straight brown hair—a simple but effective disguise. "You're Riggins's friend who came to visit the jail before the trial and offered to send food," he said. "You were in the courtroom and met Riggins and me after the shooting."

Schuyler nodded. "I remember you insisted on bringing your wife." He looked around.

A light-skinned young woman, seated on the pew next to Frye, stood with her chin up. "I'm Georgia Frye."

Schuyler blinked. There was no mistaking this woman's full lips, broad nostrils, and coarse black hair. It explained a lot. And nothing. Questions burst in his brain, but this somewhat public forum was not the place to voice them.

Reverend Boykin seemed to have the same thought. "Maybe we should disband the general meeting for now," he said with quiet authority. "Everyone go home for a meal, and we'll gather again when there is news." As the congregation dispersed, the preacher took Schuyler by the elbow. "You will come to my home, along with the Fryes and the Lawrences." It wasn't a request.

Schuyler followed the minister as he gathered his wife and leadership cohort, and they all walked the short distance to a small, tidy cabin next to the church. Seated with the others around the Boykins' dining table over a simple supper of cornbread and buttermilk, Schuyler couldn't hide his interest in the mixed-race couple, an anomaly in the modern South. He knew of plantation owners who had relationships with their female slaves, some who fathered and acknowledged children, but none who lived in open marriage.

Catching Schuyler's eye across the table, Georgia Frye acknowledged his obvious curiosity. "You're wondering how this happened."

Feeling his face heat, he shrugged. "I admire your courage. Your life can't have been easy."

"A life of ease is overvalued," Frye said. "We have been blessed in many more important ways. My life partner is a woman of grace, beauty, and godliness."

Schuyler thought of his turbulent anti-courtship of Joelle. "Well said. I pray I'll one day be able to say the same. Would you mind telling me how you met and married?"

"I grew up in Connecticut as the son of a Congregational minister." Frye exchanged glances with his wife. "Georgia, as you might expect, was a slave before the war, in the home of a family in Tennessee. Because she was the mistress's personal maid, and I had been hired as the children's private tutor, we came into almost daily contact. When I realized Georgia was absorbing my lessons and practicing on her own, I began to find ways to teach her as well. It wasn't long before nature took its course and we fell in love." His fists atop the table clenched, whitening the knuckles. "The question of slavery suddenly became very personal."

Georgia touched her husband's hand. "Before we could act on our feelings, the war started. Lemuel began to think of returning to New England and enlisting in the Union cause. He wanted me to escape and go with him, but I was afraid to leave my family—"

"So we secretly married, and I stayed on. Chattanooga fell out of Confederate hands, into Union control, but life on the plantation remained much the same. Georgia continued to serve Mrs. Maney—"

"Wait." Schuyler recognized that name. It had come up in Colonel Daughtry's war record. "General Maney's home outside Chattanooga? There was an incident there, something to do with Union sympathizers attacking and ransacking?"

"How do you know about that?" Frye's eyes narrowed. "It's not common knowledge."

"A Confederate veteran from Tupelo served in the Chickamauga campaign. He was involved in retaliation against the men who raided the Maney plantation. Let's just say I'm somewhat familiar with what happened. Go on. Were you both present during that raid?"

But Frye seemed to have reconsidered trusting Schuyler with the remainder of his story. "What is your relationship with this Confederate veteran?"

"He built the plantation I now own and run as a hotel, along with his daughters. He's dead, and I don't hold any admiration for him, if that's what you're wondering." Schuyler glanced at Mose. "Tell him, Mose."

"The Colonel died a broken old man, Mr. Frye," Mose said, packing tobacco into his pipe for a smoke. "You got nothing to worry about there. And Mr. Schuyler here, he a good man you can trust."

Frye's eyes bored into Schuyler's, much like the preacher's had earlier. After a moment his fists relaxed, one turning to clasp his wife's hand. "We were there during that raid, but I hid my wife in my room and defended it against the invaders with my pistol. I shot and injured two of them, I believe. They left in search of easier prey."

By this time, Schuyler's opinion of the "meek" schoolteacher had undergone several revisions. "I imagine so," he said with considerable respect. "Did you both stay to the end of the war?"

Frye shook his head. "I convinced Georgia we'd be safer in Chattanooga, now under Union control, and managed to get there without getting caught by Rebel patrols. Unfortunately, acceptance of our marriage was not what we hoped. I couldn't find a teaching position right away, so we sought refuge in a Negro contraband camp, where at least we were fed and housed."

"It was a *tent* city," Georgia said softly, shuddering.

"But you were free," her husband reminded her, "and we could live together as husband and wife." Frye's gaze turned to Schuyler, challenging him to object. "We found like-minded Northern friends from the American Missionary Association, who assisted in establishing a school and gave Georgia and me a purpose. We were both teachers there, sharing what we had and receiving so much more in return."

"So far all this makes sense," Schuyler said. "But how did you land in Tuscaloosa, and why have you been so specifically targeted by white conservatives?"

"When the war ended, the Freedmen's Bureau hired us as itinerate supervisory teachers. We traveled between Chattanooga, Memphis, Oxford, and Tuscaloosa, making sure federal funds from the war department were distributed to the schools there. We saw much good done, especially at first. Former slaves were hungry to learn—rightly understanding that the ability to read and write would prevent them from being cheated in business transactions, contracts, and courts of law. Many good people, needing employment and wanting to help, took on teaching positions in the face of

sometimes frustrating and undersupplied circumstances."
Frye's lips tightened. "But within a couple of years, graft
began to rear its ugly head. All that 'free money' floating
around, with little way to control its equitable dispersal. Also,
white conservatives, as you mentioned, increasingly resist
being taxed for the benefit of those they view as leeches."
He sighed. "I don't know what else we could have done, but
it was a recipe for disaster."

"We should have stayed with the church," Georgia said
quietly. "A government bureau cannot force generosity."

Frye lifted his shoulders. "We've argued this up one side
and down the other. What's done is done." He looked at
Schuyler. "This is the point at which I met your father. Are
you familiar with a quasi-secret organization called the Union
League?"

Schuyler winced. "I've never been particularly politically
aware. I assume it's a liberal group?"

"Not at first, though that's where the power eventually
went. Wealthy Northerners began by raising money for Lincoln's war initiatives, then continued to be active after peace
came, even in the South. It flourished in Alabama, particularly in Mobile."

Schuyler sat bolt upright. "Are you telling me my father
was a secret liberal?"

Frye smiled. "I doubt he would have called himself such,
but he certainly resisted extreme elements of the conservative party who were willing to split the nation wide open
to prove their point. I met him two years ago at a Union
League meeting in Montgomery. Despite the difference in
our ages and his rather lackadaisical attitude toward faith,

we found much on which to agree, and I immensely enjoyed our discussions on constitutional law."

"Constitutional law?" Schuyler stared at the young schoolteacher's stained face, searching the intelligent brown eyes behind the rimless glasses. This man had been engaged in serious conversations with his father, while he himself had been throwing away large sums of money in the alehouses and pool halls of Oxford. Almost he could not bear to meet Frye's gaze. But there was compassion and generosity there, as well as understanding. As Frye had already said, what was done was done.

"Yes, we enjoyed discussing our Founding Fathers' intent for state and federal rights," Frye said. "But another spot of common ground was our mutual acquaintance with Senator Alonzo Maney."

"Senator? You mean the general from Tennessee? The same one you and your wife worked for?"

Frye nodded. "When Tennessee was readmitted to the union in 1866, Maney ran for state senate and from there was sent to the US Senate. He was only in Washington long enough to finish out the seat left vacant during the war, then returned to reopen his law practice in Chattanooga." The teacher's thin face became carefully blank. "Your father, still being well connected in the old Confederate web, came into possession of information potentially damaging to Maney's reputation as a lawyer and politician—information that my Georgia had first uncovered during her service to Mrs. Maney. I believe that is what led to your father's assassination, as well as my wife and me being hunted like animals by the Ku Klux Klan."

Schuyler struggled to breathe. "Can you prove that?"

Twenty-One

GIL WAS GONE, taking the dragonesses with him. Good riddance.

"What was that all about?" Aurora asked as Joelle regained her seat in one of the decorative wrought iron chairs that Nathan had designed for the pagoda. "Why didn't you invite them to stay for lemonade?"

"I thought about it," Joelle said, adjusting the floral seat cushion, "but that seemed an excess of civility under the circumstances." She'd simply ignored Gil's dig about Schuyler—*Ku Klux Klan? Really?*—and let them meander back to their carriage, or broomsticks, or however they'd conveyed themselves from town.

"What circumstances?" Aurora never could leave anything alone.

Joelle looked at her sister, considering ignoring her as well. Finally she sighed. "The fact that I just gave Gil the heave-ho and mortally insulted Mrs. Whitmore rather killed the convivial atmosphere. And don't tell me not to use my whole vocabulary," she added when Aurora looked irritated. "I'm tired of pretending to be stupid."

"No one's asking you to—"

"What is 'heave-ho'?" demanded Delfina. "I want to use this Americanism."

"I don't recommend it, since it's vulgar," Aurora said. "My sister's usage of language tends to revert to hyperbole when she's fatigued or provoked—or both." She made a face at Joelle. "See, I can use big words too!"

Selah put a hand on Aurora's wrist to forestall the incipient argument. "Joelle, what are you talking about? You didn't just end your engagement in the middle of a lawn party. Did you?"

Joelle shrugged. "Actually, I did. It was every bit as accidental as the proposal."

"Well, to be fair," Aurora said, "he proposed on purpose. It was your acceptance that—"

"Pete!" Selah frowned. "That is quite enough." When Aurora subsided, pouting, Selah returned her concerned gaze to Joelle. "Are you all right?"

Joelle thought about that for a moment. She smiled. "Yes. I feel lighter than a raft of feathers. It's Gil you should worry about. I'm afraid he's not very happy with me at the moment. But I'm sure he'll get over it."

That last might have sounded slightly doubtful, for gentle ThomasAnne let out a whimper. "Oh, the poor dear boy! He must be brokenhearted!"

"You're the one who recommended I jilt him! Anyway, I would say rather that he's angry. According to him, I'm not the woman he thought I was."

"You've been trying to tell him that for years," said the irrepressible Aurora.

"I know. It's beyond frustrating that he should suddenly put on injured airs and accuse me of deception. Well, I suppose there might be a modicum of truth to that." Joelle cast a warning look at Selah, who already knew what she was about to say. "He found out I've been writing for the newspaper under a male pseudonym."

Flat silence greeted that bombshell.

"What is 'pseudonym'?" Delfina asked plaintively.

ThomasAnne began to bleat unintelligible objections behind her handkerchief.

Aurora started to giggle.

"Explain, please," Selah said calmly.

"Well, I only mention it since Mrs. Whitmore is likely to tell everyone in town. Here is what happened. I had to earn money for the books and supplies I needed for the school. The only skill I have is writing. So I wrote. And Mr. McCanless said that my articles, which were somewhat political, wouldn't sell papers under my name. So at first I did it anonymously, but then people began to demand the identity of the author, so he suggested a male pseudonym—for my protection, he said." She looked at Delfina. "A pseudonym is like a stage name for actors and singers. 'Pseudo' meaning 'false,' and 'nym' meaning 'name.'"

Delfina beamed. "Ah! I understand. My real name is Maria Gotti."

Joelle blinked. Well, all right then. She and Maria Gotti had something in common. "Exactly," she said. "Gil seems to think I've put myself beyond hope of finding a man willing to overlook the gaucherie of my finding not one, but *two* wage-earning occupations. Or perhaps it's the sin of my having lied about my identity in print." She slid down onto her backbone and pulled her sun hat down over her face. "I don't mind, because I could live the rest of my life in the cupola, scribbling stories, and be perfectly happy. As long as someone would bring food up to me and occasionally empty the chamber pot. I only regret the shame I've visited upon my unsuspecting and innocent family."

Now Selah laughed. "Don't be melodramatic, Jo. You'd have to empty your own chamber pot."

Joelle sat up laughing and flung the hat at her sister. "Seriously. What am I going to do? Those ladies are poison, and I use the term 'ladies' judiciously. What if the hotel's reputation suffers because of this?"

"We'll put Schuyler on the front lines. He hasn't an enemy in the world, and he'll think of something."

"I shall sing," Delfina said. She stood, gesturing with both arms wide, black eyes sparkling. "We will have the concert, everyone comes to listen and enjoy, and no one remembers the soo-doh-neem. The so *prestante* and talented Mr. Riggins will accompany me." She looked at Selah. "You will tell him so, yes?"

Selah nodded. "I'm sure Levi would be honored to play for you. Are you sure you feel well enough to sing?"

"It is of a necessity. Poison must not be allow to spread and harm my friends." Delfina sat down, fanning herself. "I shall fortify myself with more lemonade."

Less than a quarter mile inside the Tupelo city limit, steps dragging, Schuyler took off his hat and waved it at the carriage rattling from the west toward the crossroads in his path. He'd stayed to confer with the Boykins, Lawrences, and Fryes until the sun disappeared behind the gum trees. Refreshed in spirit, if weary of body, he'd begun the long trek back to town. If he could convince this driver, identity obscured by shadows, to stop for him and take him the rest of the way to the hotel, it would be an answer to prayer. Just as Schuyler jumped to the side of the road, assuming he was out of luck, the horses slowed and stopped.

"Sorry, I almost didn't see you," came a deep familiar voice from the carriage. "Need a ride?"

In the darkness, alone with his thoughts, Schuyler had combed through the threads of the investigation. Several elements snagged his progress. One had to do with General Bedford Forrest and the extent of his involvement in local Ku Klux Klan activity. A second, even more complicated question revolved around Gil Reese.

The fact that Joelle's preacher was passing by and picking him up off the side of the road, like the rescuer in a biblical parable, shouldn't have surprised him. He had, after all, been praying.

Schuyler walked over to the carriage, grabbed the side, and hauled himself onto the seat, stifling a groan. His back really hurt. "I'd be grateful if you'd take me to the Gum Tree. I'm staying there tonight."

There was a solid, blank silence. "Beaumont. What are you doing out on foot at this time of night?"

"I believe the order is to meet later. Are you going?"

"Yes." Reese gave the horses a flap of the reins to put the carriage in motion. "I didn't expect you to come back for more."

Schuyler hid his amusement at the preacher's surly attitude. The Good Samaritan he was not. "I didn't get a chance to thank you for intervening the other night." He released a whistle through his teeth. "They were serious about confirming my determination to join the group."

"You were an unknown quantity."

Schuyler shifted on the jouncing seat. Only to himself would he admit that walking hadn't hurt his back as much as this carriage ride was doing. "Fair enough. But that bunch of rabble-rousers doesn't seem the sort a Methodist preacher would naturally choose for his companions."

"You don't know anything about me." Reese's voice revealed resentment. "Some of those 'rabble-rousers,' as you call them, are major contributors to my salary. And others have made it clear that if I openly object to their activity, innocent members of my congregation could get caught in cross fire. I can't afford to offend any of them."

Though he had suspected some such motivation, hearing Joelle's intended husband admit submitting to coercion filled Schuyler with scorn. He bit back his disgust. "Precisely. General Forrest has promised to fund my campaign for Congress."

"Is that what this is all about? I told Joelle you'd joined the Klan, but I don't think she believed me."

Sucker punched, Schuyler grabbed the seat with both hands. "You *told* her? That you stood there and watched while I was beaten half to death?"

"I didn't go into detail. But I thought she needed to understand the lengths you'd go to for a political career, in case you ever woke up and tried to . . ." Reese cut another look at him. "You know."

"Tried to what? What are you talking about?"

Reese's voice was sullen. "She ended the engagement, this afternoon."

A wild surge of joy flooded Schuyler. "What does that have to do with me?"

"If you don't know, I'm not going to tell you."

"I'm sorry for you. I know you love her."

"I did. I thought I did. But it turns out we don't have enough in common on which to build a marriage. Tell you the truth, I'm almost relieved. Joelle is . . . difficult. She thinks more than women are supposed to. She thinks like a man."

"She most certainly does *not*," Schuyler said, remembering the bathhouse scene. "I don't know that I've ever had a conversation with her that didn't end up with me twisted into knots."

"That's precisely what I mean. I thought just looking at her beautiful face would be enough. But she's too much work. I want a wife who will cook my meals and play the piano in church and sew on a button occasionally. And have well-behaved children one day."

"Well, she can do one out of those four at least. She's a very good pianist." Schuyler laughed. If he thought about it, he could probably list many reasons he loved Joelle, but her piano skills wouldn't have been one of them.

Apparently not in a mood for humor, Reese shrugged. "I tried to protect her, but she keeps stirring up trouble. That speech in church . . . And now the newspaper. If anyone finds out—"

"What do you mean?"

"The decision tonight is whether to hit the newspaper office or take down the church again."

Schuyler's stomach lurched. "Reese, you're a minister. How can you participate in destroying your Christian brothers and sisters' place of worship?"

"They're not family," Reese spat. "That is the most unnatural idea I've ever heard. There's a reason we don't meet together. They're *different*. Their minister isn't trained in a seminary. They even practice voodoo rituals and witchcraft. And if you're really one of us, you won't spout things like that."

They pray like no church I've ever seen, Schuyler wanted to cry. *They took me in and fed me the little they had.*

But he could not speak for fear of ruining his inroads into the organization. He sighed. "I guess you're right. But it's too bad. Maybe the newspaper office is the best place to hit next anyway. McCanless should be more careful of what he allows to be printed. People read things in the press and get liberal ideas."

"Exactly. Anyway, I don't really want anybody hurt—just scared enough to stay home from the polls. An educated vote is critical."

Which was why Joelle was so passionate about training teachers. Another thing he couldn't say. So he grunted as if he agreed, letting conversation lapse until the carriage rolled up in front of the Gum Tree. "Thank you for the ride," he said, climbing down. "You didn't have to stop, but I'm glad you did."

"You never did say why you're on foot."

Schuyler laughed. "Some things are just too embarrassing to mention. Let's leave it at that." He turned to go.

"Wait. I'll come by for you later, if you want to ride with me out to the smokehouse."

Had he, against all odds, made an ally out of Joelle's former fiancé? The irony was almost unbearable. "I'd appreciate that," he said lightly. "What time?"

"Eleven thirty. It's a long ride out there."

"Fine. I'll be looking for you." Lifting a hand in farewell, Schuyler hobbled toward the hotel's front door. He had a couple of hours to write some letters, in case events went in an unexpected direction. If he didn't find out tonight who was at the head of this cabal, he didn't know what else he was going to do.

"Levi, I'm not comfortable with you leaving right now," Selah said. "Are you sure it's necessary? We've got all this male company, and Schuyler keeps disappearing."

Joelle watched her brother-in-law take Selah's hand and fold it between both of his larger ones. It was late, and all their company had gone to their rooms in the big house, leaving the family to repair to the small kitchen of the manager's house for a last cup of tea and plan for the week.

Levi's eyes were tender and regretful. "You know I wouldn't go if I didn't have to. There's a witness in Tuscaloosa I have to interview, maybe bring back with me, so I'll be prepared if this thing breaks loose again here. I'll leave on the first train in the morning and be back as quickly as I can."

Selah blinked—if she started to cry, Joelle would be really worried—seemed to get herself under control, and nodded. "All right. We'll manage."

"I know you will." Levi squeezed Selah's hand once more, then put his arm around the back of her chair. "I've asked Doc to come over every day to check on you all, and Nathan and Mose are always here when Wyatt's in school."

"Will you be back for the concert?" Aurora asked. "That's scheduled for Friday night, and Delfina is counting on your accompanying her."

Levi grinned. "Since Mr. Pinkerton is the one who pays my salary, I'm a lot more concerned with his expectations than those of our Italian songbird. But yes, I anticipate returning by Wednesday at the latest."

"I have to tell you something, Levi." Joelle bit her lip. "I never had a chance to interview Schuyler about his campaign. As Selah said, he's disappeared from the hotel for large amounts of time, and every time I see him, we get caught up in some unrelated discussion—you saw what happened this morning . . . was that only this morning?—then he runs off again." When Levi just looked at her with his patented charming Sphinx expression, she set down her teacup with a clatter. "Well? What is he doing? Where has he been? You don't even seem upset with him."

Levi shrugged. "There's nothing I can do about Schuyler's behavior at the moment, I'm afraid. Just be patient, and he'll come back to us eventually."

Frustrated, Joelle pushed away her cup and saucer. "All right. I'm going to bed. This has been a very long day, and tomorrow . . . Who knows what fires I'll have to put out, now that Mrs. Whitmore knows who T. M. Hanson is."

Twenty-Two

SOUTHERN CHIVALRY WAS ON SCHUYLER'S MIND while the world went to hell around him. He rode, brandishing a flaming torch, in the rear guard of the costumed and hooded men swarming toward the office of the *Tupelo Journal*.

This morning, when he'd updated Levi about what he'd seen so far, Levi had warned him that he'd eventually have to testify. He'd need to stay outside the violence, keeping eyes and ears open to identify participants.

But when he and Reese had arrived on horseback at the smokehouse and shouldered their way through the masked crowd inside, there was so much noise, the shadows so deep, he'd feared that identifying anyone or even recognizing individual voices might prove impossible. Shouts echoed, overlapped, grew more and more strident.

"We've got gentlewomen and children afraid for their lives and their honor!" someone yelled from behind Schuyler. "Are we going to let them live in fear, or are we going to stand up for them before some atrocity happens?"

"Now that they're in power, how do we know the Yanks won't come back down here and snatch everything away?"

"We all remember what happened during the war. Plantations burned. Women raped. Provisions stolen, crops destroyed. Businesses ruined."

"They started it! They invaded. I say burn them out before they get a stranglehold on everything."

"They're not going to let our votes count until we speak up for ourselves."

"Burn them out! Burn them out!"

The chant went up, roaring like wildfire through the little building.

To keep from drawing attention to himself, Schuyler raised his torch rhythmically and pretended to shout. Hixon stood just in front of him, with Jefcoat. He recognized the slant of Jefcoat's beefy shoulders, the left higher than the right, the result of a broken collarbone. Freshman year, their fraternity, Sigma Chi, had gotten into a brawl with Delta Kappa Epsilon. Jefcoat, more sloshed than usual, had gotten the worst of it. Schuyler himself had a white scar on his forehead, just below his hairline, from a broken bottle. What had seemed like fun at the time now struck him as the utmost in stupidity. Friendship, justice, and learning. Ha.

He watched these two men, brothers he'd once trusted with his life, lean into each other, howling with manufactured rage. As far as Schuyler knew, neither of them had ever so much as talked to a Negro for more than the time it took to request a shoe shine or a horse from the stable. Neither had served in a blue or gray uniform. Neither owned any property or was likely to, as their fathers were both hale and hearty.

And that was when he first began to realize how upside

down things had gotten. This madness, sweeping him from the building with an angry mob, out to mount waiting horses and gallop toward town, had twisted a former chivalric code into unrecognizable, almost demonic shapes. He prayed he could keep himself from being consumed.

They reached the outskirts of Tupelo, where the acknowledged leader reined in a big black gelding and raised his torch high. A tall man in black hood and cloak, whom Schuyler had yet to identify, he sat his horse with ease and authority. "Hold, men," he roared in a harsh, commanding voice obviously trained on a battlefield. "From this point we must proceed with stealth. I urge you to exert your righteous anger in precise strikes. Waste no time or effort on surrounding innocent property. Courage, men! Let each one set his hand to the plow and not look back. Let no man reserve strength that could and must be utterly spent alongside his brothers. Let us urge one another on to good works, that on the other side we may stand together in having conquered an evil enemy of the Republic!"

A roar of approval went up from the mob. Schuyler took the opportunity to lean toward Gil Reese, whose sorrel mare now shifted beside his own bay stallion. "Who is that?" he shouted. "It's not General Forrest." He would have recognized Forrest's cultured drawl among thousands. This man came from the hills, possibly Tennessee or Arkansas.

"Someone called Maney, they say. I've not met him personally. I understand Forrest requested that he come."

Senator Maney? Maybe he hadn't pulled the trigger, but Schuyler had good reason to believe this man had had his father shot in cold blood.

Sweat broke out on Schuyler's brow.

"What's the matter?" Reese asked. "You know him?"

"No, but I've heard of him." Schuyler pushed his heels into the bay's ribs and let out a whoop. "Come on, let's go!"

His outcry stirred others, and the posse surged into motion.

As they rode through town, Schuyler kept Maney in sight. Now that the time for action had arrived, only the pounding of horses' hooves on packed dirt streets broke the eerie quiet. Up Main Street the mob clattered, torches blazing, past the church and hotels, past the rail station and the taverns, then around the turn toward the newspaper office and bookstore. To Schuyler's endless surprise, not a single townsperson opened a window or door, no candles or lamps burned, in curiosity as to the intent of these midnight invaders.

By the time they reached the brick building housing the *Journal*, Schuyler had moved up to the front of the crowd, riding on Maney's left flank. The general-turned-senator slowed his mount, pulling to one side and forming his riders in a deep arch that spread all the way across the street. Lifting his torch, he addressed the crowd with a single word. "Attack!"

Quietly swinging behind the leader, Schuyler watched the row of men in the front—Jefcoat, Hixon, and Reese among them—boil from their horses, torches and weapons of all description flailing about. Metal pipes, hoes and rakes, broom handles, axes—all became tools of destruction, breaking the front windows and door in a fierce assault. Once the first few men broke into the office, the remainder of the mob dismounted and followed with a combined shout. Order became anarchy.

Schuyler realized he couldn't have moved if he'd wanted

to. This display of terrorism paralyzed him in a way that the beating he'd suffered hadn't touched. He was here, he'd seen it, he couldn't unsee it. But he could keep worse from happening, maybe.

Nudging his horse closer to the former senator, he pitched his voice just loud enough to be heard over the sounds of shattering glass, splintering wood, the horrible metallic noise of the printing press wrenching apart. "Senator Maney, a word."

Maney's head jerked around, the eyeholes of his hood spectral in the flickering light. After a startled moment, he said, "Who are you?"

Then he had the right person. Schuyler wouldn't have said he was glad, but at least he knew how to proceed. "Schuyler Beaumont."

There was another silence, a longer one. "Related to—"

"Ezekiel Beaumont was my father. I'm the younger son, something of a free agent."

"What does that mean? What are you doing here?"

"The same as you, I imagine. Trying to right some wrongs." Schuyler let that assertion simmer, then said, "And I've earned the trust of General Forrest, if that tells you anything. I know you're looking for Lemuel Frye, and I know where he's hiding."

"I have no idea what you're talking about. And I don't know Senator Maney. At least, I know who he is, but he's most likely at his home in East Tennessee. I certainly don't recognize the name Lemuel Frye nor care why or where he's hiding." Maney—or whoever he was—signaled his horse to move.

Schuyler grabbed the reins. "Wait. I understand your reluctance to take my word. But ask Forrest about me. And if you decide you want to know Frye's whereabouts, send word through Kenard Hixon. I'll arrange to meet you."

The big man laughed. "I'll give you credit for a lot of nerve, young man. Now let go of my reins before I put a bullet hole in your arm."

Realizing there was indeed a pistol aimed at his shoulder, Schuyler released the man's horse and executed a mocking salute. "At your command, sir." Giving the bay his heels, he wheeled and cantered off into the darkness, halfway expecting at any moment to be taken down by a bullet in his back.

He was almost 100 percent certain that man was Alonzo Maney. Whoever he was, he certainly knew Schuyler's father. And he was a very forceful, dangerous, and influential man.

Now that Schuyler had actually talked to him, his dread oddly diminished. He knew he could not relax his guard. But a known enemy held less power. Perhaps there was hope that he might come out of this snarl with his life and reputation intact.

Joelle sat up in bed with a start. It was broad daylight, the sun streaming with obscene cheerfulness through the crack between the drawn curtains. Some noise had awakened her, but she saw nothing immediately amiss.

She had been awake, still writing, when the sun cleared the eastern treeline, and she'd fallen into bed at last, eyes grainy and body achy and weary, shortly after that. She glanced at the notebook on her bedside table next to the guttered candle. If she was doomed to insomnia for the rest of her life, at least there might be a novel to show for it one day.

Then the noise came again, a shower of plinks against the

windowpane. Someone was throwing pebbles at her window. Only one person would do something so nonsensical and unnecessary.

Scrambling out of bed, she snagged her robe off the bedpost and yanked it on over her nightdress. She jerked the curtains open, squinting against the onslaught of sunshine. "Why didn't you just come to the front door and knock like a normal person?"

Schuyler leaned on the open windowsill. "They wouldn't wake you up, and I needed to talk to you." He was hatless, his hair a wild and uncharacteristic mess. His clothes looked like they'd been unearthed from the bottom of the rummage bin at church. The bruises on his face were now a livid purple, and he smelled distinctly horsey.

A host of excoriating remarks lined up on her tongue, but she was so relieved to see him that she found herself unable to respond in an appropriately irate fashion. "Where have you been?"

"Out and about." He gestured in the direction of town. "Reese said you ended the engagement. Is that true?"

"When did you talk to Gil?"

"Last night. There was a . . . man thing in town. He was there, I was there, it's not important. But I wanted to hear it from you. Are you upset?" His eyes were red-rimmed, but they were steady on her face. He seemed to care about her answer.

She moderated her tone in the direction of nonchalance. "I'm fine, just really tired. I couldn't sleep last night. You either?"

He rubbed his hand over a chin bristling with blond stubble. "Yes. I mean no. I'm sorry I woke you up—I was just worried. Did you hear about the newspaper office?"

"How could I? I just woke—"

"Oh, right. Well, there's been a break-in at the *Journal* office. Some mob destroyed the press and wrote awful things on the walls. I know you like Mr. McCanless, so I thought you'd want to see what you could do for him."

Joelle stared at Schuyler. "Broke in? Destroyed the press?" How could she comprehend such a thing? "That's—that's—I don't know what to say! *Why?* Mr. McCanless is such a nice man! Who would do such a thing?"

"Someone who doesn't like the things he's been printing since the new legislature took office. An article by someone named Hanson apparently hit a nerve with the Klan, and it's pretty obvious they're behind this attack."

Feeling the blood drain from her face, Joelle dropped to her knees. "Oh no. No no no."

"Joelle? Don't faint! I'm sorry, I shouldn't have sprung that on you, but I wouldn't have thought—"

A roaring sound filled her ears, and the next thing she knew, Schuyler was inside the room. She lay across his knees with her head cradled in the crook of his arm, and he was dripping water from the basin onto her forehead with a washcloth.

"Are you all right? I'm so sorry!" He dropped the cloth into the basin.

She blinked up at him. "I'm T. M. Hanson."

"I'm going to get ThomasAnne. You're delirious."

"No, I'm—I really wrote those articles." She struggled to sit up, swiping away the water dripping down her face. "Mr. McCanless said he wouldn't tell anybody it was me, but somehow Mrs. Whitmore found out, and she went right to Gil . . . What? Why are you looking at me like that?"

"So that's what Reese meant. He said something about the newspaper being caught up in trouble, right after he mentioned your speech in church, but I didn't have any reason to connect the two." Under his breath he called Gil a very uncomplimentary name. "He knew you were in danger, but he decided to hang you out in the wind and run for the hills."

She sighed. "That is *the* most mixed metaphor I've ever heard. Never mind. I knew what I was getting into when I wrote those pieces. I didn't think about anyone retaliating against the newspaper itself, though. Not physically, anyway." She put her hands to her face, sick all over again. "Sky, it's just words. Words on a page."

His mouth was grim. "Words on a page started a revolution back in 1776, remember."

"I suppose you have a point."

"Of course I do. And I'm serious—you are in big danger. If that Whitmore woman knows you're the author of those articles, the whole town knows by now. I wish you'd told me." He looked more hurt than angry.

"You told me not to—"

"I know. I already told you I'm an idiot." He looked around uneasily. "And I'm in your bedroom. I'm going to climb back out, and we'll pretend this conversation never happened." He got to his feet. "You didn't tell anybody about the bathhouse, did you?"

Should she lie to him? The silence went on too long. "I might have told ThomasAnne."

His blue-gray eyes widened. "Joelle! I'm going to have to marry you and make an honest woman of you! Which is criminal, since I never even got the benefit—"

She grabbed the washcloth out of the basin and threw it at his head.

He caught it, laughing, and slung one leg over the windowsill. "Don't leave the house without one of the men with you. I mean it."

"Where are you going to be?"

"I have a short trip to make. But I'll be back before you can say 'I'm a loose woman.'"

"I am not! Wait, Schuyler!"

"What?" He paused, looking impatient.

"Levi told me to write an article, announcing your candidacy for Congress. I have some questions."

"I'm a little busy right now," he said. "We'll do that some other time."

He disappeared, and she had to content herself with cursing his birthright as she mopped up the water he'd slopped all over the floor. He came and went whenever he pleased, leaving her lonesome and anxious and . . . itchy. A very dissatisfactory state of affairs.

Twenty-Three

SCHUYLER LEFT THE MANAGER'S COTTAGE and took the path through the garden to the back porch of the main house, sifting through his priorities as he went. He'd been a fool to think talking to Joelle would ease his mind.

When he'd told Levi he would attempt to lure Harold Moore out of Itawamba County, he'd had no idea Joelle was so deeply embedded in this snarl. Now he was forced to leave her unprotected for two days, while that bunch of vampires roamed the countryside, burning and crushing anyone who opposed their agenda. Levi insisted he'd left enough manpower established on the hotel property to keep the women safe. Still, he couldn't help worrying.

Also if Maney tried to contact Schuyler while he was on the road, the opportunity to infiltrate that top ring might be lost. Time was of the essence, but conferring with Hixon before he left was critical; if Hixon was conscious, he would most likely be found in the informal breakfast room.

Approaching the house, he found Mose sitting on the back

porch steps with Wyatt, both of them occupied in cleaning hunting rifles.

Wyatt grinned and laid his gun across his knees. "Morning, Mr. Schuyler! You just now up and around?"

"Always a day late and a dollar short," he replied lazily. "Any sign of Hixon and Jefcoat this morning?"

Mose removed his pipe from his mouth on a fragrant puff of smoke. "Yes, sir. They both inside, having a bite of breakfast. A big bite. One of the maids just took in another tray of biscuits." He grinned. "Miss Selah say she'll be glad to see the back of those two—they eating us out of house and home!"

Schuyler rubbed the back of his neck. "Hixon can put away some food. At least when he's not suffering a hangover."

"Sounded to me like there might be one of those involved too," Mose said. "Mr. Jefcoat seems to be over the worst of it."

Sighing, Schuyler continued up the steps. "Y'all going hunting, or already been? Wish I could go with you."

"We got a couple of nice coons and a wild hog last night." Wyatt pointed at the smokehouse. "Already got 'em dressed and drying. We'll go again tonight, if you want to join us."

"I'm headed over to Itawamba County in a little bit. Needed to talk to Hixon before I go. But I'll take you up on it when I get back." Comforted at the thought of those two competent gun handlers standing guard over the hotel, Schuyler opened the screen door, calling out as he entered the breezeway, "Selah! Aurora! Anybody home?"

"In here, Schuyler," came Aurora's voice from the breakfast room. "Selah took Levi to the depot in town. There's plenty left, if you're hungry."

"No, there's not," Hixon said around a mouthful of biscuit as Schuyler walked in. "Go get your own."

Schuyler took a cup off the buffet, poured it full of steaming black coffee, and stood blowing on it to cool it. He couldn't talk Klan business in front of the women. Besides Aurora and Hixon, Delfina Fabio, Poldi Volker, and both Forrests sat at the table.

The general looked well rested, perfectly groomed, and sated as a hound gnawing on a clean rib bone. He toasted Schuyler facetiously with his coffee cup. "Another of the younger set has arisen from the dead, I see. Us older and wiser heads have managed to obtain a full night's sleep!"

Schuyler took that to mean Forrest knew about the previous night's activity but disassociated himself by remaining at the hotel. He caught Jefcoat's eye, noting the unshaven chin and general air of post-debauchery. "How are you feeling? Mose said you'd been ill."

Jefcoat belched. "Who?"

"Never mind. I see you're in your usual health." Schuyler frowned at Hixon. "Kenard, if you're done with breakfast, there's something I need to show you in the stable."

"You only call me Kenard when you want something." Hixon reached for the preserves. "I think I'll stay here."

Ignoring Aurora's giggle, Schuyler set down his coffee with a rattle of porcelain. "Since I've been footing the bill for your room and board for several days, I think you owe me a few minutes of your precious time."

"Good Lord, what a bear it is before noon." Heaving a put-upon sigh, Hixon got up, grabbing another biscuit, and ambled out of the room.

"Excuse us both." With a quick apologetic bow in the direction of the ladies, Schuyler followed Hixon out onto the porch. Acknowledging Mose's and Wyatt's curious looks with a nod, Schuyler hustled Hixon back through the garden, past the pagoda and icehouse, then on around to the stable.

"Slow down, you barbarian," Hixon panted. "You're ruining my digestion."

"*You* ruined your digestion, breaking in to destroy a man's property while he slept." Schuyler jerked open the stable door and shoved Hixon in ahead of him. "I may not be able to eat again for a week."

"Are you still angry about the beating? You wanted in, remember?"

"I'm not angry about the beating, and I did want in. But what if the other side broke into *your* business and took an ax to it? Oh, that's right. You don't have a business. You just ride all over Mississippi, cadging off other people's food and liquor."

Hixon leaned against the wall, looking genuinely hurt and puzzled. "If I remember correctly, you were right there with me, riding and cadging. Now you get up on your high horse and try to make me feel bad that *my* old man doesn't—didn't fund my ventures like yours does—did, I mean."

Reminding himself that he needed this pathetic numbskull, at least for the moment, Schuyler moderated his sarcasm. "I'm sorry. You're right. For the record, I'm trying to live up to my old man's expectations and example. But I do need a favor from you, if you can manage it."

"Of course, just name it," Hixon said as if he were making some great sacrifice.

"Can you keep this just between us?"

"Don't insult me. Mum as an oyster."

Schuyler laughed. "All right. It's just that this is very sensitive. I have to leave Tupelo for a couple of days, and I'm expecting a message from a man who's very high up in the order—probably at least a Grand Titan. I told him he could reach me through you. If he does, I need you to take the message and hold it until I get back."

"You won't trust me with his name?"

"He didn't give me his name."

Hixon blinked. "Then how will I know—"

"You'll know. Just keep any messages that come for me without explanation or identification. Please, Kenard, this is life-and-death important."

Hixon nodded. "I understand. You want me to stay here?"

"Yes." Schuyler hesitated. "Hixon . . . Have you ever seen General Forrest attend one of the meetings?"

"Not since we've been here."

"But he did in other locations?"

"Maybe. I'm not sure. As you said, everyone is always masked, so it's hard to identify anyone."

"That's true." Schuyler took a close look at Hixon's vacant face. The boy might be an alcoholic slob, but he had also been a loyal friend for a long time. If Schuyler himself had made radical changes in his life, wasn't it possible that Hixon could be encouraged to make better choices as well? But what could he say in five minutes that would make any possible difference? Sighing, he whacked Hixon's thick shoulder. "Thanks for your help, old man." He swung toward the door, then hesitated, looking back at Hixon. "You'd tell me if you knew of something bad about to happen, wouldn't you?"

"Bad? What do you mean by bad?"

"Bad, as in something that would hurt the people I love. I'd appreciate it if you'd keep an eye on Joelle. She means a lot to me."

"The tall redhead?" Hixon's eyes went wide. "I'm not getting near her. She scares me. Can't understand half what she says."

Schuyler laughed. "Same here, brother. But watch her anyway. I don't want her getting in trouble."

He had to hurry. He'd forgotten to grab food for the trip while he was in the house, so he'd have to stop by the kitchen after all. Horatia could be counted on to load him up with biscuits and salt pork.

Women did like him, which was a comforting thought. Maybe Joelle did too. She was indubitably a woman.

Joelle took her time putting the room to rights. As she made the bed, her thoughts bounced from Schuyler's sudden appearance, to his information about the destruction of Mr. McCanless's office, and back again. He was gone again, leaving her to deal with the aftermath of his energy. It was like standing in an electrical storm, then trying to explain why she hadn't just gone indoors to get out of it. Perhaps she was crazy after all.

She walked to the mirror and tried to see what he saw. Masses of red-blonde hair twisted into a sleep-mussed braid hanging over one shoulder. Faded floral robe that had definitely seen better days, hanging over long, skinny bare feet. Puffy blue eyes and a pillow crease on one cheek. Oh dear. No wonder he'd left town.

Laughing at herself, she unwound the braid and picked up her hairbrush.

As for the newspaper situation, T. M. Hanson had stirred up a hornet's nest, and people were getting stung. Her instinct was to drive to town and see for herself, maybe try to help. But what if that just made things worse? And what could she do, anyway? She didn't know how to fix a printing press.

Suddenly depressed, she looked at the hasty, crooked knot she'd fashioned at the top of her head and decided it would have to do. Clothes. One had to wear clothes. By the time she'd dressed in a clean brown skirt and one of her ubiquitous white blouses, then shoved her feet into the first pair of shoes she found under her bed, it was nearly eleven o'clock. Breakfast at the big house would be over by now. But Horatia always kept food warm in the kitchen for the hotel workmen and maids.

She headed that way. Her students would soon arrive for their noontime lessons, but she would have time to find something to eat and prepare the schoolroom if she hurried.

She'd made it as far as the kitchen garden when one of Schuyler's friends—she never could keep their names straight in her mind—fell into step with her, coming from the direction of the stable.

She smiled at him. "Good morning, Mr. . . . Jefcoat?"

"Hixon," he corrected her, though he didn't seem offended. Rather, he seemed a bit rattled. His button-brown eyes skated above her head, to one ear and then the other.

When he said nothing further, she made an effort at conversation. "Did you sleep well last night? I hope you've been comfortable here at Daughtry House." He wasn't precisely a guest, but Schuyler would expect her to be kind to his particular friend.

"What? No, I—That is, I had adequate rest. And Daughtry House is very comfortable. The food is excellent."

"Horatia will be happy to hear that. I'll tell her. Have a

295

good day." She was about to escape into the kitchen, but Hixon took her by the elbow. She looked down at his hand in surprise. "I'm sorry—did you need something else?"

"Could I—could I come with you?"

Oh no. Not another one. Somehow, without the least effort on her part, men took to staring at her and following her around. And she'd just got rid of Gil. Still, she didn't want to hurt this one.

She bit her lip. "Yes, but I'm just going to get a biscuit and then teach some students for a couple of hours. I don't imagine that would interest you."

"But it would! I never was very good at spelling, and Schuyler says you're a brilliant teacher."

"He does?" That Schuyler had spoken well of her did something to her outlook on the day. A real smile took over her face. "In that case, come along. I think I have an extra speller or two in the schoolroom."

Looking as if he'd grabbed the tail end of a snake, he gave her a jerky nod and accompanied her into the kitchen.

The room was warm and aromatic with lunch preparations, instantly making Joelle's salivary glands come alive. Something in a big cast-iron pot bubbled on the stove, Horatia stood at the sink peeling potatoes, and a couple of kitchen maids prepared vegetables at the big worktable. Charmion sat in a chair by the fire, hulling a bowl of strawberries balanced on her large belly. All the women looked up at her entrance with welcoming smiles, followed by clear dismay as soon as they recognized her companion.

"This is Mr. Hixon," Joelle said offhandedly, as though bringing a guest into one of the work buildings were an everyday occurrence. "He wanted to sit in on the lessons, but I missed breakfast, so I thought I'd come through here before we go to the schoolroom."

Horatia recovered first. "Certainly, Miss Joelle. Here's a basket of biscuits still warm on the stove. Would you like butter and preserves?"

Before she could answer, Hixon blurted, "I would, ma'am. Those are the best fig preserves I've had since my grandma died."

Horatia's rare smile appeared. "I'm happy to hear that, sir. Would you be the reason I had to make three batches of biscuits this morning?"

Hixon blushed and patted his round stomach. "I'm afraid so."

Shortly Joelle and Hixon sat at the table with the two Negresses—one a decade older than Horatia, the other barely sixteen—who introduced themselves as Miriam and Freddy. Cowed by the young white man's presence, they both lapsed into tongue-tied silence.

If Charmion was intimidated, she didn't show it. Giving Joelle her friendly smile, she continued to deftly wield her paring knife and talk at the same time. "I finished hemming your new dress last night, Joelle. I brought it with me this morning, thinking you might want to try it on. That way, if something needs to be adjusted, there will be time before the party on Friday."

"Of course!" Joelle wiped her mouth with the napkin Horatia had provided. "I can't wait to see it. I'll finish lessons by two this afternoon. Will you still be here?"

"Yes. We'll be baking and preparing food for the next few days. Besides, Mama wants me to stay close while Nathan's working, in case the baby decides to come early." Charmion laughed. "We all know first babies are slow to arrive, but I can't convince them not to hover."

"I think that's a good idea." Turning to smile at Horatia, Joelle happened to catch the expression on Hixon's face. He seemed taken aback by the prosaic, intimate nature of the conversation between her and her employees. "Mr. Hixon, do you have any particular requests for the meal on Friday? We want everyone to go away raving about the service, entertainment, and victuals."

He blinked, closed his mouth. "I don't like opera, but I really like potato salad," he said, then took refuge in fig preserves.

All the women laughed, and Joelle applied herself to finishing her own breakfast. "I'll come through here later and try on the dress," she told Charmion as she took the empty dishes to the sink to rinse them. "Come, Mr. Hixon, I hear the other students in the schoolroom. You've brought this on yourself, there's no sense putting it off!"

Pushing through the connecting door, she stopped so abruptly that her new tutee plowed into her from behind.

"Excuse me!" Hixon bleated. "What's the matter?"

Pushing him back into the kitchen, Joelle followed, closing the door behind her. "I'm afraid it won't be convenient for you to join our lessons today," she said firmly. "Maybe tomorrow."

"Why?" He frowned. "You said—"

"I know, and I'm sorry, but one of the men is . . . sick. You really don't want to be in the schoolroom right now." She gave Horatia a warning glance, then Charmion. They both subsided, hiding alarm.

"Sick? How do you know?"

"Mr. Hixon, do you really want me to go into detail?"

He paled. "Never mind. I'll just wait for you outside."

"You don't have to do that."

"Beaumont told me to."

"He what?"

"He asked me to watch out for you. He's paying me."

She took an aggravated, disbelieving breath. "I'll pay you *not* to watch me. Mr. Hixon, I don't have time for this. I'm very busy, and I can't have you following me all over the place. If it will make you feel better, I have a gun and I know how to use it."

His eyes bugged. "You have a gun?"

"Yes. My brother-in-law gave it to me and taught me to handle it. Do you want me to show you?"

"No. No, no. That actually doesn't surprise me. I told Beaumont you were terrifying." He took a step backward. "Just—please don't tell him I abandoned you. He'd horse-whip me or something worse."

"All right, I promise."

"Good. But I'll be in the big house if you need anything."

"Fine. Thank you. Have a lovely afternoon," she said as he bowed and exited the kitchen.

"What was that all about?" Charmion set aside her bowl of strawberries.

Joelle shook her head. "Who is that strange man in the schoolroom?"

Horatia poked her head through the schoolroom door, gasped, and went in, shutting the door smartly behind her. After a few moments of muted conversation, she came back and took off her apron. "Miss Joelle, come and let me introduce you to Mr. Frye."

299

Twenty-Four

THAT AFTERNOON, TIRED, SORE, AND HUNGRY, Schuyler dismounted at the west side of the Beene's Ferry crossing of the Tombigbee River. He hoped he wouldn't have to wait long for the ferry to come for him. Tremont was another ten miles on the east side of the river, where he hoped to find the freedman Harold Moore and somehow convince the man to return to Tupelo. Three rain showers along the way had slowed him down some, but he'd taken only the necessary time to water and rest the horse. Otherwise, he'd pushed himself, eating in the saddle, enduring the jouncing of his wounded back because there was no other choice. Itawamba County had yet to connect to larger towns by rail, though the Tombigbee remained an important waterway for that part of the state.

After blowing the cow's horn hanging from a tree branch near the landing to summon the ferry, he set the horse to drink from the trough left for that purpose, then stood watching the water roll south on its way to the Mobile River. Reared on the Gulf Coast and steeped in the shipping industry, Schuyler had once considered investing in steamboats. Over the past few years, as his interest shifted to rail travel and transport, he'd matured enough to understand that the depressed Southern economy might never recover enough to make branch railroads a viable reality. Funny how circumstances had turned his wanderlust to dreams of establishing a quality hotel in small-town north Mississippi.

Funny how a red-haired girl anchored him to that small town. Insane how impatient he was to get back to her.

He turned to look back in the direction from which he'd traveled today. For the last hour or so he'd imagined someone followed him. Several times he'd turned, thinking he heard hoofbeats behind him, but no one caught up or crossed his path. The riverfront was quiet, had been so since Schuyler arrived. It seemed odd that he'd seen no sign of the ferry, but perhaps the operator would return shortly.

He wasn't good at waiting, but he had nothing else to do. He turned the horse loose to graze and sat down on a fallen tree trunk. Pulling out his pocketknife, he stripped a twig off the trunk and started to whittle it into a point. He had an uncle who could take such a tiny piece of wood and turn it into a rooster. The artistic bent, however, had somehow skipped his generation. Neither he nor Jamie could carve anything but useful tools like pointed sticks that could be fashioned into animal traps.

Ten more minutes went by, during which he planned what he would say to Joelle if he ever got up the courage to admit to her that he loved her to an embarrassing degree and would appreciate it if she'd lower her dignity enough to marry him. He had just about decided there were no words in the dictionary adequate to such an unlikely occasion, when he heard the distinct sound of hoofbeats coming from the west.

There *had* been somebody following him. He went to his horse and took his rifle from its holster, checking to make sure it was loaded and ready to fire.

A few seconds later a rider on a roan mare emerged from the woods and galloped toward him.

Schuyler lowered the rifle. "Jefcoat!" he roared. "You're lucky I didn't shoot a hole through your empty head. What are you doing here? Why didn't you tell me you were coming?"

Jefcoat reined his horse down to a trot, then a walk. He didn't seem disturbed by Schuyler's anger. "It was a last-minute decision. The general sent me after you."

Schuyler walked toward Jefcoat. "Why?"

Jefcoat dismounted. "Let me water this nag, then I'll explain."

Schuyler was forced to wait while Jefcoat loosened his mount's girth and led her to the trough to drink. Finally he looped the reins around a low-hanging tree branch and left the horse to graze.

Squatting in the shade where Schuyler had been sitting earlier, Jefcoat grinned up at him. "You don't look glad to see me."

"I'm frankly puzzled. I can't think of any reason the general would need me. I'm on an errand related to the hotel." That wasn't precisely true, but it was close enough.

"Well, sit down. It's a little complicated."

Schuyler wouldn't have used the word "complicated" in any connection with Andrew Jefcoat. In fact, he had to think for a second to even come up with his given name. Jefcoat came from a farming family somewhere in northeast Mississippi. The triumvirate—he, Hixon, and Jefcoat—had become friendly during Sigma Chi's freshman hazing week, and had from that point on done their best to drink their way through every tavern, ale house, and saloon in Mississippi.

But there had been little personal connection. Jefcoat possessed a sense of humor, or Schuyler would have long since ditched him. However, he would not have ascribed critical thinking or philosophical depth to his hairy, six-foot-tall, thickly built friend. Jefcoat loved beer, steak, dogs, and big-bosomed women, in roughly that order. He couldn't even remember what Jefcoat had studied at Ole Miss. Law? Possibly, though he couldn't imagine a judge or jury taking this inarticulate redneck seriously.

"I'll stand," Schuyler said, just to be obstinate. "I'm waiting for the ferry to come across."

"It's not coming."

"What do you mean, it's not coming?" Schuyler squinted across the sparkling river. "How would you know that?"

"Let's just say the general wanted to make sure you didn't get to Tremont."

Real alarm jangled through Schuyler. "Jefcoat, what are you doing?"

"I wish you'd sit down. That's the thing about you, Beaumont. You think the world revolves around you. That nobody else has a viable opinion, nobody else has an idea worth pursuing."

For the first time maybe ever, Schuyler looked right into Jefcoat's eyes—past the indeterminate color, into a soul riddled with resentment—and realized that his friend had just spoken a hard truth to him. He dropped to squat on his heels. "I wish you'd told me that a long time ago, Jefcoat. I don't know, maybe I wouldn't have listened. But I want you to know that my father's death has changed me, changed my priorities, changed—everything."

"Your father." A sour smile twitched up the side of Jefcoat's bearded mouth. "Rail baron, financial pillar of the Confederacy. Yet he still managed to come out rich on the other side of the war. Explain to me how that happens, Beaumont, outside of corruption? *My* father lost everything. Property, slaves, livestock, all of it. The Yankees stripped the plantation of every bit of food we had, tore up the machinery, then burned down the house. The only way I managed to finish college was through the generosity of one of his commanders, who saw something useful in me."

"Useful? Meaning a tool for revenge?"

Jefcoat shrugged. "Revenge is part of it. But pride and independence mean everything. It makes me sick to see our conquerors come down here and take what we built. They throw us out of office, refuse to let us grow our economy back in the only way we know how. They let stupid, ignorant Negroes lord over us. And people like your father, caving in and licking their boots, make it worse!" More than general disgruntlement laced those words. Real acrimony simmered in Jefcoat's eyes.

Suddenly something bubbled to the surface of Schuyler's memory. He lurched to his feet. "Where were you all day, the day of the opera?"

"You know where I was."

He suspected he did but hoped to heaven he was wrong. Jefcoat had met him and Hixon in Memphis that night, arriving at the opera house after the start of the performance. "Were you in Tuscaloosa?"

Jefcoat smiled. "Everybody thinks you're so smart, engineering and physics and mathematics, all that. But you're really stupid about people, Beaumont. You don't pay attention to what's right under your nose."

Schuyler heard a metallic click behind his head. He turned his head to find the mouth of a pistol at his temple. Looking up, he saw a small-framed black man in nondescript clothing holding the gun. "Hello, Mr. Moore. This is a happy coincidence, since I came all this way to talk to you. And since the ferry doesn't seem to be available, it's a good thing you already crossed the river."

The Negro smiled. "Don't get too chipper, Mr. Beaumont. You not gon' live to enjoy the rest of the day."

One gift he knew he'd been blessed with was talking, and Schuyler figured he'd better make use of it right now. "Jefcoat, you have been my friend for a long time, and I've kept you out of jail enough times that you owe me a chance to change your mind about what is looking to be one of the worst decisions you've made in your life."

"I dunno," Jefcoat said. "I've thought this situation through pretty carefully, and I believe I've got the clear advantage here. Put your hands behind your back."

Schuyler didn't move. "You realize people in Tupelo know where I am. They'll come looking for me if I don't come back by tomorrow night."

"You'll be dead by then," Jefcoat said matter-of-factly, "and I'll be long gone."

"My future brother-in-law is a Pinkerton detective. You think he won't make the connection?"

Jefcoat snorted. "You can't have a brother-in-law if you don't live to get married."

"You seem overly obsessed with my early demise." Schuyler

looked up at the gun again. "Would you mind moving that, Mr. Moore? I'm getting a little concerned that it might go off."

Moore's lips tightened. "Since he's paying me and you're not, I think I'll leave it where it is."

"That explains a lot. I suppose everything ultimately comes down to money. I wondered what would make a freedman turn on his brothers as you have done. I saw you in that courtroom, Moore, accusing Frye and Perkins and Thomas of beating you and setting fire to the livery stable. Who really put those marks on your back? Was it my erstwhile friend here? Did he threaten to do it again if you failed to help him in this crime?"

"Shut up, Beaumont, you don't know what you're talking about as usual. I don't have to beat people to make them do right. And I don't have to pay them off." Jefcoat lunged for Schuyler, pushed him face forward to the ground, and shoved a knee into his back.

"But murdering one of your best friends isn't beneath you?" Still trying to catch his breath, Schuyler found his hands cuffed.

With the toe of his boot, Jefcoat flipped Schuyler onto his back and looked down at him dispassionately. "I don't think that's going to be necessary. I'll just dump you in the river, and that should take care of it."

Panic wouldn't help. Schuyler gathered himself to act, made himself think. "Before you do that, you should know you'd be drowning a piece of information the general has spent a considerable amount of time and effort looking for. I know where Lemuel Frye is."

Both Jefcoat and Moore froze.

"Let him up," Jefcoat said.

Moore hauled Schuyler to his feet, then backed off with the gun still leveled.

Schuyler stood swaying, trying to regain his balance with his hands behind his back. The horse was too far away. His knife was in his boot, and he couldn't reach it. He'd even dropped the pointed stick he'd been whittling.

Jefcoat eyed him belligerently. "Where's Frye? It won't do any good to lie—"

"Never mind that," Moore interrupted. "I want to know where my sister is."

Finding a place to stash Mr. and Mrs. Frye turned out to be a bit more complicated than anyone could have foreseen.

"Who is looking for him?" had been Joelle's first question after she was introduced to the frail, mild-eyed schoolteacher. He had obviously been born a white man, but his skin had been darkened to make him look like a Negro from a distance.

Horatia wasn't really sure. "We've been hiding him with Reverend Boykin in Shake Rag," she said. "But after Mr. Schuyler came to visit—"

"Wait. Schuyler was there? When?" Joelle leaned against her desk. Her knees felt wobbly after the close call with Hixon nearly following her into the schoolroom.

"Yesterday," said Shug. "He came to our afternoon prayer meeting and stayed for supper."

That did not sound like Schuyler at all. "Schuyler came to a *prayer meeting*?"

"Yes, ma'am. Sure did."

"Do you know what happened to his back?"

Shug and Horatia looked at one another.

"He didn't tell you?" Horatia asked.

"There seems to be a lot he hasn't told me. Never mind, we'll get to his injuries in a minute. You were about to tell me what happened after he came to visit y'all yesterday."

Horatia nodded. "He told us the Klan is spoiling for another showdown of some sort, and he's afraid it might come back to Shake Rag. We all decided our village might not be the safest place after all for such an important witness. So we brought him here to see if you could find somewhere else to hide him and his wife."

Joelle had stared at Frye, who just blinked at her from behind his glasses. Who *was* this man?

Things only got more complicated when she met Georgia Frye. A lifetime of established taboos roared to the surface. There simply was no road map to tell her how to navigate this strange new world in which she found herself. Education was one thing, but interracial marriage seemed both bizarre and unnecessarily dangerous. She couldn't help wondering if Horatia had some of the same reservations, considering her previous objections to her daughter marrying the ebony-skinned Nathan Vincent.

There was no time to worry about it now, though. Georgia was easy to disguise as a kitchen maid hired for the party preparations. Nobody would take a second look at her, but Frye himself presented a trickier problem. He seemed neither fish nor fowl—a well-mannered white man with no trade besides that of educator, he would not pass for a servant, but because he was hunted, could not openly live in the hotel as a guest. She could hide him in one of the outbuildings— the icehouse or even the bathhouse, for example—but some guest would inevitably walk in on him, as Hixon had nearly done this morning.

Trying to get to the root of the problem, Joelle sat down with Frye at the kitchen table and listened to his account of the couple's harrowing odyssey from Chattanooga to Memphis to Tupelo. "Believe me when I say I understand your passion for teaching," she said when he'd finished his tale. "I've been exploring ways to keep my little school afloat amidst the lack of funds and supplies, not to mention the opposition of my neighbors. But help me understand your reluctance to leave the South. You could travel west, perhaps find a homestead to develop, where you and your family would be safe and you could found a school with little to no drama."

"Of course we've discussed that very thing, many times." Frye glanced at his wife, who quietly helped knead and shape bread dough into loaves across the room. "But as I told Mr. Beaumont, I have proof of certain federal crimes that my conscience will not let me ignore. I am waiting for these men to be brought to trial by the authorities so that I may testify. Until then, United States Marshals have tried to protect me with only moderate success. Twice I've barely escaped with my life. My wife's own brother is one of their pawns and can most certainly identify us both. If he discovers where I am this time . . ." Looking troubled, he shook his head. "I don't think we'd survive another attack. Mr. Riggins said if we began to suspect Shake Rag was no longer safe, we should apply to you. Miss Daughtry, these are very dangerous men, and I deeply regret putting you and your family in peril. I simply don't know where else to turn."

"Of course you did the right thing. I wish Schuyler were

here . . . but he isn't, so we'll just have to improvise. Levi will be back by Wednesday. Until then I'm going to put you in my own room in the manager's cottage. No one would think to invade my private space."

Georgia Frye turned, looking horrified. "No, Miss Daughtry, we could never—"

"Yes. You could, and you will. I insist. Otherwise, I couldn't live with myself. I'll just make up a bed here in the kitchen by the fire. I've slept here many times while the cottage was being renovated."

Frye frowned. "But what if someone comes in here early and discovers you sleeping here? Won't they consider that odd?"

"I assure you," Joelle said dryly, "this is by far one of the least odd things I've done in my life. No one will think a thing about it. Now tell me how I can get in touch with the Missionary Society about securing a qualified teacher for our school."

Twenty-Five

"BEAUMONT, IF YOU DON'T SHUT YOUR TRAP, I'm going to gag you." Crouching to remove a stone from one of his mount's shoes, Jefcoat looked over his shoulder, a scowl making a straight line out of his thick dark eyebrows. He had become increasingly taciturn during the long ride back to Tupelo, which Schuyler took as a sign of both distrust and irritation.

Schuyler, forced to ride with his hands now in front of him, manacled to the saddle horn, had been allowed to dismount and stretch his legs. He grinned at his erstwhile tavern crawl companion. "I could always sing instead, if that would encourage a more cheerful disposition."

Jefcoat snarled and turned back to the task at hand.

During the previous two hours of necessarily slow travel, Schuyler had used the time to engage his Negro captor in conversation. Besides the fact that information could generally be weaponized, he was genuinely curious about the unnatural alliance between a former slave and a demonstrably racist farm boy.

Tidbits he'd uncovered included the fact that, antebellum, Moore had risen to the position of overseer on the Jefcoat plantation. At the end of the war, he had been hired as a contractual agent between Jefcoat Senior and the labor needed to resume cotton production. Predictably, the freedman's incentive to work for pennies on the dollar made Moore's task both thankless and difficult. Still, his position was more desirable than the abject poverty of most of his peers. He had a tidy home, steady income, and little physical labor.

But Moore's internal motives interested Schuyler far more than the economics of the situation. He sensed a roiling resentment emanating from the man that superseded all logic.

"Since my friend Jefcoat doesn't seem eager for a joyful noise, Mr. Moore, perhaps you'll indulge me in a little further explanation of how your sister came to marry this white schoolteacher you seem to loathe with such evangelistic fervor. Weren't you raised in the same home?"

Moore, presently squatting on his heels, occupied in gnawing on a brick of hardtack taken from his saddlebag, gave Schuyler a scornful look. "I thought you was a Southerner. And you don't know how that works? I'm not even sure Georgia and me had the same daddy. Yes, we's in the big cabin with the other mamas and babies, but Mama was in the fields every day. When I got big enough, I went to work too. Georgia, being as pretty as she is, light-skin too, was sent to work in the house. Next thing I know she's sent to the market in Memphis, and a man from somewhere up in Tennessee bought her—at least, that's what I heard from some that came back."

"So you didn't see her again until you happened to be in Tuscaloosa at the same time?"

Moore shook his head. "No, but she'd learned to read and write somehow, and she wrote to my mother to let her know she was all right. We'd of never got those letters except Mrs. Jefcoat was a kind lady and read them to us." Moore glanced at Jefcoat, expression unreadable.

Jefcoat's shoulders lifted, and he turned his head.

"After the war," Moore continued, "my mama died, but I got a letter from Georgia saying she was in Memphis—by this time I'd learned to read myself"—his lips tightened—"and she'd married a white man."

Schuyler listened, gaze fixed on Moore's face. The rest of the story was bound to come out. He prayed Jefcoat would remain silent.

"I heard from her again," Moore said, "after they moved to Tuscaloosa. Apparently they had some kind of job as traveling schoolteachers. This new public school program funded by the government—" Jefcoat grunted as if in protest, but when he failed to comment, Moore shrugged. "I didn't expect to ever see my sister again, but two weeks ago Mr. Jefcoat sent me over to Alabama to retrieve some runaway field hands. I visited Georgia, and she seemed to be doing well. At least they was living in a cabin with four walls and a roof. That was the first time I met Frye."

"So you collected your workers all by yourself?" Schuyler gave Moore's slight frame a once-over.

"I had some help from local white men—friends of the Jefcoats." Moore glanced at Jefcoat. "Still, it took three runs across the state line to get them all. The second time, my sister's husband took matters into his own hands. I'd been sent into the Negro quarter of town to sniff out our contraband. On my way back, Frye had a bunch of local liberals waylay me and beat me."

"Are you sure it was Frye?" Schuyler asked, skeptical. "He doesn't seem the violent, coercive type to me."

"They were costumed, and it was dark, but the leader called me by name and accused me of things only my sister would know. They said I had to understand I couldn't force free men to come back to Mississippi and work under what amounted to slave conditions anymore. That if I knew what was good for me, I'd leave Alabama and never come back." Moore let out a harsh breath. "Which I confess I was ready to do. But then they offered me more money to go back for the rest—after all, those men were indentured under a legal contract—and sent along more protection. The timing was interesting, because we got to Tuscaloosa right when the rally was scheduled to start. I saw Frye in the crowd, along with the Negroes I knew from the Jefcoat plantation. I heard the speeches from Reverend Thomas and Perkins. I saw your father get shot, and I saw the riot start—but I couldn't get out of the crowd." Moore's hands were shaking. He took a handkerchief from his pocket and wiped his sweating face.

Schuyler couldn't help a certain sympathy for all the man had endured, but many of his actions seemed to have been not only greedy and self-serving, but cowardly. "I was at the hearing. I heard your claims against Frye. Some of them don't match what you just said. You told the judge you identified your attacker."

"I did!" Moore exclaimed. "I know it was him!"

"And you're dumb as a fence post," Jefcoat said suddenly. "I never did understand why my father depended on you so much. I tried to tell him I could do a better job at managing the property—which he claimed was why he sent me away to college in the first place." He flexed his big, meaty fists. "I never wanted to be sitting in a classroom. By the time I got my diploma and came back home, he'd already elevated his colored son to the overseer's house."

Schuyler, incapable at that point of coherent speech, looked from Jefcoat to Moore. He couldn't help thinking of a pair of biblical brothers fighting over their father's blessing. That had not turned out well for either brother, at least in the short run.

Jefcoat stood, his long shadow falling across Moore's smaller, folded figure. "I put those stripes on your back, you fool. You think you're so smart, but I used you to lure out the schoolteacher. None of us left with property and a name are going to stand for what's ours being ripped away by people who didn't earn it."

Schuyler stood apart, absorbed in the drama playing out in front of him. "Moore, do you know who shot my father? You said you saw it happen."

Moore shook his head. "I swear I didn't—"

"I didn't mean to kill him," Jefcoat said. His face above the beard was pasty, sweating, and his hands moved in agitated circles. "I would never shoot a white man on purpose. I was aiming at the preacher, just to scare him, but your pa moved, got in the way, and it was too late."

Schuyler stared at him. "You were in Memphis that night. With us at the opera. Drunk."

"Of course I was drunk. I got on the next train out of Tuscaloosa and found the first saloon out of the Memphis station. I never killed anybody before."

Schuyler lunged at him, manacles and all, catching Jefcoat

off guard, knocking him to the ground. The handcuffs crossed the hairy throat, pressed in, while Jefcoat's face purpled. A roaring took over Schuyler's brain as he shoved down with his wrists. The large body beneath him writhed but could not dislodge him.

"Schuyler!" someone shouted.

He ignored the voice and kept pressing.

Then he found himself wrenched sideways to the ground, several bodies holding him down. He struggled against the restraining hands, groaning in rage. "Let me go! He did it!"

Reason returned, little by little, along with vision and other senses. He recognized Levi's face above him.

He relaxed, tears leaking from the sides of his eyes. "He killed my father."

Levi, face compassionate, grim, let him go and extended a hand. "Yes. I'm sorry, brother. Come on, get up. We've got him in custody."

Taking Levi's hand, Schuyler let himself be pulled to his feet. Disoriented, he looked around and found two men he didn't recognize holding a very subdued Jefcoat by the arms. Moore stood off to the side, shaking and silent.

"Here, let's get those off you." Levi unlocked the handcuffs with a key he'd apparently gotten from Jefcoat.

"You were following me too. You didn't go to Tuscaloosa." Schuyler eyed Levi resentfully, rubbing his raw wrists. "You could have told me."

"Didn't have enough information." Levi tossed the handcuffs to one of his deputies, who proceeded to cuff Jefcoat. "We suspected Jefcoat had been in Tuscaloosa that day. A man of his description was reported at the station later. But no one saw who pulled the trigger on your father. I knew he'd follow you if I sent you this way, looking for Moore." Levi's smile was wry. "The only person I know better at getting people to blurt things out than me—is you."

"I'm glad to know I was good for something. While I was busy thinking I was about to die." Schuyler released a disgusted breath, glancing at Jefcoat and then Moore. "But am I right in thinking this thing is not exactly wrapped up? As bad as they are, those two are just pawns on the evil side of this chessboard."

"You're right. One murder solved. But we don't know who killed the judge and ordered that church to be burned. So I'm sending you on back to Tupelo to try to draw out the king, while I deliver Jefcoat and Moore to the closest federal officer. But don't worry—as soon as I do that, I'll be right behind you, watching and waiting."

At dinner that evening, in a belated attempt to practice her recently attained skill in noticing things, Joelle scanned the company seated around the formal dining table. General Forrest, Mr. Hixon, and Doc, who had been invited for the evening, were dressed in black suits with starched white shirts and black ties. The European Mr. Volker wore a more eclectic style of evening garb, his vest a miracle of gold-and-burgundy brocade, the jacket sporting matching stripes at the cuffs. The women had adorned themselves in their finest silk evening gowns, even Joelle conceding to formality by donning the dress she'd worn to the opera and allowing Aurora to style her hair in a scalp-stretching concoction of curls and braids.

She was not comfortable by any means, but at least she

didn't feel like a country cousin amongst this well-dressed crowd.

The eight-foot table itself was beautiful too, covered in a fine ivory-on-ivory embroidered cloth. The gaslight chandelier threw grotesque shadows over the food presented in silver tureens and on decorative platters, her mother's best imported dinnerware polished to a gleam. Horatia had outdone herself with yeast rolls, roasted new potatoes, capons in wine sauce, and bacon-wrapped green bean bundles. There would be raspberry tartlets for dessert, one of Joelle's favorites.

Unfortunately, she found her appetite ruined by anxiety over Lemuel and Georgia Frye, hiding in her bedroom; wondering where Schuyler was; and concern for Levi, presumably arrived in Tuscaloosa by now. Furthermore, she couldn't help thinking of Mr. and Mrs. McCanless dealing with the loss of their entire business. She could have at the very least invited them to come to dinner. Maybe they wouldn't have come, but the gesture would have been neighborly.

Now it was too late. But she would send a note with Wyatt, first thing in the morning, inviting them to tomorrow's evening meal.

Comforted with that thought, she looked around and noticed one more thing. Frowning, she turned to Hixon, seated to her left. "Excuse me, Mr. Hixon, but do you know where your friend Mr. Jefcoat has been the last day or so? I don't believe he has been down for a meal today at all. I hope he's not ill."

Caught in the act of putting most of a roll into his mouth, Hixon choked and coughed violently. Finally he was able to gasp, "Er, no. Can't say I do. I mean, I'm sure he's not ill.

Fairly sure. I don't know." He gulped his water. "Is there any wine?"

"Yes, after dinner, to go with dessert." Joelle regarded him, puzzled. Mercy, what a reaction to a simple question. "Please tell Jefcoat I asked about him, next time you see him."

"Certainly. Will do." Hixon subsided once more into his food.

Joelle, picking at her own plate, caught General Forrest's eye across the table.

He smiled. "I couldn't help overhearing. I believe I heard Mr. Jefcoat say he was going hunting this morning. The woods hereabouts are full of game, and Jefcoat seems to be an enthusiastic sportsman."

"Oh! That makes perfect sense." She nodded. "Have you had a chance to take out a gun yourself? My papa used to all but live in the woods whenever we girls would get too giggly."

"Not yet, though I plan to do so, at some point, before we leave the area. I'm fond of hunting bear, and I hear there's a big one terrorizing the livestock." He reached for his wife's hand. "But let us not discuss such masculine pursuits over dinner. My Mary Ann assures me the ladies prefer to keep dinner talk focused on lighter topics."

There was something oily about the general's tone that set Joelle's teeth on edge. She'd watched him in church yesterday too. Though he seemed sober and attentive, he wasn't a demonstrative man. During the war, Confederate newspapers proclaimed him to be a gifted horseman—even earning the nickname "Wizard of the Saddle"—a charismatic leader, and brilliant battle strategist. But she'd also read reports of relentless cruelty to the enemy. Could the villain of Fort

Pillow, who had reportedly led the massacre of nearly two hundred defenseless Negroes, have really changed?

Then again, who was she to judge whether or not a man had repented?

She turned her attention back to her meal and let Aurora and the effervescent Delfina carry the conversation.

The maids had begun to serve the tartlets, wine, and coffee, when she heard the doorbell ring. After a few moments, Mose, in serving livery for the evening, came to the dining room doorway.

Joelle went to him. "What's the matter, Mose?"

He handed her an envelope. "The man at the door said deliver it to Mr. Hixon immediately."

"At dinnertime? That's odd." She turned the envelope over and frowned at the slashing masculine script. "It's addressed to Schuyler."

"He said if Mr. Beaumont wasn't here, to give it to Hixon."

That was even more strange. "Thank you, Mose." She wandered back to the table and sat down.

By this time, Hixon had gulped down two glasses of wine and was looking about for more. When she handed the envelope to him, he took it with disinterest and laid it beside his plate, then leaned forward, peering past Joelle. "Somebody pass the wine, please."

How had Schuyler tolerated this sot for so many years? What if the message was something important?

Picking up the envelope, she laid her hand on his sleeve. "Mr. Hixon."

He flinched and blinked owlishly at her over his wineglass. "Ma'am?"

"I think you should open this, to see if it's something that needs to be dealt with. I'm not sure when Schuyler will be back."

Hixon looked fairly cross-eyed with the effort to exercise his brain. "Beaumont didn't say anything about opening it. Come to think of it, he told me to watch out for you too, but you seem to be capable of taking care of yourself. You open it—you're a lot smarter than I am." He seemed relieved to pass responsibility to someone else.

Joelle reached for one of the dinner candles and held the envelope above it just long enough to loosen the wax seal. Sliding her thumbnail beneath it, she opened the flap, removed the paper, and read it quickly.

I want your information. Meet me tonight at midnight at the smokehouse.

Heart thumping, hands shaking, she slipped the paper back into the envelope and resealed it.

Information? What did that mean? Hixon clearly knew nothing and wanted to know nothing. Obviously Schuyler wasn't here, so she couldn't simply ask him. But his warning had left her jumping at shadows all day, and the arrival of the Fryes this afternoon multiplied her anxiety.

What should she do? If Levi were here, she would go to him—but he was gone too. The next smartest person in the room sat at the other end of the table, relentlessly teasing her cousin ThomasAnne.

She got to her feet, swaying dramatically. "Oh my, I'm not feeling well. I'd better go lie down."

As she had predicted, Benjamin Kidd immediately got up and came to her. "What's the matter, Jo?" He waved everyone else to their seats as he put an arm about Joelle's waist and cupped her elbow. "No, I don't need an audience. Come in the parlor, Joelle, and let me take a look at you."

Joelle stumbled along trying to look sick. When they got to the parlor and he'd shut the door, she whirled and grabbed Doc's hands. "Ben, I'm so worried, and I don't know who else to go to. I'm afraid Schuyler is in trouble."

Twenty-Six

"GO KISS YOUR WIFE," Schuyler told Levi as they left the barn after stabling the horses. "I imagine she'll be glad to see you."

Without argument, Levi grinned and headed to the main house, where lights still blazed from the lower floor. His pace was remarkably quick for a man who had been in the saddle since sunup.

Schuyler lagged behind, still emotionally and physically drained from the events of the day. He knew he wouldn't easily fall asleep, no matter how his body ached for rest. Jefcoat's gasping bearded face—had he nearly killed a man who had been his best friend?—kept surging to the front of his mind. What if Levi hadn't stopped him?

Shuddering, he broke that train of thought and realized he'd gravitated toward the manager's cottage. It seemed he needed Joelle in times of duress, in a way he'd never imagined possible. She talked sense into him, she gave him hope and encouragement. Mostly she listened.

She could still be in the main house, where it looked like

a dinner party still raged. He could wait under her window until she came to her room, at least talk to her before he found his own rest in the barn or on the back porch.

Then he caught movement from the side of the cottage closest to the barn, heard a soft footfall. Weariness forgotten, senses alert, he drew his gun. Cover. He quickly and quietly slipped behind the closest oak tree. "Who's there?" he called softly.

"Beaumont?" Doc's quiet voice came out of the darkness.

Schuyler moved toward the cottage, still cautious. "What are you doing out here?"

"Waiting for you."

"What? Why?"

"I have a message for you. They want to meet you at the smokehouse at midnight."

"Who? I don't know what you're talking about."

"You're going to explain who, right here and now. And next time you appoint an emissary, you might choose somebody with a better head for liquor than Hixon. He's under the table, and Joelle intercepted the note from your contact—I assume someone in that den of criminals calling themselves a brotherhood."

"I can't explain, not until I know how much you know. I'm sworn to—"

"Levi brought me in a few days ago. He needed someone to keep an eye on the women, and I don't work blind."

An ally. Schuyler relaxed—marginally. "All right. I do have a contact in the 'brotherhood' that I believe is pretty high up the chain of command. To lure him out, I told him I'd give him Frye. I didn't tell Hixon anything germane, simply asked him to hold any messages that came for me."

"Well, it arrived during dinner. Being the reporter she is, Joelle couldn't resist opening it. Scared her to death, so she came to me. Here it is." Doc handed over a small envelope.

Schuyler muttered under his breath. Of course she would open it. "I'll talk to her. Is she still in the main house?"

"No. And there's something else you should know. Frye and his wife came here this morning, afraid the Klan had found them in Shake Rag."

"Good Lord! This is right in the middle of that nest of snakes!"

"Maybe that's the best place to hide." Doc's voice was matter-of-fact. "Joelle put them in her room, which is why I'm here, watching the perimeter."

"Huh." Smart girl. Brave girl. "Where is she?"

"She's in the kitchen, helping with cleanup."

"What time is it?"

"Nine thirty or ten, I would guess. How far is your meeting place?"

"Half hour's ride away." Schuyler sighed. "No time to rest."

But there might be time to speak to Joelle, just see her face and make sure she was all right, before he had to saddle up again.

Joelle stepped out of the kitchen into the yard to empty a pan of dishwater, praying and thinking and worrying all at once. When something moved in the darkness, she sloshed it all over the front of her dress, dropped the pan, and dove for the gun propped inside the door. Had General Forrest's bear come foraging for food?

"Joelle!"

"Schuyler?" She came outside, shutting the door behind her, kicking the dishpan out of the way. "I nearly shot you!"

"The story of our courtship."

"There is no courtship." She paused, all but blind in the starless night. "Where are you?"

"Right here." He was close. She could smell him.

Which made her laugh. "What have you been doing? You smell like—"

"I've been on a horse all day. Forgive me if I was so anxious to see you that I didn't stop to bathe."

"If you'd come a little closer, I'd have pitched that pan of soapy water at you."

Then his laughter rolled out, warm and so familiar that her toes curled. "I missed you," he said.

"It's only been twelve hours."

"Ah, Jo."

She didn't know who moved first, because some centrifugal force had their mouths crashing together, representative of the violence in the nature of their relationship from the beginning—one part resentment, one part longing, all of it inevitable as the tide. She reached for his shirt, yanked him closer, groaned in frustration when there was no closer to get to. He laughed, held the sides of her head, gentled his kisses until she submitted to being wooed in soft sips and brushes of the lips. And then he took her into that beautiful dark place once more, where she didn't know where he ended and she began.

"Sky," she gasped as he kissed her throat. "I didn't know . . ."

"Yes, you did. You always knew. That's why you've fought it so hard."

"I still can't—"

"You're mine." He said it with no possessiveness, just absolute certainty. "You. Are. Mine."

"No."

"Yes. Always."

She pushed him away, pushed herself away. "This is . . . Schuyler, there are bad things happening. A message came to me tonight—"

"I know. I'm going to deal with it, but I had to see you first. If I don't come back—"

"What are you talking about? Don't talk crazy!"

"I want you to know I love you. Probably always have, I just had to grow up and admit it. Maybe I shouldn't tell you now, but you seem to . . . I mean, I can't be feeling this way if there's no—" She heard him swallow. "You did kiss me back."

"Of course I did. Only a blind, stupid *boy* would overlook the insane way I've behaved over the last ten years."

"Then say it."

"No. Not until there's a ring. And a party. And maybe fireworks. Not in the dark, with dirty dishwater all over my dress, and you smelling like a stable."

He was silent for a long moment. Then, quietly, "I love you, Joelle. I'll tell you again, when it's not so dark and dangerous. But if I don't come back, if something happens, at least you'll know." He picked up her hand, brought it to his lips, and bowed. Before she could say a word, he was gone.

She picked up the dishpan and hugged it to her chest. What in the world?

Schuyler was halfway to Saltillo before he realized there was something off about that message.

He'd lit a lamp in the barn and read it over several times. He didn't recognize the handwriting, but the vague wording, the mention of the smokehouse, seemed targeted to him. Frye's name not being mentioned could mean either the author of the note didn't know it, or he was trying to hide it. No signature, no initial, no identification of the writer at all.

Though he'd been pushing to accomplish his mission and get back home, he slowed the tired bay to a walk. He'd been trying to lure Maney out into the open, but suppose Maney was equally determined to draw Schuyler away from Daughtry House. What if he'd played right into the enemy's hands? What if it was another trap, similar to the one he'd walked into at Beene's Ferry? He should have at least brought someone with him this time, but it was too late for that.

Now he had a decision. Go on, and risk capture or worse—or return to Daughtry House and lose the opportunity to confront the Grand Titan or whatever rank Maney claimed in the Klan brotherhood. Cursing the characteristic impulsiveness that seemed to consistently get him in trouble, he stopped and looked up.

The moon floated out from behind a dense cloud, appearing in a full golden orb laced by silvery rococo designs.

God was not in the moon, but the creator of the moon saw him, right where he was. That same moon shone over a Saltillo plantation, where he'd once been beaten and rescued. It shone over Joelle, her family, and a courageous schoolteacher and his wife, all sleeping at Daughtry House.

Where lies the battle, Lord? Which way do I go?

Joelle lay rigid, flat on her back, on the pallet she'd fashioned out of quilts in front of the fireplace.

Horatia and Mose, Charmion and Nathan, and the two kitchen maids employed for dinner had all gone home half an hour earlier, leaving the kitchen sparkling clean and ready to start breakfast preparations at dawn. After locking the door behind them, Joelle had washed her face and scrubbed her teeth at the sink, then opened the carpetbag she'd packed earlier in the day. Finding her brush, she took the pins out of her hair and returned it to its usual simple braid. With a groan of relief, she skimmed down to her chemise and replaced the tight dress and corset with her loosest day dress.

She'd thought she was tired enough to fall instantly asleep, but she kept thinking of Schuyler's last words.

I love you, Joelle. If something happens, at least you'll know.

Why hadn't she said it back to him? What was so hard about telling the man to whom you'd given your heart when you were a child that he wasn't the only one to feel a consuming, life-changing, God-ordained passion?

She knew the answer to that question. It was hard because it hurt. It hurt to be pushed away and disagreed with and put in second place. If you admitted that you loved, you put yourself in danger of rejection. She'd felt the pain of being sent away to boarding school, when all she wanted was to stay home with her mama and read all the books in Papa's library. She'd watched her mother wilt when Papa went away to war, his principles more important than his wife and family. Perhaps he thought of that as heroic, but to her it had seemed the height of selfishness.

Of course she loved Schuyler, but he was a warrior, a *doer* in the same vein as her father. And look how that had turned out.

She turned over, shuddering. No. She'd rather be alone than face that constant peril. *This* peril. He was putting himself in harm's way this very minute, and there wasn't a thing she could do about it.

Normally, when she couldn't sleep, she got up to write down what was bothering her. This time, though, the fear was so deeply personal, such a wordless groan of the spirit, that she could only lie there and quake in the dark.

She was finally beginning to drift off, when someone lit a lamp in the corner.

What?

Heart hammering, she sat up and saw the light flickering, but it wasn't a lamp, and it wasn't the fireplace. The schoolroom door was on fire. Now she could see smoke drifting overhead, all around, drugging her, making it hard to breathe. She crawled toward the door, under the table, knocking against chairs. Hitting her head on the table ledge, she paused to suck in an ill-advised breath full of smoke, and fell into a paroxysm of coughing.

Cover your face. Get out. Find the door.

Oh, God, please help me.

The closest wet rag was in the sink, the wrong side of the room. Crouching again, she blindly headed toward the exterior door. The schoolroom was now roaring with flames, and the fire would leap to the kitchen at any moment.

What seemed like forever probably took only a minute, for

the kitchen wasn't that big a room, but she finally reached out and felt wood against her hands. Trying not to breathe, tears rolling down her face, she felt her way up to the doorknob. She grasped it and cried out in pain, her palm instantly blistering.

Stupid, stupid, of course it would be hot! She should have brought the quilt with her, but too late for that. She had to get out now.

She got to her bare feet, lifted her skirt, and used it to protect her fingers as she first turned the key, then the doorknob. Smoke poured out behind her as she fell into fresh open air. On her knees, she rocked, trying to make herself get up and run. Her head swam, coughing racking her body again. Setting one hand and knee forward, then the other, slowly she made it out into the yard, past the worst of the smoke and flames.

She looked back, horrified to see the roof of the schoolroom cave in. The kitchen would be next. She'd barely gotten out in time.

Was the main house on fire? It seemed not. People were pouring out the back door, though, off the porch, into the garden, running toward her.

The cottage. It was clear of the fire too, as was the barn. Only the kitchen and its attached schoolroom had gone up.

"Joelle!" Selah reached her first, snatched her into her arms. "Thank God! Are you all right? Was anyone else still in there with you?"

"No, I—" She doubled over, coughing. "Everyone else went home about an hour ago." She turned toward the hill a quarter mile away, where Nathan and Charmion's little house sat. "Oh no!" She started running. "The Vincents' house is on fire! Everybody grab a bucket from the barn!"

But she'd barely gone a few yards when she saw that it was the blacksmith shop, not the house, in flames top to bottom. Hearing somebody running behind her, she looked over her shoulder to find Levi overtaking her.

"We've got to contain it so that it doesn't catch the house!" he shouted on the way by. "Go wake up Nathan and Charmion."

For the very reason that the forge fire was in constant danger of getting out of control, the smithy had been built near a small pond. While Levi organized a line of buckets from pond to forge, Joelle ran to the house and banged with both fists on the door.

"Nathan! Charmion! Wake up! The shop is on fire!"

Nathan jerked open the door. "What?" At the sight of his smithy in flames, his mouth fell open. "Charmion! Get up!" He ran back for his wife and brought her out, supporting her bulky pregnant body with a strong arm. Leaving her with Joelle, he ran to join the bucket brigade.

When Charmion would have followed her husband, Joelle held her back, made her sit on the soggy ground. "Sit here, Char, don't put the baby in harm's way. How are you feeling?"

"They did this on purpose." Charmion put a hand to her head. "Our business. Joelle, it's all gone." She started to cry, and then jumped to her feet, shrieking, "The house! The roof's on fire!"

Joelle looked over her shoulder and saw that Charmion was right. The breeze had flung sparks from the smithy to the house in spite of the water brigade's best efforts. Levi hadn't seen it yet. She ran toward him, screaming and waving her arms. "The house! Levi, the house!"

By this time the smithy fire had been doused, the building half destroyed. The fire on the roof of the house burned with fresh ardor. Charmion was going to lose everything after all.

Charmion no longer sat on the grass beside the house. Where was she?

Horrified, Joelle saw that the front door was open. Charmion wouldn't do that. She wouldn't go inside.

But she might, if there was something valuable enough in there.

Joelle looked around and realized that she was the only person close enough to have any chance of getting back out before the fire got dangerous. She ducked her head inside the dark house. "Charmion!" she called. "Are you in here?"

"I'm looking for your dress. It's right here."

"Charmion, no! We don't have time for that."

"But it's finished, and I worked months on it. We're going to need the money."

"I'll pay you! Come on!" Joelle reluctantly stepped inside. "What if you—"

Something crashed. Charmion screamed.

"Where are you, Char?" It was so dark, Joelle could barely see her hand in front of her face. Smoke was starting to seep through cracks in the ceiling. She was terrified. Not once, but twice in one night to be trapped in a house on fire. But she couldn't leave Charmion alone, not even to get help. "Can you hear me?"

There was no answer—Charmion must be unconscious. If only she had a light. Cautiously she moved farther into the room, willing her eyes to adjust to the darkness. Gradually shadows appeared, and she saw the outline of Charmion's body near the rocking chair. The glint of a heavy mirror frame lay near her head, perhaps knocked over as Charmion had fumbled around in the dark.

Heat built inside the little room, and Joelle knew she only had a few minutes to get herself and her friend out before the roof collapsed on them both. Taking shallow breaths, praying with every step, she moved toward Charmion, crunching on broken glass with every step. Squatting beside her, she saw that Charmion's gown had tangled in a hooked curve of the wrought-iron table beside the rocker, and Joelle was going to have to turn it over to get her loose.

Hearing a crackle and crash overhead, she knew time was running out. Gritting her teeth, she took the table in both hands and heaved it upward and over on its side, groaning as pain seared her palms. Charmion was free.

At that moment the ceiling buckled.

Twenty-Seven

ONCE HE MADE UP HIS MIND which direction to go, Schuyler rode hard. He pushed the bay faster than he would have liked, a sense of unreasonable urgency driving him back toward Daughtry House.

When he rode through the front gate, the house looked much like it had two hours ago when he and Levi came back together, but something was different. The stillness, he realized as he rode around the side of the house. No noise of music and laughter came from the front windows, where family and company gathered in the parlor and dining room.

As soon as he rounded the back of the house, the smell of smoke and burning embers from the cottage roof hit him in the face. In the distance he could see flames of another building, either the smithy or Nathan and Charmion's house—possibly both.

Leaning forward, he dug in his heels, begging his mount for one more burst of speed, and the bay responded gallantly. Sooner than he would have thought possible, he arrived at the pond, where a line of sooty-faced men and women, half in evening garb, the other half in nightwear, toiled at putting out the blacksmith fire.

Flinging himself from the horse, he looked for Levi and Nathan, saw that the two of them and the other men had the situation under control. Then his anxious gaze fell on the house. "The roof of the house is on fire!" he shouted and ran, looking for Joelle as he went.

She should be among the other women, carrying water, but he couldn't find her. He saw Selah, Aurora, Thomas-Anne, Horatia, even Delfina and Mrs. Forrest. But no Joelle. Charmion was missing too.

He grabbed Selah. "Where is Joelle?"

Selah looked around. "I don't know—she was right here with Charmion a minute ago! Schuyler—"

But he was already running for the open door of the house. "Joelle! Charmion!" As he stepped inside, he heard a crunch overhead and looked up. *Oh, God, save us.*

"Schuyler!" Joelle's voice came from the interior, somewhere near the back fireplace wall. "Help me get her out. She's unconscious and I burned my hands—"

Hold that ceiling, God, he begged. "I'm coming. Say something so I'll know where you are."

"I love you," she blurted.

He laughed. "That will do." He moved toward her voice, crunching on broken glass. "What have you done?"

"Me? I didn't do this. One of your dragon-breath friends apparently decided to set the world on fire. Wait! Let me help."

Schuyler lifted Charmion, staggered a little under the awkward shape, regained his balance, and headed for the door.

"Come on, I've got her. Be careful, there's"—he heard Joelle shriek—"glass everywhere."

They made it out just as the ceiling collapsed in a shower of sparks and ash.

Schuyler stood cradling Charmion, looking over his shoulder at his little love, seated on the ground picking shards of glass out of her size eleven feet. She was crying, which created white streaks on her black cheeks and made rivers of soot run down her chin onto her dress. Her braid had come loose and caught fire at some point, singeing about a third of her hair off below one ear.

She was the most beautiful thing he had ever seen.

"Doc!" he shouted. "Come here and take a look at Charmion." He carefully laid his unconscious burden down in the grass, waited until the doctor and Nathan came running, and considered himself free to tend to Joelle. He walked behind her and reached down under her armpits to help her up. "I'm sorry, but I don't think I'm capable of lifting you straight off the ground." Once she was vertical, he swept her into his arms and carried her toward his horse, placidly grazing not far away.

She looked up at him and sniffed. "You're pretty strong after all."

"I assume you don't mean I smell this time."

"Ha. Ha."

After a moment he said, "Thank you would be appropriate."

"I already told you I love you. What else do you want from me?"

He stopped beside the horse and kissed her hard. "Stop talking."

"All right." She laid her head against his shoulder. "I'm really tired."

"So am I. Can you get on, if I boost you a little?"

"Certainly. Do I look like a damsel in distress?" She put one bare foot into the stirrup and hopped onto the saddle astride. "Don't tell ThomasAnne I rode this way. She'll have palpitations."

"I don't know. ThomasAnne might surprise you. She was handling a bucket with the best of them." He called out to Levi that he was taking Joelle back to the house, received an answering shout, and headed that direction. He walked beside the horse, Joelle quiet in the saddle above him.

Finally she said, "Where did you go?"

"I thought I was supposed to go to a smokehouse at Saltillo plantation. But it turned out I needed to be here."

She laid her hand on his shoulder. "I'm glad you came back. But I meant all day."

"Levi sent me over to Itawamba County. Turned out he was following me the whole time. You know, now that I think about it, that's a lot like walking with God, isn't it? You think he's taking you into dangerous places, but it turns out he knows exactly what he's doing, and he's with you. Not that Levi is God, but you know what I mean."

"Yes," she said softly. "I know what you mean. Levi said your friend Jefcoat is a traitor. That he was the one who killed your father. Sky, I'm so sorry."

"I'll tell you about it sometime. Not tonight, not when I've just got you to myself. Now I have a question for you. Where are Mr. Frye and his lovely wife?"

"Well, it turns out we are a resourceful bunch, we Daughtry girls. After dinner, we dressed Mr. Frye in one of Wyatt's suits and hats, and put a pillow at Mrs. Frye's stomach to make her look like Charmion. Doc let them take his wagon to town, saying he wanted Charmion to stay in his office for a while, since he's worried the baby might come early."

"Whose idea was that?"

"Mine," she said modestly. "I'm sure these fires tonight were an attempt to smoke them out. I saw Hixon snooping around the schoolroom, and thought he might suspect they'd been here. I had them in my room for a while, but then I worried that even that might not be safe."

"I didn't see Hixon around tonight. Where is he?"

"I imagine he's snoozing peacefully under the dining room table. Doc put a little extra toddy in his wineglass."

Schuyler laughed out loud for the first time all day. "Resourceful indeed." They had arrived at the front door of the manager's cottage, and he halted the horse to look up at Joelle. "Listen to me, beautiful. Here's what I want to do. I want to carry you inside your room. I want to bathe and bandage your hands and feet. I want to wash your hair and brush it dry, and hold you until you go to sleep. But if I don't walk away right now, all my newfound good intentions are liable to go to, well, where they ought not go. You understand? I'll be back in the morning." He paused and winked. "After I've had a bath."

Joelle stood at the office window, watching for Schuyler. He was true to his word. Last night he had treated her like a perfect gentleman would treat a perfect lady. Carrying her into the kitchen, he'd seated her in the rocker, then brought her a bowl of water, a pile of linen rags, and some ointment for her cuts and burns. Politely he said good night without so much as kissing her hand. And left.

But he'd said he would be back. ThomasAnne claimed not to know where he'd spent the night, though she assumed he'd taken the bedroom in the main house that had been vacated by Hixon and Jefcoat (Hixon being still beneath the table and Jefcoat languishing in a Fulton jail). It was now broad daylight, fully nine a.m. Presumably he'd managed to find a bath, maybe even breakfast by now.

Joelle herself had risen with the first cry of the rooster. In spite of her burnt palms and stinging feet, she'd slept solidly, relaxing for the first time in weeks. She'd already had breakfast and been dressed and styled by Miss Aurora. She put her bandaged hand to her curly, now chin-length hair. Aurora had at first refused to cut it off, but even she could see the writing on the wall when the burnt third fell off in her hands as she brushed it. No matter, it would grow.

He had called her beautiful. She had heard that word so many times in reference to herself that it had lost all meaning. But when *he* said it, she knew he wasn't referring to the awkward, cinder-covered personage sitting on his horse, but to the girl on the inside. The one who wanted to love him well, to treat others justly, to write with passion and truth. Maybe they could be beautiful together.

There he came, walking up the path from the garden with that loose, familiar stride. And he looked so fine in dark pants and white shirt open at the throat, his golden hair blowing in the morning breeze. She heard his knock on the door and ran to open it.

She felt breathless, possibly too eager. So she scowled. "What took you so long?"

He laughed. "It's customary to greet one's suitor with a 'Good morning.'"

"Oh. Are you my suitor?"

"I think so. Unless I've mistaken you for that girl with the soot all over her face." He squinted. "No, it's you. I like your hair."

She put her hand to the curls behind her ear and twisted one. "It's really short."

"Yes, it is, but it suits you. Can I come in?" She backed up and watched him swing inside, bringing with him springtime and a handful of daylilies, which he'd held behind his back. Now he presented them. "Mose said I could give these to you."

"Thank you. Would you like to sit down?"

"I suppose." Suddenly he looked a little unsure of himself. "Where?"

She realized they were still standing in the little entryway. "Come into the office. I made some coffee."

That seemed to make him happy. Schuyler liked his coffee in the morning. She gave him the best chair, the one with the extra-long seat and comfortable back cushion, then poured coffee into the biggest cup in the kitchen and handed it to him. Seating herself across the rug from him, she looked at him inquiringly.

He was silent for a long moment, then finally blurted, "Can we call this a party?"

She blinked.

"I mean, I know we're having a real party on Friday, with music and dancing and lots of company, but honestly, Jo, I don't think I can wait that long."

"Wait for what?"

"You said a party. And fireworks. I've got the ring."

"You've got a . . . you've got fireworks?"

"Come here. I'll show you." He set down his coffee cup with a rattle of china and bolted to his feet. Grabbing her hand, he took her to the back door, which he threw open, then put two fingers to his mouth and emitted a shrill whistle.

Wyatt appeared from the barn, holding a paper canister trailing some kind of fuse. He set the canister on the ground, produced a flint from his pocket, and lit the fuse. It sizzled for several moments, just sitting there.

"I hope this works," Schuyler murmured over Joelle's shoulder. "It would be better at night, of course, but I couldn't wait."

Suddenly the canister exploded with a burst of light and color that soared into the air like a rocket.

It *was* a rocket—blue and red and orange and purple—brilliant and loud. Mouth open, Joelle watched it fly skyward, still popping and spitting color, until it disappeared over the barn. Wyatt shouted and jumped, throwing a fist into the air.

Joelle whirled. "Where did you get that?" she demanded.

"Wyatt made it. This morning. Which is why it took me so long to get over here."

She tackled him. Flung her arms around his neck and walked him backward into the office, pushed him down into his chair, and sat in his lap. "Yes, this is a party. That was a pretty fine firework. Now where's the ring?"

He looped his arms around her waist, relaxed at last. "That's my Cinderella. I wondered where she went. I can't get to my pocket."

"Oh!" She jumped to her feet, allowing him to fish in his

pants pocket. When he pulled out a small ring, she sat back down and nestled close.

Arms around her, he picked up her left hand, poor bandaged thing that it was, and held it gently. At least her fingers were free. He slid a gold band, set with a big dark-blue sapphire, onto the third finger. "This is your grandmother's," he said. "When I told her I wanted to marry you, she insisted I bring this with me."

She stared at the familiar ring. She'd admired it on her grandmother's hand hundreds of times. "Wait." She held Schuyler's face with her fingertips and stared directly into the ocean-blue depths of his eyes. "When did you talk to my grandmother about this?"

"I think it was . . . about this time last week. She was very relieved to hear you weren't going to marry the preacher after all."

"Schuyler, I didn't know I wasn't going to marry the preacher then!"

"Well, it's obvious you'd make a terrible preacher's wife." He squeezed her and nuzzled her throat. "I mean, look at you."

She lifted her chin to give him better access. "But I'll make a perfect wife for a . . . what is it that you do?"

"I manage hotels. I am an entrepreneur. We are going to make lots of money and lots of children, not necessarily in that order."

"And we are going to found a school. And maybe one day a college. And I am going to write a novel."

"And I'll read it."

"Perfect," they said simultaneously and leaned in for a celebratory kiss.

Twenty-Eight

THE REMAINDER OF TUESDAY and most of Wednesday passed for Schuyler in a love-drunk delirium. By Wednesday at dinnertime, he had begun to recover to the point that he was able to hear and comprehend words that did not proceed from the honeyed mouth of Miss Joelle Daughtry.

Over chicken and dumplings, he heard the company talking about Levi's disappearance, after the arrival of a mysterious gentleman from Chicago. This man had been closeted all afternoon with Levi in the Daughtry House library, then the two of them had left for Memphis—leaving behind a very disappointed Selah.

"I knew he would do this periodically when I married him," she told her family philosophically. "It's a good thing I have the hotel to keep me busy."

Schuyler, who now considered himself one of the family, looked at Joelle with smug self-righteousness. "I'm never leaving you." He lifted her hand, linked with his under the table, and kissed the sapphire ring.

"Would someone pass me the syrup of ipecac?" Aurora said, looking revolted. "I think I'm going to heave."

But Joelle laughed. "Don't worry, he'll leave as soon as someone starts singing opera. No offense, Delfina."

"None taken." Delfina tipped her head, considering Schuyler with dispassionate interest. "I think he is not meant to worship at the shrine of the Fabio after all."

Doc, who had stayed for dinner after checking on Charmion—she and the baby had come through the trauma of the fire with little more than shock and minor burns—winked at Joelle. "His goddess is more likely to forget he exists and go off and leave him."

"Unfortunately, that's true." Joelle rested her shoulder against Schuyler's in a gratifyingly intimate fashion. "I depend on him to come after me and remind me I'm attached. But seriously"—she thumped his ear when he leaned in a little too close for her sense of propriety—"does anybody know what's going on with the investigation? Who killed the judge? And when are they going to round up that gang of criminals who burned the church and our buildings and destroyed the newspaper office?"

Putting a hand to his stinging ear, Schuyler gave her a wounded look. "That hurt! And if you must know, the man who was here this afternoon was a federal marshal. At least, I'm pretty sure that's what Levi said. They went to get a warrant signed by a federal judge Levi knows in Memphis. As soon as they get back, I'll be called in as a witness, and of course Lemuel and Georgia Frye as well. I'm sure we'll have a proper trial eventually. As to who killed the judge, the shot came from the balcony in the courtroom, and I don't know if anybody will admit they saw who did it. Anyone who speaks out against that crowd is subject to the worst intimidation."

Everyone around the table looked at him, and Joelle sobered. "Schuyler, that means you."

He shrugged, uncomfortable that he'd drawn attention to himself. "They've done their worst to me. But we've got to stand our ground to stop the violence. Fear isn't helping anything." He hesitated. "Joelle, you know your preacher was up to his neck in it, don't you? He was present at two of the meetings I attended, and I saw him breaking into the newspaper office."

She bit her lip. "I suspected. But nobody will do anything about it as long as the leaders go unchecked."

He squeezed her hand to comfort her. "As I said, the authorities are coming. Justice is coming." He looked at the dining room doorway, where Horatia stood looking uncharacteristically flustered. "And dessert is apparently coming. What's the matter, Horatia?"

"The baby," the cook blurted, sagging against the doorframe. "Dr. Kidd, I need you to come quickly, please. Nathan ran all the way from our house to tell me the baby is coming early."

Just a few minutes shy of midnight, ThomasAnne bounced into the parlor to share the news that Benjamin Schuyler Lawrence had made a screaming, but otherwise healthy appearance. Apparently, ThomasAnne had been quietly training with Doc as a midwife for the last two months, without telling a soul.

Joelle, who had been reading on the sofa while Schuyler

kept himself awake by instructing Delfina and Mr. Volker at billiards, put down her book and listened to her cousin's excited and rather lurid description of the birth with half an ear. Aurora and Selah had already gone to bed, and Joelle began to wish she had had the sense to do likewise.

When ThomasAnne finally ran out of words and retired to the manager's cottage, Joelle got up and tapped Schuyler, presently bent over the pool table, on the arm. "Come here, please."

He looked around and gave her a slow smile that sent a slide of something delicious through her veins. "I'm not sure that's a good idea." But he handed his cue to Volker. "You're on your own, Cousin. Where are we going?" he said to Joelle.

"Nowhere dangerous." She led him into the rotunda and sat down at the foot of the stairs.

He joined her, sitting close, and picked up her hand to lace his fingers with hers. "It's really late."

"I know. I won't keep you but a minute."

"You can keep me forever."

She smiled. "I just wanted to tell you that we'll be getting a dog."

He blinked. "O—kay. Any particular reason?"

"Well, it's just I'm not sure we'll be having children. You'll need something to keep you busy."

He laughed. "What are you talking about?"

"Did you *hear* what she said?"

"Who?"

"ThomasAnne! Having a baby sounds painful!"

He propped his elbow on his knee, rested his head in his hand, and looked at her sideways. "You know you think too much, right?"

"I can't help it! I've been reading about it too, because nobody will talk to me about the—the physical part of being married, and I'm a little—well, no, I'm a lot scared." She'd asked Doc to loan her a couple of books on the subject, and what she'd learned would have curled her hair if it hadn't been naturally in ringlets already. "Schuyler, I'm sorry, but I don't think I can do this after all."

"Really?" His eyes half closed. His lips were almost on hers before she realized what he was doing.

"No!" She jerked back. "Don't do that right now! I'm serious!"

He sighed. "Reese was right. You are extremely hard work. Listen to me." He picked up her hand and kissed her thumb. "We don't have to get a dog. Hilo is mine, so we'll bring her home with us, wherever we wind up living. You like Hilo, right?" When she nodded suspiciously, he kissed her index finger. "So we'll start out slow, just you and me and Hilo." He kissed her middle finger, and she melted a little. "When you get used to me kissing you, we'll figure out the next step." He kissed the finger with the ring on it. "I guarantee you, by the time we go swimming together a few times, you won't even be thinking about children." He kissed her pinky and waited, looking at her with those ocean-gray eyes.

"I liked going swimming," she said cautiously.

"Right, then. That's all we'll do until you're ready. Jo-elle," he said, cradling her hand close to his cheek, "I love you so much that if that's all we ever do, I'd be happy just to live with you and talk to you and sleep next to you and read your book. But I think you're going to have to trust me when I say the rest of it is going to be pretty spectacular as well—fireworks, if you like. There's nothing to be afraid of."

Something flowered in her stomach, forcing out anxiety and other nasty things that her imagination had allowed to grow there. It flowered in her heart and in her mind and in her spirit. She turned her hand and cupped his cheek. "Schuyler Beaumont, I love you. I can't wait to marry you, with or without your dog."

"Whew," he said.

A NOTE TO THE READER

A Reluctant Belle PICKS UP THE STORY of the impoverished Tupelo, Mississippi, Daughtry sisters right after the completion of *A Rebel Heart*—placing it in the middle of the Reconstruction Era, five years after Robert E. Lee's surrender at Appomattox. Because Joelle is a writer and teacher, and Schuyler's goal is tracking down the gunman who killed his father in a race riot, the story necessarily winds its way through some complicated political territory. There was no way to sugarcoat the terrible racial injustices and struggles to right those wrongs that in fact imbued daily Southern life in the early 1870s.

First and foremost, however, I call myself a romance writer—and I mean that in the classic Alexandre Dumas, Zane Grey, and Jane Austen sense. I always desire for character development, satisfying story arc, and evocative setting to supersede any particular "moral." This is art, and it's not going to be perfect; it's simply a take on life as lived through one author's lens, as clearly and in as unbiased a fashion as I can bring it to you.

With that said, to make the story as historically accurate as possible, I read as many primary sources as I had time for. Those sources include journal and diary entries, memoir and footnoted biography, and contemporary newspaper and magazine articles. You may find a list of these resources on my website, if you're interested.

For those who like to know which characters were "real people," the most obvious might be General Nathan Bedford Forrest. Documented sources of the period present a strong personality, a fierce warrior in battle, consummate tactical genius, and undeniable racial bigot. There is some indication that he at least overtly underwent a change of heart toward the end of his life (because of his wife's Christian influence), but we'll have to leave that to the Almighty to judge. For the purposes of my story, Forrest had begun to publicly distance himself from the violent activities of the Ku Klux Klan, but conflicting eyewitness accounts of people who knew him survive. I chose to make him an important part of my story, but not the main villain.

A few more heroic real-life characters make an appearance in *A Reluctant Belle*, including Hiram Revels, the first African American to be seated in the United States Senate (Mississippi), and US Representative (Alabama) James Rapier. Both these men, along with other Southern black congressmen, served with grace and distinction, were generally respected and well liked, and seemed remarkably free of bitterness or resentment toward their white fellow legislators. One of the most interesting and eye-opening accounts of the period that I read was John R. Lynch's *Facts of the Reconstruction*. Lynch served as a Mississippi Representative for years during the Reconstruction, becoming the first African American

Speaker of the Mississippi House of Representatives, and eventually being elected to the US House.

Aside from those few, all other characters are entirely my creation.

Some plot elements are based on real historic events. My Tuscaloosa race riot is based on a similar incident that occurred in Meridian, Mississippi, in March, 1871. The Ku Klux Klan induction rites and the violent atrocities committed by that organization, as described in my story, are based on research gathered by Michael Newton in *The Ku Klux Klan in Mississippi: A History*. It's not light reading, but it helped me understand the political and social background—and consequences—of events of the period.

I hope the reader will understand when I say that I have couched some terminology in an attempt not to jar and offend the twenty-first-century ear. I know how some people talked back then. I know it's offensive on so many levels. But my editors and I saw no need in being deliberately inflammatory, even for the sake of historical purism. I trust the intelligent reader can read between the lines in whatever fashion you find most satisfying.

Mainly I hope you've enjoyed getting to know Joelle and Schuyler. They truly make me laugh. Every bookworm princess needs a hero to keep her from walking into walls.

I kind of know this from personal experience.

READ ON FOR AN
EXCERPT OF *BOOK 3* IN THE

Daughtry House
Series!

One

April 27, 1865
Memphis, Tennessee

His first thought when he came to was that the world was coming to an end.

Zane lay flat on the ground, where he'd been knocked off the horse, mud up his nose and in his eyes, and he turned his head to squint against the giant boiling, roaring flare on the Mississippi. Fire on the water—how could that be?

But then he'd seen hell in all its various forms over the last four years, most of them human. Maybe God had decided to start over, like he did with Noah's family. Zane wouldn't quibble with the Almighty over the need for a fresh start.

He pushed to his hands and knees, shaking his head to rid himself of the sensation of battle aftermath. The war was over. He was on his way . . . somewhere. Not home, because he didn't have a home. Just north. Somewhere beyond Mississippi and Alabama, a place where a man could live in peace.

Sounds came and went—small explosions, screams that

almost sounded human, the roar of the flames—and he fought the urge to curl up on the ground, arms over his head, knees drawn in. No. He was here for a reason. Left behind for some purpose only God knew. If he didn't believe that, he'd have given in long ago. What? What was he doing here?

Dragging in a breath that pierced his lungs and set him into a spasm of coughing, he forced himself upright, wiping the slime from his face, spitting grit out of his mouth. His ears cleared long enough to distinguish—

The screams were real. Human.

In a flash of recall, he remembered what brought him here. The man he'd followed along the river from Memphis—where was he? Where was the horse? Both frightened off by the explosion . . .

It occurred to Zane that he should have been on that boat. He stared in horror at the debacle on the river. There were people everywhere, hundreds floating past on doors and shutters and tree limbs, calling out, drowning, burning, shrieking like demons, the scene comparable to the worst wartime engagement he'd seen. Forget his quarry—he was gone by now anyway. Zane knew he had to plunge himself into this new emergency.

As he staggered to his feet, something dripped into his eyes. He reached up to wipe it away, then stood looking at his hand by moonlight and the flickering fire, rubbing the sticky moisture between his fingers. His head was bleeding. All right then.

He took off his coat, methodically ripped off one of his shirt sleeves and tied it about his forehead, then put the coat back on.

By now his senses had straightened enough that he could think. He took stock of the tragedy around him and began to formulate a plan. That was what the Provost Guard of the

Indiana Iron 44th did. Take any unorthodox situation, assess the most critical problems, and deal with them step by step. It was how he'd survived the last eight months in prison. It was how he'd made it to Vicksburg mainly on foot, how he'd secured a berth on that hell-bound steamer.

It was why he wasn't on it when it exploded.

Come on, Sabiere, he told himself. *There are people in the water worse off than you. Help them.*

So that was what he did.

The explosion jerked her awake. Aurora sat up, heart slamming in her throat. The second-floor bedroom was dark and quiet, but she could still feel the iron bedstead quivering. Cousin ThomasAnne lay beside her, snoring a prosaic, ladylike purr. How could she sleep after that concussion? For that matter, Aurora herself seemed to be the only one in the house awake.

Everyone always said she had the hearing of a bat, but had no one else felt the reverberation, the shudder of the house? Some nights she lay awake long after everyone else slumbered, listening to the hoot of the steamboats pushing upriver from exotic places like Natchez, Vicksburg, Baton Rouge, New Orleans. Now that the war was over and the Mississippi had opened to civilian traffic, the daily symphony of sounds from the landing below the bluff had thickened with longshoremen calling to the boat crews as they docked or steamed away, loaded with passengers, cotton, and other crops headed north. Nighttime was quieter, with a rhythm and music all its own: distant foghorns, the call of night watchmen, perhaps a drunken sailor singing a bawdy song on his way out of a waterfront saloon.

Now—only muffled silence, as though her ears had suddenly been stuffed with cotton wadding.

Shoving aside ThomasAnne's bony knees, she lay back and pulled the quilt under her chin. With spring slow to arrive this year, the night was sharp and cool for late April. The river had been roiling with snow melt for weeks, overflowing its bounds, flooding the planes of the delta. Though Memphis, high on its bluff, remained safe from the angry water, she breathed a prayer for the roustabouts below.

She lay awake for perhaps an hour or more, unable to shake the feeling of unease, trying to return to slumber. Maybe that disturbance had been a dream after all. She hoped it had been. But some time later, her eyes flew open at the sound of feet on the stairs just outside the bedroom door. The room had lightened, but shadows still lingered in the corners. Then, oddly, a flare of lamps penetrated the blackness beyond the open streetside window.

Scrambling out of bed, Aurora ran to lean over the windowsill. Lamplight flickered and swam along the street like giant fireflies, all headed in the direction of the river. A wagon rattled by, then a couple of horses, then more wagons. Suddenly the street was alive with chaos and noise, men pouring out of their houses, calling to one another.

"Steamboat exploded!" the words came clear at last in the melee. "Fire! People in the water . . ."

Craning to see beyond the mad activity streaming toward the bluff, Aurora spotted a stream of boats backing out into the river. Impossible to distinguish individual vessels from amongst the various sizes and shapes, but the US military packet *Pocahontas*, a midsized steamer charged with rounding up Confederate blockade runners and habitually moored at the foot of Beale Street at nightfall, was no doubt among the rescuers. That very day, Aurora and her sisters had been at the Soldiers' Home, serving members of the *Pocahontas* crew, along with paroled Union prisoners from the steamboat *Sultana*. Stopping in Memphis to unload a hundred tons of sugar, nearly as many crates of wine, and a herd of hogs, the *Sultana*'s pilot had allowed the passengers to disembark for supper. The ladies of Aurora's church had brought blankets and food, tea and conversation, to men so gaunt and ill from incarceration at Cahaba prison over in Alabama that they hardly seemed human.

But the men, clearly giddy with joy at the knowledge that they were on their way home, had seemed grateful for feminine kindnesses. Some had had the means to purchase new clothes in town, but some remained in stinking uniforms, so black with grime that the original color—blue or gray—could no longer be discerned. Aurora had held her breath and bravely smiled at each man she encountered, some who seemed hardly older than her own fourteen years, some aged beyond reality by their travails. All but blinded by pity, Aurora had ignored the revolting of her stomach and sat beside a poor man with an amputated leg and a ferocious head wound while a troupe of opera singers from Chicago, also traveling on the *Sultana*, had performed a program of comic scenes.

Could the *Sultana* be the afflicted vessel?

She thought it likely, and if so, the disaster could not be overstated. The steamboat had been monstrously over-loaded—so much so that she had nearly capsized while she chugged into Helena, Arkansas, earlier this morning, due to the passengers ganging on one side to pose for photographers on the wharf.

Or, more properly, she supposed, that had been yesterday. Dawn could not be far away now.

"Aurora?" came ThomasAnne's querulous voice. "What's the matter?"

Aurora looked over her shoulder and found her older cousin sitting up in bed, nightcap askew over curly, sandy hair straggling in plaits over her shoulders. "I'm not sure," Aurora said, turning back to the ruckus outside the window. "Sounds like a steamer up the river exploded and caught fire. Those poor people . . ."

"Oh mercy! Come back to bed before—"

"Tom, it can't reach us here." Aurora squelched her own anxiety to reassure her cousin. "It's almost time to get up anyway, so I'm going to get dressed. I'm sorry I woke you. Go back to sleep."

"Heavens, no, you can't . . ."

Ignoring her cousin's bleating protests, Aurora shucked out of her nightgown. Feeling her way in the dark, she found her undergarments, stockings, and day dress lying across the cedar chest at the foot of the bed and quickly put them on. "Go to sleep, ThomasAnne," she said soothingly and slipped out into the hallway, carrying her shoes—and stopped in her tracks at sight of her grandmother mounting the stairs. "Grandmama! What are you doing up?"

"I might ask you the same thing, young lady." Grandmama reached the landing with a thump of her ebony-head cane, an accessory which Aurora suspected was carried mainly for effect. "Turn right around and get back to bed." The old lady had once been a famous Titian-haired beauty, and she had not lost the raised-eyebrow expression of one used to commanding a retinue.

"I'm not sleepy." Aurora tipped her chin, imitating the autocratic tilt of Grandmama's well-coifed head. "Besides, it's very noisy outside. What is happening out on the river? I heard the explosion."

"You *heard* the . . . You couldn't possible have—" Grandmama buttoned her lips, then sputtered an exasperated breath. "Pish. I told your grandfather we might as well wake you girls up. Go on down to the breakfast room and find something to eat. We'll need to start making bandages and send them on to the hospital. I'll get the other girls—oh, ThomasAnne, you're up, too? Good, then. Hurry and put some clothes on."

As Grandmama stumped past Aurora to knock on her sisters' bedroom door, ThomasAnne ducked back into the room from whence her white, freckled face had briefly appeared like a lace-frilled daisy.

Aurora hurried down the stairs to the breakfast room. Finding the table laid and an array of breakfast foods—bacon, biscuits, grits, fried eggs, and fig preserves—already spread on the buffet by the window, she marveled at Grandmama's ability to pull together such a bounteous meal in the middle of the night.

Thoughts of the unfortunate souls who had undoubtedly perished in the accident, killed her appetite. But she had gone to the buffet to pour a cup of coffee when sudden thunderous banging on the front door startled her into dropping the coffee pot. Jumping up to deal with the spill spreading over the Aubusson carpet, she heard the butler, Alistair, go to the door, tut-tutting at the racket.

"Hold your horses," Alistair muttered, and Aurora heard him jerk open the door.

"Doc McGowan sent me!" came a rough male voice that Aurora didn't recognize. "Said tell the mistress to get ready for an emergency 'cause the hospital's already full—"

Aurora hurried into the foyer. "Grandmama's upstairs. I'll take the message."

The wiry young Negro at the door snatched his cap off. "Miss, Doc said not to—"

"Pish!" Aurora said, again in deliberate imitation of her grandmother. "How many?"

The man looked over his shoulder, then back at Aurora and apparently decided he'd better deliver his information fast and get back to the hospital. "As many beds as you can find, miss. Some going straight to the morgue, of course— excuse my bluntness—and the surgical cases will stay at the hospital, but the ones can easily be treated will need nurses and simple comfort. Blankets, bandages—"

"Yes, yes, we'll take care of it. I'm sure you're needed elsewhere. Thank you."

As the man ducked away, Alistair shut the door and turned to Aurora. He looked at her with reluctant respect glimmering in his dark eyes. She'd known him all her life, and he and his wife, Vonetta, the family cook, had half raised her. "Well done, little miss. I'll start down here rounding up blankets and laying out pallets, move some furniture around."

"Good. I'll go up and help Grandmama with bandages." She headed for the stairs, then hesitated, a hand on the newel. "I'm sorry about the mess in the breakfast room. I dropped the coffee pot."

Alistair responded with a grim smile. "I got a feeling we gon' have more to worry about than spilt coffee 'fore this day's over, Miss Aurora."

ACKNOWLEDGMENTS

I WOULD LIKE TO START by thanking my usual cadre of beta readers and editors who keep me from coloring too far outside the lines. My husband, Scott, first reader and sounding board; Kim Carpenter and Tammy Thompson, both of whom gallantly tolerate mixed metaphors, illogical motivations, and anachronistic and wandering prose (and frequently rescue me from corners into which I have painted myself); and my brilliant Revell editors Lonnie Hull Dupont and Barb Barnes. As always, I'm grateful to my longtime literary agent, Chip MacGregor. Your loyalty and encouragement is astonishing.

Also, I would like to mention that my son Ryan continues to bail me out with cool plot twists (perhaps the product of a slightly twisted imagination?). Where's your book, boy?

On the technical side, thanks to my friend Ronnie Redding, homicide detective with the Alabama State Troopers, who listened to my description of a Reconstruction Era race riot and helped me figure out how my imaginary sheriff would handle it. However, as usual I take responsibility for any errors or misunderstandings.

Last but not least, thank you to all the brothers and sisters who have prayed me through another long teeth-gritting season of finishing a novel. I'd be a mess without you.

Beth White's day job is teaching music at an inner-city high school in historic Mobile, Alabama. A native Mississippian, she writes historical romance with a Southern drawl and is the author of *The Pelican Bride*, *The Creole Princess*, *The Magnolia Duchess*, and *A Rebel Heart*. Her novels have won the American Christian Fiction Writers Carol Award, the RT Book Club Reviewers' Choice Award, and the Inspirational Reader's Choice Award. Learn more at www.bethwhite.net.

"Full of intrigue, grit, and grace, *A Rebel Heart* is Beth White at her finest."

—JOCELYN GREEN, award-winning author of *A Refuge Assured*

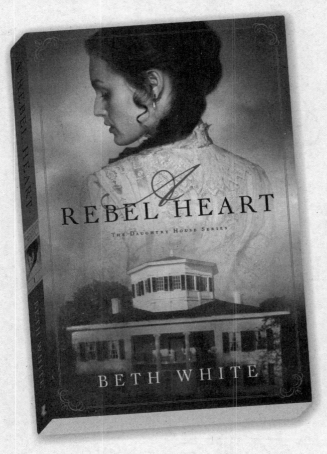

The Civil War is over, but Mississippi belle Selah Daughtry finds that former Union officer Levi Riggins has set siege to her rebel heart. Can she trust him to help her protect her home and family in these hard times—or will she lose her pride and self-respect in the process?

Revell
a division of Baker Publishing Group
www.RevellBooks.com

Available wherever books and ebooks are sold.